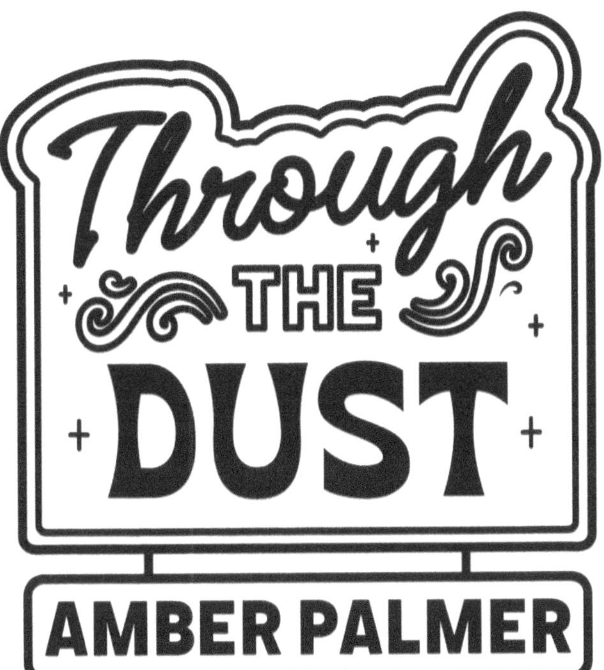
Through
THE
DUST
AMBER PALMER

Complete Editing Services performed by Heather Nix

Alpha/Beta: Liz Mayer, Rose Santoriello, Lauren Cox

Cover Design: Forensics and Flowers

To everyone who's ever been told they were too much -
They were wrong.
Be loud. Be radiant. Be unapologetically ambitious.
*Be **yourself**.*

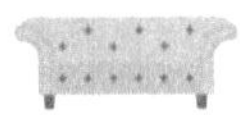

playlist

For the full playlist, scan the QR code!

Ain't Nothing About You - Brooks & Dunn
All I See Is You - Shane Smith & the Saints
Wasn't That Drunk - Josh Abbott Band, Carly Pearce
The Good I'll Do - Zach Bryan
Still Falling For You - Ellie Goulding
Any Man Of Mine - Shania Twain
Siren sounds - Tate McRae
Shameless - Camila Cabello

content warning

While this book is sweet and swoony, there are a few matters that may be sensitive to readers.

- Alcohol Use
- Detailed Sex Scenes, including intimate activities while under the influence and consensual degradation
- Parental Illness and Hospitalization
- Animal Cruelty (Don't worry! The dog is fine.)

lennox

. . .

"FUCK THE LEATHER, fuck the lace. Cheers to the ones who sit on our face!" I yelled, slamming the bottle on the rickety wooden table before bringing it to my lips. The cold beer hit my tongue, calming the nervous energy fluttering in my veins.

I was met with a declaration of cheers and groans—both sure signs that my words had done the job.

Cold beer and whiskey were the standard at the Lone Star Bar in Ashwood, Texas. Nothing could ever get better than this—bright neon lights and music too loud to carry on conversations. Add in the hot-as-hell cowboys walking around the place, and I was set.

There was a reason I was a regular here, and it wasn't for the cheap alcohol. Tonight was different, though. Or so I told myself.

Every summer, my dad taught at an intensive training clinic that brought in rich folk with horses from around the world. Each session lasted two weeks, and they were held back-to-back over two months.

Today marked the end of the first round, and we were out to celebrate. I'd already clocked at least half of our ranch hands amongst the crowd, laughing, dancing, and drinking their fill. I couldn't wait to watch them stumble around hungover tomorrow when the next group showed up.

The Lone Star hosted live bands on the weekend. Tonight, there was a local playing who'd made a big name for himself in the music scene. I'd never seen the bar so full. The whole damn town seemed to have showed up. I hadn't ever heard of him, but I hoped he was good.

My sisters, Josie and Cleo, sat beside me, shaking their heads at my antics. Not that I cared. My toasts had become somewhat of a party trick when I went out—an icebreaker. I couldn't even remember why it started or where it came from. I grew up around too many foul-mouthed cowboys who had no business speaking the way they did with me present. I had to do *something* with all the dirty anecdotes I'd picked up along the way. Plus, trying to top whatever I said last time was always fun.

Like a little competition with myself, which I always enjoyed.

"That's sure as fuck something I could toast to," the tall man to my left chuckled.

"Hear, hear!" I said, leaning over Josie to knock my bottle with his.

Lincoln Carter was the new addition to our little group. I didn't know him well, but I liked him so far. Dad hired him at the beginning of the summer to help with the clinics, and he'd done a great job the past two weeks. What I enjoyed the most, though, was the way he made my sister squirm. Lincoln hovered near the end of the table, conveniently close to Josie, and was having a damn hard time keeping his eyes off her.

On his first day here, Dad had introduced the two of them, but the universe was a funny bitch about things like that. Apparently, they'd had some sort of fling last summer in Tennessee before she'd run off and broken both their hearts in the process.

Ever since Lincoln had shown up, she'd been trying to

convince us that there was nothing between them anymore, but anyone in a ten-foot radius saw what a lie that was.

Now that Lincoln was here, though… Josie had changed. I'd been seeing less and less of her skeezy dickwad boyfriend, well, *hopefully* soon-to-be ex skeezy dickwad boyfriend. Lincoln and Josie were like a pair of fuzzy yellow ducklings: where one went, the other followed. I reckoned they'd be knocking boots before the end of the week, if not the end of the night.

"Oh my god, you're the worst," Cleo groaned. She was smiling, though, so I didn't take it to heart.

"No, I'm the best," I said, pointing toward her. "It's the reason you keep me around. I'm funny, smart, and pretty as hell."

"And annoying to boot."

I slid my gaze toward the green-eyed cowboy sitting across from me. Bishop Bryant sipped his beer, gripping it tightly in one scarred hand. He had his black felt hat pulled down, concealing him beneath the shadows.

Like, who did he think he was? An outlaw on the run? Get over yourself.

Ugh. From his stupidly hot, bearded face—because *yes*, I was woman enough to admit he was attractive—to the way he always glared at me like I was in the wrong. All of it grated on my nerves.

Bishop was the epitome of a grump. He was kind of like a mean ole bear that'd just come out of hibernation, that I just couldn't help but poke. I'd known him almost my whole life. He'd come to work on our ranch before graduating high school and spent the past twenty-three years praying at the altar of Black Springs Ranch and Douglas Hayes.

I leaned over the table, smirking as his eyes dropped to my chest. "Is that why you can't stop staring at me?"

It was dark, but I swore his cheeks heated. "Maybe we should add delusional to the mix, too. I ain't fucking staring."

He pointed the bottle my way, and I fought the urge to lick it. It'd be worth it just to see him squirm, but I decided not to for the sake of our company. "And if I am, it's because you're too damn loud."

"It's a bar, Bishop. If I wasn't loud, your old man ears wouldn't be able to hear me."

He huffed. "Yeah, that'd be *really* horrible. What a shame."

I sat back on my stool, crossing my arms. Again, his gaze dropped. It was only a second, but I saw it all the same. "You know, if you really want to keep me quiet, you could give me something to fill my mouth with and shut me up. It's worked for others in the past."

Bishop coughed, choking on his beer, while I grinned like the Cheshire Cat. He made it too easy to mess with him. Sometimes, my conscience would pop in and say, *"Hey girl, maybe we should take it easy on him,"* but then he'd say something stupid, and I'd throw her advice right out the window.

His overall disdain was fine when we were younger. I was a chicken-legged brat running around the barn and asking a million questions, but not anymore. Now I was a twenty-seven-year-old championship barrel racer who didn't feel like taking shit from an old cowboy with a stick up his ass.

Plus, maybe I liked seeing his cheeks flush with embarrassment when I said some off-the-cuff remark that made him uncomfortable. He should've known better by now that if you give me an inch, I'm gonna ride a mile.

"Christ, Lennox," he said, wiping his mouth with the back of his hand. "No one needs to hear that shit."

"Is that your problem, Bish? Feeling a little pent-up? Haven't gotten laid in a while?" I pouted, reaching out to pat his hand. He pulled away quickly, shifting in his seat. *Bingo.* "You know, that always helps me when I'm feeling wrung too tight. I just go out and find someone who looks like they'll fuck me really—"

"Don't finish that fucking sentence," he growled.

I raised my brow. "Why? You jealous?"

Bishop opened his mouth and closed it, looking more like a fish out of water than a cowboy at a bar. I was preparing to tease him when I heard Lincoln ask Josie to dance. My head turned their way, studying how she swayed gently on her stool. If I were a betting woman, I'd say she was getting ready to turn him down for a dance.

Well... as her loving younger sister, I couldn't let that happen.

Lincoln stepped back, holding out his hand for her to take. "Well, what do you say?"

"She says yes," I called out over the music.

Cleo smacked my arm. "Len, stop meddling! She's an adult—"

"Yeah, and she's acting like a child. I don't see how I'm the problem for pushing her toward something she wants. Isn't that what you were doing earlier?"

My sister chewed on the inside of her cheek. "Yeah, but you can't just butt into their conversation."

I shrugged. "I can, and I did." The sound of stools scraping against the floor caught our attention, and we glanced up, watching Josie place her hand in Lincoln's. I smiled, turning back to Cleo. "And look! It worked. I don't know what this family would do without me."

"Probably stay out of everyone's business," Bishop muttered, but I paid him no mind. I didn't have to look to know his eyes were on me. His attention was hard to get, but even harder to ignore.

If he wanted a show, then I'd give him one.

Reaching for my beer, I downed what little was left. Then I straightened my shoulders and pushed up my tits. The night was early, and the headliner hadn't even started. I hadn't been out in far too long and was ready to let loose.

Yeah, it was going to be one hell of a night.

"What're you doing?" Cleo asked.

"Is there anything in my teeth?" She shook her head. "What about my lipstick? Is it smudged?"

"No, you're good—"

"Great," I said, not letting her finish. "I'm gonna go talk to that tall drink of whatever over there," I said, nodding to the man at the next table. "Would've been embarrassing to make a bad impression, don't you think?"

Cleo chuckled to herself. "Whatever you say, sis."

"Will I see you out on the dance floor?"

My sister looked down at the bottle between her palms, picking at the peeling label. "I'm married, Len."

"Yeah, and I like men in Wrangler jeans and Stetsons," I deadpanned.

"What does that have to do with anything?" she asked.

"My point exactly."

My sister rolled her eyes. "Well, *my* point is that I'm not going to ask some random stranger to dance. I don't want to give them the wrong impression."

I rolled my lips together, dropping my gaze to my sister's hand. She was fidgeting with the finger that once housed a simple gold band. No one else seemed to notice a tan line had taken its place.

Cleo had recently moved back from helping her supposed husband and his brother at a dude ranch in Montana. When she'd come back alone, she'd made some comment about work keeping him there and her needing to be here, but she never spoke about him—never called him, either.

"I'll dance with you," Bishop said, downing his beer. "If you want."

We both looked at him in shock. Bishop hated dancing. In fact, I was sure he hated anything to do with fun. I could probably count the number of times I'd seen him smile on one hand —maybe two if I really tried.

I reached over the table, placing my hand on his forehead. "Are you sick?"

"What?" He swatted my hand away. "No, I'm not fucking sick. I was just being polite."

"Yeah, which is why I'm circling back to my original question."

Bishop pinched the bridge of his nose. "Why are you such a pain in the ass?"

I batted my eyelashes. "Because it drives you insane."

Cleo looked between us. "Listen, it's okay. I'm fine here, and I know it isn't your scene…"

"Oh no, you don't," he said, shaking his head. "Let's go see if I remember how to dance."

"I may be more out of practice than you are," she laughed, walking around the table. He took her hand, leading her to the floor before I could make another comment.

"Perfect!" I called out, forcing my voice to remain steady. "So, I'll see you out there then!"

There was a time when I would've given anything for Bishop Bryant to take my hand and hold me close on the dance floor, but that crush had been killed long ago. I wasn't the same naive little girl I was back then. Besides, I didn't even want a relationship right now. I'd taken a year off the rodeo circuit after Dad had gotten sick so that I could help around the ranch. Next year, I was hitting the ground running and wasn't planning on looking back.

Still, I couldn't deny the ache in my chest that refused to go away as I watched him pull my sister close. He said something, making her laugh as they moved around the enclosed space.

"Heya sweetheart, wanna dance?"

I slid my gaze to the cowboy standing beside me, the same one who'd been making eyes at me from across the table. Up close, he'd lost his appeal. I mean, he was cute in a boyish way —blond hair, blue eyes, and a cocky swagger that I'm sure he thought made him look cool—but there was no edge to him. There was nothing there that screamed, *"I'll fuck you into a coma."*

But I wasn't about to sit around and watch everyone else dance when I'd been the one who forced everyone to go out.

So, I smirked like I always did, hiding my discomfort, and said, "Let's go, cowboy."

lennox

. . .

THAT BOOTLEG COWBOY couldn't dance for shit. He kept stepping on my toes, and his turns were sloppy and out of control. I'd lost count of how many couples he'd bumped us into after the first song.

It didn't help that I'd worn brand-new boots. Josie had warned me not to, but I didn't listen. I never listened. At least when I showed up limping tomorrow, I could blame it on the man.

Fortunately, after two songs, Bishop and Cleo made their way back to our table, and I had an excuse to save what was left of my toes. As the music came to an end, I forced a smile. "Thanks so much for the dances! My friends are headed back, though, so I'm gonna…" I trailed off, shooting finger guns in his direction.

Maybe Bishop's onto something. Why am I the way I am?

The cowboy laughed. "Then let's go."

He gripped my hand in his, following my sister and Bishop. It would've been fine had he not grabbed his beer and set it on our table, looking around expectantly at everyone. "'Sup? Name's Case."

Case? Oh no. I had an ex-boyfriend on the circuit named Case, and he was a fuckboy supreme. Looked a lot like this guy, to be honest.

He stuck out his hand toward the others. Cleo shook it because she was polite and never wanted anyone to think anything bad about her, but Bishop stared at it like it was a hot branding iron.

And then his gaze slid to me in a *"Are you fucking kidding me?"* look.

Oops.

"I'm gonna grab some more drinks," Cleo muttered, shaking her head as she made her way to the bar. I wanted to beg her to take me.

"Ouch," Case said, pulling back and laughing. "Tough fucking crowd. You her brother or something?"

I said, "Or something," while Bishop growled, "Absolutely fucking not."

Lord, give me strength.

"He's the foreman at our ranch," I clarified. "Known him my whole life."

"Not your whole life," Bishop mumbled.

"I mean, as good as," I laughed. "What? I was like, four when Dad brought you on? Anyway, we're practically family."

The lie was bitter and horrible, like cough medicine being forced down my throat, but I swallowed it anyway.

"Black Springs, right? Heard some of the boys talking 'bout it when y'all walked in. That's a damn fine outfit. Y'all hiring?"

"Nope," Bishop said, popping the P. "Even if we were, don't think you'd cut it."

"What's that supposed to mean?" Case asked, puffing out his chest.

Bishop stared at him, the corner of his lips tipping up. "You ever rounded cattle?"

"Well, no—"

"What about branded? Ever helped with that?"

"Not exactly, but—"

"Have you ever driven a tractor? Or pulled anything in that fancy truck I'm sure you've got sittin' out there?"

Case was silent, teeth grinding together so hard I swore I could hear them scraping against one another.

Bishop chuckled. "Then why the fuck do you think I'd hire you to work on my ranch?"

"It's not your ranch, though, is it?" Case snapped back. "You may be the second in charge, but you don't have a say in shit at the end of the day."

I'll say this about the kid… He'd found his balls but found them at the wrong time.

"Okay," I said, dragging out the word. "Case, it's been great —*really* wonderful—but I think it's time you head back to your friends."

"Yeah, okay," he scoffed, grabbing his beer. He muttered something under his breath, but I didn't hear it. Or maybe I did, but I wanted to pretend otherwise.

"Lennox!"

I turned to see Cleo scurrying over with her drinks, but her eyes were wide. Panicked.

"What's up? What's wrong?" I asked, placing my hands on her shoulders.

"Ellis," she panted. "He's here. He's at the door." Her eyes slid to where Josie and Lincoln were cozying up on the dance floor.

"I'm on it," I said, stepping around her. "Stay here."

Josie needed to kick that asshole to the curb, but now wasn't the time to do it. I didn't know why Ellis was here, and I didn't care. All I wanted to do was make sure my sister was okay.

She and Lincoln stood in the enclosed area, looking at one another like moon-eyed fools, lost in their own world. I almost hated to intrude.

Almost.

I marched forward, skidding to a stop as I rested my hand on his shoulder. "Hey, cowboy, mind if I have this dance?"

I quickly gave them the rundown, telling Josie she sure as hell didn't want Ellis to walk in and see what I had. She took off toward the table, leaving Lincoln and I alone out on the floor.

The house band was saying their goodbyes, packing up their instruments to clear way for the next act. The bar switched on one of their tried-and-true playlists of old country tunes.

They'd played it so many times, I'd memorized the order. The owner never switched the songs to shuffle, even though most of his regulars had tried to show him how.

Lincoln's movements were stiff, his muscles coiled and ready to strike beneath my hands. He didn't take his eyes off Josie for one second, not until she was safely sitting down at the table with Cleo and Bishop.

I glanced up at him, envious of the way he watched her with such intensity. No one had ever looked at me like that, like they *wanted* me. Not that I had ever let anything grow past the point of lust-filled glances and heated moments in the back of my truck.

I told myself I never had the time for more, that I was too busy with life on the ranch and the circuit to share what precious moments I had with someone else. Even though we were in the heart of cowboy country, it was hard to find someone who understood.

I think they found it attractive at first—how I could hold my own in the arena and kick most of their asses while doing it. But there was some deeply rooted belief that all of that had to go away when a woman settled down. Like suddenly, it was unbecoming.

I was never going to be the type to be barefoot and pregnant, turning in my reins for apron strings while my partner was out tending to the things that needed to be done. I wanted to be beside them, fixing fences and rounding up cattle. I wanted to be seen and treated as an equal, sharing the load of life's hardships instead of becoming an accessory on their arm.

My mom always said I had too much of my dad in me. At first, I thought it was a criticism, something I always challenged her on. As I got older, though, I realized it was the best compliment anyone could've given me.

I squeezed Lincoln's hand, bringing his attention back to me. "Don't break her fucking heart."

He looked confused, brows pulling together in question. Yeah, it may have seemed out of left field to him, but it wasn't to me. "Pardon?"

I'd watched Josie, my sweet, overly anxious, falls-in-love-too-easily sister, get hurt more times than I could count. I was always there to pick her up when she was down. We'd go out to the Lone Star, and tear up the town until the cycle started over again and she caught the eye of some new heartbreaker.

It was only now that I realized we'd never done that after her trip to Tennessee. I hadn't understood what was different about that time than any of the others, how she seemed more distraught after a five-day fling than she had finding out her boyfriend of over six months had been cheating on her.

But I understood now, and I reckoned love didn't care about conventional timing.

"You heard me, cowboy. I mean it. If you break her heart, I'll kill you. There's a lot of places to hide a body on the ranch, and I won't think twice about shoving your dick back up—"

"I'm not gonna break her heart," he mumbled, sliding his eyes back toward the table. "But I'm afraid she's gonna break mine."

I followed his gaze, stomach dropping as I noticed Ellis standing where Lincoln had been moments ago. The buttoned-up cockbag leaned forward, relying on the table to steady him as he swayed on his shiny shoes.

As Josie leaned away, every muscle in Lincoln's body grew taut. We'd stopped in the middle of the dance floor, earning our share of rude looks from couples passing by. "Don't go making a scene," I warned. "You don't want to get tossed out on your ass."

"I don't give a shit about that," he said, rolling his neck as Ellis sneered down at my sister.

He said something and Josie slammed her hand down on the table. I didn't need to hear her words to know she was tearing into his ass. It would've been funny had Bishop not sat up straighter and looked over his shoulder at Lincoln and I.

Ope. This wasn't going to end well. Someone was going to end up with split knuckles or a broken nose. My money was on Ellis for the latter.

And then, just like I'd predicted, all hell broke loose as Ellis reached for Josie, pulling her off the stool and getting in her face. She reached for the hand firmly curled around her bicep, trying to loosen his white-knuckled grip.

Lincoln was gone, storming toward the table in a murderous rage. His boots thundered against the concrete floor. I followed, hot on his heels because if he didn't get to him first, I'd be the one security was dragging out, kicking and screaming.

I'd always hated Ellis, but that was because I thought he was an arrogant piece of shit who thought he was better than everyone around him. I'd never clocked him as the violent type, but sometimes, you didn't see a snake in the grass until you got bit.

Laying a hand on any woman was a mistake, but laying a hand on Josie?

Huge. Fucking monumental.

Cleo shouted for security as Lincoln pulled Ellis off Josie, internally cheering as he landed a hard blow to the fucker's nose. I stopped beside Cleo, watching with glee as blood began trickling down his upper lip. "What'd you do that for?" I asked her, grabbing what was left of my beer off the table and downing the rest.

We both cocked our heads as Lincoln pushed Ellis against a table. "Because I don't want to have to call Dad and explain why he's going to need to drive down to the county jail and bail everyone's ass out."

"Davey doesn't call the cops for shit like this," I said, just as the man in question came bounding up. He'd worked at this bar for as long as I could remember, and I'd gotten to know him pretty well.

"Hey, hey!" he called, trying to break up the fight, but Bishop put his arm out to block him. "Bishop, what the fuck?"

"Aw, come on… Let the man get a few good hits in," Bishop said, jerking his chin toward the spectacle. "He put his hands on Josie." There was a smirk on his face as he watched Ellis try to break out of Lincoln's hold. I didn't know why, or if there was even a reason, but he hated the fucker almost as much as I did.

And maybe it was the alcohol, maybe it was adrenaline, but there was something about that simple move that was stupidly hot.

I was clearly not in my right mind, because there was no way I was letting myself daydream about Bishop Bryant.

"Can't risk the bar being sued, dumbass," Davey muttered, barreling through Bishop's blockade. Lincoln stepped back with his hands up, welcoming Josie as she wrapped her arms around him. Two other men grabbed Ellis, trying to drag him out, but he broke free and made a dash toward my sister.

Lincoln tried to break their fall, but they both landed in a tangle of limbs. Ellis lunged forward, calling my sister a bitch and shouting promises of lawsuits from the top of his lungs.

Fuck that.

I stepped between them, reaching Ellis before Davey even had a chance. Without another thought, I shoved the toe of my brand-new boots into his balls. "Piece of shit," I spat as two large arms wrapped around my middle. The scent of sage and honey and very bad decisions filled my senses as I was pulled tightly against a warm, broad chest.

"Easy there, killer," Bishop chuckled. His deep, throaty tone sent shivers down my spine. "I think you've done enough damage."

I watched Davey pick Ellis off the floor and drag him through the front doors. The crowd parted, some laughing and clapping the moment his wailing faded away. Josie pulled Lincoln to the corner, fussing over him like he'd been in a knock-down, drag-out brawl when it could barely be classified as a bar fight.

"Lemme go," I said, struggling in Bishop's hold.

"Have it your way," he said, untangling himself from my middle and letting me drop.

The sound I made was somewhere between a yelp and a squeal—I couldn't be sure. I wasn't in the habit of making it.

I spun around, ready to dig into him for letting me drop, when I saw a smile on his lips. An actual smile—not that fake, public shit some people put on. No, this had wrinkles forming near his temples, his eyes full of a weird playfulness. He covered his mouth with a hand, shoulders shaking with restrained… *laughter?*

"Was that a laugh?" I asked, peering up at him. He dropped his hand and tucked it inside the pocket of his jeans. "Like, an honest-to-God *laugh*? Oh my god. Who are you?"

Bishop closed his eyes. "Why do you have to be so weird about shit?"

"Because I don't know if I've ever heard that sound from you. Should I be worried? Do we need a doctor?"

"It was just a laugh, Lennox. Nothing to make a fuss over."

I crossed my arms. "You're not programmed to laugh, so this obviously means one of two things."

He leaned his elbow on the table. "Alright, let's hear them."

"One," I said, holding up my pointer finger, "aliens have abducted you. This is some kind of body double situation."

He blinked. "*What?*"

"Or two, you've been possessed. I'd wager it's a demon, given your overall dislike of, well, everything, and your grumpy disposition."

Bishop shook his head. "Where the fuck do you come up with this shit?"

I shrugged. "Unlike some people—and I'm not naming names, of course—I read books with *words*, not just pictures. I know it's a crazy concept. Maybe if you tried it some time, you could learn a thing or two."

"Are you saying I can't read?" he asked. He seemed offended, which was weird because that was exactly what I was saying. I'd never seen Bishop read anything besides whiskey bottles and feed labels.

"I already told you I wasn't naming names, Bish," I said, raising my hand to mimic zipping my lips tight.

Out of the corner of my eye, I noticed Cleo walking up. She placed her hand in the crook of my elbow. "Let's go check on Josie," she said, chewing on her cheek. "I want to make sure she's okay."

"Yeah, I guess we'll need to settle our tabs. Davey doesn't call the cops but has a no-bullshit policy. Lincoln'll be kicked out for the night," I said.

Bishop stuck his hands in his pocket. "Well, are y'all wanting to stay? There are plenty of familiar faces here tonight. We could probably catch a ride if you wanted to."

I shot Cleo a grin, ecstatic because I wasn't ready to go home. There was a restless energy coursing beneath my skin. I wanted to set it free, to see where it would take me.

"Don't you think we should probably cut our losses and go home?" She pulled away from me, fidgeting with her fingers like she had earlier.

I reached out and grasped her hand and gave it a quick squeeze. Her eyes met mine, verging on panic or hope. I couldn't tell which. "Do you want to go home, Cleo?"

"I don't know, Len." Her voice was little more than a whisper. I barely caught her words over the din of the crowd.

I pulled her in tight, aware of Bishop's curious gaze bouncing between us. "You say the word, and we're gone, okay?"

"Sure," she said, nodding slowly. "But maybe we could get a few shots?"

I clapped my hands together. "Fuck yes, we can! That's my girl. What's your poison? Whiskey is my personal favorite, but there's also tequila—"

"Tequila," she blurted out. "Lots of tequila."

Bishop groaned. "This is gonna be a long fucking night."

I turned toward him, standing taller as his eyes slowly raked over my body. He dragged a thumb across the bottom of his lip, shaking his head.

Yup. The alcohol was getting to me, but that didn't mean I couldn't have fun with it.

"Oh, you have no idea."

bishop

. . .

I HATED THIS GODDAMN BAR. It was too bright, too bold, too mainstream, too fucking loud. Or maybe it was the two girls standing in front of me, shooting tequila like it was water and chasing it with beer.

Since Josie and Lincoln had said their goodbyes and driven off in my truck, I'd been sitting here, regretting my choices as I watched Lennox and Cleo get more drunk by the minute. They were giggling and laughing and screaming out the lyrics to every song played. At one point, A Bar Song by Shaboozey came on and they sang so loud that the entire bar joined in.

"Y'all are gonna regret this in the morning," I muttered, taking a long sip of beer.

"Liquor before beer, you're in the clear!" Lennox yelled, laughing even louder.

Goddammit.

Cleo turned to me, blushing. She and I were closest in age, only five years apart. I'd never known her to come out of her shell often—she was the quietest of the three Hayes sisters. Always dependable, always taking on more than she should ever have to.

I guessed even the most strait-laced people needed an outlet for whatever they were running from.

But the hellion beside her? The twenty-seven-year-old who was trouble wrapped in a pretty fucking bow? Yeah, this was par for the course with her.

Lennox Hayes and I were like fire and ice. She burned hotter than a thousand fucking suns and had the temper to boot. I was the dick who acted unaffected but was anything but. That woman had a way of getting under my skin like no one else had. She drove me crazy, slipping further into madness with each moment we spent together—which was way more than I liked.

When Lennox wasn't out on the road, she earned a paycheck at the ranch. We didn't agree much, especially not when it came to work. Most of our conversations ended in one of us shouting at the other that they were an idiot before storming off.

I loved my job, loved living on the land I worked my ass off for, but it had its downsides. No matter how hard I tried to escape a particular blonde pain in my ass, I couldn't. She was there wherever I went, pestering the fuck out of me.

If she could make it a career, she'd be a millionaire.

"What time does this guy go on?" I asked, cursing as the bartender brought another tray of shots.

I swore I was going to be the responsible adult and stay sober, but I couldn't do it. Not anymore. Not when Lennox just licked a line of salt off the rim of a shot glass before tipping it back. My eyes remained locked on her throat as it moved, swallowing the liquor in one go.

Guess I was adding "lookin' too hot" to the list of offenses against the Lone Star, too. Christ Almighty. Getting drunk should never look that fucking sinful, and I suddenly found myself wondering if I needed to go to church.

I looked at my watch. Yeah, I really should have insisted on leaving. It was already ten, and the band was just getting ready to play. I was going to hate myself in the morning, but I was starting to wonder if lack of sleep would be my only regret.

The intro to The Stroke by Billy Squier blared through the speakers. Lennox yelled, turning in her seat as the lights on the stage began flashing. Cleo, for all her momentary excitement, seemed to shrink in on herself as three figures walked on stage. They picked up their instruments as the crowd went wild.

I was getting too old for this shit.

"Lennox! What're you doing?" Cleo asked. I glanced over, mouth drying up as her sister stood on top of the rickety stool her perfect little ass had just been perched on. "You're gonna fall!"

"No, I'm not!" Lennox called, shimmying her hips to the beat of the song. It was hypnotic. I couldn't look away if I wanted to. Her hands ran along her body, fingertips brushing her hips. They climbed up and up and up, twisting in her hair and exposing the column of her neck. "I've done this a thousand times."

"Lennox, stop playing around," I said, slipping off my seat and circling the table.

She looked down at me and smirked. "*No.*" Her blue eyes dared me to do something, burning with the same stubborn fire I saw every time she pushed my buttons.

My hand itched to make her, to throw her over my shoulder and find someplace quiet to turn her ass red. Or maybe I'd do it right here, where everyone could see what a fucking brat she was.

A small crowd had gathered around our table. Most were young bucks who didn't know their ass from their elbow and sure as fuck wouldn't know what to do with a woman like Lennox. She'd chew them up and spit them out without a second thought.

"Get down," I seethed.

The stool rocked as she crouched down. I didn't know how

she kept herself so stable. "Or what?" she asked, letting her fingers play with the collar of my shirt. That simple touch sent blood rushing to my cock, and my thoughts spiraling out of control. This moment, that look she was giving me, would be etched into my skin and my memory until the day I died. "What're you gonna do?"

"Stop being a pain—"

My words stopped as she reached forward with her other hand. She grabbed my hat and placed it on her head with smug satisfaction. "If you want me to get down, Bishop," she said, running a finger along the gold chain around my neck, "then you better make me."

I barely heard the grumble of disappointed men behind me, too aware that Lennox Hayes was wearing my hat.

My. Fucking. Hat.

And then she pushed to her feet as a single spotlight swung to the middle of the stage, lighting up a man standing dead center. His shoulder length hair was tucked beneath a hat, and he was smiling at the crowd.

"Well... goddamn, Ashwood!" he called out as his band struck their first note of the night. The crowd cheered, going wild as he scanned the crowded bar. "It's been a while since I've been home. I'm glad y'all still know how to party!" The man pointed toward Lennox when she cupped her mouth and yelled. The man laughed and said, "Someone buy her a shot on the band!"

As if summoned by fucking magic, three men raced forward to put theirs on the table.

"She doesn't need any more fucking shots," I muttered, turning to shoo them away.

Instead, I was stopped by Cleo's gaze, staring in horror up at the stage. Goddammit, what the hell was happening right now, and why was everything going to shit?

But as quickly as her face fell, she scrunched her nose and

hopped down from her seat. "I—I'm fine," she said, waving me off with a watery smile. "Just need the bathroom. Take care of her for me, yeah?"

And then she was gone, disappearing into the sea of cowboy hats and raised beer bottles as the band played their first song.

"Fuck this," I said, surging toward Lennox. She was sorely mistaken if she thought her bratty attitude would keep me from going toe-to-toe with her. If anything, the way she acted only made me want to pursue that more—to punish her for the way she was acting and openly defying me.

Lennox yelped as I gripped her thighs, trying my damnedest to ignore the feel of her smooth skin against my callouses. Her dress rode up as I tossed her over my shoulder, and my fingers slid beneath the fabric.

Fuck. Fuck. Fuck. What the fuck was I doing?

"Bishop!" she scolded, beating her fists against my back. "Put me down!"

Without thinking, I brought my palm down on her ass hard three times, turning her angry protests into a muffled moan. That noise went straight to my dick, which was growing harder by the second.

I grasped her waist, sliding her down my body until her feet rested on the ground. Her eyes met mine the moment she felt my erection through my jeans, pupils blown from either anger or lust. I couldn't hide it. Truth be told, I wanted her to feel it, for her to know what she was doing to me. Our chests rose and fell to the same staccato beat, lost in a rhythm we couldn't escape.

I let my gaze drop, instantly regretting my decision. The top of Lennox's full breasts spilled slightly over the neckline of her dress. Each ragged breath she took drew me in closer, and I couldn't stop myself from reaching up and tracing the line.

Her lips parted as the tip of my finger brushed across the heated flesh. My hands were weathered, riddled with callouses and scars from years of hard labor. If I grabbed her own and examined it, I'd find the same, but this? This part of her was unmarred, a creamy expanse of skin that practically begged me to mark it up.

"You just gonna stare at my tits, cowboy?" Lennox asked. It wasn't her usual bravado. Her voice wavered as if she was trying to gain control of the situation, but she knew it was out of her hands. "Or are you gonna do something about it?"

I met her gaze. "The things I wanna do can't be done in public, killer."

She licked her lips. "Tell me anyway."

This was stupid, so fucking stupid, and reckless, to boot. There was no future in which Lennox Hayes and I would ever be more than one night.

But maybe one night was all we needed.

Even I couldn't deny that fighting with her got my dick hard. Her snarky comments and devil-may-care attitude were unlike any other woman I'd ever met. She wasn't the type to be tied down, and I hoped she never was. Lennox deserved to run as free as the Mustangs in Montana.

I stepped forward, brushing her long hair over her shoulder, lingering at the crook of her neck. Her pulse was erratic, thrumming just beneath the surface of her skin. I let it ground me as I wrapped my hand gently around her throat and softly squeezed. She was still wearing my hat. I should've taken it from her but couldn't bring myself to. Not when she looked so fucking good wearing it.

"You wanna know what I'd do to you?" Lennox nodded, barely able to move in my grip. I leaned forward, enjoying the way her eyes fluttered close as I whispered, "It's taking everything in me not to throw you over my shoulder again and haul your bratty ass to the bathroom. I wanna lock the door, force you to your knees, and stuff that smart fucking mouth with my cock until your make-up is ruined. And then I'd fuck you bare against the wall, hard and fast, letting you scream for more. I bet you'd beg me to come inside your hot little cunt, wouldn't you?" She whimpered, fidgeting in her seat. It filled me with a smug sense of satisfaction. "Yeah, you'd thank me for filling you up, killer. It'd turn you on to know I'm leaking out of you whenever some other mother fucker tried talking to you."

"Fuck," she cursed, reaching for my belt to pull me closer.

But I smirked, stepping away and leaving her needy. Lennox opened her eyes, ready to smart back, as Cleo came back to the table with red-rimmed eyes and a bucket of beers. She forced a smile, wavering slightly as she looked toward the band on the stage. "I brought more drinks!" she called, handing us each a beer.

I didn't feel the same buzz I felt earlier. Now, all I could feel was the phantom beat of Lennox's racing heart as I held her like I owned her.

I hated how much I wanted to feel it again.

lennox

. . .

I WANTED to fuck Bishop Bryant. And not just in a casual, one-night random rendezvous. I wanted everything he'd whispered in my ear and more. I wanted to be wrecked so thoroughly that I didn't know my name when he was done.

Who'd have known the grumpy cowboy had it in him? I sure didn't. He showed a side of him tonight that I never knew existed. One I desperately wanted to explore, to see what other sordid things he could come up with in his slutty little mind.

I stood up on the stool to mess with him. Maybe I wanted to piss him off a little, provoke him just a little bit so he would either lighten up or leave me alone. In the end, the result was better than I ever imagined.

After Cleo returned to the table, we sat and watched the concert without much fuss. I didn't even finish the beers Cleo brought. I wanted to go up to the front, to let the vibrations from the speakers run through my body. Maybe it would kill some of the restless energy consuming me since Bishop whispered in my ear, but Cleo begged to stay. She said something about having too much to drink and needing to stay by a trash can in case she threw up.

I wasn't gonna argue with that logic because I definitely didn't want to be the one dealing with the mess.

Bishop had returned to his seat behind me. I didn't have to look his way to know he kept his eyes on me. It felt like pinpricks all over my skin, an icy chill forcing all my hair to stand on end, which was annoying, seeing as I'd just shaved.

By the time the band finished, I was ready to crawl out of my skin. It didn't matter how good the concert was. I couldn't focus on anything but the way Bishop touched me. Every inch of my body burned, needy and desperate.

"Yeah, you'd thank me for filling you up, killer. It'd turn you on to know I'm leaking out of you whenever some other mother fucker tried talking to you."

That was the type of talk you read about in books, not from the foreman on your parent's ranch. I didn't even know Bishop could string that many words together. He usually kept his conversations as straight to the point as possible—more of a one-word kinda guy.

He didn't even know that he'd perfectly summed up every filthy fantasy I'd ever had.

I loved rough sex, craved it even, but most of the men I'd been with couldn't find my clit with a map. They cared more about chasing their own orgasm than helping me reach mine. Then, and possibly the worst part of it all, was how they had the audacity to turn to me and ask if it was good?

Dude, don't make me laugh. I didn't even come. Get out of here with that bullshit.

Somehow, though, I knew Bishop was different than the rest. I *knew* he would be the best sex of my life, which meant it was ridiculously unfair that he was who he was. I mean, there was no way we could sleep together. That would just be stupid. Reckless, even.

Exactly why I wanted to do it.

I saw Bishop talking to one of the ranch hands while they closed their tabs. He'd quickly sought out our ride after Josie and Lincoln left so we wouldn't have to worry about it later. Thank God for that, because Cleo and I did not have the right mindset to plan shit.

She may have had one too many beers. Or maybe it was the shots? And I'd been dirty talked into a quiet submission. Who knew that was a thing?

I was standing off to the side near the band's merch table. Cleo had run to the bathroom for what seemed like the tenth time in five minutes. I didn't know if she was getting sick or had broken the seal too early.

"Come on, come on," I said, checking my phone. It was only midnight. Under normal circumstances, I would've hung around for at least two more hours until the bar officially closed, but not tonight.

Tonight, I was wound up so tight that I knew I'd have to reach into my bedside table for some help before I even had a chance at sleep. It was hard not to think about how unsatisfying my vibrator would be, especially knowing the real thing was so close.

The door behind me opened, letting in a burst of hot Texas summer air. I groaned when it didn't close immediately, hating how humidity clung to my skin. As if sexual frustration wasn't enough, now I had to deal with this? "Hey, buddy," I said, turning around. "Mind keeping that door—"

My words died when I noticed it was the band's lead singer. He opened the door so his crew could load their instruments inside a large, white trailer. "Shut?" he finished for me, smiling. He was tall, with dark hair plastered against his neck and a thick mustache. I couldn't remember his name, but it was something Wilde. It was kinda dumb, but Cleo mentioned it was a stage name. They'd gone to school together. Seeing how many women were screaming it earlier, I guess it didn't matter much. "Maybe if you weren't standing so close to the band exit, it wouldn't be a problem."

I tapped my chin. "You make a good point. I'll take it into consideration," I said, returning his smile. I gestured toward the stage. "Y'all were great up there. It's been a while since we've had a decent live band play."

"Oh, that's a damn shame. I got my big break up there. Couldn't help but come back for the end."

"The end?" I questioned. Don't get me wrong, he gave one hell of a performance, but not one that screamed it was the end of his career.

He reached behind him, scratching the back of his neck. "Yeah, we're taking a break for a bit, but I wanted to come back here for a final show. That was the deal. Kind of a full circle moment, ya know?"

"Now, that's the real shame," I said, shaking my head. "I'd definitely go to another concert if given the chance."

The guy was hot; I'd give him that. What struck me as odd was how he didn't look the part despite his music being authentically country. I didn't know what it was. His clothes fit the bill —jeans, boots, and a well-loved Brooks and Dunn t-shirt—but there was something about him in general that didn't seem to match the persona he'd curated. It was like he thought just because he was from a small country town, he had to act the part, too.

The man smirked, pointing at me. "I know you," he said. "You're the barstool girl."

I grimaced. "Barstool girl? That doesn't sound very sexy or cool."

"Ah, you're right. I should've come up with something better."

"I guess that's why singers have songwriters," I laughed. "You just have to have the voice to sing their words."

He shifted on his feet. "I'll have you know I write all my own—"

"Hey Len, are you ready to—"

Cleo walked up and came to an abrupt halt when she saw the man standing in front of us. They stood in silence, staring at one another in pure shock.

"Cleo?" he asked, taking a step forward. "I-Is that really you?"

My sister drew her shoulders back, clutching the strap of her purse tighter. "Lawson, right?" There was an edge to her tone I'd rarely heard her use.

"Yeah, I guess it is," he said, dipping his head. "It's been—"

Cleo cut him off, turning to me. "Are you ready to go? Bishop is waiting."

I looked behind her, confused to see Bishop happily talking to the same man he had been earlier. "He's talking, Cleo. He's fine."

"Okay, well, maybe I would like to go," she said, averting her gaze.

There was a nauseous feeling in the pit of my stomach, some kind of sister intuition that sensed something was wrong. "Yeah, of course," I said, faking a smile as I turned back to Lawson. "It was nice meeting you."

"Wait!" he called out, stepping forward once again. I looked down at Cleo, giving her the option to stay or go, but she shook her head. That was enough for me.

As Lawson tried to talk to Cleo, I put one arm around her shoulder and used the other to whistle at Bishop. He looked over, brows furrowed as I waved. "Let's go!"

"Cleo, wait! Can we talk?" Lawson called out behind us.

"Doesn't look like she wants to talk, asshole. Take the hint," I said, pushing my sister through the front doors.

"I just need a moment—"

I turned around, pushing Cleo behind me. She stumbled, catching herself on my waist. "Listen, dickwad, I don't know why she doesn't want to talk to you, and I don't care. *She. Said. No.*" I enunciated each word, making sure to drive my point home.

Lawson dug his heels into the floor, blinking at us with wide eyes. He ran his fingers through his hair, forcing it to stand on end. "I just—" he began before promptly closing his mouth.

"Wise choice," I said, just as a group of fans yelled out his name. They swarmed him, swallowing him in the crowd as I helped Cleo out the front door.

She clutched her chest, sucking in deep breaths that nearly broke my heart. And then the first tears fell, taking her mascara with them. "What do you need, babe?" I asked, forcing myself to stand still. I wanted to draw her close, to comfort her in the way our mom always did—with big, warm hugs and open ears, but stayed where I was.

Cleo wasn't a fan of being touched unless she initiated it. She tolerated a lot of it at the best of times because our family was an overly affectionate bunch, but she was different. And in times like these, when her anxiety was spiraling out of control, I knew going near her would only make things worse.

"What the hell is going on out here?" Bishop asked, storming out of the bar with our ride on his heels.

I stepped in front of him, stopping him before he could make a scene. "I don't know, but drawing attention to her like the big, dumb, angry brute you are won't do anything to fix it," I hissed. "Just leave her alone for a minute. Let her catch her fucking breath."

Bishop looked like he was ready to argue, but thought better of it. Cleo leaned forward, resting her hands on the railing around the outside patio. She dropped her head and closed her eyes. I could see her lips moving, counting down from ten and then back up to get her breathing under control.

I walked over to Cleo, resting my ass against the post. We

stood in silence as I kept watch over her. She was always the strongest of the three of us, putting us before herself in every situation. The only time she did anything for herself was when she moved out of town, but I wondered if that hadn't backfired in some spectacular way.

It wasn't like she talked to me about anything, and I knew she barely said anything to Josie. Cleo was a vault—locked up tight and refusing to budge.

"Well, note to self... Never suggest going to see a band without learning everyone's full background information, particularly in relation to my sisters," I said.

Cleo huffed. "That might be a good idea."

I kicked a rock beneath my boot, watching it roll across the uneven boards. "Do you wanna talk about it?" She turned, giving me a look that said, *What do you think?* But I just held up my hands. "Hey, I had to ask. I didn't know if this was the moment your wall broke and you were ready to let someone in."

"I'm not that bad," she mumbled. "I just don't have anything worth saying. Our story... I don't know, Len, it's complicated."

"Will you tell me one thing?"

"Maybe." She cracked a smile. "We'll see."

I nodded, chewing on the inside of my cheek. "Did he... Did he hurt you? Because I swear to God..."

"Not in the way you're thinking," she said. Her gaze flitted to the spot where her ring once sat. "He would never."

"But he did hurt you?"

Cleo was silent for a second. "In a way, yes," she said with a sigh. "Can we go home? I'm already regretting all the tequila."

I laughed. "Whatever you want, sis."

bishop

. . .

THE NIGHT HAD TAKEN A TURN, sobering considerably since the stage lights went dark at the bar. I rode up in the passenger seat of Keith's truck while the girls sat in the back eating soft tacos they insisted we pick up.

A small-town Taco Bell drive-thru on a Saturday night was my own personal kind of hell. It'd taken us over thirty minutes to even grab our food, all while Lennox and Cleo complained about being hungry.

I was too, just not for food.

As the girls kept to themselves, I shot the shit with Keith, talking about all the work we had to do to prepare for baling hay in the upcoming weeks. We were already behind, but given the wet spring we'd had, we still needed to hold off.

Keith pulled through the massive black gate that marked the beginning of the ranch, driving up the winding road until he reached the main house. "Want me to drive you down to your cabin, man?" he asked, resting his hand on the steering wheel.

"Naw, it's a pretty night. I'll walk," I said, hopping out. I hurried to the back, opened the door, and lent a hand to help the girls down. Cleo took it with a smile, said goodnight, thanked

Keith for driving us, and then she walked into the house without looking back.

Meanwhile, Lennox had taken one look, eyeing me like I was covered in cow shit and hopped out on the other side. I half expected her to have disappeared by the time Keith drove off, but there she was, standing beneath the full moon in all her glory.

Goddammit, she was beautiful.

"Whatcha staring at, Bish? See something you like?"

I scratched my beard, wondering if I should answer her honestly or not. It felt like boundaries had been pushed at the bar, but none that we couldn't take back. Now, the question was where to draw the line? Harmless flirting and teasing were fine. It went hand in hand with the same shit we did now.

But saying what was on my mind felt like it bordered on inappropriate. We weren't in the bar anymore, letting the scent of alcohol and cigarette smoke cloud our decisions. Instead, we were standing on her ranch and my home. By all accounts, we should have gone back to hating one another the moment we crossed the property line.

"Sure do, killer." Lennox blinked, looking taken aback by my honesty, which made two of us because I hadn't expected it to slip out so easily. "Even if I shouldn't."

"No, you shouldn't." She cocked her head to the side. "But aren't you tired of doing what you *should* do? Don't you ever wanna be a little reckless?"

I laughed. "Never been one to throw caution to the wind. There's too much to lose."

She took a step forward. "Like what?"

"All this," I said, spreading my arms wide. I tipped my head back, breathing in the Texas air. It was hot and humid as hell, but something about it centered me. It was my anchor. When I looked back to where she'd just been, I realized she was now standing a few feet away. "I don't wanna lose this."

"What makes you so sure you will? I mean, I don't think Dad's gonna toss you on your ass anytime soon."

"Eh, I don't like the unknown," I said, shoving my hands in my pockets. It was taking all I had not to reach out and pull Lennox closer, not to wrap her silvery blonde hair in my fingers and tug her head back. "Not my thing."

"How do you know it's not your thing if you haven't tried it?" she asked, sweeping my face with curious eyes.

"You ever just know something without knowing why you know it?" She nodded. "Okay, well, it's like that."

"You need to live a little, Bish. Life on the sidelines is dull. You're gonna be too busy watching it pass you by."

"Shit, killer," I said, laughing. "Where did that come from?"

Lennox crossed her arms over her chest, popping her hip out in that sassy as fuck way she always did. "I'm full of great wisdom. Just because you're too busy brushing me off as a kid doesn't mean I am."

"Don't I fucking know it," I mumbled. The way I was looking and thinking about her now was far from the way I did when she was a brat running around the barn. She annoyed the shit out of me growing up, and I never let her forget it.

Lennox stepped forward, plucking the hat from my head and setting it on her own. "Isn't there a rule about this?"

"You know there is," I said through gritted teeth. I struggled just I had at the bar when she'd done the same damn thing, wanting to pull her into the shadows and have my way with her.

She smiled. "What would you say about being a little reckless, huh? How does that sound?"

"What'd you have in mind?"

Her smile was infectious, and I knew I was fucking done for. "Were you all talk earlier?"

"Fuck no," I growled. One of my hands landed on her hip as the other wound in her hair, wrapping it around my fist like I'd imagined doing all night. "When I say I'm gonna do something, killer, I fucking do it."

Lennox let out a soft moan that went straight to my dick. "Is that right, Bish? You think you're up to the challenge?"

"What challenge would that be? 'Cause it sure won't be making you come. I could do that shit without thinking."

"I prefer actions over words," she whispered, our lips a hair's breadth away. I leaned forward on instinct. *A taunt*. The barest hint of a kiss.

This wouldn't be anything more than sex—one night of our dirtiest fantasies coming to life. Come sunrise, things between us would go back to normal, and we'd go back to fussin' and fightin'.

But not tonight.

"You want actions, huh?" I asked, just before throwing her over my shoulder like I had earlier. I let my hand ride up, brushing the inside of her thigh. Her panties were soaked, the wetness coating her skin. Goddamn, this was better than any dream. "I'll show you actions."

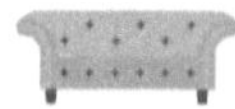

WE WERE on one another the moment we reached my cabin. I tore through the door, slamming Lennox against the nearest wall. Picture frames fell to the floor with a clatter as she latched onto my neck, licking and sucking, while I lifted her dress above her hips.

A pair of bright blue underwear caught my eye, though the center was a deep navy where she'd soaked through. "Goddamn, baby. This all from me?"

She moaned as I pressed myself against her aching center, moving her hips against my belt buckle. "Needy girl," I panted, pulling back to watch her grind down on the metal like a wanton little slut.

I slipped my hand between us, pulling Lennox's panties to the side. The sight of her bare pussy was nearly enough to make me come in my pants. Her lips were slick, coated in her arousal, and glistening in the light coming from the small lamp in the corner. God, I wanted to taste it, to make her come so hard she drowned me in it.

Reaching down, I slid my thumb along her folds, watching with an open mouth as I parted her. Wetness coated my digit, and I brought it up to her clit, rubbing in slow circles. She moved her hips, chasing her pleasure. "Please, Bishop… Oh my God. Yes, right there."

It was the hottest thing I'd ever seen.

"This pussy needs someone to take care of it, huh? Bet those other mother fuckers you've been with didn't know what it needed."

"No," she said, gasping as I pressed harder on her center. "They didn't."

"That's a damn shame. I could watch this for hours, watch you soak my jeans as you come from this alone."

"Bishop, please," she said, pressing against my chest. Her pupils were blown wide with lust.

"You want my cock? Is that what you're looking for? Need something to take away that ache?"

Lennox whimpered, nodding her head as I loosened my hold on her waist. She landed on her feet, undoing the clasp of my buckle before sinking to her knees. Her hairline was beaded with sweat, like she was physically burning up.

"Thinking 'bout my dick got you hot, killer?"

"Fuck yes," she said, pulling on the zipper with shaky hands.

I let my pants fall around my thighs, reaching inside my boxers and freeing my cock. Her mouth dropped as I stroked myself, wiping the bead of moisture at my head with my thumb. She licked her lips. "You want a taste of what you do to me?"

Lennox opened her mouth without question, sticking her tongue out for me to run the pad of my thumb along the gentle ridges. She hummed in pleasure, dipping her eyes to where my cock jutted between us. With the other hand, I brought it forward, letting the crown rest there. "Such a dirty little slut, aren't you, Lennox? Letting me use you like this?"

She let out a needy noise as I pushed in further. I was trying so hard not to blow right here, but I'd never seen a prettier sight. It'd been too damn long since I'd had a set of lips wrapped around me, and none of them compared to how she felt.

"It's nice to see this mouth can do more than talk shit," I said, picking up a slow, steady pace. Lennox was kneeling at my feet, hands gripping her own thighs like she was trying to restrain herself. Something about that sight made me cocky, how she was willing to let me do anything I wanted.

We may not have ever gotten along, but this showed she trusted me. For some reason, that made my chest ache just a bit.

I pressed in further, holding my cock in her mouth until her eyes watered. I'd told her I wanted to watch her makeup run down her face, and I was determined to deliver. "You look at me while you have my fucking cock stuffed down your throat." Lennox's eyes snapped up, lined with pretty tears. I pulled back, loving the sound she made as she gasped for breath.

"Oh God," she said, covering her mouth and scrambling to her feet. She pushed past me, running to the kitchen.

I turned to follow, tucking myself back in my boxers, when I heard her retch. "Shit, shit, shit," I cursed, trying to step forward. In all my haste, I tripped over my jeans. They'd fallen to my ankles and gotten tangled there. I caught myself on my couch, kicking them off in a hurry.

As I rounded the corner, I saw Lennox hunched over my sink. She held her hair back with one hand while the other was braced on the edge to hold herself up. I ran my hand down my face, feeling like the world's biggest ass.

I fucking knew Taco Bell wasn't a good idea.

"Go away," she said, holding her arm out. Her hair fell back around her face, sticking there as she retched again.

"Not a chance in hell," I muttered, padding over and holding it back for her. This shit didn't bother me. If I couldn't handle bodily functions and foul smells, I couldn't do my job. I came home covered in some variation of animal shit and blood more times than I liked.

I ran my free hand along her back in circles until her body seemed done purging everything from her system. It didn't look like she'd consumed much today. She rested her forehead against the cold porcelain, sucking in a ragged breath. "Stupid fucking tacos," she groaned.

I couldn't help but chuckle. "Come on, killer. Let's get you cleaned up."

Lennox tried to protest as I bent forward and scooped her up, but it was weak. I sat her down on the edge of my bed, stepping back to examine the situation. The neckline of her dress had fallen victim to vomit splatter. She didn't protest as I pulled it over her head and threw it on the floor.

"I can't sleep naked, Bish," she said, pouting as she wrapped her arms around her middle.

"Yeah, yeah, I know. Gimme a second," I said, going to my dresser and pulling out a plain white shirt. "Alright, let's put this on."

Lennox raised her hands as I slid it over her body. It came down below her thighs. If this was a different situation, I would've loved seeing her sitting on my bed and wearing my clothes. The sight shouldn't have looked as good as it did, and I mentally berated myself as I walked to the bathroom and grabbed a warm washcloth.

She didn't speak as I came back, gently washing away any

lingering traces of her being sick. "I don't have all the fancy shit you probably use to take off your makeup, so this is gonna have to do."

"Ugh," she said, closing her eyes and curling into a ball when I was done. "My face is going to hate me in the morning."

I chuckled. "Oh, I think your head might hate you more. It's gonna hurt like a bitch."

Lennox opened one eye, glaring. "Thank you, Captain Obvious."

"Anytime," I said, with a little salute. "Let me get you some water and medicine so we can lessen the damage."

The best thing about living on the ranch was the well water. I didn't have to worry about filling a filtered pitcher or any of that shit. I went back to the kitchen, grabbed an insulated glass, and filled it to the brim.

By the time I got back to my bedroom, I was greeted by Lennox's snores. Her mouth was open, letting out a sound I didn't know someone so dainty could make. I momentarily leaned against the doorframe, watching her chest's soft rise and fall.

The night might not have ended as expected, but I was okay with that. Seeing her here, in my bed, was somehow gratifying enough. Come tomorrow, I knew she'd wake up hating me.

lennox

. . .

Four Months Later

"FUCKING PIECE OF SHIT," I cursed, tugging at the rusted bolt lock on the gate. I'd told Dad we needed to replace it for months, but did anyone ever listen to me? Nope. They sure didn't, and now the stupid thing was stuck.

I stepped back, hands on my hips, scrutinizing the gate. My horse, Strider, stood beside me, munching on some grass. He lifted his head, huffing in annoyance. "What?" I asked, turning his way. The bastard had been judging me all afternoon. He was ready to be back in the barn with his friends and was pissed that we were still at least three miles from home. "Please feel free to step in anytime if you think you can do a better job."

He just stomped his feet and went back to eating, leaving me to figure out how I was going to do this.

It didn't help that it'd rained last night. My boots slipped in the mud each time I pulled on the stupid gate. I'd nearly fallen on my ass three times in the past five minutes alone.

"Come on, come on, come on," I muttered, moving forward and tugging again. My hands ached from the rusted metal. I'd forgotten my gloves in the barn this morning and was too proud to turn around to get them. "Why won't you just—"

"Need a hand?"

I stilled at his voice, turning slowly to scowl at the man looking down at me. Usually, I was attuned to his presence. My internal warning bells began ringing whenever we were within ten feet of one another. It had come in handy over the past few months since I'd vowed to ignore Bishop Bryant until the day I fucking died.

The universe had given me a lot over the course of my life, but keeping me from going there with the man in front of me was probably the greatest opportunity of all.

But here I was, fussing over a stupid gate instead of paying attention to my surroundings. The only good thing about that infuriating man showing up was seeing his massive gelding, Titan. He looked mean as hell, just like his owner, but he was a softie with a penchant for sweet treats at the end of the day.

"No," I said, crossing my arms. "And if I did, it wouldn't be from *you*."

Bishop looked up toward the darkening sky. "There's another storm rolling in. Think you can get it open before that happens? Or are you gonna be showing up to dinner like a soaked rat?"

"Thank you for the weather report, Captain Obvious," I said, giving him a mock salute. "This wouldn't have been an issue if Dad had replaced the gate like I told him three months ago."

"And just like I told him and you, there are more important things to spend money on. We needed patches done on both the barn roof and the enclosed arena. Thankfully, he listened to me."

"Oh yes," I said sarcastically, "the mini fridge and brand-new coffee maker were a necessary purchase. They were very valid."

"Hey, your dad bought them because of the boys working so hard during the clinic," he said, laughing. "Who am I to turn away free gifts? Seems a bit rude."

My hands curled into fists at my side. "Dammit," I cursed at a bite of pain, bringing my palm up to examine it. I'd cut it this morning moving some old barbed wire. I hadn't even realized I'd done it until I felt blood drip and looked down. I had no choice but to crudely wrap it in a clean strip of cloth I'd torn off my t-shirt.

"Where the fuck are your gloves?" Bishop bit out. He dismounted Titan and stormed over, taking my hand in his. "What'd you do?"

I ripped it back, holding it close to my chest. "I left them in the barn this morning. It's fine." I'd cleaned the cut the best I could and re-wrapped it when I stopped for lunch, but it wasn't a great job. I knew better than anyone how important it was to take care of your hands when working. Dad was going to chew my ass out for not being more careful. It was something he'd drilled into us as kids, or at least tried to.

Bishop pointed in my direction. "Doug's gonna have your ass for this. How long has he been telling you to keep a spare pair of gloves in your saddle bag, huh? You know the rules."

He needed to get out of my head. "Oh my god, crypt keeper. I don't need a lecture. I just need this damn gate open. So, if you could go ahead and ride away into the sunset, preferably to never be heard from again, that'd be great," I said, turning my back to him. I started forward, really hoping I wasn't about to slip and fall on my ass, when I was suddenly lifted off the ground.

"Let me go, you cockbag!" I yelled, kicking my legs out to no avail. He chuckled, setting me down beside Titan before walking to the gate. "It's not gonna budge!" I called out, running my hand along the gentle giant's forehead when he leaned into me. I looked over at Strider, who watched me lazily. "*Traitor*," I muttered. "You couldn't warn me he was coming?"

"Wanna bet?" Bishop asked, rolling up his sleeves to reveal his ink-covered skin.

Smug asshole. I hoped he couldn't do it, even though I knew he likely could. Bishop, much to my dismay, was a mountain of a man. Every inch of him was muscle, sculpted by hard work on the ranch that kept him crossing my path like a pesky horsefly.

I tried looking away, turning my head toward the open fields surrounding us, but failed miserably. The moment he gripped the latch and pulled, he let out a groan that sent goosebumps cropping up along my skin. His weathered tan chaps framed his ass perfectly, drawing me in. I was no better than a man, gawking at something that was never mine to have.

"I can feel you staring, killer," he said, peeking over his shoulder. "Should I be worried about you taking that little knife hanging from your belt and stabbing me with it?"

I pretended not to look his way, staring at the thick grime beneath my nails instead. "Killing you would be too much effort, and you're not worth it. Honestly, I don't see how your big ass head can fit inside your hat. Why would I be staring at—"

With one final tug, the bolt came flying off. Bishop flailed, trying to catch himself on the gate, but failed. It filled me with a stupid amount of joy when he landed flat on the ground with a thud. His breath whooshed from his lungs, followed by a string of curses so foul I reached up to cover Titan's ears.

Not Strider, though. That traitor could fend for himself.

Bishop pushed to his feet, glaring over at me as I bent forward, laughing so hard I had tears in my eyes. "Shut your fucking mouth," he said, craning his neck to check out his mud-covered ass. He strode forward, ripping open his bag in search of something to clean up with.

Spoiler alert: Unless he had a portable shower I didn't know about, he'd be riding back to the barn in mud-caked jeans. The thought brought me more joy than it should have.

I wiped beneath my lashes. "I take it back. I'm *so* grateful for your help," I said, trying to catch my breath. "Not only do I get to go tell Dad we need a new gate, but I got to watch you roll in the mud like a pig. Best. Day. Ever."

"I didn't roll around in the mud... I fell. There's a damn difference, and you know it." He pulled a small towel from his satchel, trying to clean himself up.

"Is there?" I asked, walking backward toward the gate. I needed to tie it to the post to keep it open so we could drive cattle to the next pasture on Monday. "Because from where I'm standing—"

Except, suddenly, I wasn't standing. I was falling, landing on my ass in the giant puddle of mud Bishop created because karma was a bitch.

"Standing, you say?" he boomed, heckling me in a way only he and the voice in my head could do. The sound of his laughter might as well have been nails on a chalkboard for how it got under my skin. I had half a mind to march over and push him back down, making sure there wasn't an inch left clear of mud.

But that would only get me thinking about what it'd been like to have the full force of his attention on me, and I didn't want to go down the road again.

"Will you get out of my fucking head?" I called, pushing to my feet. God, I felt disgusting. Mud clung to my clothes from the waist down, dripping in wet, sloppy puddles at my feet. Riding like this would be shit, and unlike Bishop, I didn't have a towel in my bag.

Bishop held up the offensive item. "Need this?" he asked, taunting me by waving it in the air. "I'll be nice and share with you. I think a couple of spots might be dry...*ish.*"

"No thanks, gramps, I would rather soil my saddle than accept your help," I muttered, walking over to Strider and mounting up. His ears twitched, excitement sparking in his black eyes when he realized our work was done here.

Bishop put his boot in the stirrup, swinging his leg over Titan's back. The pair of them were almost impressive. Both were ridiculously large and imposing—broad-chested and easily towering over anyone who stood too close. It was always funny to watch brand-new hands gawk up at them on their first day.

However, sometimes, it was annoying how they revered him like he was God's favorite cowboy. Bishop worked his ass off, don't get me wrong, but so did all the workers we employed. I think his overall take-no-shit attitude and ever-deepening scowl made people see him as more powerful than he really was.

"Don't be like that, killer," he said, bringing Titan next to Strider. "You don't have to hate me, you know."

I held my hand up. "I'm gonna stop you right there, Bish. I know I don't have to do anything. I hate you because it's enjoyable, because I have fun getting under that thick skin as much as you do." I adjusted myself in the saddle, blowing out a breath.

I clicked my tongue, letting my spurs graze Strider's flank. He loved to run and he was born to do it. It made us a great team on and off the circuit. Before Bishop could respond, Strider and I took off, leaving him behind.

bishop

. . .

FRIDAY NIGHT DINNERS were a big thing on Black Springs Ranch. Every week, the Hayes household gathered around their massive dining room table at seven on the dot. Not that anything bad happened if you walked in late, but Doug would absolutely give you shit about it if you didn't have a good reason.

In all the years they'd included me in their tradition, I'd only been late four times. It'd been fine, seeing as Doug had been with me for each, and he couldn't very well say anything when it'd been his doing.

But tonight marked number five, and I knew I'd get an earful when I walked through the door. It wouldn't matter if I told him I had to shower and change clothes because I didn't want to ruin the cream-colored chairs.

Lennox had beaten me to the stables, made evident by the sound of Strider noisily munching on his dinner from his stall. I was just grateful we'd made it back before the thunderstorm rolled in. While Titan was a massive fucker, he wasn't fast by any means. He hated when I made him go any quicker than a lope.

But the rain was coming down in a steady deluge by the time I'd made it back to my cabin and showered. Normally, I'd walk to the main house, but no way in hell was that happening tonight.

My old white truck was parked beneath a covered awning on my front lawn. I hurried out, sighing as I settled into the patched leather seats. It'd seen its fair share of wear and tear since Doug passed it down to me so many years ago.

When I'd started on the ranch, I had five bucks in my pocket and a chip on my shoulder. My mom kicked me out of the house at seventeen. With nowhere to go, I decided to walk out here and ask for a job.

I'd gotten to know Doug by working at Tractor Supply. He'd stop by to pick up feed and shoot the shit until his wife called asking where he was. I'd come to idolize him in a lot of ways. He was the type of man I wanted to become—dependable, kind, and hard-working—and I was determined to prove myself worthy.

I didn't want to think where I'd be if he'd turned me away.

Turning over the ignition, I listened to the comforting hum of the diesel engine. I rested my forehead against the steering wheel, praying for patience, which I knew was already in short supply. I'd need all I could get to make it through this dinner.

I followed the gravel road to the main house, parking next to Lincoln's truck. I was glad he and Josie had gotten together. He'd become a damn fine addition to the ranch's ranks, holding his own and not needing someone to constantly oversee him.

Though, I did notice there were a few times he'd disappear into his and Josie's new office, only to come out grinning like the damn devil.

"'Bout damn time you showed up, son!" Doug boomed as I stepped into the foyer. He stopped in the doorway, holding a big salad bowl for the table. "I was about to send Lincoln to look for your ass."

"No need," I said, toeing off my boots. I looked down, scrutinizing the bowl of greens. "The fuck is that, though?"

Doug rolled his eyes, ready to smart off as his wife, Ruby, came up behind him and wrapped her arms around his middle. They were complete opposites. Where she was fair with soft edges, he had hard lines and leathered skin. Her blonde hair was cropped around her shoulders, loosely swinging as she kissed his cheek.

It was crazy how much Lennox and Cleo took after Ruby, while Josie was the spitting image of her dad. All three girls, however, seemed to inherit their dad's mile-wide stubborn streak.

"Doctor's orders," Ruby said. "This one talked the girls into bending the rules on his red meat restrictions too many times over the summer, but that shit stops now."

It didn't matter how long I'd been an honorary member of the Hayes household; I was still caught off guard by two people so disgustingly in love after so many years of marriage. As a kid, the only relationships I saw were incredibly one-sided. Maybe it's why I was so damn jaded as an adult.

I'd never been in an honest-to-God relationship in all my forty years. There'd been casual hook-ups and shit—I wasn't celibate—but when it came to dating, I was clueless.

The closest thing I'd found was the ranch. I was married to my work and dedicated to it like most people would be to another. My job would always come first, and a lot of women didn't understand that. Not that I blamed them by any means. They deserved more than coming in second, but I'd never found anyone worth putting first.

"Criminal," I laughed, shaking my head and clearing my thoughts. No point in dwelling on things that didn't matter.

"That's what I said," Doug muttered. "But they don't seem to care."

"We don't!" Cleo chimed in, carrying a tray of grilled chicken. "You'll thank us someday."

"Highly unlikely," he called back. "Get in here and help me with these women. They're ruthless, and Lincoln's switched sides."

I removed my hat, hanging it on one of the designated hooks. "Yes, sir."

Lincoln set down two pitchers of sweet tea in the center of the table. "Sorry, Doug. I sleep next to one of those women at night, and I'm not looking to change that," he said. "Josie'd have my fucking balls."

"Smart man," Ruby said with a smile. "I knew I liked you."

"Castration seems more like my thing," Lennox said, striding out of the kitchen. "I did learn how in 4H as a kid, I bet it's like riding a bike." Her hair was still wet, pulled back in a low ponytail. She wore a distressed Black Springs Ranch t-shirt that looked to be about three sizes too big, nearly swallowing her body whole.

I tried not to gawk, to look away, but all I could think about was how she looked wearing my shirt not long ago. Suddenly, my pants felt tighter. I adjusted myself, trying to be discreet, but Lennox caught me.

Her eyes dipped to my crotch, jaw ticking as she met my stare. I couldn't tell if she was pissed or turned on or both. It was impossible to know with her.

Doug chuckled. "Baby girl, I pray for the man who decides to bunk beside you. He's gonna have to be strong as hell."

Lennox smirked. "He sure will. I won't accept anything less."

"Ain't that the fucking truth," I mumbled beneath my breath.

"What was that?" she asked, craning forward.

I shook my head. "Nothing. Just talking to myself."

Lennox tutted, taking her seat. "Heard that happens with old age."

"Lennox Rose!" her mother scolded. "Where are your manners?"

"When has she ever had them?" Cleo asked, taking the seat beside her sister. "She's always been a little rough around the edges."

Lennox swung her arm around Cleo's neck, pulling her close. "You love my rough edges. Admit it."

Cleo laughed, pushing her away. "Never said I didn't."

"Never said she did, either," Josie chimed in, dropping down beside Lincoln. She jumped, looking Lincoln's way before rubbing her thigh. "What was that for?"

"For instigating shit," he said, reaching for a cherry tomato from the bowl. He popped it into his mouth, wiggling his eyebrows in taunt.

"Like you always do?" she shot back.

"I'm an angel," he said, holding his hands above his head in a gesture I thought was supposed to be a halo.

As the group continued to bicker while piling their plates, I couldn't help but smile. Grateful didn't even come close to covering how I felt to have a seat at their table. It was like this every week—same shit, different day.

"Is that a smile?" Lincoln asked, pointing a finger my way.

"Fuck off," I said, leaning forward to knock it away. "I don't do that shit."

"Oh, we know," the table said, damn near in unison.

"Everything ready for tomorrow, Bishop?" Doug asked, pouring a glass of sweet tea. I was almost positive that wasn't on his prescribed list of shit he could drink, but I was willing to bet Doug would rather die than cut it from his life.

"Sure is. Lincoln and I are going into town in the morning to pick up a few last-minute things. I checked with Cook earlier, and he has all the food prepped."

"Great," he said, looking down the table at his wife. "Don't even think about limiting me tomorrow. If this is my last rodeo, then so be it."

She rolled her eyes, but nothing but love was shining back at him. "It won't be your last, so just stop that, Charles Douglas Hayes."

"Oh shit, Daddy. You just got government named," Lennox snickered. Doug hated his full name. Thought it was too stuffy for a cowboy, and that he didn't look like a Charles.

"And I've already done it to you once, young lady," Ruby warned.

Tomorrow was Doug's birthday. Usually, when the girls tried to make a big fuss out of it, he shut it down pretty quick, but this year was different. He'd fully embraced the mayhem they'd planned. He only had one condition: it was used to show the workers how appreciative he was of their work.

Every hand was off work tomorrow except for feeding the horses and mucking stalls. Doug said it was the least he could do, seeing as their workload often tripled during the four months or so that made up the workshops.

Doug was making a real show out of it, too. I hated to think about the cost of it all. Everyone could bring their friends and family to celebrate with them. Events were scheduled all day, which meant a quick way for the hands to make or lose some of the money they'd earned. Cowboys liked betting as much as they liked beer. He'd bought enough food to feed a small army and hired a band to play that night.

Honestly, Doug and Ruby had put these things together before, but I'd never seen anything this scale. It made me wonder if maybe Doug was really scared he might not live to see another birthday roll by. His health had been a point of concern for the past six months, and the girls had been worrying themselves with his care.

Doug brought Lincoln to Texas and offered him a permanent

position because he wanted to ensure that all aspects of his legacy were covered.

"Yeah, I can't wait to kick Bishop's ass *and* take his money," the man in question said, leaning back in his seat. He was like a goddamn puppy—so full of energy and jokes. It was exhausting sometimes.

I kicked his foot beneath the table, earning a chuckle. "I'd like to see you try."

"I'll do more than try. Be sure to have your wallet ready. Maybe pull out some extra cash when we're in town tomorrow just to be safe."

We ate through the rest of our dinner much the same, ribbing one another until our sides hurt from laughter. There was only one rule at the dinner table: no talking business. It was a welcome reprieve for all of us, knowing we could walk in, sit down, eat a damn fine meal, and not have to worry about talking about the same shit we dealt with every day.

As Ruby pushed to stand, Cleo cleared her throat. She looked up and down the table before her gaze fell to her lap. "I have some news to share," she said, pausing as Lennox reached over and grasped her hand.

"Sweetheart, is everything okay?" her mom asked, concern etched into her features. She and Doug shared a look, and he shook his head. Clearly, he didn't know what was going on either.

"I know I've been back in Texas for a while now, and there've been a lot of questions I haven't had answers to," Cleo said, straightening her shoulders. "But I wanted to let you know I'm not going back to Montana."

Ruby put a hand over her chest. "You're staying in Texas?"

Cleo nodded. "Yeah, Momma. I am."

"Oh, thank God," Doug laughed. "I've been wondering when I'd walk out to find your bags packed in the foyer."

Lennox raised her hands above her head, trying to bring a

lightness to the confession that felt like anything but. I admired that about her. She used her loud as fuck nature to divert the attention of others her way when things got heavy. "The Hayes sisters are back, baby!"

"What about Thomas?" Ruby asked, brows furrowing.

Josie swung her gaze down the table. "Mom…"

"Are you guys going to get a place in town? We'd love to have you close, to gift you a plot of land like we have for your sisters—"

"Momma, seriously—"

"We're getting divorced," Cleo said in a rush. "Thomas is staying in Montana with his brother, or at least that's what he told me. I don't know, and I don't care. He can rot in hell."

lennox

. . .

THE WHOLE TABLE went silent as the full force of our sister's news settled. Josie and I were the only two who weren't surprised. I'd had a sinking suspicion ever since I noticed that her wedding band had been replaced by a tan line.

Men who believed women were property, who ruled with iron fists and sharp-edged words, deserved a one-way ticket to the deepest parts of hell. It'd become somewhat of a joke within our family that the ranch was big enough to hide bodies if the need arose, but I knew damn well if Thomas ever stepped foot on this ranch again, he wouldn't be leaving.

That was both a threat and a promise.

"Lincoln, why don't we—" Bishop began, pushing to his feet and gesturing at the table.

"Right! Yeah, let's do that," Lincoln agreed.

Both men picked up what they could carry from the table and brought it into the kitchen. Within moments, they were gone, leaving us alone with our parents. They stared at Cleo in shock, trying to process the gravity of what she was saying.

"What'd that fucker do?" Dad asked, voice deadly low. I'd never heard him speak like that before. For all his empty threats about violence or kicking someone's ass if they broke our hearts, I'd never actually seen my dad follow through on any of them.

Josie moved to Cleo's other side, and I hoped it was enough to show her that we weren't leaving. Our sister looked up at Dad, tears pooling as she began to speak.

I could barely stomach hearing it again, but I would do it for her. Josie and I sat there, each of us holding Cleo's hand as she spoke of the abuse she'd endured over the past fifteen years. It'd been slow, starting out as little comments here and there designed to chip away at her value. How he'd made her feel worthless, had diminished the way she viewed herself until she no longer recognized the haunted woman in the mirror.

By the time she was done, Mom was crying, and Dad looked like he was ready to commit murder. The house was eerily silent. I didn't know how long we'd been there or where the guys had run off to, but I was grateful Bishop had the sense to vacate the premises.

"Yep, I'm gonna fucking kill him," Dad whispered, staring down at his empty plate. "I swear to God..."

"I'm sorry, Daddy," Cleo said, gripping my hand tighter when he lifted his gaze. "I'm so sorry. I didn't want to disappoint either of you and I—"

Dad's face fell, draining of color at her words. He and Mom were instantly out of their chairs, wrapping their arms around her shoulders. Josie and I kept hold of her hands, never letting go. She needed this, needed to know that no matter what, her entire family stood behind her.

"Baby girl," he said, pressing his cheek to the crown of her head and closing his eyes. "If there's anyone who should be apologizing, it should be your mom and I. *We* failed you. We didn't..." His voice broke as the tears began falling. I knew he was barely holding himself together and would fall apart the moment we were out of his sight. "We should've known. And we should've ensured you knew you could always come to us, no matter what."

"You girls are our priority," Mom said, meeting each of our eyes. "And you have our support no matter what. I don't care what it is or what has happened. You. Come. First." Her words were enunciated as she moved to press a kiss to each of our heads.

The tension in Cleo's body vanished as she let herself relax into our hold. She'd been so worried about what Mom and Dad thought, which Josie and I had told her was utterly ridiculous. I didn't have blind faith in much in this life, but when it came to our parents?

We'd hit the freaking lottery.

"What if we watched a movie together?" Mom asked, pulling back. She tried to discreetly wipe her eyes, but it was no use. "Like we used to when you girls were little."

Cleo nodded, turning to check on Josie and me. "You don't have to—"

"Oh no, you don't," I said, wiggling my finger at her. "I can already tell you're going to say something stupid about us not needing to stay."

"Which is *so* not happening," Josie piped in. "We're staying."

Our sister smiled, and it felt real for the first time in ages. Nothing but genuine relief shone in her eyes. Being the eldest, I knew she felt trapped in the façade of being perfect and strong in front of Josie and me. Sometimes, I appreciated it.

When we'd found out about Dad's heart condition, I'd nearly crumpled to the floor with no intention of ever getting back up. I didn't know what to do at even the thought of living without him. He was my hero, my role model, my everything.

And while I knew giving up was never an option, nor what he would've wanted, I don't know how long I would've let myself wallow in my grief if it hadn't been for Cleo.

I didn't have many skills outside of horsemanship. There'd

been a time when Dad asked if I wanted to take over his training clinics. The question had been met with a resounding no because, at the time, I'd been too preoccupied with my rodeo dreams. By the time I realized I wanted to be involved with the ranch, he'd already decided to train Lincoln to take over.

So, I did what I did best. I made myself invaluable, pitching in wherever I could. No job was too small or too dirty or too complicated. I never complained, never balked, never questioned. And when Dad started involving me in damn near every choice he made, it did one extremely valuable thing I'd never expected.

It chapped Bishop's ass.

In terms of ranch hierarchy, Bishop was just beneath Dad when it came to the daily operations. He'd earned the title of foreman, and I wasn't looking to take it from him. But the two of them shared the load. If anything happened to my dad, Bishop couldn't make those decisions alone.

Enter me.

But all that was just precaution. It was a way to make sure that in the event of something happening that might upset the balance, this place could still run properly until someone stepped into his role. I still had plans of going back to the circuit, winning another couple championships, and adding a few more buckles to my shelf, but until I knew Dad was okay, I'd be here to help with whatever he needed.

The scent of popcorn wafted in from the kitchen. We all looked up to see Lincoln and Bishop rounding the corner with big family-sized bowls filled to the brim. They sat them down on the coffee table.

"Cheddar ranch, kettle corn, and regular butter," Lincoln said, pointing toward each bowl.

"Well, you just thought of everything, didn't you?" Josie asked, rising on her toes to kiss his cheek. He blushed, which was honestly both ridiculous and stupidly cute at the same time.

It seemed like they'd been together much longer than they had. I mean, it'd only been a few months ago that I'd listened to them have sex in the barn after they finally solidified their relationship. A fact that, try as I might, I still hadn't forgotten.

"Yeah, yeah. Cowboy Casanova is great," I said, stepping around them for the couch. I plopped down, turning on the TV. "But the real question is… What are we going to watch?"

"Why don't you ask Cleo?" Bishop said, crossing his arms. He stood out of the way, watching as my mom and dad cleared the table. "Maybe she has something in mind."

"It's funny," I said, grabbing a handful of the cheddar ranch popcorn. "I don't remember directing the question at any singular person. It's almost like *anyone* could answer."

"Right," Bishop sighed, shaking his head. "Well, I'll see y'all tomorrow. And Lincoln, don't make me come looking for you. I don't want another view like I got the other morning."

Lincoln just laughed, winking in Bishop's direction. "I'm not even sorry." Josie elbowed him, and he rubbed the spot. "What? I'm not."

"Maybe if you ever want us to do that thing we were doing," she said, lowering her voice, "you will be."

Lincoln looked at Bishop and gave a little salute. "Right. I'm totally sorry. Won't happen again."

"Where are you going?" Dad asked, walking back into the living room.

Bishop pointed over his shoulder to the door. "I was just gonna head out so you guys could—"

"Absolutely not," Dad said, shaking his head. "You're a part of this family, Bishop. Dunno how many times I have to tell you that. So, unless you have something better to do, I'm gonna kindly ask you to sit your ass down and join us."

I looked around the living room, taking note of every filled seat, except for the one next to me.

Oh no, no, no. This cannot be happening.

Bishop and I spoke at the same time, both leaning forward.

"Dad, I don't think there's room—"

"Naw, really, it's fine—"

My father held up his hand, silencing us both. "There's plenty of room on that loveseat next to you, Lennox. You just need to scoot your ass over."

Josie and Lincoln grabbed a blanket off the back of the couch and cuddled beneath it. I heard their fit of giggles, holding up my middle finger when Dad turned around to push Bishop toward me.

Josie mouthed, "Sorry," and ducked beneath the covers as I sent popcorn flying her way. I looked toward Cleo, silently pleading for her to switch seats so Bishop could sit next to Lincoln, but she shook her head.

Traitors, the lot of them.

"You're all going to hell," I hissed through my teeth. "See if I ever do anything for you again."

Cleo leaned over and patted my hand. "Don't worry, you will."

I leaned back, crossing my arms. I hated when she was right. It was the principle of the matter, anyway.

"You want one of these?" Bishop asked, holding up a blanket.

I held out my hand. "Give it here."

"How 'bout asking nicely?"

"You're right. I shouldn't ask the elderly for help," I said, brushing past him to get my own. There was no way I was sharing with him. "You need a boy scout to come help you get across the living room?"

"I'm not fuckin' elderly," he muttered, groaning as he took a seat. I stood there, trying my hardest not to laugh when he rubbed his knees.

"Yeah, you're the picture of youth. Tell me, how are your joints?"

"Fuck off."

"You first," I said, taking my seat. I curled up in the blanket, trying to distance myself as much as possible. "This is *my* house."

"And I *tried* to leave," he whispered harshly, taking me aback. I was used to him giving sass, but there was an edge of anger in his tone that took me by surprise. "But here I am. So, we're gonna sit here and watch this movie like two fucking adults and deal with it."

"Fine," I shot back. "You stay on your side, and I'll stay on mine."

"Gladly."

I could feel my sister's eyes on me, watching closely for any hint as to what Bishop and I were discussing, but I didn't dare turn their way. Sometimes, I felt terrible for keeping secrets from my sisters, but then I remembered they'd both done the same to me.

Suddenly, I didn't feel so bad anymore. I'd sworn an oath to take that night with Bishop to the grave, and I damn well intended to keep it.

bishop

. . .

"WHAT CRAWLED up your ass last night?" Lincoln asked, tossing the grocery bag in the back seat of his truck.

"What do you mean?" I asked, following suit.

The two of us had gotten up at the ass crack of dawn to head into town. Doug and Ruby had given us a mile-long list of things to pick up before the party began. We were almost done, thank God. I didn't have the patience to grocery shop, even on the best day, so I usually ordered them and picked them up.

Saved me a shit ton of money, too, since I'm not going in on an empty stomach and buying everything in sight.

"With Lennox last night. I don't know, man. It seemed kind of tense."

"Things are always tense with her," I growled. "What the fuck's the difference?"

He rested his forearms on top of the truck bed. "That," he said, pointing at me. "You're all snippy and angry—"

"I'm always snippy and angry," I interrupted.

"No arguing there," he muttered. "But y'all were at each other's throats all night."

"You're imagining shit."

"Am I?" He raised a brow. "Because at one point, she literally kicked you off the couch. You spent the rest of the night sitting on the floor while she glared daggers at the back of your head and then laughed as you limped outta the house."

Alright, well, he had a point there, but it wasn't my fault. Lennox kept digging her feet into my thigh, fidgeting and fussing about not being able to stretch out. Every time she did it, I'd knock them away. It wasn't until the last half of the movie, after both her parents had fallen asleep, that she was able to throw me off the couch.

If we'd been anywhere else, I would've ripped her from her seat and bent that infuriatingly hot little ass over my knee, and turned her ass red. It was the wrong thought because I shouldn't—*I couldn't*—think of Lennox that way. Not anymore.

Not ever again.

Still, it remained there all the same, keeping me up nearly all fucking night. I wanted to act on it so badly, to pull myself free and see if she'd wrap her pretty little lips around my length agai—

"Dude, what the fuck?" Lincoln asked, bringing me back to the present. He was waving his hand in front of my face, smiling like a jackass. "Wanna talk about it?"

"Can you get your nose out of my business and help me get this shit done?" I knocked his hand away and finished piling the groceries into his truck in silence. There was nothing to talk about. Not as far as I was concerned.

And it needed to stay that way because I struggled enough with keeping my mind off Lennox as it was. Last thing I needed was Lincoln making shit worse.

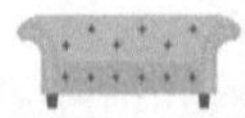

BY THE TIME we pulled up to the ranch, Lincoln's truck was loaded down with so much random shit. He stopped by the barn, where a large group of hands stood talking.

I pointed their way. "Y'all doing anything?"

"No, sir. We just finished feeding," Keith said, stepping up beside me. He was one of the best workers we had—he kept his head down, didn't start any shit, and was loyal to boot. There were times he'd gotten offers to work at other ranches in the area, but he stayed with Black Springs instead.

"Great," I said, filling my hands with bags and handing them to him. "Take this to Mrs. Hayes and Cook to see where they want it to go."

Keith laughed. "Already on it. Cook's been bitching about the lack of pickles for the past thirty minutes. This'll make him happy."

"Thank God," I muttered. Cook was a great guy, and he did a damn good job at what he did, but he was a bit dramatic when it came to his food. I'd watched him throw things at the hands when they tried combining shit he didn't think belonged together.

Once, he'd run over and ripped a ketchup bottle out of someone's hand because they tried putting it on their steak. Though, I didn't try to stop him on that one. What kind of person does that?

The other workers brought wheelbarrows to carry the bags to the big open field where Cook was set up. He began hollering when it came his way, smiling like someone had just told him he'd won the lottery.

"You've saved the day, boys," he boomed, clapping Lincoln and me on our shoulders and squeezing. "I can't thank you enough."

"You can thank us by not breaking our bones," Lincoln said, disentangling himself. "You can't expect us to rope shit if we have dislocated shoulders."

"Yeah, he needs all the help he can get," I said, pointing toward Lincoln. "He thinks he can beat me at the tie-down competition."

Cook glanced at Lincoln, raising a prominent, bushy brow. "Really?"

"Hey! I'm a damn good roper," Lincoln protested.

"I'm sure you are, but..." Cook trailed off, turning back to his prep station. "You haven't seen Junior here, have ya?"

"Of course, I have. We work together every day."

"Day-to-day shit is different than competin'. I mean, hell... Anyone can cook a meal, but when push comes to shove, they can't do what I can," he said with a smug smile. "I've watched Junior here since he came to the ranch, and I can tell you right now that you're gonna lose every dollar you put up."

"I will not," Lincoln said, puffing out his chest.

"Nothing to be ashamed of, son. He's just better." Cook turned around, sifting through the bags until he found his giant ass jars of pickles. "Good luck, though!"

Lincoln watched with an open mouth as Cook stormed away, barking to someone chopping onions to drop everything to take care of the jar instead.

"Who knew he loved pickles so much?" I asked, covering my mouth to hide my laughter.

"Fuck off," Lincoln said, straightening his shoulders. "I'm gonna win."

"Whatcha gonna win, baby?" Josie asked, coming up behind Lincoln. She wrapped her hands around his waist as he wrapped his arm around her.

"Bishop and I are going head-to-head for the tie-down roping later, and no one thinks I can beat him." He looked down at her. "But you do, right?"

Josie smiled, not skipping a beat. "Of course you can," she said, raising up on her toes to kiss his cheek. "You can do anything you set your mind to." When he looked my way, clearly thinking he was hot shit with Josie backing him, she widened her eyes and shook her head.

She knew damn well he couldn't beat me.

"Yeah, that's right, I can. Wait..." Lincoln paused, gripping her chin when she tried to pull away, laughing. "Are you doing that thing where you just tell me what I want to hear?"

Josie placed her hand on his chest. "Yes, but it sounded more convincing this time, didn't it?"

She squealed as he bent forward, throwing her over his shoulder and smacking her ass. "I'll see you out there soon," he said, looking my way. "I just gotta take care of something real quick."

"If it's quick, you're not doing it right!" I called back, earning his middle finger before they disappeared into the barn. "Lovesick fools."

I looked around, noting how different the ranch looked today. It was all done up for the party, long white tents with clusters of tables beneath them for people to hang out and eat and shoot the shit. Cook had made almost everything you could ever want, but his barbeque had everyone lining up.

Bar tents were marked with a red top, making them easy to find in a massive crowd. That was great, seeing as I couldn't fucking stomach being around so many people without a bit of liquid courage.

Doug even built a big stage in the middle of it all, ready for a band to play. In the meantime, several speakers were placed throughout the tents and up by the barn, where most of the events were being held.

When Doug's training clinics took off, he'd built a massive, covered arena, so there weren't any excuses not to get out and ride. It'd come in handy over the years, especially when he decided to throw a party on a whim. And when Lennox started barrel racing, she'd spent almost every day out there.

I returned to the barn, noting the red tent outside the arena entrance and heading straight for it. Sure, it might not even be noon, but I was off the clock and intended to make the most of it.

"Lemme get a beer," I said, pointing to the one I wanted. I waited, tapping my fingers along the bar top, stopping only when I heard a familiar voice to my left.

Fucking Lennox.

"Let me get another," I said, grabbing and drinking the first beer.

She was in her element, standing in the middle of a group of workers, laughing at something one of them said. They all looked like doe-eyed idiots staring at her like she was the center of their world. I was willing to bet she could tell any of those boys to climb on the back of the rankest bull they could find, and they'd do it without question.

I could blame it on their age, but it likely had more to do with the skin-tight jeans she had on. Lord knows that was my fucking excuse.

When I turned around, she stared at me over their shoulders, watching my every move. Her blue eyes raked down my body, stopping on the buckle at the top of my jeans. The same buckle I'd worn four months ago, the one she'd fought desperately to get off on.

I couldn't wear the damn thing now without thinking of the heat in her eyes. I could've sworn it was almost the same look she was giving me now, but I wasn't close enough to be sure.

I slowly walked toward the barn entrance, not stopping myself from listening to their conversations.

"You gonna put on a show today?" one of the guys asked. He was a new hire who had only been at the ranch for a few weeks. I think his name was Justin.

"Not today, boys," Lennox said, batting her eyelashes. "I'm here to drink, listen to some good music, and watch cowboys fall on their asses."

Each of them laughed, going around in a circle and making sure she knew what event they were participating in. Christ, did these guys really fall for that? Did they think that was enough to make her crawl into the back of their truck for a quick fuck?

I'd fire them right now for being so stupid if it were my choice.

One bold idiot stepped forward, removing his hat and holding it close to his chest. "You mind if I buy you a drink, darlin'?"

You've got to be fucking kidding me. How cliché. Had he taken lessons from Lincoln? The sonofabitch wielded that name like a weapon when it came to Josie, and now they were likely fucking somewhere in the barn.

Lennox flicked her gaze to mine, curling her lips at the annoyance I knew showed on my face. Subtlety was never my strong suit. I couldn't hide shit.

"I'm not a cheap date," she said, curling her hand around his bicep.

He blushed a deep shade of red. "That's okay with me."

I tipped my head back with a groan. God, help me. It was an open bar. No one was buying anything.

Their whole interaction was like watching a newborn horse try to stand. Lennox would chew him up and spit him out without giving him a second thought. I didn't want to deal with the fallout when he got his heart broken.

At least, that's what I told myself, anyway.

She needed a man, not a boy. One who could put up with her shit and give it right back. Who was older and had experience and—

"Probably best not to get drinks with the boss's daughter," I said, stopping them before they could make it to the bar tent. "Don't you think?"

The kid gulped, looking up at me. I could see the hopes and dreams of settling down with a Hayes sister dying in his eyes. If it wasn't so damn sad, I might pity him. "I was just gonna buy her one drink, sir. Nothing else. Honest."

Lennox tightened her hold on his arm, digging her nails into the fabric of his button-down shirt. She was gearing herself up for a fight, preparing her body and mind for those sharp-tongued words she loved to wield. "I don't see how this is your business, Bishop. You don't have a say in how I spend my time or who I do so with."

"It *is* my business when you lead this poor kid on, leaving him high and dry. I don't have time to watch him mope around like a puppy. I need all the hands thinking sharply, party be damned."

And maybe because I didn't want to watch him slobber over her like he had a chance. He would never know what it felt like for her to press her lips to his. To be consumed by the thought of her kiss.

But I did. And God help me, I wanted to do it again. I wanted to bend her over the nearest surface, to feel her body shudder under my touch as I brought my palm down on her ass. She had folded when I'd done it last time.

A perfect little brat.

The boy straightened up, stepping away from Lennox as she glared daggers my way. *Maybe he's got some smarts after all.* "Sorry, sir." He turned to Lennox, barely meeting her eye as he tipped his hat toward her. "Ma'am, have a good night."

We both watched him scurry back to his friends, who were already entering the arena to watch the first event. I couldn't help but laugh as he cleared the corner. Judging by the furious jab against my chest, it was the wrong thing to do.

"What the hell was that?" Lennox hissed, turning on me in an instant. "You had no right—"

I tipped my chin in his direction. "You really wanna be with someone who scares so easily? He scurried away like a little mouse."

"For fuck's sake, I wasn't going to *be* with him," she said, crossing her arms. "He was going to buy me a drink—"

"At an open bar?"

"—and then I was going to find my friends and watch cock-sure cowboys like you fall on their asses and lose their money." She barreled through like I hadn't said a damn word. "But you had to go and ruin it."

I let her insult slide because we both knew I wouldn't lose. She was grasping at straws, trying to come up with the smallest jab to fuck with my head like she always did. "You don't need anyone to buy you shit, killer. You're more than capable of doing that on your own."

"Doesn't mean I have to," she shot back. "Besides, he was cute! I liked the way he blushed when I touched his arm."

"Maybe for a puppy," I said dryly. "Doesn't really seem like your type."

She scoffed. "What would you know about my type?"

"I know enough," I said, stepping forward. Her sweet, honeyed scent filled the space between us. "And we both know a kid like that wouldn't be able to keep up with a hellion like you."

"What is it about him that you're opposed to, *Grandpa*?" she said, challenging me.

I gestured toward the arena. "He looks like he's twelve and, by the sounds of it, has never talked to a woman before. That's all I need to know."

"You're so stupid," she said, shaking her head. "It was about pleasant company and some innocent flirting, a concept I'm sure is completely lost on you."

"It's not lost on me," I snapped back. "I just think you need to be toying with someone more age-appropriate, which may be a concept lost on *you* instead."

Lennox paused, staring at me like I'd grown three heads. Maybe I had. That was the only explanation as to why the fuck I was standing here arguing with her about who she spent her time with.

The briefest hint of hurt flashed in those haunting blue eyes before they hardened. Lennox straightened her shoulders, lips curling into the tiniest smirk as she stepped forward. I'd gone too far with my age comment. I knew it was a low blow after everything, but it was too late to take it back now.

All I could do was watch her land the killing strike.

"You know… You're right. I should find a nice, *age-appropriate* cowboy to spend my time with. Maybe then someone would finally give me a fucking orgasm."

And then she walked away, leaving me standing in a crowd, not knowing whether I wanted to fuck her or fight her.

lennox

. . .

I STOOD BY THE CHUTES, watching Lincoln and Bishop warm their horses in the holding pen near the arena. They were relaxed, talking and laughing as they took turns throwing loops at the training dummy in the ring. Josie was beside me with a big, goofy grin when Lincoln did a lap and winked at her.

"Ugh. Y'all are so gross," I said, resting my boot on the bottom rung of the fence. "Can't you keep it together in public?"

Josie laughed. "I don't know. It's kinda hot that everyone knows we're head over heels for one another. PDA might not be your thing, but it does something for me."

"Oh, yeah. I'm well aware of your exhibitionist tendencies," I said sarcastically. Since Josie and Lincoln had started dating, I'd found out more about their sex life than I ever wanted and had already been stuck listening to them once. "Do you guys even check your surroundings before getting it on?"

"Most of the time, we're alone!" she said, cheeks blooming red. "But I'll admit that it's not always the first thing on our mind."

"Don't I know it," I muttered. "I don't think I'll ever get the sound of your screams outta my—"

She clamped a hand over my mouth. "I already said I was sorry about that." I licked her palm, and Josie pulled back before rubbing it along her denim-clad thighs. "You're so gross!"

"That doesn't mean I've stopped having nightmares," I told her, visibly shuddering.

"You are so dramatic. Leave me alone, I'm happy and in love."

"Bleh, gross," I said, scrunching my nose. As much as I hated to admit it, their relationship was on track to rival our parents'. Those two were disgustingly head over heels for one another. "But I'll let this go this time because you're my sister. Just don't tell Lincoln because I'm not quite ready to give up my leverage over him yet."

She nodded once. "You have yourself a deal."

"Have you seen Cleo this morning?" I asked, biting down on the inside of my cheek. "I know last night was rough."

Josie sighed. "Yeah, she's been helping Cook down at the pits. I think she's just trying to stay busy. Mom's been watching her like a hawk."

"I hate that she felt like she couldn't tell us," I said. "It's one thing to keep things from Mom and Dad, but neither of us would've judged her."

"Yeah, but you know things aren't always that simple. Once you speak your truth, it's out there. You can't take it back. I mean, they were married forever. They had us all fooled."

I knew she was right, but it didn't make me feel any better about the situation, especially thinking about the pain she'd been in for God only knows how long.

"Oh, look! Here they come," she said, pointing toward the alley.

Bishop and Lincoln rode forward as the announcer called their names, drumming up excitement with news of their little competition. Money exchanged hands around us as people laid down their bets. They were the last two riders for the tie-down event.

"Who's up first?" I asked. Seven Nation Army by The White Stripes blared through the speakers as Lincoln's horse, Boots, stepped up. He pranced in place, eager eyes darting around the expanse of the arena. "Guess that answers my question."

Josie leaned her head on my shoulder. "I almost feel bad for him. He'd have a real shot if he was going against anyone else."

"Yeah," I said, sighing. "I hate that you're probably right."

Bishop's been the reigning champion since Dad started throwing these big get-togethers. No one had ever been able to beat him, nor had anyone come close. At least Lincoln would give him a run for his money.

Lincoln nodded, and the chute burst open. A little piebald calf ran toward the other side of the arena. The moment the calf was far enough ahead, Boots gave chase. Dust filled the air as Lincoln threw a perfect loop around the calf's head, quickly wrapping the rope around his saddle horn and jumping down.

"Go, go, go!" I called out above the noise. My hand came down on the fencing with each word. It felt like the entire audience was holding their breaths as Lincoln flew off his horse and ran toward the calf.

He reached for the animal, flipping it on its side before grabbing its two hind legs and one from the front and tying them together with a short, looped rope he held in his mouth. Boots backed up, eliminating the slack in the rope tied to his saddle.

Lincoln's hands shot up, and the buzzer sounded. His time is displayed on the large clock hanging over the chutes. 7.45 seconds. It was a damn good time, one that absolutely smoked the other contestants. He blew a kiss at Josie as he mounted Boots. They stepped forward, loosening the slack and waiting the required six seconds to see if the little calf squirmed free.

As he walked back toward the arena entrance, he stopped by where Josie and I stood. She climbed to the top of the fence, grabbed his hat, and placed it on her head. "That sight never gets old," he said, kissing her quickly.

"Want it back?" she asked.

He shook his head no. "Naw. It looks better on you."

I laid my forehead against the fence and groaned. "You two really are the worst."

Lincoln reached over and patted the top of my head. "Don't be jealous, little sister," he said as I knocked his hand away. "One day, someone will claw into that pit you call a heart—"

Josie smacked his arm. "Lincoln Carter!"

I cracked a smile. "I mean, he isn't wrong. It's pretty scary in here," I said, tapping my chest.

That was one of the things I liked best about Lincoln. He wasn't afraid to say what was on his mind, and he was sarcastic as shit. Honestly, how well he fit in with us was a little scary. Lincoln and the Hayes family were a match made in cowboy heaven.

"I'll see you in a minute," he said, pulling away and heading back.

"Poor guy," I whispered, watching him clap Bishop on the back. "He doesn't even realize he lost."

"It's okay. I'll make him feel like a winner tonight," she said, laughing when I made a vomiting noise.

"Boundaries, Josie! Boundaries." The music queued up again, and Josie hopped down. The crowd went wild as the familiar beat of The Stroke blared through the speakers.

You've got to be fucking kidding me. I was going to kill him.

Memories from four months ago came flooding back, and I remembered the heat in his gaze as he watched me dance on my stool to this very song. How he'd whispered the filthiest things in my ear and got me to drop my guard for what was supposed to be one night of the most mind-blowing sex either of us had had.

And then I remembered the pain and embarrassment of

waking up the following day to find him sitting in a chair in the corner of his room, watching me sleep like he was afraid he'd committed a crime.

Well, fuck that. I narrowed my eyes, barely able to make out Bishop from inside the darkened alley between the chutes. There was a slight smile on his lips beneath the brim of his hat. Titan pranced in place, large nostrils flaring as his rider leaned forward and whispered something into his ear while running a large hand along the gelding's neck.

Bishop had always cleaned up infuriatingly well. Gone was the dirty t-shirt and jeans he wore daily. In their stead was a rust-colored button-down I'd never seen him wear. His pants were starched, fitting too nicely to his muscled thighs. It was unfair how quickly I'd toss my anger out the window during a moment of weakness. Damn, I'd love to run my tongue along the lines of his tattoo peeking out beneath the fabric.

And then there was that slutty fucking gold chain around his neck. Who knew it would be so hot?

As Bishop rose to full height in his saddle, our gazes collided. I shifted on my feet, finally acknowledging the blooming ache between my legs that'd begun when I'd seen him earlier.

I fought the urge to look away as his eyes scanned the length of my body. I wasn't about to give him the satisfaction of my embarrassment. Whatever effect he had on me needed to stop. It was getting out of hand. His attention lingered, wrapping me in an invisible embrace that made me uncomfortable.

"Hey beautiful," someone whispered. Two arms landed on the fencing, caging me in. I recognized the voice, scented the beer on his breath as I dropped my gaze from Bishop.

"Carson," I said, trying to inch closer to the fence. Josie watched me from the corner of her eye, but I shook my head. That dick wasn't worth the scene I knew she'd cause if I asked.

He stepped forward, letting the arm between my sister and

me drop away. "You haven't returned any of my calls," he said, lifting the corners of his mouth. Once upon a time, I'd thought the blond-haired, blue-eyed cowboy was adorable. He had dimples for days and was talented with words, but all of that went down the drain pretty quickly when I realized half the town also shared my sentiment.

"You've been calling?" I asked, turning to face him. "I haven't gotten any."

"Really? Let me see your phone. Maybe something isn't working right—"

"Oh, no. See, that's intentional, Carson. I haven't gotten any of your calls because I blocked your phone number." Josie stifled her laughter next to me. "It looks like things are working just fine."

Carson chuckled, shaking his head. "That won't do, Lenny. You gotta forgive me sometime. I miss that smart mouth."

I snorted. That was what got me into that mess in the first place. Being attracted to people who can give it as good as they can take it wasn't always the best practice. Some of the best narcissists in the world have a silver tongue at the ready.

That was how I'd gotten into this mess with Bishop. I'd let my attraction take things too far and then got burned, so I was done listening to my body's suggestions. "I don't have to do shit, Carson, and neither do you. Your wandering eyes and traveling hands can browse and sample the goods at any other market, but this one's closed."

Carson said something, but I turned back around toward the show. I was done with the conversation. Bishop's eyes quickly looked away. He focused straight ahead, a muscle in his jaw flexing as the chute opened and his calf ran out. I held my breath as the calf reached the vantage point, and Titan broke the barrier. When Bishop threw his loop around the calf's neck, Titan dug his hooves into the ground.

Dad always taught us about the sacred bond between a horse

and its rider. One had nothing without the other; that connection could make or break you. Sometimes, during the clinics, someone would ask what that looks like. Dad would always bring in Titan and Bishop to show off. They were the gold standard to which he held the others. It wasn't exactly fair, seeing as I'd never seen a better pairing.

Bishop jumped down, flanking the calf to the ground. He was so focused, so angry, so hot. Even though I couldn't see them, I could imagine how the muscles in his arms flexed and strained beneath his shirt.

He reached for the loop in his mouth, making quick work of his tie before throwing his hands in the air. The buzzer stopped, and the crowd went wild, but Bishop didn't indulge them. He kept his head down as he mounted Titan and waited to see if his knot would hold.

Of course, it did.

The clock flashed 7.53 seconds and Lincoln came running out to claim his prize. I let out the breath I'd been holding since realizing Bishop had hesitated half a second before the barrier fell. Had he done it on purpose to give Lincoln an edge? That wasn't like him. They had been ribbing each other for weeks about their little competition.

But then, what else could it have been?

bishop

. . .

"OH MAN, THAT WAS GREAT," Lincoln said for what was likely the hundredth time since we'd sat down for lunch. The fucker hadn't shut up about beating me, and it was grating on my nerves. If he didn't learn to shut his mouth quickly, I'd teach him how.

"Lincoln, baby," Josie warned, using that sickly sweet tone that turned Lincoln to putty. "No one likes a braggart."

He turned toward his girlfriend, staring at her with big brown eyes. "Not even a little bit? You're going home with a winner, darlin'."

"Double or nothing next year," I said, pointing my bottle in his direction. "It was an off day."

Off day my ass, I thought. I knew exactly what had happened.

I'd taken one look at that smug fucker Carson Wells talking to Lennox and had internally lost my shit. He'd worked on the ranch several times, and I was grateful to see him drive away each time.

He did alright on the back of a horse, and his rope skills could get the job done, but he ran his mouth more than anyone

I knew. Always went on and on about chasing skirt or his next big gig. I couldn't trust him as far as I could throw him.

His presence surprised me since I'd told him not to step back on the property the last time he worked for us. He was far more trouble than he was worth. If Doug found out he was here, it'd probably cause a fight.

He didn't find Carson's antics funny when they often concerned his youngest daughter. The kid had a mouth on him and didn't care who heard him talking about his latest bunkmate.

My gaze drifted to Lennox. She was sitting beside her sister, talking animatedly to a girl from town. I didn't know what they were talking about, but Lennox spoke with her hands and made large gestures that kept gaining my attention.

So far, she'd nearly smacked Josie three times in the past five minutes. I told myself it was a safety hazard to look away. If I let her keep my attention, maybe I'd save a life or something.

But that seemed to always be my problem where she was concerned. I was constantly looking when I shouldn't have been. No matter how many times I told myself I'd only been distracted because of Carson, I knew it was a lie. The way he'd leaned in to whisper in Lennox's ear, how he'd caged her in against the fence, had taken my focus.

She could handle herself. That was never my concern. What bothered me was the sense of familiarity between them and how she didn't flinch in his presence like she did with me.

"Whatever you say, old man," Lincoln chuckled.

"I'm not that fuckin' old," I muttered. "We're only a few years apart."

"Four," he corrected.

"Same difference," I countered. "I could still kick your ass in a fight."

Lincoln held up his hands. "And I have no interest in finding out the truth, so I'll let you have it."

Cleo, who Cook had been running ragged all day, groaned as she dropped into the chair beside me with a plate of food. "God, I'm starving," she said, digging her fork into a pile of potato salad. "Remind me never to volunteer when Cook asks for help. I don't know how anyone keeps up with him and his standards. He's nuts!"

I laughed, taking a sip of beer. "Naw, I think you'll still help. That's just who you are."

She blew out a breath and grumbled, "Well, maybe I don't want to be that person anymore. Being nice doesn't get you anything."

I lifted a shoulder in a shrug. Cleo wasn't wrong, but she wasn't right, either. People often mistook kindness for weakness, and sometimes that got exploited. After dealing with the shit from her ex, I reckoned she was pretty familiar with that concept.

"You did a damn good job with this coleslaw," I said, gesturing toward her plate.

Cleo stopped mid-bite. "Uh, thank you," she said with a small smile. "How'd you know I made it instead of Cook?"

"I've eaten it enough throughout my life to know."

"Guess you got me there," she said. "I'm pretty sure that was one of the first things mom taught me to make just so she didn't have to chop things anymore."

I laughed. "I wouldn't put it past her."

"Neither would I! She hates it. That's why there are like five of those easy-chop things stuffed in the cabinets. I swear, it was love at first sight whenever they came out."

"Are you talking about me?" Ruby asked, sitting down beside Cleo. She reached over and snatched a piece of brisket off her daughter's plate. "I won't apologize for my love of those little choppers, and I won't hear of you talking ill against them either!"

"Oh god, I hate those things," Doug said, setting his beer on the table. "They are a bitch to clean. I always cut myself."

"They give you gloves!" Ruby said.

"Those are for cutting, not washing. It shouldn't be that big of a hazard, and wearing gloves seems silly, Rubes."

"Do you wear gloves when you work?"

"Well, yeah," he said.

"Do they protect your skin when mending all those barbed wire fences?" Ruby asked, raising a brow. I laughed, knowing damn well she had him right where she wanted him.

"Yes..."

"Then why wouldn't you wear them when handling sharp objects in the kitchen?" she asked, leaning back in her chair.

Doug sighed and closed his eyes. "Alright, honey. You've made your point. I'll wear the gloves."

"Oh, no. I think you should go without them now. Since they're silly and all," she said, dipping her chin.

He grabbed a chair and brought it over before sinking down into it. "Boys, if I could give you one piece of life advice, it'd be this... Never try to win an argument with your wife. It doesn't matter how small it may seem. Just let it go. It ain't worth it."

"Don't I know it," Lincoln said, sipping his drink. "I tried arguing about the color of our bedding, which was the worst three hours of my life."

"I don't know why you don't like the pink..." Josie mumbled. "It's not neon or anything."

"You know damn well it has nothing to do with the color and everything to do with the fringe at the bottom. It's a pain in the ass in the washing machine." Josie lifted a brow, and Lincoln sighed. "*Right*, sorry."

"Well, at least one of you can take that wisdom to heart," Lennox said, returning to the group. "It's not like Bishop will ever get to use it."

"Lennox Rose," Ruby said. "What has gotten into you?"

She met my gaze, shrugging. Her claws were sharpened, ready to strike. "What? It's the truth."

"Yeah, it is," I said, narrowing my gaze.

Ruby laid her hand on my shoulder. "Don't mind her. She's been in a mood for the past few months."

Didn't I fucking know it. I'd been waiting for the day when this tension between us would break, and we'd get back to normal. Never thought I'd find myself missing the days before I knew what it was like to kiss her.

"More like the past twenty-seven years," I said back, trying to smile. It was forced and felt wrong, but I did it anyway. I hated remembering how old she was. How I'd woken up the following day at war with myself because what we'd almost done had crossed every damn line I'd ever drawn, and yet it'd felt so right at the time.

How could something like that possibly be bad? It wasn't fair.

But I needed to remember that nothing had changed at the end of the day. I still prioritized my work and this ranch above all, and no one—not even the twenty-seven-year-old hellion across from me—could change that.

Ruby laughed. "True. All my children are stubborn, but that one is a step above the rest," she said, looking toward Lennox. "Takes after her father more than I care to admit. He was hard to keep up with when we were kids, you know? Always on the go, always wanting more. I see that in her."

"I dunno, Ruby. After what I just saw, I think she's a little more like you than you think."

"Y'all realize I can hear you, right? Like, I'm sitting right here," Lennox said, leaning back in her chair. She tried to put on a tough front, but her eyes softened the moment her mom said she was like Doug.

All those girls had a soft spot when it came to their dad. He was the center of all their worlds, and I hated wondering what would happen when he wasn't here. They were all strong enough to survive, but his loss would be a wound that'd never fully heal.

Hell, I didn't know how I'd recover myself, and we weren't even related. It never mattered when it came to Doug.

I'd learned early on that blood didn't define family. It was determined by who showed up for you day in and out when shit got tough, the ones who rallied behind you and lifted you up until you could stand on your own two feet. I'd expected to be treated like an outsider here, but it'd never happened. Instead, I'd been offered a seat at their dining room table and shown a kindness I wasn't sure I had even deserved.

"I'm well aware, daughter of mine. But at least you know I'm not talking shit behind your back."

"Mom!" Lennox exclaimed, laughing. "Is that supposed to make it better?"

Ruby shrugged. "I don't know, but it's the truth," she said, bringing her glass of wine to her lips. "What time does the band go on? I'm ready to hear some live music."

It was around four in the afternoon now. We still had a few hours of sunlight left before the stars came out. People were already hustling back and forth on the stage to prepare for the show.

"Around seven, I think," Doug said, turning over his shoulder to stare. "I dunno. It was all a little last minute, so I think they're just making sure everything is good to go."

"What do you mean, last minute?" Josie asked. "This thing has been planned for months."

"The band I originally booked canceled like three days ago. Said they'd broken up a month ago. Guess our little shindig had gotten missed when they made their cancellations."

"That sucks. You seemed excited about them," Josie said.

"Who'd you get instead?" Lennox said, propping her elbow on the table and resting her chin on her palm.

"Well, I guess the kid I spoke with was the singer. He seemed pretty confused about why I was calling at first. Then I explained the situation, and he said he'd refund the full amount I paid and still do the set."

"That's nice of him," Cleo said, furrowing her brows. "But how's he going to do that if the band's broken up?"

Doug shrugged. "I don't know. Guess he made some calls and told them what happened. They agreed to do one last show. Ain't that cool?"

Lennox forced a smile, looking at her sisters. "Sure is, Dad. Out of curiosity, what's the name of the band?"

Doug opened his mouth to answer, but was interrupted by a tall shadow looming over our table. Dread settled in the pit of my stomach as we all turned to see who it was.

Shit. This wasn't gonna end well.

"Lawson! How the hell are you?" Doug said, pushing to his feet. He rounded the table and shook the singer's hand.

Lawson smiled at Doug, but his eyes kept darting to Cleo at my side. I looked her way, half-expecting her to have lost all the color in her face. Instead, she looked like she'd just eaten a hot pepper. Her cheeks were flushed red, and there was an unmistakable anger in her eyes.

"I'm great, Mr. Hayes. Just wanted to stop by and give my congratulations in person before heading on up there."

"Have you eaten? There's plenty of food to go around for you and the band."

"Not yet, but we'll be sure to grab something before we head out," Lawson said. He kept his words polite and friendly, but he couldn't stop his gaze from wandering to the angry blonde to my right.

Cleo was damn near vibrating. Her knee bounced erratically under the table, shaking her whole body. I didn't know what happened between them, but I didn't like it. She'd been through enough and didn't need this dick messing things up for her.

"This is my wife, Ruby," Doug said, motioning toward her seat. "And these are my girls, Lennox, Josie, and Cleo."

"It's so nice to meet you, Lawson," Ruby said, giving him a sugary smile.

All three girls stared at him, not knowing what to say or do. Lennox was ready to kill someone, while Josie shifted uncomfortably in her seat, and Cleo looked like she'd rather be anywhere else. Even Lincoln seemed to sober as he eyed Lawson suspiciously.

"We've actually met before, Mr. Hayes," Lawson said, rubbing the back of his neck. "Cleo and I went to high school together."

"Un-fucking-believable," Cleo scoffed, rolling her eyes.

Doug furrowed his brows, leaning forward to examine Lawson closer. "Huh. I don't remember anyone with that name in Cleo's graduating class."

Lawson dipped his head. "Yeah, Lawson's a stage name. My agent thought it'd be a good idea, so I ran with it."

"You're Marsha Wilde's boy, aren't you? Grady?" Ruby asked, smiling sadly. Lawson nodded, averting his gaze. "I was so sorry to hear about her passing. She was a good woman."

"Yes, ma'am, and thank you. She was something special," Lawson said. He rocked back on his heels, peering around Doug to look at Cleo. "I'd love to catch up if you have time—"

Cleo pushed to her feet and grabbed her plate. "Sorry, I'm busy."

"I can talk while you walk," he added quickly. "You know, just wanted to say hi and—"

"And now you have," Cleo said, sucking in a breath. "I'm sure you have better things to do, anyway."

"I don't," he said. I didn't know their history, but even I could see a lot of hurt between them. Doug started picking it up, too, gaze darting back and forth between them like he was onto something. "The show doesn't start for another hour, and I'd love to catch up while we wait."

"I've got to get back to Cook. I told him I wouldn't be gone long. I'd say maybe next time, but I'm sure you'll be gone by the morning."

"Oh shit," Lennox laughed. Josie jabbed her in the side, averting her eyes when Lawson and Cleo both looked their way.

"Actually, I'm home for good. Now that the band's on a break, I thought it'd be a good idea to move back. I never got the chance to go through Mom's things when she passed, and there's a lot to do around her place."

Silence hung heavy in the air as Cleo's chest rose and fell. "You're not leaving?" she asked, clenching a fist at her side.

"I'm not leaving," he said, softening his voice. "So, if you can't catch up tonight, I understand, but I'd love to get together sometime—"

"DADDY!"

We all turned in time to see a little girl fling herself toward Lawson. He caught her in time, lifting her in his arms and kissing her forehead. "Hey baby girl, what're you doing here? I thought I told you to stay backstage."

"Well, Momma said Uncle Ben needed your help, and she asked me to go find you." She smiled wide, lifting her little hand and tapping the tip of his nose with her finger. "And so that's what I did!"

"Daddy, who're they?" the little girl asked, resting her head on Lawson's shoulder. The resemblance was uncanny. They shared the same light brown hair that looked golden in the sun and the brightest blue eyes I'd ever seen. You could tell they belonged to one another even if you'd only gotten a glimpse in passing.

Cleo stared at the pair in wide-eyed shock. Her hand trembled, causing the plate she was holding to waver. Lennox stood, taking it from her with a reassuring smile before throwing it away.

"They own this ranch, honey. We're here to celebrate this gentleman's birthday," Lawson said softly, motioning toward Doug. He looked toward Cleo, but she hadn't moved.

"I love birthdays!" she said, throwing her arms in the air. "They're my favorite day."

Doug chuckled. "You know what? Me too. Mine's been pretty good so far."

"Are you gonna listen to my daddy play?"

"I sure am," he said.

"Yay! He's the best. My momma loves listening to him play, too. She says his music is pretty," she said, turning toward Cleo. "I like your dress. Blue is my favorite color."

Cleo cleared her throat and forced a smile. "Thank you. It's mine, too."

"Mommy and Daddy did my whole room in blue. It's my favorite room ever."

I couldn't be sure, but I swore I saw a tear slip down Cleo's cheek. She wiped it away quickly. "You're so lucky to have them," she said quickly, turning to us. "I don't mean to be rude, but I need to get back to work."

"You good?" I asked, reaching out to stop her. It was a stupid question, but I'd hate it if I didn't ask.

"Yeah, it's just a lot," she said.

I dipped my chin. "It is. You know where to find me if you need me."

Cleo placed her hand on my shoulder, whispering thanks before disappearing into the crowd. She wasn't headed toward Cook, and no one stopped to question her motives for leaving. Even if Doug and Ruby didn't know why, everyone at this damn table could see there was history between them.

Lawson shifted on his feet, looking ready to go after her, but stopped as his daughter spoke again. "Daddy, let's go find Mommy."

"Alright, baby girl," he said, adjusting his hold before facing us. "I hope y'all enjoy the show and have a good night."

They walked back toward the stage without another word, leaving us all silent. To no one's surprise, Lennox broke it.

"Well..." she drawled. "I think we know why he did the show for free now."

lennox

. . .

ON PRINCIPLE, I stayed toward the back of the crowd with my family as Lawson's band took the stage. They'd been performing for about an hour, and the sun had finally set.

After they'd gone on, Josie and I tried to find Cleo. We looked everywhere we could think of, but it was like she'd simply vanished. Then we started calling her over and over to see if she would answer. It wasn't until the thirtieth attempt that she finally told us to leave her alone and that she'd talk about it later.

I didn't believe a single word, but if it made her feel better, then I'd go along with it.

Mom and Dad had been on the makeshift dance floor for nearly every song, leaving Bishop, Lincoln, Josie, and me behind. We'd drunk our fair share, poking gentle fun at the couples that looked like newborn foals who didn't know how to work their legs.

"That looks so painful," Josie said, grimacing as one guy stepped on his partner's toes for the fifth time. "Her poor feet are going to be destroyed. Thank God you can dance because I wouldn't marry someone who couldn't."

Lincoln wrapped his arm around her shoulders. "If I didn't, I'd have taken lessons just for you."

Josie scrunched her nose. "I don't think I'd like someone else teaching you, so nevermind. I'd endure it, but only because you're a quick learner."

"Is that the *only* reason?"

"Oh my god," I said, tipping my head back. "Don't start. Go dance and say all that lovey-dovey stuff out there."

Josie and Lincoln laughed, but he pulled her into his arms. "What do you say, darlin'? Wanna go show'em how it's done?"

She smiled, not saying a word as she dragged him out with the crowd. They bumped into our parents, and my heart ached as I watched how happy they seemed. Don't get me wrong, I was over the moon for them. Mom and Dad had been through so much over the past year. So had Josie and Lincoln. They all deserved to smile and laugh and settle into their forevers.

But lately, I'd found myself envious of that kind of simplicity. I didn't really know what I was doing with my life outside of rodeo, which had already taken a sideline with how much of a shit show the year had been. My days consisted of working, eating, and going to bed, only to wake up and do it over again.

I had no spark, no drive, nothing pushing me toward the greatness I always thought I'd achieved.

Except for Bishop.

As much as I hated being around him, the thought of making his life difficult seemed to be the only thing I could focus on. It helped take my mind off the perpetual doom I felt over my future. The thought of burrowing so deeply under his skin made me smile. He was just too easy to piss off. Maybe that was why I did it. Mom always said when I was little I'd rather have negative attention than no attention at all, guess not much had changed.

I didn't want to think about any other reason.

Bishop had been relatively quiet since Cleo left our table

earlier, spending his time eyeing everyone around him like he was keeping watch. Only Lincoln's incessant pushing and prodding seemed to bring him out of his shell.

Or maybe it had something to do with the multiple glasses of whiskey being pushed his way.

"And then there were two," I said, picking up my bottle and downing it. It soured on my tongue, leaving a bitter taste behind. "Why is it always us?"

Bishop shook his head. "Fuckin' beats me. I figured you'd be up and out of your seat by now."

He was right. Under normal circumstances, I would've left without a second thought. So why was I still here?

I couldn't ignore the restless energy coursing through my veins like it had the night he and I had almost gone too far. I didn't know why I felt the need to act on it. It wasn't like it'd never steered me wrong. In fact, there were many times I'd woken up regretting my actions.

It wasn't too late. I could still wander into the crowd and find a cowboy for the night. One I could lose myself in and avoid damaging my pride further. There sure wasn't a shortage of them. I could literally throw a stone in any direction and hit a good-looking man in tight jeans and a pair of boots. But therein lay my problem.

I didn't want just any cowboy. I wanted one specific pair of boots kicked off by the foot of my bed. I wanted the one next to me, as stupid as it might be. Just for one night. Just to get it out of my system, so we could squash whatever the fuck this was between us once and for all. He could preach to me all day about how we shouldn't for any number of reasons, but it didn't eliminate that stupid, reckless feeling.

Our age difference, the fact he worked for my dad, the fact we both knew it wouldn't change anything... None of it mattered. Honestly? It only made things worse. It felt forbidden, and I wanted him even more because of it.

I found myself thinking about that night more than I cared to admit. Though, I usually dragged myself out of the thought right before I'd thrown up—everything that came after that was a fucking disaster. My whole body tingled when I remembered what it felt like to have his calloused fingers dig into my skin, or the way he'd slapped my ass. He always exuded such control. Seeing him try to force me into submission got me all sorts of hot and bothered.

Something knocked into my chair, and I blinked to clear the haze. Bishop was staring at me, his brows furrowed in question.

"What?" I asked, straightening my back.

"Dunno. You had a weird look on your face. Wasn't sure what was happening."

"It must be difficult to understand the concept of being lost in thought, what with all that empty space up there," I said, reaching over to tap his temple.

"Fuck off," he said. "There's at least one or two little Bishops up there running the show."

I turned to him in shock. "Did you just make a joke?"

Bishop chuckled. "I've been known to do that a time or two."

"Well, I've never heard one before."

"Naw, I never let my guard down around you. That'd be too dangerous." He turned his head, letting his eyes rake over my body. There wasn't anything soft or sweet about it. Nothing but raw heat blazed in those dark green depths.

"Sounds vulnerable," I said. My voice came out all raspy and strange, like I'd forgotten to breathe in the moments that passed.

"Sometimes it is," he admitted.

"Maybe you should try it sometime."

"Telling jokes?"

"No," I said, shaking my head. "Being vulnerable."

Bishop ran his tongue along his teeth, looking down at the hand wrapped around his cup. "I thought we already talked about that. I have rules I don't break," he said, lowering his voice. "Not even for a pretty little cocktease like yourself."

"Fuck," I breathed, clenching my thighs on instinct. What was happening right now?

He closed his eyes, letting out a shaky breath. "Shit, sorry. I—I don't know why I said that—"

I leaned over, placing my hand on his thigh like he'd done to Cleo earlier. It'd made me stupid jealous, even though I knew I had no right or reason to be. They were closer in age, eliminating what seemed to be his biggest concern.

And yet, he couldn't keep his eyes off me. Even in the months since our fight, even when he thought I wasn't paying attention, I knew he was looking my way. I wasn't stupid, and I wasn't blind.

Bishop's nostrils flared as he glanced down at my hand. "The fuck are you doing, Lennox?"

"I dunno," I admitted. "Maybe it's the alcohol—"

"Definitely the alcohol."

I smiled. "Or maybe it's the fact that despite my best efforts to be utterly repulsed by you and everything you do—"

"*Ouch*."

I smacked his arm. "Will you stop interrupting me? That's rude!"

"Nope. I can't," he said. My breath caught as he lifted his gaze to mine.

"Why not?" I asked.

A muscle in his jaw fluttered as he answered. "Because that's the only thing stopping me from telling you to move your hand. I shouldn't like it as much as I do, but I'm feeling selfish tonight."

"You should be selfish." I moved my hand back to his thigh, squeezing slightly.

"Lennox..." he warned. "We can't go down this road again. You're too young—"

"I'm a legally consenting adult."

"You're drunk."

"So are you," I said, leaning forward in my seat. "So is everyone else here."

"That doesn't make this any better. Remember the last time—"

"Don't you wanna know what I taste like?" I whispered. Bishop's eyes flared, watching as I trailed my fingers up his leg. "You didn't get the chance before, did you? I bet you've been dreaming of it, huh?"

"Christ, you don't play fair," he bit out. "You're a fucking brat who is used to getting your way."

I smirked. "Sure am."

He raised a brow. "And you think this is gonna work? That you're gonna get me to give in and break all the rules for you? You must not know me well enough. My control is unwavering."

I glanced down at his crotch, where the outline of his very hard dick was visible through his jeans. "Doesn't look like you're the one in control anymore."

I tried to move my hand, but he shot out, quickly gripping my wrist. "You think I'm not in control?" he asked, smirking when I nodded. "That's cute. Killer, I could have you bent over this table, begging to be fucked if I wanted to. And before you try to tell me no, tell me this instead… If I reached between those sweet thighs, would I find your panties soaked? Your cunt aching to be touched? Would you give me those desperate little whimpers you gave me the first time I touched you?"

I tried to stifle my moan as I shifted forward to put pressure on my clit. It was, in fact, needing the contact. It'd been too long since I'd been with someone who wasn't powered by batteries. He was talking to me like my parents weren't standing nearby, which was ridiculously hot.

The way Bishop looked at me, knowing he was right, was enough to make me give in.

"Tell me what you're thinking about," Bishop ordered, sitting back in his chair. He looked cool, calm, and collected—like we were discussing the weather or something incredibly mundane.

"That I'll beg if you ask me to," I said without hesitation, keeping my voice low. "That I'll get on my knees right here and now—"

Bishop looked away, and I let my words falter. My stomach sank, embarrassment creeping in hard and fast like it had the morning I'd woken up in an empty bed. It wasn't a feeling I was accustomed to, especially not when it came to sex. I was used to getting my way both in and out of the bedroom. With Bishop, it seemed to be my default setting—like I was always one step away from either wanting to burn his cabin to the ground or bury myself in a hole to hide.

Before I could backpedal, he spoke. "I didn't say to stop," he said, tone stern. "And I don't want you on your knees."

"Where do you want me, then?" I asked, licking my lips.

Bishop leaned forward, bracing his elbow on the table. He opened his mouth but quickly shut it as screams rang out from the dance floor. We both jerked our heads toward the commotion, rising out of our seats to see what was happening.

I couldn't make anything out over the rapidly forming crowd. Was there an accident? Was someone hurt? As someone shouted for an ambulance, I hoped the fear creeping up my spine was wrong. Someone probably twisted an ankle, that's all.

And then the band stopped, cutting the music just as a single wailing cry pierced the air. A sound I would recognize anywhere.

"*No, no, no,*" I said, pressing my hand to my heart as if it could stop it from breaking.

"Lennox—" Bishop began, sticking out his arm to stop me from running forward, but I was too quick.

I darted past him, urging my body to run faster than ever. Bishop's footsteps sounded behind me, solidifying my anxiety.

He wouldn't have taken off after me if his mind hadn't gone to the worst possible scenario like mine had.

He grabbed my hand, pulling me back as I got to the crowd. I tried to fight back and struggle out of his hold, but it was useless. "Let me go," I said, panic rising with each wasted second.

"I'm trying to help you," he barked. I didn't know what he meant until he stepped in front and tugged me through the crowd. He shouted at the onlookers, forcing them out of the way so we could pass.

I couldn't breathe or think about anything other than seeing what was on the other side of the crowd. If it wasn't for Bishop's skin against my own, I wouldn't have made it without collapsing.

As Bishop broke through the last line of people, his steps faltered. He spun around, taking me in his arms as I tried to step around him. "Look at me," he said, but I shook my head.

"Let me through," I cried. "Let me see—"

"Goddammit, Lennox... Look at me," he growled. His hands flew to my face, forcing me to meet his gaze. "I need you to breathe, okay?"

My vision clouded, the world going blurry around me. It wasn't until his thumbs swiped beneath my eyes that I realized I'd started crying. "I can't," I said, gasping for air. "Bishop, I can't..."

"You can," he said, trying to keep his tone even, but he couldn't. There was a shake there that hadn't been before.

"Lennox!" Josie cried, pulling me away from Bishop. "We need to find Cleo," she said in a rush. "Her phone is off, and we need—"

But I'd stopped listening when I looked past her shoulder and saw Lincoln. He was hunched over someone, frantically performing CPR. My mom was on her knees beside him. She had her arms wrapped around her middle, crying for the person to wake up.

"—meet us at the hospital," Josie finished, tugging on my arm. "Are you listening?"

I couldn't. Not as Lincoln shifted, and I saw my dad's face come into view.

Then I screamed.

bishop

. . .

THE DRIVE to the hospital was long and silent. Lennox and Cleo sat in my back seat, holding onto one another, as I followed Lincoln, Josie, and Ruby up ahead. Given the severity of Doug's condition, he'd been immediately airlifted to a facility in Dallas that could treat him properly.

I kept the radio low, total quiet made me uncomfortable, especially when I could hear the girls' soft sniffles and couldn't do a damn thing about it. My gaze darted to my rear-view mirror too often, keeping an eye on them like it could make a damn bit of difference.

I'd never felt so helpless in my life.

Hearing the heartbreak in Lennox's scream had nearly broken me. I'd held her to me as long as I could, squeezing her tightly as if I could stop her from shattering further. It was only when the paramedics began loading Doug onto the stretcher that I knew I had to jump into motion.

When we pulled up to the hospital, both girls jumped out and ran through the doors as Josie ushered a distraught Ruby in after them. Her eyes were re-rimmed and swollen. Unfocused.

Lincoln and I followed, but neither of us said anything. He

looked stricken, his face pale and arms still shaking. By the time the ambulance had made it out to the ranch, he'd given Doug CPR for over thirty minutes.

The paramedic said it was the only reason Doug was still alive.

We quickly made our way inside and found the elevator. We rode in silence up to the ICU. The moment the doors opened, the girls headed straight to the nurse's station.

"Hi, we're here to see Douglas Hayes? He was airlifted." Cleo asked the woman sitting behind the counter. "We just drove up from Ashwood."

"Let me check," she said, typing his name into their system. It was silent for a long moment as we all waited on bated breath. "Unfortunately, he's still in surgery, and visiting hours are over."

"Please?" Josie asked, voice breaking.

"I'm so sorry," she said. To her credit, she sounded genuine. "Even if things were different, I can't let six of you in—"

"We can wait out here," I said, gesturing toward Lincoln and me. His eyes darted to Josie, and I could tell he didn't want to let her out of his sight, but that was too damn bad. "If that helps."

The nurse pursed her lips. "I can't let you in until he's back from surgery," she said carefully. The girls' shoulders dropped. "But I can bring you back two at a time once he's settled. How about you all get some coffee downstairs in the cafeteria? It will likely be a long night."

"Thank you," Cleo breathed. "Can I leave my number with you?"

While they exchanged contact information, I looked toward Lennox. She stood off to the side, chewing nervously on her thumbnail. All the light I was used to seeing in her eyes was gone, replaced by an unfocused and glassy look as people moved around her.

I wanted to go to her, to let her know it would be okay, but I couldn't tell her that. I didn't know what the future looked like or if he'd come out of surgery at all. There was no fucking crystal ball, either.

"You alright, man?" Lincoln asked, nudging my shoulder.

"Yeah," I said, rubbing the back of my neck. "Good as we can be, ya know?"

Lincoln nodded. "I get it."

Cleo turned and began ushering everyone toward the elevator. Lennox was the last to move. Lincoln and I fell into step behind everyone as she wrapped her arm around her mom, holding her tightly when the doors closed.

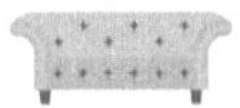

I SHIFTED in the shitty waiting room chair, pulling my hat down over my eyes to block the disgustingly bright light overhead. It was around five in the morning. Lincoln and I had been out here for a couple of hours while the girls took turns sitting in Doug's room once he'd gotten out of surgery and settled in. Ruby hadn't left his side since the nurse called them back. Not that I blamed her one bit. It was the only thing that'd seemed to knock her out of the state of shock she'd been in since leaving the ranch.

Thankfully, everything had gone smoothly with no complications—doc's words, not mine—and Doug would make a full recovery. There'd been a blood clot blocking one of his arteries, and they'd been able to go in and remove it without much fuss. Though, they did say they wanted to keep him in the hospital for at least a few days.

When I'd gotten the word, I'd sent a message to our work chat, updating them on Doug's condition and letting them know we'd all be out today. They all gave their best wishes and told me they'd take care of the ranch in our absence. I wasn't worried about them. We'd built a damn good crew, and I trusted them to get their shit done.

No, I was worried about Lennox. I was torn between staying and trying to be there for her, I was probably the last person in the world she'd want hanging around. I should head home so the family could be together and focus on Doug.

Just a few more hours of sleep, I told myself, *and then you can go home.*

I was sure Lincoln would stay, which was fine. He was family now. The team and I could handle just about everything we needed to on our own. The only concern I had was the branding coming up. Our spring calving season yielded one of the largest herd additions we'd seen in a few years. We would need all hands on deck to get everything done on time. Hell, I might need to hire a couple more hands depending on how things went here, but that was a problem for future Bishop to figure out.

I heard the shuffling of feet before someone plopped down beside me. I was about to peek out from under the brim of my hat, already annoyed I was awake, but then I smelled her.

The soft scent of honey and vanilla filled the air, invading my senses. I'd recognize it anywhere. It was fucking imprinted in my memory. Sometimes, I swore I could still smell it on my pillow at night, like it was haunting me.

Today, though, I savored it.

My muscles relaxed as I settled back into my spot. Neither of us spoke as Lennox shifted, causing our knees to brush. I expected her to jerk away, but she didn't. If anything, she leaned into me.

I don't know how long we stayed like that, quietly searching for comfort in a place that offered none. I was almost asleep when she whispered, "I want to go home."

I tilted my hat up to get a good look at her. Her blonde hair, loosely curled earlier, was now piled on top of her head in a crudely secured bun. She wasn't wearing any makeup, though there were still dark smudges near her eyes, like she hadn't been able to get it all off. I'd never seen her look so tired, so distraught. There was no fight left in her. She was just sitting there, vulnerable. Exposed. Raw in every sense of the word.

Seeing her that way made my chest ache. I wanted to take her in my arms and make it better. Not that I even knew how or what to do—I'd never been the type people turned to for that kinda stuff, but she made me wish I was.

"You wanna leave?" I asked, my voice rough from exhaustion.

Lennox nodded her head, keeping her focus straight ahead. "I can't..." she began, but her voice broke. "It sounds horrible, but I can't see him like this. I've been staring at the man in bed for hours, but he doesn't look like my dad. That guy looks frail and sick, and all it does is remind me how quickly he can be taken away from me. I mean, he was laughing and joking less than twelve hours ago, and now we're here—"

Tears began rolling down her face, and I let instinct take over. I sat up straighter and pulled her close. Or I tried to. One of those stupid armrests was between us, but thankfully, I could lift it out of the way. She leaned into me, letting me take on the full weight of her body.

"What're you doing?" she asked, looking up with red-rimmed eyes.

"I dunno," I said honestly. "You were crying. Felt like I should do something."

Her laugh was hollow, but I took it as a good sign. "Is this a pity hug?"

"Do you want it to be?" The last thing I felt toward her was pity, especially now, but this was new territory for us. There'd never been a moment I could think of when she and I had ever hugged.

Lennox was quiet for a moment. "It probably should be, right?"

"Probably," I agreed.

"I don't really want it to be—"

"Then it isn't," I said. "This is whatever you need it to be."

Lennox settled into my arms, laying her head on my chest. Her fingers fiddled with the button along my shirt collar, and it felt natural.

It was unbelievably terrifying. I was sure she could make out the frantic beating of my heart as I ran my hand up and down her back. "You just let me know when you wanna go."

She nodded. I could feel her hesitation before she spoke. "Can we stay like this a little longer?"

"As long as you need."

lennox

· · ·

"PSST... LENNOX."

I tightened my hold on my pillow. "Go away," I groaned, nuzzling into the warm cushion. It smelled nice. Masculine. It reminded me of home, which is where I wanted to be. I didn't even remember falling asleep, but I knew I was beyond exhausted. The last thing I remembered was…

Oh, God. Bishop.

I'd fallen asleep on Bishop.

I jerked up, pushing off his chest. He groaned as my weight left his body. I tried not to think of how cold I felt suddenly, trying instead to open my eyes. The harsh fluorescent lighting above was blinding, and I blinked to adjust to the brightness.

"What's happening?" Bishop asked, looking around the room. He stopped as his gaze landed on me. His voice was gruff and full of sleep. It reminded me of how it'd been last night, how he'd opened his arms to me without question.

When I'd wandered in here, I hadn't been looking for comfort but an escape. I just needed a few minutes to gather my thoughts after spending hours going in and out of Dad's room. There was only so much more I could take of listening to the doctors talk about his condition. It was all so clinical, as if this was just another day. I guess it was, for them, but it sure as hell wasn't for us. Seeing them come and go like our world hadn't just been upended made me wildly uncomfortable.

The waiting room had been quiet. Only a few other people were strewn out around us, huddled together and waiting for news like we were. I noticed that some of those faces were still here. Though, there were many more than there had been last night.

Josie stood above me, holding a tray full of coffee. I greedily took one, closing my eyes to savor the liquid gold on my tongue. She handed one to Bishop next and then Lincoln, who sat up and greeted her with a kiss.

"Thought you guys might want some caffeine," she said softly, looking every bit as tired as I felt.

"Did you sleep at all last night?" I asked, patting the seat next to me.

Her shoulders slumped as she sat down. "An hour or two. More than Cleo and Mom, though."

Guilt gnawed at my conscience. I shouldn't have left them. I shouldn't have walked away to find some peace when my mom and sisters didn't. "How long was I out?"

"Just a few hours," she said. "It's only seven."

"I'm sorry," I said, in a rush. "I didn't mean to fall asleep."

Josie put her hand on mine. "I'm glad you did," she said. There was no hint of annoyance, only complete understanding. That was one of the things I loved most about Josie. "Cleo is booking a hotel room nearby. Not that Mom will sleep there, of course. She's been pretty vocal about not leaving his side."

"Not surprised," I said, taking a sip.

"Nope," she said. "But at least she'll have a place to shower if she wants to."

"Makes sense," I mumbled. "Have the doctors been in this morning? Do we know how long he'll have to stay?"

"They're about to do rounds, I think. I wanted to come get you so that you could see him."

Did I want to see him again? Could I handle it? I wasn't so sure. It was a shitty and selfish thought, but I was scared.

As if reading my thoughts, Josie put her hand on my knee. "It's okay, Lenny. You don't have to—"

"No," I said, shaking my head. "I wanna see him."

She smiled. "The nurse will make an exception to let us all back there. I told her we're all family, and not having everyone together has been hard. I don't know if she's convinced, but it worked anyway. Let's go."

Josie took my hand and led me through the grim hallway. Lincoln and Bishop fell into step behind us, nearly barrelling into me as we abruptly stopped outside Dad's door.

"—goddamn wires. Why're there so many?"

"He's awake?" I asked, staring up at my sister. "Why the hell didn't you lead with that?"

"He wasn't when I left," she said, quickly pushing open the door.

Everyone looked up as we entered, but my eyes went straight to Dad. He was sitting up in his bed, hair sticking up a hundred different ways. His skin was still pale, especially under this shitty hospital lighting, but there was a definite flush to his face that hadn't been there hours ago.

"There they are," he croaked, offering a watery smile. "Bishop, why're you lingering outside? Get your ass in here."

I turned over my shoulder, noticing Bishop was still standing outside the room. I narrowed my eyes at him and he stepped in awkwardly, the door snicking shut behind him.

Looking back toward the bed, my chest tightened. "Dad," I whispered, shoulders slumping as I stepped forward. Tears threatened to spill down my cheeks, but I tried to hold them at bay.

Oh god, he was awake. He was okay.

He took my hand, running his thumb over my skin. The callouses there were a comfort, a reminder that he was still here, that we had more time.

"Hey, Lenny Bug," he said, smiling.

And then the tears fell. I couldn't hold them back anymore. It didn't matter what the doctors had said. I'd spent hours trying to rid myself of the anxiety plaguing my body, but now he was awake and it was the first ounce of relief I'd felt.

I dropped into the chair beside his bed, resting my forehead against his hand. "I know this fuss isn't all about me."

Lifting my head, I glared at him. "You know damn well it is, old man. You scared us."

"I'm not going anywhere for a long time," he said. "Don't go countin' me out now."

I pressed a kiss to the back of his hand. "Wouldn't dream of it."

The door opened, and a tall man in a white jacket walked in. "Whoa, full room," he said, eyes widening as he looked at each of us. "I'm Doctor Rhodes," he said, offering a smile. "Looks like I'll be your cardiologist for the time being."

Dr. Rhodes stepped forward, shaking each of our hands. He was definitely more likable than the doctors we'd seen last night, not to mention much better looking. He had short, dark brown hair and hazel eyes that leaned brown over green.

Not like Bishop's.

"How's everyone doing this morning?" he asked, reaching for Dad's chart at the end of the bed. His eyes scanned it quickly before looking over to me. "Do you mind if we switch places for a minute? Promise it won't take long. Just need to check his vitals."

"Oh, yeah. Of course," I said, quickly pushing out of my chair. I tucked a loose piece of hair behind my ear, knowing I probably looked like a mess.

I stepped beside Josie, who obnoxiously wiggled her

eyebrows as Dr. Rhodes listened to Dad's chest. "He's cuuuute," she said, dragging out the word.

"Shut up," I muttered, nudging her side. "You're worse than your boyfriend."

I mean, he *was* cute—handsome, even. He was the kind of guy you expected to see on an episode of Grey's Anatomy. Maybe if the circumstances were different and we'd met anywhere else, I'd have flirted a bit. I'd never dated a doctor before; there were plenty of fun roleplaying scenarios I could think of. But I wasn't thinking about a man in a lab coat, not really.

I was still craving the warmth of Bishop's body on my skin.

As the doctor finished, he stepped back and placed his stethoscope around his neck. "What's the verdict, doc?" Dad asked. "When can I get outta here?"

"Well, Mr. Hayes, do you want good or bad news first?"

My stomach dropped as Mom reached over and took Dad's hand, the two of them bracing each other for the worst. "Give it to me straight," my dad said. "Bad news first."

Dr. Rhodes nodded once. "Alright then. We'll need to run a few more tests to check on the status of your heart and get a better idea of what's going on there. And I'll have to ask these lovely ladies," he said, gesturing toward us, "to ensure you stick to your diet. I have a hunch you haven't been as strict as you should be. This is your health, Mr. Hayes. No more red meat. No more bacon."

Dad huffed. "Might as well take me out to pasture now," he mumbled.

The doctor smiled. "I know that isn't what you wanted to hear, but the good news is that we can get you out of here within a few days, depending on the test results."

"Really?" Mom asked.

"Really," Dr. Rhodes said. "I won't lie, it won't be all rainbows and sunshine. There'll be restrictions, and you'll need to take it easy for a while. Unfortunately, that'll be non-negotiable."

"I'm a rancher," Dad said proudly. "I can't just take days off. This little vacation alone is gonna put us behind."

"I understand that. I respect it, even. I grew up on a ranch not far from here, so I'm not a stranger to the hard work and dedication it takes to do what you do, but can I be frank?" Dad nodded, and Dr. Rhodes quickly looked around the room before answering. "You're going to have to make a decision, Mr. Hayes. You can take my advice and live out the rest of your days with your beautiful family here, or you can tell me to go to hell and get back to work, in which case I'd wager you'd only have six months."

I squeezed Josie's hand as though that could change his words.

"Six months?" Dad asked. There was a tremble in his voice that hadn't been there moments ago.

Dr. Rhodes pursed his lips. "It doesn't have to be that way, but like I said, I have first-hand experience with how difficult the life of a rancher is. You're up before the sun, working hard to provide for your family and taking care of animals that are helpless without you, and then you don't walk through the door until night falls. The job is stressful and isn't for the faint of heart—which, unfortunately, you now are."

My parents looked at one another, a lifetime's worth of hard work and memories between them. They were locked in a silent conversation as the gravity of the situation came into focus.

My dad could choose his passion, the career he'd worked his ass off for, and the empire he'd built brick by brick. Or he could choose to live out the rest of his life by retiring and leaving the work to the next generation.

It would either be him or the ranch, and I hated not knowing what he'd choose.

Dad pulled his gaze from Mom's, taking a moment to look at

each of us standing near the end of his bed. His bottom lip tensed for a moment, and I knew him well enough to understand how difficult his decision would be. He'd always said he'd rest when he was dead, that the devil himself would have to tear him from the saddle to reap his soul.

As a kid, I remembered being so captivated by his dedication. Dad loved that ranch with everything he had, and he'd given more than his share of blood, sweat, and tears to turn it into what it was today. I'd wanted nothing more than to follow in his footsteps. I wanted to have something I was proud of. Something I never wanted to leave.

"I'm not ready to go yet," he said, looking down at his hands. "And if that means I gotta give some things up to make sure I'm around for a little bit longer, I guess that's what I'll have to do."

I closed my eyes, letting my forehead rest against Josie's shoulder. I heard Cleo's sniffle from her other side. It was the best and worst case scenario happening all at once. None of us wanted to see our father walk away from something he loved, but we damn sure preferred that over spreading his ashes in the wind.

"I was hoping that'd be the case," Dr. Rhodes said. "I'll order the tests now to get the ball rolling. We'll start in a few hours, after you've gotten to catch up with your family and get some food in your system."

"Thanks, Doc," Dad said, reaching out and shaking Dr. Rhodes's hand.

"Just doing my job," he said before heading toward the door. He stopped and tapped the frame. "Keep it quick in here, though. I'm already breaking the rules by letting everyone in here. Fifteen minutes, okay?"

"Of course," Mom said, wiping away her tears. "Thank you."

Dr. Rhodes dipped his head and closed the door behind him, leaving us all in relative silence.

"Well, that fucking sucks," Dad said, sinking back into his pillows.

For the first time in twelve hours, I laughed. Considering where we were and the news we'd just gotten, it felt wrong but I was also wildly happy that this wasn't the end. Josie and Cleo joined in, and it wasn't long before everyone in the room followed suit.

"Douglas Hayes," Mom chastised, tapping him lightly on his arm. She wiped the tears from beneath her eyes.

"Well, it does," he grumbled. "I wasn't planning on being forced into retirement. There's a lot of things we'll have to rethink. We'll have to hire more hands, and—"

"We'll take care of it, sir," Bishop said, stepping up. "We've got a good crew now, so it's nothing we'll have to rush to figure out."

Dad was quiet for a second. "You're gonna need some help, Bishop. You can't run this place on your own."

"He won't be alone, Daddy," Josie said. "When I get back, I'll still run the books and schedule while Lincoln takes over the training schedule full-time. We don't have any clinics until the beginning of the year. Besides, y'all were already planning on having him cover the smaller seminars. It'll be fine."

Lincoln nodded, placing his hand on Josie's shoulder. "Hell, yes, it will. Like Bishop said, you've built a damn good team here. I'm happy to pitch in with whatever you need."

"And I can help," I said, piping up. I mean, I was already doing the damn job anyway. Might as well make myself useful. "I don't have anything else going on right now."

"Listen, I can take care of it," Bishop said, annoyance seeping into his tone as everyone chimed in. "Nothing has to change."

For some reason, his words rubbed me the wrong way. Didn't he understand that change was already happening whether we wanted it or not? Bishop was hyper-independent. He always had been, often biting off more than he could chew.

He and Dad had gone to verbal blows with one another on multiple occasions when Bishop would take on too many responsibilities and didn't delegate.

His dedication was admirable. I'd even go as far as to say it was one of his best qualities, but it was only a matter of time before that quality got his ass hurt. Dad always said when you didn't ask for help, you were usually asking for trouble instead. It couldn't have been more accurate.

Operating a ranch wasn't an easy feat. Caring for the animals and mending fences were only a tiny part of the daily operations. Bishop and my dad worked together to make sure everything ran smoothly. There were a hundred different things they had to oversee.

I turned and looked at Bishop, narrowing my eyes. "I didn't realize you could do two people's jobs simultaneously."

"Done it before," he said, shifting on his feet. "And I can do it again."

"You don't have to, though. And instead of taking the help and saying thank you, you're being a stubborn ass about it," I argued.

"I thought you were heading back to the circuit?" Josie asked, stealing my attention.

I shrugged. "Yeah, but I've got plenty of time before the season starts." There was a good six months before my next ranking ride, and that was more than enough time to get things settled here before heading back on the road. But I didn't understand Josie's question. It was almost like she was hesitant to lean on me for help.

My sister wasn't hard to read. She wore her heart on her sleeve, even though she liked to pretend she didn't. Each time her mind kicked into overdrive, she had these little tells. One of which she was doing right now.

Josie worried her lip. "Are you sure?"

"Uh, yeah," I said, chuckling. Was she serious? Of course, I was sure. In fact, I had zero hesitation. "Seeing as I'm already doing the job, I didn't think my offer to help would be a big deal."

"I know, I just don't want to tie you down with something you don't want to do. That's all." Her smile was weak, which could be from any number of things. Tensions were high. We were all exhausted and running on one to two hours of sleep. So, why did my mind instantly twist her words into something that left me feeling bitter?

"We don't need her," Bishop interjected. "I can run shit just fine. If I need help, I'll ask Lincoln or one of the other hands."

Don't cry, Lennox. Don't. Fucking. Cry.

No, I wouldn't shed another tear in front of him. Not if he was going to act like working with me was the worst thing to ever happen to him. News flash, I didn't like it any more than he did. He was an overbearing asshole, even on the best day.

But this wasn't about either of us, and I'd work with him every day if Dad asked me to.

I guess whatever common ground we'd found was over and done with. It was almost funny how quickly we had gone from falling asleep next to one another to standing here at odds.

"We're already stretched thin," Josie said slowly. "We need all the help we can get."

Dad was sitting silently, gaze bouncing between us at the foot of his bed. I fought against the urge to shrink back when it landed on me. If Dad didn't want me helping with the ranch, he could tell me himself.

"Lennox is the best rider out of y'all," he said, clearing his throat. "She already knows the ins and outs of what needs to be done. Figure it out however y'all need to for the time being. If things are that bad after a month, we'll re-evaluate."

I looked over at Bishop. He ran his tongue along his teeth, and I could tell he was holding back that temper I was so familiar with. Good. That was something I could work with. In fact, I preferred it to whatever the hell had happened last night.

Nice Bishop freaked me out and made me feel weird things I couldn't explain. Judging by his pinched expression, he thought the same.

"Have I made myself clear?" Dad asked sharply.

"Crystal," I said, dipping my chin.

Bishop was still silently fuming, staring at a spot on the far wall like it held all the answers to his problems.

"That gonna be a problem, Bishop?" Dad asked, yet again. "I didn't say all that to listen to crickets chirp."

"No, sir. I've got it," he said, rolling his shoulders back. "If it's alright with y'all, I'm going to step out for some air. Anyone need anything?"

"No, we're okay. Thank you, Bishop," Mom said. "We appreciate you."

He gave her a tight-lipped smile, avoiding me as he dipped his head and stormed out the door. There were a million things I wanted to do, and most of them centered around tracking him down and giving him a piece of my mind, but that would have to wait. I didn't have the energy to worry about what our new normal would look like.

Not today, anyway.

lennox

. . .

I STOOD next to Cleo beside the kitchen sink. We were cleaning up after breakfast, and our routine was flawless. She washed, and I dried—which was perfect, considering I hated washing dishes. Bits of food were always stuck to the plate, and even the thought of touching one of them made my skin crawl.

It'd been nearly a week since we'd left the hospital. Josie stayed behind with Mom since Cleo had to return to work. Before moving to Montana, she'd taught first grade at Ashwood Elementary and loved it. Cleo had the perfect disposition to work with kids day in and out. Over the summer, the principal had found out she was back in town and had been begging her to come back. She'd told her no over and over again, but Mrs. Cox wasn't one to give up. Eventually, my sister agreed to come back as a substitute, but that'd quickly turned to full-time employment when she informed them she'd be staying permanently.

It'd been one of the first genuine smiles I'd seen from Cleo in a long time.

The school year was in full swing now, and while they were able to find a sub for the Monday and Tuesday following Dad's hospitalization, no one else was available to fill in for the rest of the week. Thankfully, this gave us the opportunity to get Mom and Josie settled in Dallas before coming home and collapsing ourselves.

Being in this big house was strange, just the two of us. I couldn't remember the last time it'd been so silent. Growing up, it was always full of noise. After all, it was filled with three boisterous girls who spent their days running up and down the halls screaming at one another about God knows what.

But now it felt empty and cold.

I'd never thought much about what would happen when our parents weren't around anymore because I'd never let it even be considered a possibility. Death was inevitable, but not for my parents. I always thought they'd live forever.

For the first time in twenty-seven years, I was forced to face the ugly truth, and I hated every minute of it.

Cleo and I had done what we could. We invited Lincoln and, much to my dismay, Bishop over for dinner every night. Lincoln was grateful and had come over each time since Josie was gone. I think he hated being alone just as much as we did.

Bishop, on the other hand, never showed up.

Working with him had proved to be just as challenging as I expected it to be. Every morning when I showed up to the barn, his office was empty, and Titan was gone. I started waking up earlier and earlier in hopes of catching him, but I never could. I was almost ready to camp out in the damn stalls to confront him.

Whatever this thing hanging between us was weird. We were like one of those indoor rollercoasters you rode in the pitch dark. Was there a huge climb coming up? A sharp turn or a drastic drop? No one knew.

Setting my feelings aside, which was hard to do because I took *everything* personally, my main annoyance was his insistence on doing everything himself. Try as I might, I did care about him. How could I not? He'd damn near always been in my life.

Burnout was a real thing, and it had dangerous consequences. As a kid, I remember my parents fighting about Dad's long working hours. Mom always kept him in line and never backed down when he argued with her.

Bishop didn't have that, nor did he like anyone calling him out on his shit.

The thing was, even through my anger, I found myself pitying the man. He was someone who always seemed to live in fear. A set of rules were his best friend, and he would never dare to color outside the lines. No wonder he didn't understand how good it could be if he set his pride aside.

"What's on your schedule for today?" Cleo asked, wiping her hands on a clean dishrag. Her hair was down, dusting the top of her shoulders. She'd cropped it short at the start of the school year to keep it out of the way. I didn't get it. I'd always thought shorter hair was harder to manage but to each their own.

I blew out a breath, turning and leaning against the counter. "I don't know yet. I guess I'll head to the barn and see what needs to be done. I might go out and check the stock tanks to make sure they're still full, or I could go check fencing."

Cleo tossed the towel down on the countertop. "Bishop still giving you hell?"

I rolled my eyes. "If you consider him completely ignoring and avoiding me hell, then yes. It's more annoying than anything because we're supposed to be working together, you know? But I haven't seen him since Sunday. Even Lincoln tried to talk to him, but he just shrugged him off. I don't know what's going on with him."

"It's hard. So many things are changing, and so fast, too."

"Well, it sure doesn't give him the right to be a dick," I grumbled. "I'm the one who's sworn to hate him forever."

Cleo cocked her head to the side, studying me. "And why is that, Lennox?"

"What do you mean?" I asked, trying to keep my voice even.

"Why do you hate him?"

"Because it's Bishop," I said, shrugging. "I've always hated him."

Liar, liar, pants on fire.

"No, you haven't," she said, turning to grab her travel cup from the cupboard. "Y'all have always fought like cats and dogs, sure, but I've never seen real hate between y'all until a few months ago."

"We don't need her."

"I don't know what to tell you," I said, wiping my hands on my jeans. "Things change. People change. Maybe it's always been there."

Cleo tapped her fingers against the countertop. "I don't know. You guys seemed pretty comfortable at the bar." I quickly turned on her, narrowing my eyes. She was smiling as she lifted her cup and took a sip. "And it's funny… You didn't come home that night, even though we were dropped off at the same time. I can't help but wonder—"

I surged forward, clapping my hand over her mouth before she could finish. Her eyes widened in surprise. "Don't say it," I said. "Don't even go there."

She ripped my hand away and pointed at me. "You had sex with Bishop!"

"No, no, no," I said quickly. "We did not have sex."

"You did *something* with him, though! You didn't come back to the house until the next afternoon."

"I was in the barn, you know that." Much to my dismay, the entire family knew about my getting trapped in the barn while Josie and Lincoln *rekindled* their relationship. Speaking of nightmares, those sounds still haunted me.

"And why were you in the barn?" She leaned her hip against

the counter. "Because I know damn well you didn't sleep in there."

"There's a couch in the loft," I said slowly, looking everywhere but at her. Cleo had an uncanny way of coaxing the darkest secrets out of people, and I'd fallen victim to her schemes more than once. "And Strider would be an excellent cuddle buddy."

"Probably not as good as a six-foot, four-inch giant of a man who gives excellent hugs, but go on."

I crossed my arms. "Well, if you like his hugs so much, why don't you spend the night with him?" I mumbled, realizing my mistake too late.

I looked up, finding my sister grinning as though she knew she had me cornered. Why the heck would that have been what I latched onto? Why would I even be concerned if I had nothing to hide?

"And what if I did, huh? What then?"

"Are you trying to use reverse psychology on me? It might work on Josie, but it won't on me." I hoped I sounded convincing because I wasn't sure I felt it.

She lifted one shoulder. "Are you sure?"

"Absolutely." *Okay, maybe it was a little bit.*

Ugh. I damn sure didn't want to think about him in the way I did, but I feared it was too late. My interest had been piqued. Every time I tried to shove those pesky feelings down, firmly locking them into a cute little box at the back of my brain, it shook and rattled until I had no choice but to let them escape. His filthy mouth had set me aflame, and no amount of special private time with my favorite vibrator had been able to give me that toe-curling goodness I was looking for.

I really needed to get laid. And not just laid, but a blow-your-back-out-and-make-you-forget-your-name kinda sex.

Cleo sighed, topping off her coffee. "No, I'm not going to lecture you, but I'll say this… I've never known you to not go after what you want. You're far more stubborn than your sisters."

"I don't want him," I countered.

My sister walked to our breakfast nook, grabbing her purse. "Whatever you wanna tell yourself, Sis." I followed her to the living room, stopping when she did in the mud room. "Oh, and don't forget Dad'll be coming home today. Mom wants to keep it simple for family dinner tonight."

"Sounds good. Maybe I can make some chicken soup and load that bitch up with veggies," I said, resting against the doorframe. "I know how much he loves it."

"I think he'll love that," she called over her shoulder. "Let me know if I need to pick anything up from the store on my way home."

"Will do," I said. "Have fun! Teach those kids to fight the patriarchy or whatever you do."

She rolled her eyes. "They're six, Lennox."

"Never too early to start empowering the next generation!"

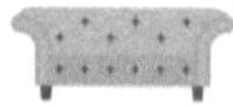

IT WAS around noon by the time I wandered into the barn. I'd spent the morning cleaning up the house, making sure it would be up to Mom's standards. I didn't need her coming home and worrying about the fluffiness of the pillows or the fact we'd missed a single shelf with dust.

Strider poked his head out of his stall, nickering as he saw me approach. I ran my hand along the soft white spot between his eyes. "There's my boy. I'm sorry I haven't been around as much this week. I promise we'll be back at it soon," I cooed. He leaned down, pushing his nose into my pocket. I smirked and stepped back. "Ahh, I think that's a new record."

Sticking my hand into the pocket, I pulled a peppermint and

laid it flat on my palm. His ears perked the moment he snatched it up. Noisy chomps filled the silence, and I laughed. He was a fiend for the things, could always scent them out the moment they were taken out of the wrapper. "Figured that might sweeten you up a bit. Now... I have one more," I said, patting my pocket, "but I'm going to save that until after our ride, alright?"

He huffed, clearly annoyed at having to wait for his treats, but he'd have to suck it up. He was only fifteen, and yet he acted more and more like a grumpy old man when he wasn't on the circuit.

"I'll be right back!" I called, heading across the hall to get my tack. I had a few hours to spare before getting back to the house to prep dinner and was too restless to sit around and do nothing. Besides, I didn't need Bishop to tell me what needed to be done here. This ranch was my home, and I wanted to take care of it.

Strider was waiting for me by the time I got back—the picture of obedience. I rolled my eyes, knowing he was anything but. We were a well-oiled machine at this point, and he knew if he cooperated, I'd spoil him with much more than a single peppermint.

Within minutes, I was leading him out of the barn. I sucked in a deep breath, savoring the fresh air. City folks might call it weird, but I loved the smell of ranch life. Sure, there were a lot of gross things we came across, but to me, it was just home.

Horse shit equaled money. It meant we still had a job and employees who depended on us. I hated to think what would happen if that scent went away.

I reached down and patted Strider's neck. He pranced on the spot as he stared out at the open fields. Black Springs was just about as flat as flat could be, but that didn't mean our views were lacking. The sunset was almost perfectly framed by the large oak trees lining the closest pasture.

I was always told I'd get sick of small towns, that my personality was too big and I would get bored. People swore I would be the sister that walked away from all of this for the big city. Don't get me wrong; there were times I loved making the drive and trying things we couldn't get in our little town, like an unlimited choice of restaurants instead of the same five I was used to in Ashwood.

I'd been to a lot of places over my short twenty-seven years, thanks to Dad's clinics and my own time on the rodeo circuit. Everything from beautiful and charming little towns that reminded me a lot of our own to the big and bright lights of Las Vegas. But all of that paled in comparison to the ranch. I was always happiest when I crossed the county line and drove under the big black arches at the start of our property line.

I moved forward, riding through the gate leading to our back pastures. As I reached down to lock it behind me, Strider threw his head back and knickered. "Hold on, boy," I said, struggling with the chain. "Almost... there..."

But he didn't listen. I barely had time to grab the saddle horn before he took off at a dead run. I cursed, wondering if something had spooked him, but when I looked forward, I saw exactly what he was excited about.

Titan and Bishop were headed toward us. We were too far apart to get a good read on him, but I noticed he pulled up on the reins to slow down. And then the bastard diverted and headed to his house instead.

Oh, hell no.

I urged Strider forward, gaining on them quickly. Bishop may have had the bigger horse, but mine was faster. There was no competition. We caught up to them quickly, riding in silence until we stopped outside his cabin.

"What the hell are you doing?" he asked, lowering his black hat. If I hadn't known better, I might've thought he was just shielding his eyes from the sun, but I wasn't stupid. He was putting yet another barrier up.

"I could ask you the same thing," I said. "Seeing as you've been avoiding me for a week."

"Been busy. Got shit to do."

I chuckled, but there was no warmth. "Ah, so I see we're back to using as few words as possible. Lovely."

"Don't see why it matters," he muttered. "Back to business as usual. Like it should be."

The words shouldn't have stung, but they did. "Business for who?" I shot back. "Because last I checked, we were supposed to be working together out here, and yet I can't even get you in the same room, let alone to look at me."

Bishop shifted in his saddle. "That's not true."

"You literally haven't looked at me once this entire conversation."

"Cause it's a waste of time. You followed me out here."

I slammed my hand down on the horn. "Goddammit, Bishop. Stop acting like a dick. I know it's your default, but avoiding me is a little fucking childish, don't you think?"

He turned, lifting his chin to stare at me from beneath the brim of his hat. His eyes were cold. Hard. Unyielding. I didn't know whether it turned me on or left me feeling queasy. "What do you want from me, Lennox?" he spat my name like a curse. I hated the way it felt. My pride urged me to turn around and leave him in the dust, but something told me I needed to stay to hear whatever he had to say. "I don't want to be around you. I mean, for fuck's sake, we'd never get anything done. All we do is fuss and fight. We sure as hell don't work well together. Especially not with whatever weird shit we had going on."

"So, what's the answer then? You're telling me that you can't separate your feelings from your *job?*" I laughed harshly, temper rising to the surface. "Give me a fucking break and get your shit together."

"Can you?" Bishop asked, knocking me off kilter. He guided Titan closer, and I could smell his sweat-slicked skin. His long-sleeved shirt was soaked, clinging to his body in a way that almost made me jealous. Tattoos peeked out from the cuffs, deliciously dark lines I wished I'd been able to study before.

I'd never given them much thought since he'd had them for as long as I could remember, but now I couldn't stop picturing what it'd be like to watch the ink ripple as he worked my body.

"Every time we're alone, we step closer and closer to the line we know we shouldn't fucking cross. Nothing has changed since the morning you ran outta this cabin."

"Why?" I asked through gritted teeth. "We had agreed to one night of meaningless sex. One. Night. No more, no less."

"And what about the night of your Dad's birthday, huh? What was that about? Spare me the bullshit about it being just one time." He looked away, and I was grateful for the reprieve. My heart was beating so hard that I almost wondered if he could see it, if he could tell how far he had thrown me off whatever course I'd set out on.

"Call it a moment of weakness! I don't know, Bishop, and I certainly don't care." I was on a roll today with my lies. First Cleo, and now Bishop. I cared about whatever this was more than I cared to admit. I could blame it on my pride if I wanted to, but it was more than that. It was some soul-deep thing I didn't want to acknowledge, an unrequited crush from years ago.

As he ground his teeth together, a muscle flexed along Bishop's chiseled jaw. I already hated myself for what I was about to say, but I said it anyway. Maybe it would kill whatever hope I was holding onto.

"I know working alongside me is apparently a real hardship—"

Bishop rolled his neck. "That's not what I meant, and you know it."

"I don't, though. You've given me no reason to believe otherwise, have you? I've tried to talk to you every day, to figure out how to work through whatever this is, but you've been gone before the sun even comes up. This is stupid, Bishop."

He stared down at me, eyes burning with something I didn't quite understand. "This job is the only thing I have, and I can't risk losing it. If that means I have to stay away from you to keep it safe, then so be it."

I ignored the flash of fear in his eyes. "Well, I hate to tell you this but you're gonna have to cowboy it the fuck up and do what's best for the ranch we *both* love."

"Lennox..." He lifted his hand, looking like he was going to reach for me, but then he stopped as I shook my head and turned Strider around.

"Dad's coming home today," I called over my shoulder. "For his sake, don't be fucking late for dinner."

And then I ran.

bishop

. . .

I WALKED through the door of the Hayes household five minutes before seven, hoping it might earn me some brownie points if I was early to dinner. I would've been here sooner, but I was too busy overthinking and wearing a hole in the carpet of my living room as I paced back and forth.

The interaction with Lennox earlier had taken up space permanently in my brain. Guilt had gnawed at my conscience since I watched her ride away. I forced myself to watch until she was nothing more than a little dot in the distance, leaving Titan and me standing in my yard wondering what the fuck had just happened.

The prospect of seeing her tonight had me reaching for my phone a thousand times, ready to tell Doug and Ruby how sorry I was that I couldn't come to dinner because I was a coward. Lennox's disappointment was heavy. It weighed on my shoulders and twisted my stomach into knots. I didn't realize how much her anger would eat me up.

This was different than the other times we'd bickered because there was true hurt behind both of our words. We both ached for something we couldn't have, but I was terrified to risk what I already had. This job was a sure thing, and before I complicated things with Lennox, I hadn't ever had to worry about it before. She didn't understand that, and I didn't hold it against her. I was grateful she'd never had to make the choice.

I sucked in a breath, relishing the scent of freshly baked bread and whatever pumpkin-spiced candle Ruby had burning throughout the house. Doug's surprisingly hearty laughter filtered through the air, and the tension in my muscles lessened slightly.

But not nearly enough.

The past week had been a mixture of worrying about how he was doing and when he'd be back home. I think Ruby had gotten sick of me texting her every day for an update, but she sent them anyway—even if one was just a picture of Doug flipping off the camera with a message that said, "Get back to work."

"Will you stop fussing over me?" he asked. I rounded the corner, watching him bat away Cleo's hand as she tried to fill his cup with water. "I'm not completely useless, you know."

"Oh, I know, Daddy," she said, holding the pitcher of water out of his reach. "I'll tell you what... If you can get it from me, I'll let you fill it yourself."

His eyes darted between his daughter and the jug, clearly trying to decide whether this was a battle he could win. "Fine."

"That's what I thought." She looked up and found me staring, waving me inside. "Look, Bishop's here. Maybe the two of you can see who is grumpier."

"I've got him beat," Doug grumbled.

I shook my head, forcing a laugh over the lump forming in my throat. "I dunno. I've been told I'm pretty unmanageable at times."

Doug said something sarcastic, still fussing over something Cleo had done, but I'd stopped listening and turned away at the sound of approaching footsteps.

Lennox rounded the corner with two plates of fresh bread in her hands. Her hair was up in a twist, the bright red clip standing out against her silvery blonde strands. She'd changed into an old Wrangler t-shirt that nearly hid the little black shorts she had on beneath, leaving her long, tanned legs on display.

It reminded me of the way my own shirt had dwarfed her body, how I'd had to fight myself from getting hard at the thought of slowly lifting it to find her perfect pussy bared to me beneath the fabric.

Get it the fuck together, Bishop. You can't be foaming at the mouth over her at dinner.

My head knew that, of course, but my dick? Not exactly. And that didn't take into consideration the pathetic thump of my heart hiding in my chest.

Despite my insistence on keeping things between Lennox Hayes and me professional, I was failing miserably. I spent nearly every waking moment over the past few months thinking about her in some capacity. It started as a fantasy, a way for my mind to safely explore the boundaries of what could've happened that night without crossing any lines. For a while, I was okay with knowing that was all it'd ever be.

But as time marched on, that changed. I watched the witty, sarcastic banter we had turn to something full of anger and pain. We were alike in so many ways, both of us building up our walls and using words as a weapon to keep others away. She'd proved time and again that hers were sharper than I ever imagined.

The worst part was knowing I had no one to blame but myself.

She wanted to know why I'd stayed away all week? Without Doug on the ranch as a reminder of who she was, it would've been too damn easy to give in. I was weak for her. I didn't know how much longer I could stop myself from acting on the things I wanted.

Lennox Hayes was a goddamn lightning strike to my heart.

She'd cracked the wall I'd carefully erected, letting in dangerous ideations that threatened to send me to my knees. I didn't know what she saw in me. A woman like her may have thought she wanted a grumpy old man to show her a good time, but that was all it'd ever be.

A good time.

A one-night stand. A fling. A single, reckless moment that would become a fun anecdote she'd tell her friends about down the road.

But for me, it was sickeningly different. It'd become obvious after our first kiss that she would turn my world upside down. That was why I needed to keep my distance. If I had to act like an outright dickhead to do it, to protect myself from her unintentional destruction, then I was willing to do that.

It'd killed me to ignore her, but she deserved more than an emotionally stunted forty-year-old man who'd never been in a relationship.

Her eyes flicked to meet my own, as if she could feel me staring. They lingered, and for a moment, I swore I stopped breathing. It was like I'd forgotten how to perform essential bodily functions. My chest grew tight as I tried to suck in a lungful of air, suspended in this awkward tension hanging between us.

A loud clattering from the kitchen broke the connection, and we both looked away. I blew out a sharp breath, running my hand along the back of my neck in hopes of releasing my tightly coiled muscles to no fucking avail.

"You just gonna stand there all night?" Doug asked, gesturing my way. "Go get your dinner and sit down. I'm starving. You won't believe the swill they serve at the hospital. It's disgusting. I can't believe they give that to sick people."

Ruby came around and laid a hand on her husband's shoulder, patting it lightly. "You just didn't like it because it was healthy," she said, rolling her eyes. "I ate it all week with no complaints."

"What if that was the last thing I'd ever eaten, Rubes? Serving that to people who're on their deathbed should be illegal."

Josie walked out with two bowls of steaming soup, setting one in front of her father and the other on her own placemat. "It's a good thing you weren't dying then, isn't it?"

"But I could've," he argued. "And then you all would feel bad about denying me one last meal before I died."

Lincoln chuckled, pulling out Josie's seat before dropping into his own. "Doug, sometimes I wonder where your girls got their sass from. Then you go and open your mouth, and it hits me." He reached forward and plucked a steaming piece of bread from the plate, pointing it toward the head of the table. "They're just like you."

At Lincoln's words, a knowing smirk crossed Doug's lips. "And that's the best compliment you've ever given me, son."

I slunk away into the kitchen, avoiding any more of the conversation in favor of grabbing my own meal. It was silly and stupid, but there was something about Doug and Lincoln's easygoing relationship that made me nervous.

Doug and I had always worked as a team. The work was more manageable when we split the load. Sometimes, I needed an extra hand on roundups or branding, and he'd pitch in. Other times, he'd need help with his training clinics and I'd tag along —which was few and far between, seeing as I didn't really have the temperament to handle idiots with kid gloves.

Since Lincoln had started at the ranch, he and Doug had been spending more and more time together. We all worked great together, but sometimes I felt like a third wheel when they got to talking, so I'd make up some excuse and let them do their thing. He was family, and I was... what?

How long would it be until they realized they didn't need me at all?

It'd crossed my mind on more than one occasion that maybe

I'd been a placeholder all this time for Doug's eventual son-in-law. Black Springs Ranch had been in the Hayes family for damn near a century, so why would he let someone who didn't belong run the place?

That's what I desperately wanted Lennox to understand. If something went tits up with us, I was the one who would lose absolutely everything. I had nothing and no one outside of this ranch, while she would still have the full support of every single person in this house. Doug would fire me, kicking me out of the only home I'd ever known. And maybe worst of all? I would lose *her*.

As I rounded the corner, I found Lennox standing at the kitchen sink. She was staring out the window toward the barn, her fingers tapping gently against the porcelain fixture. Her eyes had a faraway look, like she had the weight of the world on her shoulders, but I clocked the tension in her body the moment she was in my line of sight.

I did that. I pushed her away and told all the same lies I told myself as a reminder not to cross the line. All I wanted to do was to walk over and tell her how sorry I was, how much of a fucking idiot I'd been, and hoped she would forgive me.

But I couldn't. I didn't deserve it, anyway.

"Dinner smells good," I said, grabbing a bowl beside the stove. Her response was a simple hum, but she didn't turn around, so I tried again. "It's one of my favorites."

"I'll be sure to remember that," she said. There was a tightness to her voice I wasn't used to. I didn't like the way it made me feel.

The corner of my mouth curved up, trying to inject an edge of humor to my tone. "Why's that? Gonna treat me with it from time to time?"

Lennox turned over her shoulder, keeping her eyes downcast. "No. So, I can stop making it on Friday nights."

"In that case, it's my least favorite dinner. This is barely edible. It'll be so hard to get it down."

Lennox raised one of her perfect brows. "Fingers crossed you don't choke on a carrot. That'd be such a shame. I don't know the Heimlich, so you'd be shit out of luck."

"It would," I agreed, filling my bowl. "Who else would take your verbal punches and roll with them?"

A noise that sounded suspiciously like a snort came from her mouth. "Maybe Lincoln would give you mouth-to-mouth," she said, finally turning to face me.

Lennox was beautiful, but she looked tired. There were dark circles under her eyes that reminded me of how she'd looked in the hospital, and the guilt kicked up again. I'd pushed her away when she needed someone the most, had ignored every dinner invitation over the past week, and let myself selfishly stew over my own problems instead of putting her first.

I was a goddamn asshole.

I scrunched up my nose. "Naw, I'll take my chances with the devil. I don't want Loverboy's lips anywhere near mine."

"Probably a good choice," Lennox said, pushing off the sink. She sauntered forward, keeping her eyes locked on mine as she reached for the last bowl on the counter behind me. Our bodies brushed, and I forgot how to breathe.

We were locked in a stalemate, neither of us moving. She was all I could think about—the softness of her parted lips, the memory of her lust-filled eyes staring up at me, the scent of her sweet perfume clinging to her skin. I wanted to throw our dinner on the floor, grab her waist, and drown in the taste of her. I wanted to make up for the last four months, to punish her and punish myself, and most importantly... I wanted to give in.

Is this what it felt like to go insane? Hell, maybe I was already there—so far gone I didn't know which way was up. Maybe Lennox Hayes had well and truly fucking destroyed me.

But as quick as it had happened, it was gone. Lennox pulled

back, narrowed her eyes, and tapped her foot expectantly. "Do you mind moving your giant ass out of the way, Grandpa? Dad'll riot if he has to wait any longer, and none of us want that. He's been bitching non-stop since they got home."

As if on cue, Doug hollered from the dining room, "What the hell is taking so long? My stomach is about to eat itself, and then all this shit will have been for nothing."

"Hold your horses, we're coming!" she yelled, pushing me aside to get to the stove pot. "Bishop's been taking up the whole kitchen with his big ass head."

"Y'all have about ten seconds to get in here, or I'm starting without you."

"Yeah, yeah. You always talk a big game, old man," I called over my shoulder. I stepped out of the way so Lennox could move past, but she chose to go around the island instead.

Alright, then.

I followed on her heels, both of us taking our places at the table while Doug muttered something under his breath and took his first bite. We all laughed when he groaned, praising his daughter for the wonderful meal and saving him from the evils of bland hospital meals.

He asked about our weeks, steering away from anything that would constitute business talk while we ate. I stole glances at Lennox the whole time, wondering if she would rat me out for being a total dickhead, but she never did.

Instead, she laughed and joked as Cleo told everyone how one of her students had brought their pet frog to school because they wanted to show it to the class. Then Lennox chimed in about one of the goats staging a breakout from their pen and how it'd taken her and three hands to wrangle them all back in and rig the panels so they couldn't be knocked down.

By the end of the dinner, Doug's eyes were shining joyfully at being back home with his kids. He loved the ranch fiercely, but he loved his family more. That's one of the things I admired the most about him, one of the things I'd always been inspired to become. And it had always been the thought of his possible disappointment that kept me from going after what I wanted. I wanted this, and I hated having to choose between the possibility of whatever this was with Lennox and the life I'd worked so hard to build.

Something had shifted this afternoon when Lennox had tracked me down. I'd felt it the moment she'd ridden away, and left me standing there with nothing but her haunting words to keep me company.

While I was still concerned with Doug's opinion, I didn't think it was holding me back anymore. I thought that this life on the ranch was all I ever wanted, but I would give anything to stop Lennox from looking so goddamn sad.

lennox

. . .

IT'D BEEN two weeks since Dad had come home. Two weeks of endless doctor appointments, check-ups, and monitoring vitals. Two weeks of everyone reminding him that he needed to take it easy and recover properly to get back in the saddle. Two weeks of getting up before dawn to stop him from sneaking out of the house out of old habit.

I looked at the clock on the oven, loathing the little green numbers that read just past 5:00 AM. It'd been quiet when I woke up this morning. Too quiet, honestly. I'd snuck into my parent's room to make sure Dad hadn't headed out already, but he was still in bed with his arm draped over my mom's waist.

As a kid, I'd slept in this room a million times when I had a nightmare or if I was having an emotionally draining day. Each time, I didn't think about how they'd scooted apart without question to let me snuggle between them. They were just Mom and Dad, providing the comfort I desperately needed.

Looking at them as an adult was different, though. I didn't just see them as my parents, but rather as people who were helplessly and disgustingly in love with one another. They'd built a life they were proud of, had raised three wonderful children, and still clung to one another like no time had passed.

In a world full of fuckboys and wandering eyes, would I ever find that kind of love? I'd always tried hard not to judge myself based on what I'd accomplished by my age, but relationship goals seemed different for some reason. Mom and Dad were already married with kids at twenty-seven, yet I was more committed to my favorite perfume than a person.

Well, sort of.

Only one person came to mind, a person I'd desperately tried to shove out and lock the door behind, but he kept breaking through all the same.

Bishop had been acting strange since I'd confronted him. It was like he wanted to move past whatever war we were waging by loosening the reins he always held so tight. He'd started including me in the morning meetings, where he gave job delegations to the ranch hands and went over things that needed to be done. He even held me back to ask about hiring a few more hands for the branding this weekend.

It was a complete one-hundred-and-eighty-degree shift from how he'd been. There were moments I caught him staring at me from across the room. Each time, I held my breath, wondering if it was going to be the moment he made good on all those longing looks and said, "fuck it," before storming over to kiss me.

And when it never came, I couldn't fight the pang of disappointment as he walked away with his head down.

His hot and cold nature was driving me crazy. I couldn't tell whether his restraint should be celebrated or ridiculed. Was I any better, though? Could I fault him for not knowing what he wanted or for not wanting to upset the balance at the ranch? His dedication to my dad was the one thing I couldn't hate.

Suddenly, the kitchen lit up, and I blinked to adjust my sight. Dad was standing in the archway, staring at me with his hand on the light switch. He was in his work clothes—worn Wrangler jeans that looked like they were on their last life and a faded blue button-down shirt. It was one of his favorites, but the buttons were constantly popping off because it was so old.

I leaned back in my chair, folding my arms over my chest and raising my brow. "Going somewhere?"

Dad rubbed the back of his neck. "Yeah, uh... I heard you in here and wanted to have coffee."

"I smell bullshit," I said, gesturing toward his outfit.

He lifted the collar of his shirt and brought it to his nose, inhaling deeply. "I don't smell anything," he said, giving me his best smile. "Are you sure it's bullshit you smell and not one of your mom's frilly little candles?"

"Oh, I'm pretty sure," I said, grabbing my favorite red mug. Dad had gotten it for me, much to Mom's dismay, a few Christmases ago. There was a small middle finger engraved into the side of the clay with the words Fuck Off right above it.

Dad didn't say anything as he went to make his own coffee. We had two separate machines because he liked to make his so strong and bitter. I didn't know how he drank it like that. "How long have you been up?" he asked, reaching for a cup of his own.

I glanced at the clock, seeing that over thirty minutes had passed since the last time I'd looked. "Mm, I made my pot around five," I said, tracing my finger along the edge of the breakfast table. "I had to get up a little earlier since you'd nearly succeeded in escaping house arrest yesterday."

He smiled, taking the seat across from mine. "Well, I have to keep you on your toes, don't I? Wouldn't be much fun if I stuck to a routine."

"Actually, it'd be pretty great. Maybe I could get some sleep without having to patrol the halls for an old man who should be in bed right now," I deadpanned.

"Go easy on my heart, Lenny Bug," he joked. "I dunno how much more it can take."

I dropped my gaze, letting the truth of his words settle. "I wish you'd stop saying that."

There was a beat of silence before he spoke in a soft tone. "It's just a joke, honey. I don't mean anything by it."

I lifted my shoulder in a shrug, keeping my eyes on the worn groove along the edge of the table. I remembered the day I'd made the indenture. Josie and I ran around the kitchen, chasing one another while Cleo did her homework in the living room. She'd told us to stop running, that someone would get hurt if we weren't careful, but neither of us listened. All it took was one misstep, and I went careening into the table.

There were so many tears shed that day. Blood was all over the table and my clothes. It looked like something straight out of a horror movie. I'd never forget the look on Mom's face when she rushed inside at Cleo's ear-piercing scream. She ran me straight to the hospital for stitches along my upper lip. I lost both of my front teeth, which, thankfully, were already loose.

By the time Mom and I made it back to the ranch, I'd worried myself sick thinking about how mad my dad would be that I messed up the brand-new table. Instead, he'd left the cowboys in charge of the chores and came home to watch Cleo and Josie. They'd all made cards that said *Get Well Soon* and decorated my bedroom with a string of colorful teeth cut from construction paper.

For some reason, Mom called it extremely disturbing, but I'd thought it was the coolest thing ever.

Neither of them ever yelled, though. They didn't raise their voices or make me feel horrible about being a kid who had an accident. It quickly became an inside joke, a Hayes family anecdote we still laughed about to this day. I loved that they never patched the table because while it had hurt like hell, what came after was still one of my favorite memories.

Except now, it didn't fill me with joy or excitement because I couldn't stop thinking about how many more times we'd be able to laugh about it as a family.

"I know that's your nature, Dad. You like to make light of serious situations and turn them into jokes, so it takes the gravity out of the scenario, but there's no way to turn this. You're literally the glue that holds us all together, and I—" my voice broke, and I quickly reached up to wipe away the tear that slipped free. "I don't know what I'm gonna do when you're not here."

Dad's face fell, his dark, hooded eyes full of remorse. His Adam's apple bobbed as he swallowed, staring down at his weathered hands. "Joking about it is the only way I keep going, Lenny Bug. It's the only way I can pick myself up in the morning and continue about my day, because if I don't, then I'm filled with fear. Sure, some of that is for me—I don't wanna die, you know. But mostly, I'm terrified for everyone I'd leave behind," he whispered, laying his hand flat for me to take.

"I'm scared about your momma being alone for damn near the first time in her life and how empty this big ole house will feel for her when y'all fly from the nest. I'm scared about what'll happen to the ranch, and if I've prepared Bishop and the boys for the highs and lows they'll experience because, let's face it, running a ranch is fucking tough." We both shared a watery laugh. "And I'm scared for you girls because I wanna watch y'all grow old, too. I wanna see you hit every milestone y'all set for yourselves—whether that's in a career or marriage or babies or even just finally ticking off everything on your to-do list. I wanna know y'all are fulfilled and happy and taken care of."

If my heart were made of glass, it would've shattered in my chest. "Dad..."

"I'm sorry I've hurt you, bug. Believe me, that's never my intention, but it's all I've got right now. The ability to work, to throw myself into my job and take my mind off all this shit, has been taken away from me. I don't have anything..." His words trailed off, and I squeezed his hand to let him know it was okay. He wiped at his eyes and chuckled. "Especially since none of y'all have given me any grandbabies yet."

I rolled my eyes playfully. Neither of our parents meant anything by their pestering. They didn't care if we had a school bus full of kids, had none at all, or chose to be animal parents instead. They just wanted us to live the lives we wanted, the ones we built brick-by-brick until we had shelter from the storm.

"Well, the way your middle child is going…" I said, letting the implication land.

Dad shook his head. "They're crazy kids. If they keep going at it like bunnies, they'll end up with a bunch of babies. Think Lincoln knows that?"

We both broke out into a fit of giggles until the tears we'd shared in grief turned into ones from laughter instead. As we came down and settled into a comfortable silence, Dad reached out and gave my hand three pats.

"We're all scared, bug, but just because we're scared doesn't mean we should stop living. We shouldn't let that fear consume us. Shouldn't stop laughing over stupid shit, or going after what you want, or dancing in the kitchen at"—he looked toward the clock—"5:57 in the morning with your dear old dad."

"What?" I asked, laughing.

Dad pushed to his feet, fishing his phone out of his pocket. He smiled as he found the song he was looking for. "We can't blast it like we used to when you were little, but I think we could make this work, don't you?"

I Loved Her First by Heartland began playing through the speakers, and I fought the urge to cry for what seemed like the hundredth time this morning. It was our song. The song he taught me to dance to, the one we always said we'd play at my wedding if I ever found someone I thought was worth marrying. I hadn't listened to it since he got sick because I focused on the negative, letting the 'what ifs' control the narrative and steal my joy.

Dad was right, and not just about his illness, but about being scared in general. I wasn't one who often feared the unknown—I was an *ask for forgiveness rather than permission* kinda gal—but that had shifted in the past year. Instead, I found myself avoiding the hard conversations and holding myself back from what I really wanted because I didn't want to rock the boat.

But no more.

"Come on, bug. Indulge an old man," he said, and this time, he held out his hand.

I took it, letting him pull me to his feet. He held me in his arms, and I laid my head on his chest, comforted by the steady beat of the heart beneath my cheek. We swayed in the kitchen far longer than either of us intended, letting song after song play until the playlist ended. Silent tears slowly slipped down our cheeks as we clung to one another. It was cathartic in a way I never imagined.

For a moment in time, I wasn't a twenty-seven-year-old woman walking an unknown path who was terrified of losing her father. Instead, I was just a girl dancing with her first love as we watched the sun rise over the peak of the barn.

bishop

. . .

"KNOCK, KNOCK!" I looked up and saw Josie standing in my doorway. She had a stack of paperwork in her arms, looking at me with an apologetic smile. "I need you to look through the supply order. I think I have everything we'll need, but I need to submit the feed orders tonight before we leave for the day."

"Alright," I said, letting my shoulders drop. That wasn't too bad. "I can do that."

"And I need you to prep your expense report, too," she added quickly, cringing when I groaned. "I know, I know! There's still like a week left before the end of the month, but if I don't start asking for it now…"

"I fuckin' hate paperwork," I muttered. "I've got too much shit on my plate as it is."

We'd already decided to move the branding from this weekend to two weeks from now. It was later than we had liked, but Lincoln was out of town with a clinic. We couldn't afford not to have him, even though I knew Lennox could easily step in to help.

Doug and I sat down with Josie after he came home to talk about the finances. We could afford to hire some temporary help and had already sent out the call. There were a few cowboys coming out today, so I could see their skills. The last thing I needed was some idiot who didn't know their ass from their elbow.

"Like I said, I know you hate it, and it's a pain. Believe me, I don't like having to hound grown men to do their job, yet here I am," she deadpanned.

"You've never had to hound me—"

Josie rolled her eyes. "We have this same conversation every week, Bishop."

I leaned back in my chair. "You're grumpy when your little boy toy is away. Were you always like this?"

"Nope, but when you're used to having sex every day—"

I plugged my ears. "Never mind! Forget I asked."

She smiled, backing slowly out of the door. "That's what I thought. So, make sure that report is on my desk by month's end, or else I'll plop my ass right there," she said, pointing at the sad-looking folding chair in front of my desk, "and tell you all about the time he put his fingers in my—"

"Thanks, Josie!" I shouted, trying to block the image of her and Lincoln out of my mind. "I'll be sure to get right on that."

"See that you do, Bishop!" she said, waving over her shoulder.

I blew out a breath, running my fingers through my hair. "Fuckin' Hayes women, I swear," I muttered, getting up to refill my coffee.

I wasn't used to sitting behind a desk for long periods. Computers and I didn't exactly get along. Doug was better at using the damn thing than I was—something he constantly felt the need to tease me about. Josie had been about as patient as I could've asked for, but lately, paperwork had gotten out of control.

Ever since the summer when she found out her ex-boyfriend was stealing funds from the ranch, Josie had run a tight ship around here. We were expected to hand in our receipts the moment we had them, and she promptly filed them away for reconciliation.

It wasn't that I didn't have what she needed, it was just that I often got sidetracked and let things pile up until I had to go through everything at once. As much as I didn't want to admit it, maybe I did need help.

"Bishop!" Dallas, one of our newer workers, shouted my name from the alley. "You got someone here to see you."

I checked the time, kicking myself for not paying attention. "Gimme a minute," I called back, grabbing my hat and locking my office behind me.

"Kid's early," I said, stopping beside Dallas, who stood at the barn entrance with his hands on his hips. "I like that. We need more people to show that kinda dedication." We watched as a beat-up red Dodge came slowly up the drive. An orange and white cattle dog stood on shaking legs in the truck bed.

Well, I sure as shit didn't like that.

I'd never had a dog of my own, mostly because I was hardly ever home, and it seemed like they took way too much time to train, but we'd had dogs here at the ranch over the years. Lennox was always partial to them. Always bringing them home and crying because she'd found them on the side of the road.

That was the unfortunate thing about living where we did. People would drive out here and dump the animals they didn't want, leaving them behind without a second thought.

I fuckin' hated people.

The guy hopped out of the truck, and I already knew he wasn't the one for us. He was tall and lanky, yapping on his cell phone. His clothes looked way too tight, and the aviator glasses he was wearing nearly dwarfed his face. There was something cocky in the way he stood, examining the ranch as though he was judging us.

There was an anxious whine as the dog seemed to glance

between the owner and the drop from the tailgate. He leaned over to slap the side of the truck, ushering out a curse and command to be quiet. The dog flinched before laying down with its head on its paws, and my stomach dropped.

Dallas gave me a knowing look and shook his head. "Oooh, boy. Need me to call back up?"

"Naw, I can handle this," I said, toeing my boot along the trim line that broke up the concrete from the dirt. "This won't take long."

"I'm sure it won't," Dallas said, laughing as he got back to cleaning the stalls.

I stepped forward, raising my hand in greeting. He gave me a simple nod of his chin like we'd been friends for years. Fat fucking chance. And then he hung up his phone and tucked it away in his pocket.

"Nick?" I asked, meeting him halfway.

He smiled. "Yeah, man. How ya doin'?"

I already knew I wouldn't hire him, but call me curious... I wanted to see what he thought he knew.

"You bring your rope?" I asked, keeping my voice even.

"Sure did," he said. "It's in the truck. Need me to get it?"

I widened my stance. "Well, I'm not gonna loan you one, if that's what you're asking."

"Alright, man. Whatever you say. You got a horse for me, though, right?"

I dipped my chin. Not that he would need it. We wouldn't make it that far. "Told you I would."

"You don't say much, do you?" he asked, shaking his head. "Man, I heard you were a hard guy to work for, but—"

"That's an odd thing to say at a job interview, don't ya think?" I asked, tilting my head. "You're more than welcome to hop in your truck and get the hell off the ranch I run."

Nick's eyes widened in surprise. "Nope, we're all good here."

"That's what I thought. Grab your rope and your gloves,

meet me in the round pen over there," I said, pointing toward the area we used to break horses. Lincoln and I had gone to auction before he left and came home with four we thought had real potential. There was one of them that was really giving us a hard time, though. She was stubborn as hell and reminded me of Lennox.

As Nick followed me, his dog started barking. It was a real high-pitched noise that had him turning around and shouting for her to shut up. I picked up my pace, trying my damndest not to hit him right here.

Unfortunately, so did Nick. He came jogging up behind me. "Sorry 'bout her," he said, chuckling. "Damn, bitch won't shut the fuck up."

I didn't say anything; I just clenched my jaw tighter. *Little prick.* If this was how he treated his own animal, there was no way in fuck he could be trusted to take care of anything he didn't have a vested interest in.

Three other guys were working the pens, excluding someone in the center, and gently loping one of the more docile fillies of the group. I didn't recognize who it was until I caught a glimpse of blonde hair beneath a baseball cap. "Hey, boss man's coming!" they called out, raising their hand. "And is that fresh meat I smell?"

The dust settled, and Lennox turned, narrowing her eyes as Nick and I came closer. At least she was wearing a pair of fucking gloves today. She gave me a tentative smile as the horse stopped in front of her.

I stopped along the railing, resting my elbows on the dusty posts. "She giving you any trouble?" I asked.

"Are you talking about me or the horse? Because we've both been perfect angels, haven't we, girl?" Lennox reached out, letting the filly step forward and nuzzle her palm.

"We had to talk her out of starting with that one," Keith said, pointing toward the pissed-off looking stallion two pens over. His chest heaved, and his nostrils flared as he stared at the railing like it was a cage. I supposed it was, in a way. "He's one mean son-of-a-bitch. Bit Reggie while we were unloading him."

"Probably best," Nick said. "Pretty little things like her should be watching from the sidelines, not putting themselves in danger."

Reggie and Keith looked at one another and chuckled. "Fresh meat's about to be dead meat."

I watched Lennox transform from the hard-working rancher's daughter to the stone-cold vixen who chewed up and spit out weak little shits like Nick. She glanced up through long lashes as she stepped forward. Her lips curved, morphing into a seductive smile with each sway of her hips.

"Is that right?" she asked, bracing one hand on the railing and the other on her waist.

"Sure is," he said, stepping up beside me. "Especially with that big brute over there. We wouldn't want you getting hurt now."

Usually, I'd step in and say something, but that wicked little spark in Lennox's eye said she could handle it herself. I believed her too. Hell, I wanted her to show this fucker what she was made of and prove him wrong.

"Do you think you could handle him?" she asked, dropping her voice.

"I know I could."

I'd give it to the kid. He had confidence in fucking spades. It was hugely misplaced, but maybe he'd find somewhere to fake it until he made it.

Or maybe he was about to get his ass handed to him by a five-foot-seven blonde who terrified most men around here.

Only time would tell.

"Well, I'd love to see what you've got," she said, gesturing toward the gate panel. "Maybe one of us will learn a thing or two."

"Oh, you will, for sure," he said. And then the motherfucker slid his glasses to the tip of his nose and winked before going through the gate. "Now, climb up, and let me show you how to do it, sweetheart."

Part of me wanted to stop it, to tell the kid to pack it up and head home. But the other part wanted to see Lennox's plan come to light and watch her come up on top. He said he'd broken over thirty horses on his resume, so what could it hurt?

Lennox perched up on the top panel, giving me an eye-level view of her perfect ass. I tried hard not to stare, to keep my focus on the kid who was probably about to be run over by the tank of a horse on the other side of the fence, but goddamn, she made it difficult. She kept wiggling her hips, either trying her best to get comfortable or to kill me.

They both looked the same to me.

She looked down with a little smirk, as if she could sense my gaze on her. "Eyes on the prize, old man," she said, nodding toward the idiot in the ring.

"They're already there," I muttered, letting my gaze linger far longer than necessary. Not that she'd noticed. She was damn near vibrating with glee as Keith asked Nick if he was ready. There was something about it that tugged at my damn heartstrings.

Seeing her so happy, I realized, made me happy.

"Alright, sweetheart, you ready?" Nick asked, running his rope through his hands.

Lennox giggled. "Oh, I am so ready."

Nick nodded his head to Keith, and he let open the small gate separating us from the raging stallion ahead. The other boys came up behind, urging the horse forward. He threw back his head and charged toward Nick with a huff.

The kid's eyes widened before he threw himself out of the way, landing in the dirt with a thud. I swore I heard the breath leave his lungs as the stallion turned back toward him.

Lennox's hands came up to her face. To anyone else, it probably looked like she was concerned, but she wasn't.

She was laughing.

"Oh no! Are you okay?" she called.

Nick scrambled up and widened his stance. "I'm good!" He threw his arms out and slowly inched forward, not taking his eyes off the animal in front of him. "Woah, woah, woah," he cooed. His hands were shaking. "Calm down now, boy."

"Oh, he's gonna get himself killed," I muttered, shaking my head. The kid had no idea what he was doing.

"I'll step in before that happens," Lennox whispered back. "Really make him eat his words."

As if on cue, the stallion charged, and Nick jumped out of the way. He tripped over his own feet, stumbling into the fence post. Before he could recover, the animal reared on his hind legs, coming dangerously near striking Nick down. He cowered on the ground, rolling into a little ball.

"Shit." Lennox jumped down from the rail, running to pull Nick away from the fencing. I surged forward, damn near tripping over myself to step in front of them.

If I died for this idiot...

The animal landed on all fours, bobbing his head as I stepped forward with my arms out. I kept my gaze locked on his, even though I wanted nothing more than to check and see if Lennox had cleared the area. "I don't like him either, boy, but you can't kill him, okay? That'd put us in a whole mess of trouble."

The horse stomped its feet, moving nervously from side to side.

"They're good, B!" Reggie called, which was good enough for me. I slowly back away from the pissed-off creature. He wouldn't do anything to me, but I didn't feel like taking chances today.

Keith got the gate, swinging it wide so I could slip through quickly. The stallion reared up and took off when his hooves touched the ground. He circled the pen, snorting and throwing a fit that he was still locked up.

"Holy shit, boss man," Reggie said, clapping my back. "We got one hell of a job on our hands with that one."

"Can't wait to see you get your ass in there instead," I said, picking my hat up and wiping the sheen of sweat from my forehead.

I looked over to see Lennox bending forward to check on Nick. He was sitting with his head between his knees, taking deep breaths.

"Christ," I said, shaking my head and walking over. I nudged him with my boot, and he looked up. "Thirty horses, huh?"

Nick's eyes widened slightly, suddenly remembering he was here for a goddamn job interview. "N—none *that* mean," he stammered.

"Clearly," I said, glancing down. "Listen, kid, I don't think I have to tell you this isn't gonna work. So, why don't you head on out."

He stared at me, slack-jawed for a moment, before pushing to his feet. "You let me go in there without knowing how crazy that thing is!"

I held up my hands. "I'm not the one trying to impress a pretty lady by being a jackass. Anything that happened in there… That's on you."

"You could've told me no."

"And you're a grown-ass man who should know better than to think with his dick. I'm not your father, and I'm not your friend. You decide to show off, then you better be ready to deal with whatever consequences are thrown your way," I snapped back. "Now, get your shit, and get off this ranch."

Nick's eyes darted to the truck as his dog started barking. It was standing excitedly as Josie approached the truck with a water bowl. "Stupid bitch," he muttered beneath his breath, storming their way. Lennox and I quickly followed, not knowing what he would do.

"Hey!" he called out, snapping his fingers. Josie looked his way, her eyebrow raised in question as we approached. "Get the fuck away from my dog."

"Excuse me?" she asked, crossing her arms over her chest. "She was thirsty. I was just giving her water."

"She's fine," he spat, knocking the bowl off the bed of his truck. The dog yelped, skirting back. Josie stepped out of the way just in time, looking between the panting dog and the spilled water on the ground.

Oh shit. I knew she was on the move before I felt her.

Lennox pushed past me, marching over to Nick. "Hey, dickhead!" He whipped around, leering down at her as she stopped in front of him. He tried to open his mouth to smart off, but she was faster.

She slammed her fist into his nose in a quick jab.

His hands flew to his face, covering his nose as blood began spilling down his face. "Ow! Oh, God. What the fuck?"

"Maybe think about that before being a complete and total asshole to someone who is trying to help your animal. Why the fuck are you coming to work on a ranch when you can't even recognize that?"

I couldn't help but smile because I'd thought the same thing.

"She's just a fuckin' dog—hey! What're you doing?"

Lennox pushed past Nick and stood near the end of his truck. "Come on, sweet girl. Let's go," she called. The dog didn't even hesitate. She hopped down and circled Lennox's feet before laying down beside her.

Nick watched all of us for a second. "You can't steal my dog!" He cried. "That's illegal!"

"I'm not stealing your dog, Nick. Looks like she's running away to a better home," Lennox said, running her fingers along the top of the dog's head.

"Callie!" Nick called, snapping his fingers. "Get over here!"

The dog didn't move.

No matter how many times he called her name, Callie didn't budge. She ducked her head behind Lennox's knees, refusing to look at her old owner.

"You know what? Fuck this. Thanks for taking that bitch off my hands," Nick called out, stepping into his truck and slamming the door.

Lennox surged forward, but I grabbed her around the waist and pulled her into me. "I'll hit you again!" she called out, thrashing in my hold. "Get the fuck off my ranch!"

Nick's truck peeled out of the drive, kicking up rocks as he gassed it forward. I spun around, ensuring anything flying our way would hit me first. Even if I hated the reason why, I loved the feeling of her being against me. I loved how she squirmed and fought in my grip, and I couldn't help but imagine it in a different scenario.

"What a dick," Josie said, shielding her eyes from the sun. "Where'd you find him?"

Lennox slid down my body, shrugging out of my grip. Every part of her was vibrating with anger. "Yeah, what the fuck was that?" she asked, spinning to face me. "Did you not field him before inviting him out there and putting our animals at risk?"

"Ray Johnson referred him to me. The kid had worked for him the past few summers and did a good job, so I figured it was safe. You know damn well if I'd met him before today, he wouldn't have made it this far." I stepped forward, towering over her. "You were the one that challenged him to step in the ring with that fucker."

"I knew he was an idiot, not that he was a piece of shit that probably abused animals!"

We stared at one another, chests heaving and thick tension rippling through the air. You could almost cut it with a knife. That was always the issue with us. The moment dissipated before we knew it, and she smiled. I followed suit, unable to help myself.

"How's your knuckles?" I asked, glancing down at her hand.

Lennox raised it between us, examining the irritated skin. "It's been worse," she said, shrugging. "The pain's well deserved."

A cold, wet nose brushed against my other hand, and we looked down to see Callie sitting near our feet and staring up at us. She didn't have a tail, so it looked like her whole butt was wagging like crazy.

Lennox crouched down, scratching the pup behind her ears. "She has two different color eyes."

I got down on their level. "Well, I'll be damned." The right eye was a soft brown, but the left was a brilliant blue. It almost looked like it was glowing. There was just a dusting of a darker color along the top of the iris. "You're a pretty girl, aren't ya?" I asked, looking up at Lennox out of habit.

She stared down at me, lips slightly parted. I couldn't tell what she was thinking, but for the first time, I didn't care. I wanted to act without thinking. I wanted to be a bit fucking reckless. I wanted—

Callie jumped up, licking my face. I laughed, letting her get a few hits before gently pushing her down. "Alright, alright, alright," I said, standing up.

"I think she'll fit in around here just fine," Josie said, stepping beside us. I'd almost forgotten she was here. I was damn glad I remembered before I did something foolish, like kiss her little sister until I'd forgotten my own name.

lennox

. . .

I STROLLED THROUGH THE BARN, giving each horse who stuck their head out of their stall a good chin scratch and kiss. Callie strolled beside me with her tongue lolling out to the side. She'd settled in perfectly around here, though we'd have to watch her around the cattle. That heeler in her came out strong, and she nipped at their heels the first time she'd seen them.

Strider's stall was last, and he was impatiently waiting for me. He immediately dipped into my pocket, where I stashed his treat, nudging me when I didn't pull it out quick enough for his tastes.

"You know you're spoiled, don't you?" I asked as I fed him. He happily munched, closing his eyes as I reached for the spot behind his ears he loved so much. "None of the others got treats."

He bobbed his head as if to say that was their problem and not his.

I gave him one last mint before switching off the large overhead light in the alleyway. The dimmers kicked on, leaving a low glow behind. It was just enough that I could easily navigate my way to the stairway at the entrance and climb to our old hay loft.

For the longest time, it'd sat unused after Dad had built the addition to the barn, moving everything downstairs for ease of access, so I figured I'd repurpose it. Now, it was my personal little haven.

Unlike my sisters, I hadn't picked a plot of land to build on. Josie was the only one to begin construction, which made sense, seeing as she and Lincoln were ready to start their life together. Of course, my parents had given me the same proposal, but I'd turned them down. I knew the offer would stand when I was ready, but I didn't like the idea of building something and sitting in it all alone.

Until that day came, I had the loft. I'd thrifted most of the larger furniture—the velvet orange couch was my favorite—and utilized a lot of hand-me-downs from our storage units. Dad had built a few custom bookshelves along the walls for me to put little knick-knacks on. Pictures of our family were posted throughout the years, along with a few of my riding trophies and ribbons from high school.

The wooden posts looking out over the alleyway were wrapped in hundreds of fairy lights, giving the space a soft glow that felt magical. I refused to install a big overhead fixture, opting for a standing lamp with a red fringe along the shade.

It was all random and quirky, but it was one of my favorite spots on the ranch.

Callie trotted up the stairs behind me. I needed to get her a nice dog bed for the corner. Maybe one that was fluffy and soft and—

She didn't hesitate to hop on the couch before I could correct her. The moment she closed her eyes and curled in on herself, I knew I couldn't. She looked so content, so peaceful. If that meant I needed to keep an industry-sized lint roller up here, then so be it.

"I could use a snack. What about you?" I asked her. She lifted her head, staring at me in wonder as I pulled a bag of popcorn from the locked cabinet that doubled as a pantry. I wasn't big on sweets, but I kept a few bags of M&M's and some Sour Patch Kids for emergencies.

I popped the packet in the microwave and pulled out the spicy ranch seasoning I used to dust over the top. The scent of buttery goodness filled the air. It was one of my favorites, reminding me of midnight movie premieres in our shitty small-town theater with my dad. He and I had similar movie tastes. When Mom didn't want to go, he knew I would.

Were all the movies age-appropriate? Probably not. He'd definitely snuck me into an R-rated horror movie once or twice over the years, but now they were my favorites. Plus, I didn't think I was too messed up from watching a masked killer torture the same person in five movies.

As I turned on the TV, I almost thought about packing it up and asking Dad if he wanted to watch it in his den. But he looked so tired when I kissed his cheek after dinner. He clearly needed the rest.

Callie and I snuggled up on the couch together as the famous opening scene came on. She tried talking me into a few bites of popcorn, but it'd taken one internet search to talk me out of it. Instead, I grabbed the bag of carrots I'd plopped in the mini-fridge earlier in the week and snuck her some of those.

Hopefully, that would keep her sated until I got her something else.

We were about halfway through the movie when a loud banging noise came from downstairs. Callie went on alert, stalking off the couch to peer over the railing into the alley below. The lights were still off, but I could hear someone or something moving.

Maybe watching scary movies at night in a building filled with perfect hiding spots for a killer wasn't the best idea.

Callie let out a low growl just before music filtered through the space, echoing off the concrete floors and rising to meet me in the loft. It was an old-school country, the kind my dad and Bishop listened to religiously.

Maybe Dad had gotten restless and gone for a walk. Maybe he wound up in his old office, reminiscing on his prime. But it was strange he hadn't called up and let me know he was here, which meant one of two things: Either there was a killer on the loose who was hellbent on framing someone, or Bishop and I were the only two people awake on this ranch right now.

For some reason, the latter scared me more than the former.

At least with a random psychopath, my chances of having my pride stomped on were slim to none. Sure, I had to worry about murder, but I'd watched enough films to know what to do.

Bishop, on the other hand, was lethal. He could be a killer on his own, except it wasn't my life he was taking, but something far more dangerous. He could obliterate me and walk away unscathed while I lay with the scattered pieces of a broken heart.

Which was stupid because for Bishop to break it, I would have to give him the power to do it. A few misplaced kisses and some—admittedly very hot—heavy petting didn't mean anything, did it?

Sure, I hadn't been able to stop thinking about him. And okay, *yes*... Maybe I had daydreamed about what it would feel like to have the full weight of his attention, time, and energy directed toward me all day, every day.

But that was normal, wasn't it?

I mean, he was stupidly attractive—I'd never, ever questioned that. Honestly, it kind of pissed me off how handsome he was. He had that whole ruggedly handsome, grumpy cowboy thing going on. It was stereotypical, but I couldn't help but laugh at how well it fit him. The man hardly ever laughed or smiled, and when he did, it was usually either at someone else's expense or a temporary lapse in judgment.

People said you never forgot your first love, but what about your first crush? There had to be some kind of special bond that linked two people together, right?

Callie whined as I quietly crept down the stairs. I tried telling her to stay in the loft or be quiet. On the faint chance there really was a crazy person in my barn, I didn't really want her getting hurt if shit went tits up. But my new bestie must have had a death wish because she was being noisy as hell.

I peeked around the wall, breathing a sigh of relief when I saw the light spilling from Bishop's office out into the alley.

Perfect, Lennox. Now you can go back upstairs and finish your movie in peace. There's absolutely no need to go and check on the annoying and infuriatingly hot cowboy.

I took a step forward.

You're just going to piss him off if you go in there and run your mouth.

I took three more steps. I liked the idea of antagonizing him a bit. I liked his anger, his fury, his attention.

No, really. It's best to turn around and take your ass back to the loft. If Bishop is up this late, it probably means he's in a crap mood.

And now I was standing just outside his door, peeking through the opening. Bishop was wearing what he had been earlier in the day. His hair was slightly ruffled, likely from him scratching at his scalp after taking his hat off. His shirt was unbuttoned at the top, showing off the smattering of dark curls along his chest.

He leaned back in his chair, head tilted back. His eyes were closed. There was a single unopened beer resting on his desk. Condensation dripped down the glass bottle, pooling at the base.

That wasn't a good sign. Bishop and beer were a love story for the ages. I was half-convinced he'd come out of the womb with a Banquet in his hand.

He tossed something on his desk before running his hands over his face, whispering to himself. It was a worn-down pack of cigarettes. The carton that used to be white was stained yellow, with dirt smudges and weathered edges.

Weird. Bishop used to smoke like a freight train, but I hadn't seen him with one in years. I remembered telling him how gross it was when we'd left the bar on my 18th birthday. The stench filled the cabin of my truck, and it'd taken forever to get out. From the looks of it, the pack he threw down had seen better days.

He stared down at them. The harsh lighting from above made the dark circles beneath his eyes more prominent. He kind of looked like that corpse from Hocus Pocus, but only if he was a cowboy who clearly hadn't been getting enough sleep.

I hated that I wanted to know what was keeping him up, that I even cared in the first place.

I hated that I wanted to make it better. Even if I didn't know how to even begin to do that. I wasn't usually the type of person people turned to in hard times. In fact, they often dismissed me as being unable to help. I was the baby of the family, so naturally I wasn't capable of handling big feelings.

To be fair, I didn't ever blame them. I wouldn't have sought me out, either. Big emotions made me feel awkward. One time, when one of Josie's boyfriends broke her heart, she cried on my shoulder, and I just kind of awkwardly patted her back until her tears dried up. None of that had changed over the years.

Until now.

I leaned in on instinct, wanting to drift closer, but that'd been a mistake. My foot caught on the door, and I tripped. My hand landed on the wall with a soft thud. I closed my eyes, hoping he hadn't noticed, but the sudden brightness told me otherwise.

I cracked one eye open, peeking at the massive man standing

in front of me. Bishop had one hand braced on the door, scowling at me like I was an intruder. I guess I kind of was. We'd never have crossed paths if I'd minded my business and stayed in the loft.

"What're you doing out here?" he asked, looking around me down the abandoned alley. "Shouldn't you be asleep?"

"I could ask you the same thing. I heard rest is important for the elderly."

"I'm not really in the mood for the jokes, Lennox," he sighed, looking up into the loft. The soft glow of the fairy lights and my television lit up the space. "Sorry. I didn't know you were in here. I must've been distracted."

I bit the inside of my cheek. *Don't ruin a perfect moment, Lennox. No jokes. No snark. You can do this.* "It's fine. I was just watching a scary movie and then heard you moving around, so I thought I was about to be murdered."

The corner of Bishop's lip lifted a fraction. "No homicidal maniac here."

"Just the regular kind?"

"Pretty much. Wouldn't say I'm functioning on all cylinders," he said, slipping his hand into his pocket. The music played softly in the background as he ran a hand along the back of his neck. "I'll get outta here. Should probably get some sleep anyway."

"Or you could join me." The words left my big, fat mouth so quickly, as if it were easy. "Sorry," I said with a breathy laugh, trying and failing to shrug it off. "You literally just said you needed to get some sleep. I just thought..." I trailed off, twisting my hands in front of me.

Bishop reached out and ran his finger along my jawline. He tipped my chin up gently so that I met his eyes. "You thought what?"

"I just thought you might want some company," I said, swallowing my pride and whatever stubborn bullshit I was holding on to.

"You and me alone in an abandoned barn?" he asked, quirking a brow. "That seems like a recipe for disaster, killer."

Killer. He hadn't called me that since Dad's birthday. Before everything had gone horribly wrong, we'd been on the precipice of giving into this raw energy between us. The way it rolled off his tongue, decadent and low, sent shivers down my spine.

"Well, we aren't alone," I whispered, licking my lips because they'd suddenly gone bone dry.

Bishop's gaze darted down, tracking the movement with expert precision. "Is that right?"

Had his voice dropped lower, or was I just imagining things?

"Mmhm," I said, nodding. "I mean, we are surrounded by animals. And you'll have to share the couch with me *and* Callie."

He glanced down at the dog sitting at my feet. "I think I could make that work."

"Are you sure? She kind of hogs the space."

He leaned in, and I caught a faint whiff of cologne. Since when did he wear cologne to work? I mean, I sure didn't put perfume on when I was getting ready to shovel shit for hours at a time. "I'm a big man, killer. I'm used to taking up space."

Oh boy, I was in fucking trouble now.

"Well, if you're sure," I said, stepping back. I needed a bit of distance, just a moment to clear my head. I didn't know what to do with this softer side, especially not toward me. Bishop was compassionate and hardworking and dedicated, but he was also gruff and brash and had zero patience. Most of the time, the latter was his default.

It seemed only in the quiet moments that he let that other side slip out and show itself. Like right now, in a silent barn filled with sleeping horses and no one around but us.

Bishop reached up to turn off the lights, but I stopped him. "Aren't you gonna grab your beer?" I asked.

He turned and stared at the bottle, hesitating for a moment before shaking his head. "Naw. I don't need it."

"Wait... What? Did you, Bishop Bryant, just say you didn't need a beer?" I reached up, placing the back of my hand along his forehead to check for a fever. Clearly, he must be on his deathbed to make such a bold claim. "Is there such a thing as a fever being so hot that it nearly feels cool to the touch? That's the only explanation I can think of."

Bishop gripped my wrist, gently pulling it away from his face. "It's nearly midnight. Why would I need a beer?"

I narrowed my eyes into tiny slits. "Have you been abducted by aliens again? It's weird they tried for a second time when their first was wildly unsuccessful."

"Nope. No aliens, no body snatching. Just Bishop."

"Just Bishop," I repeated slowly. He still had hold of my wrist, his thumb sweeping gently across my pulse point—which was embarrassing because I could feel it racing. I was too aware of the contact, how close we were, and how much closer I wanted to get.

"That's right." He gave me a small smile and nodded toward the stairs. "Now, let's see what gore fest you're up there watching."

"I'll have you know it isn't a *gore fest*," I said, walking backward. "Scream changed the horror genre, okay? It is witty and well thought out. And the cast, Bishop! The cast is so good. And—"

"And you have a weird thing for the mask?"

I couldn't help but laugh. "Are you asking me if I have a mask kink?"

He lifted one shoulder. "What if I am?"

I didn't know how to respond, so I said, "I wouldn't call it a mask kink... But maybe a Ghostface kink? Is that a thing?"

He chuckled. "Can be, I guess."

As I turned to climb the stairs, I realized Bishop's face would be eye level with my ass. Did I put a little extra swing in my hips? I don't know. Maybe. Maybe I was the one who was going insane because what the hell was I doing alone with Bishop in my loft about to watch a scary movie? That sounded like a recipe for disaster.

Or the start of a really fun night…

bishop

. . .

MY COCK WAS STRAINING against my jeans as Lennox pressed play on the second film. In fact, it'd been hard since I saw her standing in my office doorway wearing a sleepy smile and long legs on display.

I'd never considered myself a leg guy, but I couldn't stop staring at Lennox's. She constantly fidgeted, causing her muscles to ripple beneath her tanned skin. There were a few scars from accidents over the years—some I remembered and some I wanted to explore.

We'd started out with an arm's length of space between us, but Lennox had been right; her damn dog hogged the fuck outta the couch. Our bodies had been touching for the past hour. I felt every single twitch she made, every small sigh, or scared gasp.

At one point, she'd screamed and gripped my thigh so hard that it nearly took my breath away. Not because it'd hurt, but because I was surprised by how much I liked it. And then I'd started thinking about what it would be like for her to slide her hand up to my cock, for her to stroke and squeeze me until I felt like I was ready to come in my goddamn pants from a daydream like a teenager.

It didn't matter what I thought about—apparently, reciting football teams didn't work like they said it did in movies—I was still rock fucking hard. I laid one of her fluffy pillows in my lap to hide the bulge threatening to break free, hoping it would be enough to keep her from asking too many questions. After the first movie ended, I should've called it a night and walked home. It was late enough. We both had work tomorrow, and it sure as hell would've made me feel like less of a creep.

But here we were.

"You're good to start the second one, right?" Lennox asked, snuggling into the couch. She reached for the blanket that'd fallen to the floor earlier and draped it across her body. "I know it's late."

"Yeah, it's fine," I said, laying my arm along the back of the couch. I tried to convince myself it was comfortable, but it wasn't. The angle was all wrong and way too high. It did, however, mean that every now and then, when one of us moved, my fingertips grazed her shoulder.

I'd call that a win.

"You sure?" she asked, raising her brows. "I know how grumpy you are on a normal day. I shudder to think what you're like sleep deprived."

I snorted. "You've seen me running on a couple hours of sleep more times than you think."

"Is that the secret?" Lennox turned to face me, plopping her hands in her lap. Her knees brushed my thigh. "You're just always running on E?"

"Naw, killer. I'm just a dick who is easily annoyed. I can't stand ninety-five percent of the people I'm surrounded by."

"Five percent are in your good graces? They must be impor-tant. Who makes the cut?" Lennox looked so eager. I didn't know how she had so much energy all the time. It was almost exhausting.

Yet another reminder of the thirteen years between us. She was so young and had her whole life ahead of her, and I was an old bastard set in my ways.

I shifted under her gaze. My arm dropped lower, skimming her shoulder. "I don't have a list. I was just pulling numbers outta my ass."

"But there has to be a list. Like, if you were trapped on a desert island and could bring any five people with you, who would they be?"

A question like that wouldn't stump most people, but I wasn't most people. I didn't have anyone who didn't already belong to someone else. No one for me to put first or vice versa. It felt pathetic to admit that.

"Are we gonna watch this movie?" I asked, trying to change the subject.

Lennox pushed out her lower lip in a pout. "Why won't you tell me?"

"Why does it matter?"

"Because I want to get to know you," she said matter-of-factly.

"You've known me damn near your whole life. I'd say you know more than most," I sighed.

"But I don't know you, know you. Like I don't know what your favorite color is—"

"Red."

"—Or if you prefer sweet or savory foods—"

"Always savory. Sweets upset my stomach."

This time, she reached out, placed her hand on my chest, and gave me a small shove. "Okay, smartass, can you let me finish a sentence?"

I waited to see if she'd move, but she didn't. Her touch lingered, fingers absentmindedly fiddling with the buttons of my shirt. If I was smart, I'd have told her it wasn't a good idea to touch me, that I was barely holding onto my restraint as it was, but she didn't need to know that.

And selfishly, I liked the way it felt.

"I'm just telling you the things you said you wanna know," I said, peering down at her.

"What if I wanna know everything?" Her large blue eyes scanned my face, slowly dropping to my lips before flicking back up. She was holding steady in a taunt, a fucking temptation I was close to giving into.

I dropped my arm, pinning myself between her body and the couch. She glanced down at the spot my hand rested on her waist. I toyed with the hem of her t-shirt, slipping beneath the fabric when she didn't object.

"I'll tell you anything you wanna know," I answered honestly. "As long as you ask. I'm just not that good at talking about myself. Not much interesting there."

Lennox shifted forward, letting her fingers drift along my skin. She trailed them through my chest hair, watching and waiting for me to tell her to stop.

I didn't have it in me anymore.

It was a horrible idea—truly terrible—but I couldn't stop myself. I didn't care about all the 'what ifs' and 'shouldn'ts' tonight. For the first time in my life, I wanted to be selfish.

"I dunno about that," she whispered. "I think you're kind of terrifying."

"Terrifying?" She nodded. "I didn't think there was anything that could terrify you."

"Not much does," she said, and there was an undeniable hint of honesty in her voice. "I've always been what people call 'reckless and irresponsible.' I'd call it fearless, but…"

"But?"

Lennox licked her lips, and I ached for her touch. To know what it would feel like to have her swirl her tongue around my tip and—

"But you scare me more than anything. I can't stop thinking about you, and it's—I don't know—it's fucking me up. If I'm not thinking about how infuriating your snarky little comments are or trying to convince myself that giving in would be a cataclysmic mistake, I'm thinking about what it would be like to kiss you and—"

Lennox didn't finish her sentence. I didn't let her. Before I knew it, my mouth was on hers, and we were moving. I clung to her waist, gripping it tighter as she swung her leg over, trying to straddle me.

"Lennox..." I breathed, but she wasn't listening.

"Stupid penis pillow," she mumbled, yanking it from my lap and throwing it across the room.

Penis pillow?

But then she was on top of me, grinding down onto my hard length in a way that was downright pornographic.

Fuck. It was better than I ever imagined.

Her lips came down hungrily on mine, tongues eagerly exploring one another until we were consumed. She groaned into my mouth as my fingers dug into her hips. I hoped they bruised. I hope she left this loft with my fucking mark imprinted on her skin.

Lennox breathed my name as I pulled myself away to place slow, languid kisses along her jawline. Her skin was just as sweet as I remembered, and like a man starved, I devoured her.

Her hands slid from my shirt and up my shoulders until they were wound in my hair, pulling me closer. She tipped her head back, letting me run my tongue along the column of her neck.

"Fuck, killer... You taste so good," I whispered, letting a low groan loose as she moved her hips. *Shit, now I really was going to come in my pants.* "You gotta slow down."

"What?" she mumbled, pulling back just enough to look down at my pained expression. "Oh my god, don't tell me you don't want this now. Don't go back on your word and—"

I brought my hand between us, wrapping it around her neck and lightly squeezing so she stopped talking. "Did I say I was going back on my word?" I growled, enjoying the way her eyes widened in surprise. She melted into my touch. So pliant. So fucking beautiful.

Lennox shook her head, and I leaned in. "I just needed you to stop grinding that perfect pussy on me because I am so close to embarrassing myself."

She glanced down between us, a devious smile spreading across her lips. "Bishop Bryant, are you gonna come in your pants?" Her hips rolled again, and I bit back a moan. "You flatter me."

I squeezed tighter. "You're a fucking brat."

"Tell me something I don't know, Bish."

"I haven't been able to stop thinking about you since that night in the bar," I said, leaning in to kiss her. "Haven't been able to stop wondering if you only came home with me because you were drunk or if you really wanted to. Haven't—"

"I didn't get sick because I was drunk," she panted. "I stopped drinking after you whispered all those dirty words in my ear because I wanted to remember everything."

I furrowed my brows, and I dropped my hand to her waist. There was no way she'd sobered up. I remembered her clinging to her beer like it was a lifeline. "What? But you got sick?"

She grimaced. "Alright. Not the best topic of discussion in the middle of a hookup, but I guess we might as well get it out of the way. So, you know how we picked up Taco Bell on the way home? Cleo and I had been starving because neither of us had really eaten that day. I'd scarfed down three soft tacos, but she'd said hers had tasted funny and didn't finish."

Oh no.

"Apparently, I should've followed her cue because the tacos combined with leftover alcohol on an empty stomach had my gag reflex kicking in, and… Well, let's just say they weren't a great combination."

"You weren't drunk?"

"I hadn't had a drop of liquor in over two hours by the time we got home," she said. "I was perfectly in control of myself"—she leaned in and pressed a kiss to my left cheek—"and my actions"—another kiss on the right—"and my desires…" This time, she gently pressed her lips to mine.

"What about now?" I asked breathlessly.

Lennox smirked, circling her hips in a slow taunt. "No alcohol in sight."

I quirked a brow. "What about tacos? Should I have a hazmat suit on hand?"

"Haven't touched them in four months—which is truly a travesty because they used to be one of my favorite foods."

Lennox ran her hands up her thighs, looking up through long lashes as she gripped the hem of her shirt. I sucked in a sharp breath as she slowly—so fucking slowly—lifted the fabric over her head and let it fall to the floor.

"Christ, killer…" I whispered, running my gaze across her nearly naked body. "You're fucking gorgeous."

Even though it was dark, I didn't miss the blush creeping across her cheeks. She smiled, preening under my attention as she leaned back, putting herself on display for me. Then she moved, rolling those fucking hips and drawing a noise out of me that I didn't recognize. That body would be the goddamn death of me. "Gee, Bishop… The way you're reacting might make a girl think you like what you see."

I bit out a harsh laugh, letting my hands travel up her thighs to her hips, holding her in place. "Well, you're topless and grinding down on my dick like it's an Olympic sport."

Lennox's lips parted in an O shape. "How close am I to getting a medal?"

The tingling in my spine told me she was pretty fucking

close to going for gold. What the hell was wrong with me? "You're such a brat."

"What're you going to do about it, old man? You gonna spank me?"

Yeah, I fucking am.

Lennox screamed as I lifted her off my lap and draped her across my knee. I ran my hand beneath the hem of her shorts, palming the plush curve of her ass. My fingers swept along the edge of her panties.

Fucking. Soaked.

I liked being in control, and I liked the thought of punishing her smart mouth and making her beg even more. Throughout my years, I'd found that some women believed they enjoyed being bratty and dominated more than they actually liked the reality of it.

But Lennox was made to smart off. She loved the way I took control, the way I promised the mixture of pain and pleasure.

"These shorts have to go," I said, reaching for the elastic band and pulling them down her legs. She was left in nothing but a scrap of pale pink fabric that barely covered her ass. "Too many fucking layers." I reached over, lifting her blonde hair out of her face. I wanted to watch every expression flicker across her face.

"So, you are going to spank me?" she asked breathlessly, peering at me from over her shoulder.

I smiled, running my hand along the length of her spine. "I want to," I said honestly. "I know we didn't talk about this last time, but if this isn't something you like…"

Lennox laughed. "Being spanked by you would be a highlight."

"That so?"

She nodded. "I liked the things you said last time. The names and wicked promises…"

I squeezed her ass, and she moaned. "You like the thought of being a slut for me, killer?"

And then I struck. My palm landed against her soft flesh, and the sound echoed throughout the barn. Her eyes flew open, a gasp leaving her lips as she bucked against my hold.

"Answer me," I grit out. It was getting hard to control myself when all I wanted to do was find out how perfectly I fit inside her.

"Y—yeah," she breathed. Her body squirmed, and I felt the heat radiating from her aching center. She wanted this. She wanted *me*.

"Of course you do. Your panties are soaked, and I've barely touched you."

"Says the man who nearly came in his pants five minutes ago because we were making out," she barked back.

I landed three smacks quickly, her cries going straight to my cock. "Your smartass comments have repercussions now, killer. Better watch it if you wanna be able to sit down tomorrow."

"If it hurts, will you kiss it better?" she asked.

I raised my brows and dropped my gaze to her ass. "Oh yeah? Is that what you want?"

She bit her lip. "Maybe."

I'd have to file that away for later because that was something I absolutely wanted to explore, but I didn't have the patience tonight. Leaning forward, I let my fingers graze the wet spot on her underwear. She squirmed around, searching for the friction that'd ease her suffering.

"Please…"

"Please, *what*? What does my little slut want?"

"God, why is that so fucking hot?" she whispered, rolling her head to the side. "You're killing me here."

"I'm just teasing you like you teased me. For fuck's sake, you've paraded around here for months, taunting me with someone I couldn't have, but now I've got you right where I want you." I pulled her panties to the side, sucking in a breath at the sight of her glistening cunt.

Jesus Christ.

Lennox Hayes had me in the palm of her fucking hand, and she didn't even know it.

"Please, Bishop..." she whimpered. "Touch me."

And it was the sound of my name in that desperate fucking tone that broke the final tether of my self-control.

lennox

. . .

"HOLY SHIT," I gasped, closing my eyes as Bishop slowly circled my clit. It was blissfully agonizing, the sweetest torture, as he watched me rock against his hand, searching for the right amount of pressure. I was embarrassingly close to coming from a few light touches, but it wasn't enough.

I wanted more, but I could feel his hesitation.

"Tell me to stop," he whispered.

"What?"

He paused for a moment, touch hovering over the spot I wanted it most. "Tell me to stop, Lennox. Tell me it's a bad idea. Tell me this is reckless. Tell me we shouldn't be doing this for any number of fucking reasons that I can't even think of right now."

"But I—"

"Because if you don't," he said, interrupting me. "God help me, I don't think I can. Not unless you tell me to."

I turned and peeked at him from over my shoulder. His gaze was locked on my ass, on the spot where I was exposed. "Do *you* want to stop?"

I was afraid of the answer, but I had to know. Was Bishop

doing this for me? Or did he want this just as badly as I did? All signs pointed to yes, but his hesitance caught me off guard, and I didn't want to be just another regret.

If he genuinely didn't want this, I'd get dressed, and we could go our separate ways without too much hurt clouding our relationship. It'd be awkward, sure, but we would get over it because it was a decision we made together.

Not something he decided at eight in the morning after he sat in a corner and watched me sleep all night.

"No," he said, shaking his head vehemently. "But I worry you don't."

I blew out a breath. "Bishop Bryant, when have I ever done something I didn't want to do?"

He cracked a smile, slowly looking my way. "Never."

I pushed to my feet, and he leaned back on my sofa, giving me space. His eyes shamelessly raked over my body, taking in my peaked nipples and soaked panties. Slowly, I hooked my fingers in the waistband and pushed them down my legs.

I loved my body and had never really been ashamed of it except for a few awkward years in junior high. For some reason, standing naked in front of Bishop made me nervous. He looked like some kind of cowboy king with his arm casually resting on the armrest and his legs spread wide, showing off the impressive —and slightly terrifying—bulge beneath his jeans. His green eyes lit up as they slowly traced every dip and curve until they settled on my own.

"Come here," he said roughly.

I stepped closer, feeling my arousal coat my thighs. Maybe I would've been embarrassed by it if Bishop hadn't reached out and placed his hands on my hips. They traveled up my waist and stomach, stopping just beneath my breasts.

Neither one of us was breathing, not as he leaned forward slowly and placed a kiss along my belly. I couldn't look away, and neither could he. I was sure he felt me trembling in his touch, thrilled that it was happening and altogether terrified of what we would be when we were done.

"You're so beautiful, Lennox," Bishop said. His tone was reverential, awed. There was something about it that nearly had tears pooling beneath my lashes. "You know that, don't you?"

I nodded because suddenly, my voice was gone. I didn't know what to do with this moment of raw honesty. There were no walls between us, no boundaries to cross. We laid ourselves bare before one another, and I recognized him as the same man who'd comforted me at the hospital.

And if I wasn't already feeling some type of way about him, this softer side would've sealed the deal.

Not that I'm ready to handle those emotions yet. That'll come later when I'm alone and can properly process them.

He kissed slowly up one side of my ribs before switching to the next. His hands slid up, cupping my breasts and rolling my nipples between his fingers. I closed my eyes, gasping as I felt his mouth against my skin, flicking his tongue over the hardened peaks.

"Fuck." I couldn't stop myself from wondering what it'd be like to feel his touch elsewhere, for him to devour me. "I want this, Bishop," I said, threading my fingers through his hair and pulling it away. "I want *you*. I don't want you to stop."

A crease formed between his brows. "Are you sure?"

"Don't make me repeat myself," I said, rolling my eyes.

He chuckled, reaching behind to swat my ass. "Oh, I'll make you repeat yourself plenty of times tonight."

Bishop lifted me up, laying me on the sofa as we switched places. He settled between my thighs, forcing them apart and giving him unrestricted access to see every part of me.

"Look at that pretty pussy," he groaned, running his finger along my entrance, teasing me slowly. "Gotta take my time even though you're being a wanton little slut, grinding against my hand and wanting more. I don't wanna hurt you—"

He pressed on my lower stomach as he finally slid inside, and my eyes rolled back in pure bliss. "What if that's what I want? What if I told you to make it hurt?"

Bishop paused. "I'd tell you you're in luck because I've never been very conventional with the things I like, but this isn't the kind of pain I'm into. I wanna make sure you're comfortable, even when you're out here naked, begging me to touch you."

"You want to touch me, too," I countered. It was getting difficult to focus on what I was saying while his fingers lazily dipped inside me, curving and stroking and driving me mad. "I've seen how you watched me, how badly you've wanted to feel me. I know the kind of power I hold."

The smile he gave me was nearly blinding. It nearly knocked my breath away and made me forget what was happening. I'd never seen him smile like that, so full of pride and happiness and something else I couldn't understand now.

"Make no mistake... I'm in control right now," he said lowly. "And I'm gonna take my time, killer, because you're right; I've been watching and waiting and wanting, and I'm not gonna fuck this up because I don't know if I'll ever get this again."

I didn't have time to analyze his words before he added another finger, stretching and filling me. He didn't hesitate for a single moment, and the moment he realized I was okay with the intrusion, he wasn't gentle. This was the side I'd expected from Bishop—unyielding and entirely in charge. We were surrounded by the obscene sound of my arousal and the pornographic moans coming from my mouth.

"That's right. Squeeze my fingers with that perfect cunt. Show me how much you like them inside of you. Fuckin' beg me to come." His eyes volleyed between my legs and my face like he didn't want to miss anything. The way that man worked my body had my toes curling against the velvet cushions within minutes.

How was he so good? Was it the taboo thing? The fact I'd

had a crush on him nearly my entire life, and now something was going down? I didn't know what was happening, but I didn't want it to stop.

He was enjoying every minute of this, enjoying torturing me and making me feel good.

"That's right, killer. You're going to come on my hand like a good little slut, aren't you?" He gripped my chin when I didn't respond, forcing me to look his way. "Answer me."

"God, yes," I moaned, writhing in his hold. "Please, make me come."

Dear God, his voice was nearly as dangerous as whatever the hell he was doing with his fingers. He held me down and whispered the dirtiest praises as an orgasm ripped through my body, leaving me a quivering mess.

Before I'd caught my breath, he pulled his fingers free and brought them between us. I could see my arousal coating them, shining beneath the warm, yellow lights.

And then he put them in his fucking mouth, closing his eyes and humming like he'd just gotten a taste of warm peach cobbler.

It shouldn't have been as hot as it was, but something ignited inside of me, begging for more of the earth-shattering orgasm he'd just given me.

I pushed him back, enjoying the sound of his quiet laughter as I reached for the button on his jeans. He held his hands up, watching me desperately struggle for it to come undone. "Easy there, killer," he said, making quick work of the stupid thing and lifting his hips to shuffle out of them.

Then he worked on his shirt, going too slow for my liking. "Come on," I said, tapping my foot against the floorboard.

"Someone's impatient," he muttered. "Didn't anyone ever tell you good things come to those who wait?"

"Pfft. That's just what people tell kids to make them behave, and we both know I never behaved."

He shook his head. "Yeah, but—"

"Bishop," I said, cutting him off. "I'm sure whatever wisdom you're about to spew is insightful, but a little more stripping and a little less talking would be ideal. My nipples are so hard, they could literally cut glass, and I really want you to fuck me so…" I tapped my wrist like I was checking the time. "Could you hurry it up?"

"You little shit," he said, pulling the shirt over his head and exposing his stupidly hot body. Seriously, this man was ripped from years of working on the ranch. A large tattoo started at the top of his shoulder, dipped onto his chest, and went down his left arm. I'd seen glimpses of it before, but never the full work of art.

I reached out, tracing the black and grey lines of a beautiful landscape. A river ran through a set of trees, and what looked like a small cabin nestled on the banks. And, because I knew Bishop better than most, I made a little noise when I noticed the horse tied outside to a hitching post.

"It's beautiful," I said, pulling my hand back.

He dipped his head. "Thank you. It took fucking ages, but my artist is amazing. Couldn't have done it without her. She's truly brilliant."

I opened my mouth to say something else, but he placed his pointer finger over my lips and hushed me. "I thought you said you wanted less talking?"

"I do, but even I can appreciate a masterpiece."

Bishop puffed out his chest. "I've been working hard on my—"

I reached over and threw his penis pillow at his face. He caught it, smiling and tossing it down before grabbing my waist and lifting me toward him. I didn't know how he could move me around so easily, as no other guy had before.

Then again… No other guy I'd been with had muscles like Bishop. Seriously, how was he so jacked? Was he chugging raw eggs in the morning? I think I'd seen that in a movie once. Was that still a thing?

Bishop sat me down on his knees, and I could make out the bulge beneath his snug blue briefs. His expectant gaze drifted down, lifting one brow as he said, "Take out my dick, killer. I wanna see it in your hand, wanna feel—" His words cut off with a hiss as I reached beneath the band and pulled him free.

"What the fuck, Bishop? How does this thing not get in the way of riding or working or, I don't know, regular everyday activities?"

Honestly, I would've been worried about what he was working with if I hadn't felt it when we almost hooked up four months ago. I mean, just because he was a bigger guy didn't mean he automatically had a bigger dick.

"You're good for an old man's ego," he said, leaning forward for a quick kiss. "Now slide down on me. Let me fill that tight little cunt."

I saluted him before reaching down and notching him at my entrance. "Yes, daddy."

I didn't know if he groaned at my words or the fact his tip had slipped inside. "Fuck, fuck, fuck, wait..." he said through gritted teeth. "Condom."

Fuck was right because I didn't have one, and I was willing to bet neither did he.

"I have an IUD," I whispered. "And I get tested every six months. Rodeo circuit life," I said when he looked at me in question.

"I don't really wanna hear about that shit when it's my dick you're about to come on," he panted.

"Are you jealous?" I asked, realizing I sounded just as breathless as he did.

"Of all the wasted years? Yeah, it's not a fucking great reminder, Lennox," he scoffed. "I'm fine with this if you are. I haven't been with anyone since I was last tested, but I don't wanna pressure you."

Of all the wasted years.

His words were a lightning strike to the heart. They were further proof that he'd been fighting this as long as I had, even if my silent pining went farther back than was appropriate.

I circled my hips, letting him slip in further. "Does that answer your question?"

"Fucking tease," he said, gripping my waist and bucking his hips up.

The sensation took my breath away. I leaned over and dug my fingers into his shoulders as he worked me down his length. "Holy shit," I gasped.

"Almost there," he whispered, moving slowly. And then I felt his legs beneath me, felt how full I was, and I knew I'd taken every inch. "Good fucking girl," he praised. "Taking all of me like the perfect little slut you are."

I really shouldn't like that as much as I did, but it was like a dopamine hit straight to the brain. Each time he said it, my body reacted like I'd just won the lottery.

We worked in tandem, each of us lost to the other's pleasure. I loved watching his lips part with each ragged exhale, and his pupils dilated until almost all the green was gone. He was just as lost to this sensation as I was, and I never wanted it to end.

Sweat slicked our bodies as we moved. Bishop pounded up into me, pistoning his hips in the most deliciously brutal way that had my head falling back and stars dancing across the back of my eyelids.

"I'm so close," he groaned. "Your pussy is too good, too"—*thrust*—"fucking"—*thrust*—"good."

I felt his hand drop between us, and at the slightest brush against my clit, I was gone. I detonated, clawing at his body as he rode me through my orgasm. He followed me over the edge as I collapsed against his chest. We were a mess, but I didn't care.

Bishop wrapped my hair gently around his fist and tugged my head back. And then he leaned in and kissed the crook of my neck, moving along my collarbone.

"That was beautiful," he whispered, lingering against my skin for a moment, eyes closed as he sucked in a deep breath. I chalked it up to my emotions being all over the place after an earth-shattering climax, but there was something so tender about the way he looked that my chest ached.

"I think you're kind of beautiful," I admitted, leaning in to kiss him.

It should've felt weird, even though we'd just done a lot more. There was something about kissing in the heat of passion that looked different when the dust settled after a storm. I worried he'd pull away or push me off, but he only drew me closer.

"Did I fuck you stupid?" he asked, pulling back with concern. "Are you concussed in any way? Seeing double, perhaps?"

"What? No! I'm serious."

He shook his head. "Killer, we need to get your eyes checked. Something isn't right."

I wound my arms around his neck. "I've got twenty-twenty vision, baby. I see just fine."

Bishop blinked in surprise before his eyes softened. "Say that again."

"That I've got twenty-twenty vision?"

"Not that. The other thing."

I scrunched my nose, trying to figure out what he was talking about when it hit me. "Baby?"

He nodded. "That's the one. Repeat it, killer."

I held my hand up. "Wait, why do you get something cute, and I get that?"

Bishop smoothed the hair away from my face, tucking an

errant strand behind my ear. "Because that's just how it works. I said it, and it stuck." He shrugged. "It's not my fault you're all ragey. I'd rather fist-fight a grizzly bear than you."

"A grizzly, huh? Wow. I didn't realize I was so scary," I said, flattening my hand against my chest. "Well, I guess you're forgiven, then."

"You're not gonna say it again, are you?"

I snuggled into his chest, contentedly listening to the steady beat of his pulse. "Not yet, Bish. Not yet."

I wanted to say it, desperately so, but there were things we needed to talk about, things I needed clarification on before I could fully cross the line with him. For all my reckless and impulsive behavior, Bishop was the overthinker, and whatever happened between us just now would play repeatedly on his mind. It wouldn't surprise me if I woke up in the morning and he was gone, leaving nothing more than an ache between my legs as a memory.

I desperately hoped I was wrong, but honestly... Only time would tell. In the meantime, I needed to protect my heart until I was sure Bishop would go all in with me like I was ready to be all in with him.

bishop

. . .

I HAD sex with Lennox Hayes, and now she was asleep in my arms, drooling on my chest.

We'd stayed curled up on this tiny velvet couch, talking and touching and kissing until we'd apparently fallen asleep at some point during the night. It sure as hell wasn't comfortable, either. Every muscle in my body ached as I woke to soft-spoken voices instead of the blaring alarm sound I'd used since I was a kid.

Call me old-fashioned, but I still used an alarm clock. I only used my phone as a backup in case we lost power. It wasn't until I blinked away the sleep that I realized where I was or what I heard.

"…seen Bishop this morning?"

"No, but he could've ridden out early. He was bitchin' about the fences down by the gate last night. Said they needed fixin' ASAP."

"Naw, Titan's still here. Think he's sick?"

There was a pause, and then both men laughed. "He's worked through the flu before."

Fuck, fuck, fuck.

Lennox and I had fallen asleep on the couch.

In the old hayloft.

And now the barn below was crawling with employees and likely, her family.

Goddammit, Bishop. This is exactly why this was a horrible idea. Now the entire ranch is gonna know you fucked the boss's daughter.

Panic took hold as voices filtered through the space—mundane conversations about what they had for breakfast or their weekend plans. Given the amount of people filtering in, I guessed it was around seven in the morning. How were we supposed to get out of here without raising suspicion? It was one thing for her to waltz down the steps and go about her day, but not for me.

I looked down at the woman lying on my chest. She was so beautiful, even with a thin line of drool spilling from her lips. A large window near the stairs filled the space with sunlight.

Everything looked different in the light of day. The loft was cozy enough that the small amount of clothes and random pillows around the floor made the space look cluttered. I'd seen Lennox's room once in my life and knew this was standard operating procedure. She thrived in chaos, in an organized disorder.

Sometimes I'd ask her where something was just to be a smartass, and she would mouth off the exact location with her arms crossed and an "I fucking told you so" look on her face.

The shelves were filled with trophies and ribbons from her early riding days. There were random knick-knacks in the mix—some I recognized and some I didn't. Only Lennox would have a goddamn disco ball as a shelf ornament.

In the past, I'd never cared much about how women decorated their spaces the morning after a hookup. I was quick to thank them for a great time, get dressed, and go about my day, but this was different.

I wanted to wake Lennox up and ask her about every object that piqued my curiosity. I wanted to watch a smile spread across her face as she vividly recalled the memories—because that woman could tell a story like nobody's business—and imagine myself by her side.

More than anything, I wanted to stay here and watch her sleep, but I knew I couldn't. The barn had gone silent apart from the horses chuffing in their stalls. Morning feeding was long over. If I slipped out now, I could probably make it to my cabin before anyone else came looking for me.

Worst case scenario, I could tell whoever I ran into that I'd been up all night with food poisoning to buy myself a little sympathy.

No one ever questioned that shit.

Slowly, I disentangled myself from Lennox, grabbing one of her pillows and sliding it beneath her head. She made a little whimpering noise that had me second-guessing, leaving her behind, but time wasn't on our side. It wasn't like I didn't know where to find her. We'd see each other later today anyway.

When I was dressed, I squatted down and pressed a kiss to her forehead. "See you soon, sweetheart," I whispered, stopping as I realized the term of endearment had slipped free so easily.

What in the hell had this woman done to me last night? Suddenly, I was a worn piece of string wrapped so firmly around her finger that I'd do almost anything she asked me to. Maybe I always had been.

For all the shit we gave one another, if Lennox had asked me for something, I would've given it to her. It didn't matter the time or the place, or the circumstance.

I'd do anything for her.

As I tip-toed down the steps, though, that sense of elation came to a staggering halt as I looked through open barn doors and saw Doug walking out of the house. If you hadn't been there, you wouldn't know he'd had a heart attack recently.

Some color had returned to his skin, and he was as ornery as ever—always trying to sneak out to the barn for a ride. Most of the time, one of the girls corralled him back before he made it out there. Although, he'd managed to get his horse saddled last week and was ready to mount up before Josie came storming out of her office looking like a wet hen.

He lifted his hand in greeting as Ruby came out of the house behind him. She looked over, waving before she ushered him into the car. As they drove away, I couldn't help but feel guilty.

Guilty for feeling like I was going behind Doug's back and falling for his daughter, for not walking away when I knew better, and finally... Guilty for not knowing if I was about to break Lennox's heart and lose her for good.

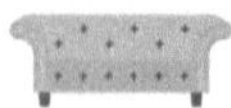

I SIPPED AT MY BEER, staring at the paper on my table. It'd been a long day, and now there was a thunderstorm raging outside. It'd been going strong for the past few hours, which meant this weekend would be miserable rounding up cattle in the mud. We would have to take extra precautions, extra time we didn't budget for, but that was part of being a cowboy. You adapted. You made shit work when Plan A went to shit.

After grabbing a quick shower at my cabin this morning, I'd thrown myself into work. The fence was mended, and I'd taken a ride out to check the stock tanks in the back pastures to make sure they were in good standing until we brought the herds in.

My mind was a goddamn mess right now. I couldn't stop thinking about Lennox and how great our night had been. For the first time, I felt this heavy weight lift off my chest. I could breathe again. The crazy thing was that I didn't even realize how hard it'd been before. It was a night and day difference.

The last night we'd spent together had ended in a goddamn disaster. It felt like years, rather than mere months. I still hated myself for the way I handled things, hated myself for the things I'd said. It'd taken me damn near a month to look myself in the mirror again. I couldn't see myself without seeing the way I'd hurt her.

Even if she hadn't said it, I knew. I could fucking feel it.

I'd hurt myself, too.

When I'd spent the night watching her sleep, I'd almost given in. I'd almost crawled into bed, pulled her into my arms, and said to hell with scaring her off. I wanted her. She wanted me. It should've been simple, but I'd gone and ruined that for both of us.

So, why was I such a chicken shit now that I had a real chance to turn things around? I felt like I was playing tug-o-war with myself. On one side were my responsibilities and loyalty to Doug, and on the other was my hope for the future and feelings for Lennox.

The two could easily exist together, but I had a mental block I couldn't get past, so I decided to write a pros and cons list for my dilemma.

Was it stupid and childish? Maybe, but for some reason, I hoped seeing the reasons for both written down would solidify my decision, but it hadn't—not yet, anyway.

I glanced at my phone screen, sinking back into my chair with a sigh as the screen came up blank.

No notifications.

Since I left Lennox this morning, I'd been checking it obsessively. Lennox hadn't called or texted once. The heaviness I'd felt before was steadily creeping back in. Had I already fucked this up?

When I brought Titan back to the barn, Strider stood in his stall, staring at me over the wooden door. It almost felt like he was judging me, so I may have tossed him a few sugar cubes to get in his good graces again, but I didn't think it worked.

He looked royally pissed off the entire time I brushed Titan out and gave him a late supper. I felt his judging gaze the entire time I locked up the barn. I swore he knew what was going on in my head and was silently telling me what a dumbass I was.

Believe me, buddy... I already know.

I tapped my pen against the table, groaning as I stared at the crinkled paper. I'd balled it up and tried throwing it away for the past hour, but had no such luck.

Pros:
- So goddamn pretty
- Smells nice
- Rides like a pro
- Can keep up with me (work shit)
- Keep me on my toes
- Good at sex
- Can't stop thinking about her

Cons:
- Doug
- Migraine inducing
- Smart ass mouth
- Too damn young
- Will push all buttons
- Might lose job—see line one
- Can't stop thinking about her

Seven and seven for each. A fucking draw.

"I thought these lists were supposed to make shit better, not worse," I muttered to myself, taking a sip of beer. Even that seemed to taste funny. Clearly, I shouldn't be doing any of this shit right now because I was a mess.

The sound of a diesel engine caught my attention, and I

noticed a bright light coming down the caliche road leading toward my cabin. It was going too fast, too reckless given the weather, but they didn't slow. They came to a screeching halt, headlights streaming through the window.

Whoever it was, better have a damn good explanation for pulling straight up and not using the carport. Given the season, my grass may have been dead right now, but that didn't mean I didn't care how it looked.

BANG. BANG. BANG.

I jerked my head toward the entrance when their fist thudded loudly against the wooden door.

"Bishop!" Lennox called, and for a split second, relief flooded my system. But then it dried up like the fucking desert as she said, "Open this fucking door, you coward!"

What was she doing 'out here in the middle of a thunderstorm? I hurried out of my seat, reaching my door in five steps before ripping it open.

Lennox stood in the pouring rain, looking like she'd just fallen in the ocean and drug herself back up to land. The small awning was hardly offering protection from the storm, but she didn't care. Her eyes narrowed to thin slits, but the startling icy blue color was glowing with undiluted fury.

She pushed past me, tracking in mud and soaking my floor with the water dripping from her clothes. And then she stood in the middle of my living room, arms crossed and not giving a fuck.

I checked outside, seeing her truck still running, and a bright ass light bar across the top was focused on the door. "Uh, your truck is—"

"I don't give a shit about the truck, you stupid prick!" she yelled.

"Alright," I said, slowly closing the door. I'd learned early on that pushing Lennox's buttons was all fun and games until she reached the point of no return. Once that happened... It was best to mind your balls because she would absolutely try busting them. "Mind telling me what you do give a shit about then?"

She let out a frustrated growl before storming over and jabbing her finger in the middle of my chest. "You! I give a shit about *you*. Maybe that makes me the fucking fool in this scenario, but here we are. Here I am, making the big gesture, laying it all out on the line for your old ass."

"Woah, woah," I said, placing my hands on her shoulder. She promptly shrugged them off, and I held them up in a promise not to touch her if that wasn't what she wanted. "Slow down, killer—"

"Don't call me that," she hissed.

"Alright, Lennox… What's going on here? I don't understand what's happening."

Lennox snorted. "Of course you don't. You're completely oblivious to everything and everyone around you—living in your own world."

I rolled my shoulders, trying to ease some of the tension tightening my muscles. I didn't know if I'd ever seen her this mad before, and I'd held her back from getting into a shit ton of fights over the years. Whatever this was—whatever I'd done—it surpassed anything I'd experienced.

For all her teasing, Lennox wasn't ever inherently rude or insulting to others. She could be passive-aggressive as hell sometimes, but I felt so out of my depth with this wave of anger.

"Lennox—"

"Why did you leave this morning?" she asked, jutting her chin out in a show of strength. One that might have worked if I didn't know her so damn well. It wobbled slightly, and she was clenching her jaw so hard I thought it might pop. When I didn't answer her quickly enough, she repeated her question, accenting each word with a sharp jab. "Why. Did. You. Leave?"

I rubbed at my chest. "I—I had work. I just—"

But she wouldn't hear any of my excuses or even think about entertaining them as she said, "You could've woken me up. You could've said goodbye, but you didn't. You just got dressed and slipped out without a word. I mean, my God, at least when Josie left Lincoln in Tennessee, she left a note that said she was sorry, but I didn't even get that." Her words were coming fast, and she paused to catch her breath before beginning again. She clutched the back of her neck. "I knew this was gonna happen, so I guess I shouldn't be surprised, but I fucking am. Silly me. I thought that maybe, just maybe, last night would've meant something to you, but—"

"It meant everything!" I bellowed, unable to stop myself. I ran my fingers through my hair as she blinked in confusion. "Jesus Christ, Lennox. I know you think I'm a callous dick, but do you honestly think I'm so cruel that I'd be so devil-may-care with your body? With your heart *and* mine?"

"Then why did you leave? Why didn't you text me?" Lennox tried holding her voice steady, but it broke on the last question. "Why didn't you say anything at all?"

I blew out a breath and hung my head. *Bishop, you're such a fucking idiot.* "When I woke up this morning, there were people in the barn. Neither of us had set an alarm, and I heard the hands questioning where I was. I panicked. You got me there, but it wasn't just for me. It was for you. For us. I didn't know what people would say if I came traipsing down the stairs from your loft, and I sure as hell wasn't about to out us without talking to you first."

"Is there an us? Because you've been the one to backtrack every time we've tried sorting this out."

"I don't know, Lennox! That's the point. We deserved a chance to sort that out ourselves."

"But you left!" Lennox stepped forward, cheeks flushed and eyes glowing. "Do you know how cheap I felt waking up this morning, excruciatingly sore, overly exhausted, and yet ridiculously happy? Until, of course, I realized that you'd snuck out like I was nothing but a cheap fuck," she shot back, running her hands through her hair. "God, I am so stupid. I can't believe I actually thought you'd gotten over your bullshit. I don't know what I'm doing here."

I'd had enough talking. Enough fucking games. I surged forward, bracketing her face with my hands and pulling her closer. Her eyes widened in surprise, but beneath all the bullshit, I saw a spark of hope ignite.

"You are anything but a cheap fuck, Lennox," I whispered harshly before crashing my lips to hers. She pushed against my chest only for a second before her arms wound around my neck.

Last night was gentle and reassuring, but this was something else entirely. It reminded me of the first night we'd kissed after the bar, how desperate and eager we were for one another. But where there'd once been confusion, I only felt clarity.

And that clarity was Lennox Hayes.

lennox

. . .

The Morning After

OH GOD. Everything hurt. Why did everything hurt? I wasn't even drunk by the time we got home. At least not if we were talking about alcohol.

Bishop and his dick, on the other hand, was another matter entirely.

Sure, I'd only tasted it for a minute before Taco Bell chipped away at my pride. Food poisoning was a bitch, but I was confident in my ability to ask for a chance to redeem myself. Especially after sneaking into the bathroom and freshening up. I know I didn't take my makeup off before going to sleep. I probably looked like a mess.

I had no idea what time it was, or even where my clothes and purse were, but I didn't care as I burrowed deeper into his pillow and sucked in a deep breath. He smelled delicious. It was all masculine and rugged—sage and firewood and fresh coffee.

I could picture him sitting in the middle of a wide field in worn chaps, brewing a cup over an open flame before the sun came up. A moment of perfect stillness.

I stretched out, reaching across the bed for his warmth, but found none. I cracked an eye, hating how bright his room was already. Did he not own curtains?

The spot beside me was empty and looked like it had been for some time. Not completely unsurprising. He wasn't the type to lounge around in bed all morning, even if we'd both had a long night.

Dad normally cooked breakfast on Sunday mornings, but I was content to skip it if it meant spending more time here. There was something so strange about being in his space. Most of the time when I woke up in a strange place, I hightailed it out of there before the sun came up. I didn't stay around for awkward conversations or the "should I call you?" conversations. I was never interested in that.

But this morning, I was struggling to get out of bed, and it wasn't because of a hangover. The awkward, bumbling nineteen-year-old me would've died at the thought of being here. Though I'd deny it until the day I died, I was a bit obsessed with Bishop. I might even still have some of my old diaries that featured full blown fantasies about the hot, older cowboy if I looked hard enough.

If only that version of myself could only see where I was now.

"Morning."

I jumped, clutching the sheets to my chest as I glanced around his room. Bishop was sitting in the corner, eyes dark and hair mussed. It looked like he'd been up all night. He was shirtless, showing off the thick patches of hair along his chest and the small line dipping below his pants. I could make out the general outline of his tattoo, but it was still too dark to see it clearly.

"Hi," I said, a little breathlessly. "Sorry, I didn't know you were here."

"Where else would I be?" he asked, staring down at his

hands. Something felt off. Alarm bells were ringing in my head, telling me to get out while I could, but I didn't listen.

"I dunno, honestly. Your side of the bed was cold, so I assumed you'd gone up to the barn or something," I chuckled, hoping to lighten the mood.

Only he didn't join in.

"I didn't sleep next to you. Didn't want to give you the wrong idea."

I straightened my shoulders, sitting up a little taller than normal. "And what idea would that be? That you like to sleep?"

"No, I wanted to make sure you didn't start throwing up again all over my bed." I waited for the punchline to a joke that never came. A smile, maybe. Any sign to show he wasn't dismissing me like I was some casual fuck.

That version of Bishop was one I'd come to know well over the years, but this felt different. He was launching straight into being a dick, which was a bit jarring considering his dick had been in my mouth hours ago.

"Last night shouldn't have happened."

"You mean the Taco Bell?" I scrunched my nose. It was going to be so long until I could look at the late-night favorite the same way. "You were right. It was a bad call—"

"No," he said, cutting me off. His eyes were trained down. He wouldn't even look at me.

"Okay... I'm not sure what's happening here, Bishop. Did I do something wrong? I mean, last night I had your dick down my throat and now you won't look at me. I didn't think bodily fluids would fuck you up this much."

He let out a weary sigh, rubbing the back of his neck. "Christ, Lennox. No, it wasn't the throwing up. I don't give a shit about that. I just mean that whatever was gonna happen last night, it can't happen again. It was a—"

"Oh no," I said, throwing back the covers. My legs were a

little shaky, and my stomach felt like it could betray me at any second, but I pushed through anyway. "You're not about to lecture me like I'm a child. We are two consenting adults and there was nothing wrong with what did or did not happen."

Okay, maybe I wasn't okay. Either the room was spinning, or the food poisoning was coming out in full force now that I was awake. Where was my stuff? I didn't remember where I put it. At this point, was it even worth staying to find it? I'd rather sit at the DMV for hours to get a new license than listen to him tell me this was all a mistake.

Damn. Let a girl leave with a little bit of pride left intact.

"I'm not lecturing you, but it was still a—"

"A mistake?" I asked, waiting for him to tell me that wasn't exactly what he was about to say, but nothing came. He just stared at the wall with a clenched jaw. "Jesus, you can't even look at me?"

"No."

The word was like a slap. It rolled off his tongue so easily, unyielding and resolute.

Well, fuck that.

I'd been told a time or two that I had a bad temper, but I always laughed it off. Sure, I might have gotten into a few fights over the years. And yes, I did put sugar in my high school exes gas tank because I caught him making out with Sarah Sheffield before school one day. In my defense, though, he'd just asked me to prom two days before and I could not let the injustice stand.

Somehow, this moment felt ten times worse than any other.

I stormed toward Bishop and gripped his chin. "If you're going to be a coward, then you're damn sure going to look at me while doing it."

His eyes were so dark they seemed almost cruel. The beautiful forest green I loved was gone, replaced instead by a black expanse that sent my fight-or-flight reflexes into overdrive. It was the first time that he'd truly looked at me all morning, and I hated it.

"Is that what you think? That I'm being a coward?" he asked harshly, gripping my wrist and breaking the hold. I let him, too stunned to reach into my arsenal of verbal comebacks like I'd been prepared to do seconds ago. "Listen to me carefully, Lennox, because I don't want you running to your father and causing trouble. Anything that happened between us," he said, motioning over his shoulder toward the living room, "meant nothing. It was a line we shouldn't have crossed, and I'm thanking whatever higher power is out there this morning that they intervened before things got out of hand."

"Oh my God, do you hear yourself?" I shot back. "I don't know how they did things back in your day, but in mine... two consenting adults can sleep together without acting like it's the end of the world or needing a wedding proposal. You didn't ruin my virtue or some shit."

My pride was taking one hell of a blow this morning. It would've been easier to walk out the door like none of this mattered and moved on with my life. Nothing between us needed to change. Bishop and I could, hypothetically, go back to how we were before.

But I'd never done things the easy way, and he had pissed me off. "That wasn't what I fuckin' meant," he scoffed.

"Then what did you mean, Bishop? Did you think I was going to run and tell my dad we'd almost slept together?" When he didn't answer, I rolled my eyes. "Give me a fucking break," I muttered.

I looked down, realizing just how much his shirt dwarfed me. It smelled like him. Something that, no matter how much I enjoyed it, was forever tainted. Now, it just reminded me of bad decisions and embarrassment.

I needed out of his clothes, of his space, and his presence right now, or else I just might combust.

"Lennox, stop. Let me get your clothes." He pushed to his feet, but I'd already ripped the fabric over my head. I balled it in a fist and threw it in his direction.

"Is seeing me naked horrible, too?" I asked over my shoulder, scouring the ground my for my dress. Thankfully, I was still wearing my underwear, so that was one less article of clothing I needed to hunt for.

"I just don't see why you couldn't have kept it on before—"

Aha! There it is.

I reached for the pile of clothes, quickly pulling on my bra. When I grabbed my dress, I was met with the faint stench of day-old vomit.

Fucking fantastic.

It didn't matter. I'd just have to cowgirl the fuck up and wear it home. There was no way I was going to ask for his shirt back.

As I turned around, I realized I probably looked like a mess. I certainly felt like one. Even if I hadn't looked in a mirror, I could still feel remnants of last night's makeup dried to my skin— though I had the briefest memory of him gently trying to get it off before I passed out.

"Where's my phone and purse?" I asked, crossing my arms over my chest. His eyes dropped, taking in the swell of my breasts as he sucked in a deep breath.

Bishop hesitated for a moment before motioning toward the living room. "By the door on the hook."

"Well, you were certainly ready to kick me out, weren't you?" I asked, storming past him.

"Lennox, goddammit, can you wait for just one second?" I could feel him at my back when I reached for my purse. I did a quick check, just making sure everything was inside. Phone, wallet, keys, taser—the usuals.

Thank God. I'd rather die than come back to this cabin.

"I don't think there's much point in that, do you? What's

there to talk about? Do you want to insult me some more?" I spun around, nearly knocked off balance by how close he was.

Bishop ran his hands through his hair, tugging slightly on the ends. I waited for him to say something—to say anything, really—but was met with silence yet again.

I shook my head. "That's what I thought. Enjoy the solitude, Bishop. Hope it's worth it."

lennox

. . .

I HADN'T BEEN LYING when I told Bishop I was stewing since the moment I woke up. I'd spent the damn day in a silent rage, throwing myself into work. The entire house was spotless, cleaned from top to bottom—even my own bedroom, which I don't think had ever been that organized.

When my parents got home from their doctor's appointments, they didn't recognize the house. Because they knew me as well as they did, they immediately launched an inquisition about what was wrong.

"Did someone get hurt? Are you fighting with one of your sisters?" It wasn't until my Dad hit the nail on the head with, "Whose ass am I kicking for breaking your heart?" that I felt my bravado slip just a hair.

But instead of breaking down and telling my Dad that I was an idiot who'd foolishly opened her heart, I cracked a joke about my Adderall hitting hard and how I didn't want to let it go to waste. His raised brow told me he didn't believe me, but it was enough to stop the questioning.

When I finally trudged to my room and flopped down on my bed, I was so exhausted that I hoped to fall asleep quickly. But no. Of course, that would be too easy. Instead, I stared at the glow-in-the-dark stars on my ceiling until I finally let myself cry.

I wasn't much of a crier. Never had been. That'd been more Josie's reactionary emotion while I was the hothead of the family. I'd been known to cuss and fight and break things in a fit of anger—all of which I'd been working on in therapy since I was a kid, but things still slipped.

The tears flowed and flowed until I worried they wouldn't stop. They matched the torrential downpour outside. I hated the way my chest ached. How I vividly recalled the immediate sensation of rejection when I woke up alone this morning.

But the sadness quickly gave way to anger, and before I knew it, I was storming out of the house, hopping in my truck, and driving through the storm until I reached Bishop's cabin. I didn't think. I didn't hesitate. I just reacted.

I didn't know what I expected from my little temper tantrum, but it sure wasn't this.

Bishop wound his fingers through my hair, pulling me to him like he'd been drowning, and I was a breath of fresh air he desperately needed. Our mouths moved against one another, tongues sweeping in and claiming. He nipped at my lip, drawing it out as he pulled back to rest his forehead against mine.

"I'm scared," he whispered, green eyes brimmed with silver. "I don't know how to do this. I don't know how to be the partner you want—the one you deserve—because I have been on my own for so long, but goddammit, I wanna try if you'll let me."

He kissed me again, softer this time, but I felt just as much heat behind it. I felt his conviction, his earnest words, and his tender truths. We were both a mess, but we could be a mess together.

Maybe we could make something new, something tangible, something absolutely fucking epic.

"You can't keep doing this to me, Bishop. You can't keep

being so hot and cold. You can't keep things to yourself or make decisions on your own that concern me as well, because you will lose me if you do. You'll lose whatever this is or could be," I mumbled against his lips.

"I know, sweetheart. I know, and I—"

It felt like he'd reached in and stolen the air from my lungs. "Wait…" I said, interrupting him. "Say it again."

"I know?"

"No, the other thing."

Bishop paused, lip quirking up. "You like that, huh?"

I nodded. It often sounded condescending as it fell from men's lips—like they looked down on me, like I was less than they were. But when Bishop had said it, it felt right. "I think you're the only one who's ever used the word sweet while talking about me, but okay."

"Well, clearly, they've never tasted your pussy before, or else they'd know there's no other word for you," he growled against my lips as he kissed me fervently.

"Oh, they did, but I still never earned the distinction," I said, choking back a laugh.

He lifted one shoulder in an arrogant shrug. "Their fucking loss is my gain."

I pulled back, quirking a brow. "It doesn't bother you that I said that?"

"What? That someone else has tasted you?" he snorted. "Lennox, I'm not a saint. Neither are you. We're grown-ass adults. I don't give a shit about what you've done in the past. I'm only concerned with your future." His fingertips danced along my still-drenched skin, leaving goosebumps in their wake. "But from here on out—" he kissed my shoulder, hand sliding into my back pocket "—I'm the only one who gets that honor."

His words terrified me. I wanted to believe them, but something was stopping me. Bishop was an honest man—an honorable man. He would never intentionally hurt me, but that didn't mean it wouldn't accidentally happen if he thought it was what was best for me.

And that was where my hesitation lay.

"You're talking a big game for someone who seemed terrified to take that step days ago," I murmured. "Don't make promises you can't keep."

"I'm not—"

I placed my finger on his lips. "Actions, Bishop. Show me, don't tell me."

"You want actions?" he growled, nipping my digit lightly, and I nodded. "I'll show you fucking actions."

Bishop leaned forward, grabbing my thighs and hoisting me in the air. I wound my legs around his waist. Neither of us cared that my clothes were soaked. We wouldn't need them for long anyway if his hard dick was any indication.

He slammed me against the wall, grinding himself against my center as he captured my mouth. His hips rolled in measured strokes, and my head fell back on a moan. How did it feel this good? We hadn't even done anything yet.

"You like that, killer?" he asked, trailing kisses down my neck. He bit down on my pulse point so hard I knew it'd bruise. Maybe I should have cared, but I didn't. Not as his tongue swirled over the hurt.

"Yes," I gasped.

"I've barely touched you," he said, clicking his tongue. "What a needy little slut you are. Look at you grinding down on me."

"You're the one digging yourself into me."

He laughed, but it was harsh. This wasn't the same man who had been ready to shed tears ten minutes ago. It reminded me of the first time we kissed and how he'd taken control of the situation and my body. He exuded confidence, the epitome of big dick energy.

But hey, at least he had the package to back it up.

"I'm just giving you what you want, isn't that right? You wanna be fucked. You wanna be filled."

"Bishop shut up," I said, tugging on his hair. He hissed, and the sound sent an electric current to my already aching core. "You sure talk a lot for someone who mumbles one-word sentences every day."

I grappled for his shirt, pulling it over his head in one swoop. My eyes trailed along his tattoo, across the dark hair along his chest, and down the trail disappearing beneath his jeans. He followed my gaze, smirking when he realized I was staring at his dick.

He let me go abruptly, and I stumbled, steadying myself on his forearms. "What're you doing?"

Slowly, he popped the button of his jeans. "There's something I've wanted to do since the moment I carried you into this cabin, something we never got around to four months ago."

My lips parted as he worked his zipper down.

"But I'm done fucking my hand to the thought of your lips wrapped around me, so..." he paused, pushing his jeans down his thick, muscular thighs. My mouth watered as the outline of his length came into view. "You're gonna drop to your knees like a good girl." Our eyes met, and I knew the slickness between my thighs wasn't only from the rainwater. "Then you're gonna reach inside my boxers and pull out my cock."

I licked my lips, and Bishop tracked the movement. "And then what?"

He stepped forward, slowly wrapping my hair around his fist and tugging my head backward. He leaned forward, his facial hair scraping against my cheek as he whispered, "And then I'm going to fuck this pretty face of yours."

I'd never dropped to my knees so fast in my life.

I wasn't sure what was happening. Sure, I'd asked a few partners to pull my hair or slap my ass a time or two, but it was always half-hearted. None of them were ever dominant in the way I needed. Even when they tried, it felt awkward and forced, which made the moment so unbelievably unsexy that it ruined the whole mood.

Eventually, I gave up asking and went with the flow. It was okay—nothing to write home about, obviously. But this was a night and day difference. Bishop didn't just talk the talk. He walked it, too. That edge came so easily to him. I was in awe of the way my mind and body wanted to please him, to obey him—even when I wanted to see how far I could push his buttons first.

Slowly, I lifted my hand and dipped inside his boxers. He hissed at the contact, but never took his eyes off me as I pulled him free and gave him one long stroke. Pre-cum leaked from the tip, and I leaned in to lick it away.

"Shit," he groaned, weaving his fingers in my hair. He pushed in, and I laid my tongue flat, running it along the silky skin. "That fucking mouth."

Bishop tightened his grip, guiding my head down on his length until I felt it at the back of my throat. It wasn't even all the way in. He held me there, enjoying the sight as my eyes began to sting.

He pulled me off, letting me catch my breath. A string of saliva connected my lips and his tip. "Can you go farther, killer? Can you take me all the way?"

"I can take it," I gasped.

"Are you sure?" he asked, stroking himself from root to tip. "I dunno if you can."

"I said I can do it," I pleaded, replacing his hand with my own. "Let me show you."

Without waiting, I slid him between my lips, not stopping until I met resistance. Bishop watched me, lips parted as I pushed further, taking him down my throat until my nose brushed against his pelvis.

"Fuuuuck." The word was long and drawn out as I struggled

to keep him there. I felt his hands on my head again, guiding me and setting a tempo. He was carefully testing the limits, figuring out what was comfortable and what wasn't.

He pulled me off, panting as he said, "Put your hands on my thighs, killer. And tap if it's too much."

"Yes, daddy," I said, nodding and doing what he asked.

He groaned, and as he slid between my lips this time, he was not gentle. He wrapped my hair around his fist, pulling on the strands as he fucked my mouth with short, measured strokes that nearly made me dizzy. I felt his muscles coiling beneath my hands with each thrust, savoring the knowledge that I was the one doing this to him. Tears leaked from my eyes, but I focused on my breathing and the sounds he made.

Was it the daddy thing? Honestly, I'd seen the few times he'd tensed when I'd let the teasing name slip. Maybe it was just another way to get on his nerves, but if saying it got him this worked up… Well, what was a girl supposed to do?

My pussy was dripping. I needed something. I needed to be touched. Bishop seemed lost to his own pleasure, so I lifted one hand from his thigh and slipped it between my legs, shamelessly grinding myself down on my own fingers to soothe the ache.

The moment I brushed my clit, I moaned around his length, nearly coming on the spot. God, it felt so good. I imagined they were *his* fingers, *his* tongue, *his* cock.

"Needy little slut," he panted, pulling me off and ripping my hand from between my legs. My fingers were slick, shining with my arousal. "Did I tell you to touch yourself?"

I shook my head.

"Words, Lennox."

"No."

"What'd I tell you to do?"

My chest rose and fell, breasts aching as he stared me down. I forced my eyes wide to look like I was actually nervous that I'd disappointed him, but I wasn't. I wanted him to test his limits, just like he'd been testing mine. "To keep my hands on your thighs and let you use me."

The growl that came out sent goosebumps skittering across my skin. Bishop hadn't said it, but I knew that was what he meant. "That's fucking right. But you didn't listen, did you?"

"No." And then I smiled, biting my lip before whispering, "What will you do to me?"

Bishop reached out, gripping my cheeks and forcing my mouth open before sticking my fingers inside. I tasted myself, desire landing sweet on my tongue.

"Bad girls don't get to come, killer," he muttered. "And from where I stand, you look like a naughty girl."

"I guess you'll have to punish me instead. Really make sure I learn my lesson."

He cocked his head to the side. "Is that what you want? To be taught a lesson? For me to tell you what a needy little whore you are?"

"Yes, daddy," I breathed.

lennox

. . .

EXCITEMENT RACED THROUGH MY VEINS, making my heart quicken faster than any drug as Bishop pulled me off the floor and tossed me over his shoulder like I was a rag doll. I laughed, beating his back even though I knew it was useless. He was completely and totally in control.

Striding into his bedroom, he threw me down on the bed, towering over me. The space was dark, but then lightning tore through the sky, illuminating the space with astonishing clarity.

For all his toughness, Bishop's eyes held an inherent reverence as he stared down at me, and for some reason, it made my chest ache. It was gone in the blink of an eye, stolen from me by the darkening of the sky once again.

He reached for my waist, flipping me over and positioning me so that my ass was in the air. I waved it like a taunt and was met with an excruciating smack. "Ow! Dammit, that hurt."

Bishop covered my body with his own, his hard length digging into my ass. "I told you that bad girls get punished. Do you want me to stop? Say the word, and I'll step back. No harm, no foul."

"No, I'm good," I said. "Just surprised me, is all."

He rolled his hips. "You sure?"

I dropped my head against the comforter, soaking in the scent of him—the worn leather and thick smoke that seemed to envelop me like a warm embrace. It was terrifying to realize how comfortable I was with him—not just with my body but with my heart.

And if I was going to give it to someone, why couldn't it be him?

"Yes, baby," I breathed. "Yes, please."

Bishop moved my tangled hair out of the way, kissing the nape of my neck. He hummed as his tongue swept out, running along my skin. "You taste so sweet," he murmured. "All this temptation, all my fantasies, and you surpass them all."

His hands moved beneath my t-shirt, lifting it over my head and discarding it at our feet. Then he peeled my shorts and panties down my legs, pressing open-mouth kisses along my body as he went.

Never in my life had I felt this turned on and yet cherished at the same time. Bishop was worshipful with his touch. Every caress carefully considered. How the hell had this man never done this before? How was he such a natural?

The question was on the tip of my tongue, but then I felt his lips trail against the globes of my ass, his hands spreading me wide, and I went still.

"Hold yourself open for me like this," he ordered, voice strained. I turned over my shoulder, watching his nostrils flare with desire. He lifted his gaze, holding it for a moment before he spoke again. "Don't make me ask twice, killer. I promise it won't get you what you're looking for."

I was too far gone to care what I looked like or that I'd given up too quickly. Reaching behind me, I did as he asked, spreading my cheeks wide so that he could see all of me.

I felt so exposed. There was nowhere to hide from him like

this. All of me was on display, like a private showing for his pleasure only.

Bishop let loose a low growl as he ran the tip of his finger along my folds, coating it in my arousal before sliding up and up. My breathing hitched as he traced the ring of muscle no one had ever breached before. I'd always been curious, but other than my own experimentation with a few small plugs, there'd never been anyone I trusted not to hurt me.

Until now.

Until him.

"Has anyone ever taken you here?" he asked, slowly tracing my ass.

I gasped as he pushed forward slightly. "N-no."

"Never?" he asked. There was a note of awe in his tone. I couldn't see him; I didn't want to risk him stopping whatever kind of magic he was working back there, but I could imagine what he looked like. Lips parted, pupils blown, heaving chest.

And I'd done that.

"Never," I breathed, squeezing my eyes shut. It was hardly an intrusion, and yet I already felt so full. And it was just the tip. How the fuck did people handle more?

"We'll have to change that," he said gruffly, pressing further before retreating. "But not tonight."

"Why not?" I asked, turning and pouting. I didn't know why I was complaining because there was no way I could handle it right now when I was already so sensitive, ready to detonate at the slightest touch.

"I don't have the patience to be gentle anymore, killer," he said, reaching into his boxers and pulling himself free. He lifted his gaze, meeting my own as he stroked up from the base. "I need you so fucking badly."

"I need you, too," I whispered. I didn't want to think about everything we'd admitted tonight, the lines we'd crossed that we'd never be able to take back. It was terrifying, but I was sick and tired of running from what I wanted.

No matter how scared I was, it wasn't enough to stop me from diving into the deep end with him.

Fuck it.

"Please, daddy. Fuck me."

I saw the moment his restraint broke, felt the bruising grip that landed on my hip as he dragged the head of his cock through my soaked pussy. He knocked my hands away, spreading my cheeks himself. With each pass, he made sure to brush my oversensitive clit.

"You're so fucking wet," he said, watching my arousal coat his length. "Christ, sweetheart. You're dripping down your thighs. I bet you are hurtin', aren't you?"

I nodded furiously. "Yes."

"Bet you wish I would quit teasing you, huh? That I'd fill this perfect fucking cunt and fuck you like the little whore you are..." He trailed off, letting out a ragged exhale as he pressed the tip inside.

"Bishop—"

He smacked my ass. "Who owns this pussy, Lennox? Who's gonna fuck you until you scream, gonna fill you up until you're overflowing and marked as mine?"

"You!" I cried out at his words, twisting my hands in his sheets.

"That's a good fucking girl," he said, pressing down on the center of my back so that I couldn't move. "And you're gonna take it all, aren't you?"

I didn't have a chance to respond. I didn't need to. He plunged forward in one hard thrust, stilling as our bodies connected. Bright lights danced behind my eyelids to the tune of his ragged breaths. God, how I wanted to see it. How I wanted to watch the way he came undone for me.

"Where's your phone?" I asked.

"What?" he bit out, fingers digging into my skin. "Why the fuck do you need a phone when I've got my dick inside you?"

I ducked my head, second-guessing myself for only a moment. "I want to record us," I mumbled into the sheets. Thank god it was so dark in here, or else there'd be no hiding the heat in my cheeks.

"You wanna make a sex tape?"

"For us, yeah," I said. Honestly, I couldn't believe what I was saying. I'd always been super careful about this kind of thing, especially with our family being prominent in the area and my career. The last thing any of us needed was a sex scandal, but I had always loved the idea of filming myself getting truly fucked. And I trusted Bishop more than anyone I'd ever been with. And while I hoped we'd have a lot more opportunities to do something like this, I also wanted something just in case it was the last time. "I mean, we don't have to right now. We could talk about it some more—"

I moaned as he slipped out, missing his touch instantly. For a moment, I thought he would tell me I'd gone too far and crossed a line, but the sound of feet padding against old hardwood faded, and I looked over my shoulder to see him walking back in with his phone in hand.

He glanced between me and the phone, raising a brow. "You really wanna do this, sweetheart?"

"If you do," I said, forcing the shake from my voice.

Bishop nodded once, fingers moving across the screen as he pulled up the camera. "It's too dark," he muttered in frustration. "Gotta turn on a light."

"Just use the flash."

His brows furrowed. "I don't know how to do that shit."

"Give it here," I said, holding out my hand. Bishop handed it over, and I turned it on, pressing record before returning it. Then I quickly flipped back on my stomach and wiggled my ass in a taunt. "Please fuck me, daddy."

"Fuckin' brat," he whispered, stepping up. I could feel him moving behind me, wondering if he was still messing with the camera or something else.

My eyes slid closed in relief as he slowly pushed into my aching center. "That's right, killer. Get my dick wet." He let out a low groan, taking his time as he continued to work inside of me. I wondered if he was having more fun than he let on. If this was a fantasy we'd both shared and had never experimented with.

"I can't wait for you to see this," he whispered as our bodies grew flush. "Your pussy is so goddamn needy, sweetheart. She's practically sucking me in. Won't let me go."

Oh yeah. He was loving this just as much as I was.

The storm raging outside these four walls matched the one inside my chest. I was swept up in the moment, in Bishop's touch, in the toe-curling way he began to move.

Within a matter of seconds, I felt his restraint slip.

He slid his hand from my waist to the middle of my back, pushing me into the mattress as the speed of his thrusts increased. As he slammed his hips into my ass, he stole all the breath from my lungs. "Oh my god," I cried, scrunching the sheets in my fist.

"God has nothing to do with this," he panted. "I'm the one making this tight cunt weep for me."

He shifted, canting his hips downward and hitting that elusive spot most men couldn't find. There was so much pressure building in my abdomen that I couldn't hold back anymore. "Bishop, I'm gonna—"

And then he was gone, tossing the phone down on the bed as he grabbed my hips and flipped me onto my back. Sweat dripped down his temple, but he didn't move to wipe it away. Instead, he jerked his chin toward the phone. "Grab it and fucking watch."

I scrambled for it, holding it with shaky hands. I knew if we ever did end up watching this again, it would probably give us motion sickness, but I didn't give a shit. Not as the light high-lighted my wetness on his dick, and he gave it one long stroke before lining us back up.

With thinly veiled restraint, he took his time pushing back inside. Watching it through a small screen while knowing it was happening to me was a wild, out-of-body experience. And knowing we'd both been so close, and yet he was putting on this show for my benefit, was so goddamn hot.

"Did I say you could come yet?" he asked, brushing his thumb over my clit.

My response came out in a whimper because how was I supposed to control something like that when he continuously hit all the right spots. If I came, it was his fault.

But I knew this was part of the game, so I played along. "No, daddy."

Bishop gritted his teeth, the muscles in his neck and arms bulging as he forced himself to go slow. He let out a frustrated growl before knocking the phone from my hand and leaning over to kiss me. I greedily savored every forceful flick of his tongue against my own, wanting to live in this moment forever.

"You're lucky I can't hold out anymore," he panted. "You just feel too good, sweetheart. Too fucking good. Goddamn, I could live here forever. Could end the day with my cock lodged inside this tight little cunt, and start the morning with your pathetic little whimpers as I fuck you awake."

Holy shit.

I blinked up at him as he pulled away, increasing the speed and pressure of his thrusts. Each one sent me higher, preparing my body to sail right off the edge without care or caution. I reached between our bodies, letting my fingers graze the top of my pussy. It wouldn't take much, but I wanted to hold out as long as possible because it felt so good.

"Fuck, fuck, fuck," he cursed. "I need you to come, killer. I need—"

I applied pressure to my clit, working it in quick strokes. It didn't take long before my back arched, and ecstasy coursed through my body from head to toe. "Bishop!"

The thunder rolled, and lightning crashed as our orgasms peaked at the same time. I could feel his cock twitch inside of me, filling me just like he'd promised. Wetness seeped between us as he slowed his thrusts, burying his face in my neck as he cried out my name.

"Lennox, Lennox, Lennox…" My name had never sounded so reverential before. Like I was the most precious thing in the world.

The weight of his body on mine was comforting. He ran his hands up my arms, intertwining our fingers as I wrapped my legs around his waist, locking him in. Neither of us wanted to move, content to lie in the aftermath of what we'd just done.

I didn't know how long we lay like that, tangled in one another's embrace. It wasn't until the sweat on our skin began to dry, and I let out a little shiver, that he shifted his body to stare down at me. He leaned in for a kiss, which I eagerly returned.

"So beautiful," he murmured.

"You can't even see me properly," I pointed out. The light from the living room barely illuminated the space, and other than a random lightning strike here and there, it was mercifully dark.

"Don't need to see you," he said, pressing his lips against mine. "I just know."

I didn't know why that made my chest swell, but it did. Most of my confidence was just false bravado. Growing up as the baby to two older sisters meant I learned how to fake it until I made it pretty early on in life. It started as a way to stand out and get attention, but it turned into a coping mechanism as I got older.

"Most people only see me as a good time," I murmured, breaking the silence. "And a lot of that is my own doing, but it doesn't ever lessen the pain I felt, you know? Like, I was good enough to fuck, but not bring home to your momma."

Bishop let out a sound of annoyance. "I don't wanna talk about you fucking other guys when my cum is still dripping out of your pussy."

I barked a laugh. "My point is that you always treated me with respect—even when annoyed. Even when we were at odds, volleying insults toward one another like we were playing table tennis." I turned toward him, feeling the weight of his gaze. "I think that's why I always had a crush on you. It was like I could be every version of myself and know it wouldn't change how you saw me."

Rough, calloused hands ran along my arm. "You had a crush on me?"

"Mmhm," I said, shifting in his arms. "For a long time, honestly. It's kinda embarrassing."

"We need to have a discussion about your horrible taste in men," he grumbled, but I didn't miss the way it sounded like he was smiling.

"I'm not worried about it," I said, closing my eyes.

"Why's that?" he asked softly, running his fingers along my skin.

I burrowed myself deeper in his embrace, pressing a kiss to the hollow of his throat before whispering, "Because you're the only one I want," as I let sleep pull me under.

bishop

. . .

THE SCENT of bacon pulled me from the edge of whatever comatose state I'd been under, followed by the low sound of Eric Clapton over my old FM radio. It was staticky and never worked when you wanted it to, but sometimes if you hit it just right, it'd start playing the local 'oldies' station.

I opened my eyes, groaning as a direct line of sunlight parted the curtain and assaulted me. But that couldn't be right. The sun couldn't possibly be up right now. I never slept in. Rolling over, I checked the clock, startled when I saw it was damn near eight.

My body was like a well-oiled, yet occasionally dirty, machine. I'd wager that ninety-seven percent of the time, I operated like usual, but the other three percent sometimes fell short. I'd been doing a lot of that lately. Especially seeing as this was the second morning in a row I'd slept in.

Of course, the fact that both of those times happened when Lennox had been asleep in my arms had nothing to do with it. Or it had everything to do with it. For the first time, I felt safe enough to truly let myself rest.

Either way, that was something for future Bishop to sort out.

I sat up and swung my legs over the edge. My bare feet landed on the old hardwood floor with a thud. One late morning could be explained by some bullshit excuse, but not two. I didn't know how I was gonna explain this shit.

I grabbed a pair of shorts from the clean laundry basket on my chair and slipped them on. Normally, I was good at putting my shit up, but yesterday had caught me off guard. I hadn't expected Lennox to bring the chaos with her through the door.

Peering out the window, I noticed Lennox's truck sitting on my damn lawn. She'd left the thing running last night, lights and all, so I slipped outside when she drifted off to sleep to cut it off before it died.

Our clothes were strewn across the floor haphazardly. It reminded me of our night after the bar, how different that morning when she'd gathered her stuff and left in a rush was compared to this one. I spent damn near every day regretting the things I'd said that day. Even if I thought they were true then, it didn't excuse how I'd hurt her.

Now, I had the chance to make things right. I wanted to show her I was in this for as long as she'd let me be. We hadn't talked about that, and I wasn't gonna push the issue, but I secretly hoped she wouldn't cut me loose too quickly.

When I rounded the corner into my small kitchen, I paused. Lennox was standing in front of the stove, transferring bacon to a paper plate. She was swaying slightly to the beat of the music, humming under her breath as she worked.

And she was wearing my favorite fucking shirt.

It was threadbare and worn, but I still remembered the day Doug gifted it to me on my first day of work. Despite being too small for me now and the BSR logo being little more than faded lettering, I couldn't bring myself to part with it. It was the start of my new adventure, my new life.

Suddenly, I didn't give a flying fuck what time it was. I leaned against the threshold and watched her.

The shirt came to a stop just below Lennox's ass. She opened the cabinet, rising on her tiptoes to reach two coffee mugs up top, and I couldn't keep quiet anymore. A low groan escaped, and she stilled, turning over her shoulder with a shy smile.

"Hi," she breathed. Her long hair was piled on top of her head in a mess of blonde and silver strands, showing off the biteable skin along her neck.

I stood in front of her in two strides, framing her face with my palms and giving her a kiss. "Hi," I said, pulling back. Those blue eyes I couldn't stop dreaming about were hazy as she stared at me. "How'd you sleep?"

"Great. Your bed is seriously comfy. It was like laying on a cloud."

"Ah, I learned early on that a cheap mattress isn't worth the gas you waste going to pick it up. You can't do shit on a ranch if your back is too fucked up to move, so I'm alright spending a little more to make sure that doesn't happen," I admitted.

"Noted. You're definitely going to need to spill your secrets, though, because I think I've fallen in love after just one night," she said with a little nod, turning back toward the bacon and busying herself in the silence.

I might have fallen in love after just one night, too, but I wasn't talking about the goddamn mattress.

I stepped forward, wrapping my hands around Lennox's hips and pulling her close. "I'll tell you anything you wanna know. All you have to do is ask," I whispered in her ear. Goosebumps spread over her skin as I let my lips trail along the edge of her hairline and down her neck. She smelled like me after spending all night in my arms and my sheets.

I fucking loved it.

She turned, placing her hand in the middle of my chest, and

pushed me away. Her cheeks were flushed, the reddish-pink hue reminding me of the color her skin turned after I smacked it the other night.

I tried to come right back, but she brought the spatula between us and pointed it at me. "The bacon's gonna burn if you don't stop," she said.

I plucked the utensil out of her hand and lunged forward, gripping her waist and setting her on the counter next to the stove. She squealed and protested, telling me to stop, but I didn't. "I don't give a fuck about the bacon when my new favorite meal is sitting in front of me. Besides," I paused, grabbing the last two pieces off the frying pan and plating them, "it looks like you were already done."

Lennox dropped her head against the cabinet with a thud while I situated myself between her legs, showing just how much I wanted her. I wasn't sure what had gotten into me over the past few days. I'd never thought about sex as much as I did when I was with this woman. Now that I'd tasted her, I couldn't get enough.

I dropped to my knees, pulling her forward a couple of inches so her bare pussy was in front of my face. I pressed kisses along her thigh, making my way toward that sweet apex between her legs. "Bishop…"

My name was a goddamn prayer dripping from her lips as I let my tongue trail lazily across her exposed clit. I loved how it peeked out between her lips, demanding attention I was all too happy to give.

I looked up from between her legs, enjoying the way her chest heaved. She bit down on her bottom lip as I sucked. A stifled moan broke free, igniting the fire in my blood.

I didn't give a shit what was happening outside this moment —didn't care that I had workers looking for me, or that we both had a mile-long list of things we needed to get done. Not when her legs began to quiver as I slid two fingers into her aching cunt.

Lennox blew out a breath, and I paused. "Sore?" I asked, and she nodded.

"It's, uh, been a while. She isn't used to so much attention," Lennox admitted.

God, I loved that.

"Want me to make it feel better?" She nodded again, that same heated flush creeping across her cheeks. "Let me take away that ache and replace it with something better, sweetheart."

I didn't wait for her reply as I softly took her clit between my lips, rolling and sucking on it until she was squirming in front of me. My fingers moved in slow thrusts with each slight lift of her hips. I matched her tempo, letting her find what felt good and taking notes for the future.

"Oh god," she whimpered, tangling her hands in my hair. The grip stung slightly, but the pain felt so good. The pain meant she was getting exactly what she needed from me. "Bishop... Oh my god."

Her praise was the only encouragement I needed. Before long, I felt her pussy clench and her legs shake as she came with a soft moan. It was taking everything in me not to stand up and fuck her senseless, but I could exhibit a little bit of self-control. If there was one thing I wanted to make clear, it was that I wasn't in this for the physical shit.

Don't get me wrong—I could spend my entire life making Lennox come, but this was different. It was something more.

I wanted to stay up too late talking and spend lazy mornings between the covers. I wanted to take her grocery shopping and make a list of all the snacks she liked. Most of all, I wanted her to know that I'd be by her side come hell or high water.

Pressing a quick kiss to the inside of her thigh, I pushed to my feet. She watched as I brought my arousal covered fingers to my lips and sucked. Those blue eyes grew molten, just as they had the last time I'd done it. I was glad it wasn't a one-time thing because I was looking for any excuse to taste her.

"Breakfast is the most important meal of the day," I taunted, throwing her a wink before I helped her down.

Lennox chuckled, shaking her head as she grabbed two paper plates and loaded them with cold, limp bacon and potatoes I hadn't noticed until now. "And people say I'm the troublemaker," she said, looking around. "Will you grab two forks?"

"No one really gets to see this side. Work is work, and I don't have many friends outside of it." She turned around with a bemused look, walking past me toward the small dining table. "What?" I asked, following her.

"I can't believe you think you don't have friends," she said, plopping into one of the old wooden chairs. I handed her a utensil, watching as she ravenously dug into her breakfast. "I mean, I get you're the boss and everything, but that doesn't mean you don't have friends."

I pulled the chair out next to her and took it, following suit. "Eh, they're obligated to be nice to me. I submit their paychecks."

"Not true," she fired back. "Those hands aren't obligated to do anything but follow orders and get shit done. They're nice to you because you're nice to them. Tell me, how often do they ask you to do something, and you turn them down?" I opened my mouth to tell her it never happened, but she stopped me. "And don't tell me they don't because I've heard it."

Okay, fair point. She had me there. I was asked at least once a week to come to their monthly poker night. Just yesterday, Keith told me they'd be holding it this weekend since we were rounding up cattle and moving them closer for branding. "Maybe a time or two."

"So, why don't you go?"

"I don't know. Figured they were just asking to be nice. Who wants to hang out with their boss after work?" It's not like I was much fun to begin with. I wasn't what people called the life of the party.

Lennox raised her brows and clicked her tongue. "Well, don't let Douglas Hayes hear you saying that shit because he might think you don't like him."

"That's not what I meant—"

She placed her hand on mine, a soft smile on her lips. "Relax. Don't overthink it. I wasn't stirring the pot, just proving a point."

Her point made my eyes sting a bit, but I pushed away the nagging thought and dug into my food. Even if it was cold, it was still good. When I told her so, she just laughed and told me breakfast was one of the few things she could confidently cook without fear of burning the house down.

I had to keep my mouth closed before I told her something stupid, like how I'd gladly eat this meal for the rest of my life if she was by my side.

"So, what'd you tell everyone we were doing today?" I asked, setting my fork down and reaching for the glass of water she'd set out earlier.

Lennox pursed her lips. "I might have told them you had the shits again."

I coughed, trying to clear my throat. "How'd you know about that in the first place?"

She shrugged and smirked. "The hands talk, you know. I just pay attention."

I dropped my head in my hands. "I'm never gonna live this down."

"You're not," she agreed, pushing to her feet. "But you'll get over it."

My fork clattered to the floor as she grabbed my plate. We both bent forward at the same time, and I knew what was coming before I could stop it. Our heads knocked into one another, and we both pulled away, cursing and laughing as she stumbled back in shock. "Christ, are you okay?" I asked, wiping my mouth and moving toward her.

Lennox rubbed at the spot and waved me off. "I'll be fine," she said, trying to move back, but I stopped her.

"Let me." I crouched down, trying for the utensil, but she was too fast.

"What's this?" she asked, holding a crumpled paper. As she unfurled it, I peered over her shoulder, and my heart sank. Oh god, I made that stupid pro/con list last night. I must not have thrown it away before she stormed inside. Of course, I'd forgotten all about it.

Shit, shit, shit. I'd already fucked this up before it'd even begun. All I could think about was the way she'd angrily stormed out months ago. She'd have every right to do it again. I held my breath as her eyes scanned the lines, shoulders already slumped in defeat.

"A pro/con list?" Lennox asked, gazing at me from over the top of the paper. "Really?"

"Lennox, let me—"

She started laughing before I could say anything else. Was it funny to her? Or was this some kind of mental defense she was locking into place before she set my cabin on fire?

"Oh my god, Bishop. You're fucking adorable," she said, placing the plate on the table and walking toward me.

I stared at her in confusion. Other women likely would've started throwing shit at my head by now, but not her. She just cupped my cheek, letting her thumb run across my cheekbone. "You're not mad?"

Lennox shook her head. "No. I wish you'd talked to me about how you were feeling, but why would I be mad when the pros are so clearly in my favor?"

"I was just trying to get it down on paper and make it real, ya know? I know that sounds stupid, but…" I trailed off, shrugging slightly. "It helps me think things through."

"I don't care how you process, baby. I just care that you're mine at the end of the day."

I turned my head and kissed her palm. "You don't have to worry about that."

"Good, because now I wanna talk about just how"—she paused, looking over the paper—"good at sex I am."

bishop

. . .

MY WEEK WAS SLOWLY TURNING into a shit show.

Since it was nearing the month's end, most of my time was spent typing up these damn reports for Josie. Honestly, it wasn't hard to put together. What was making it such a pain in the ass was how many times I got called out to various parts of the ranch to fix problems that needed my attention.

"Bishop, the tractor broke down in the middle of a field."

"Bishop, have you ordered the vaccines yet?"

"Bishop, coyote tracks have been spotted near one of our pastures."

Bishop, Bishop, Bishop.

The only thing keeping me sane was knowing Lennox was there to lighten the load. When she couldn't, then I could always count on her to be waiting at my cabin when I dragged my tired ass through the door.

Tonight was no exception. I'd gotten a call about an unexpected calving right before I was going to call it a night. One of our hands, Travis, had been headed in when they heard our new momma's birthing cries. He'd been with her for about thirty minutes before he realized she would need help delivering.

When he called, he told me he had it handled, but there was

a tremor in his voice. Although I knew the kid grew up around this life, Travis was still new. It wasn't fair to anyone if I had him handle it all alone. Much to Titan's disappointment, I'd turned and ran for the pasture to help him pull the calf.

Now, we were all headed back in. The baby was lying across the kid's lap, with the momma following us closely. Usually, we'd leave them out with the herd, but I felt better bringing them in just in case they ran into any issues.

"Where you want'em, boss?" he asked as I grabbed the gate.

"Let's put them in the birthing pen for the night. We'll sort the rest out in the morning."

He nodded and headed through. "Looks like poker night's already started," he said, picking up his pace. "Guess an angry heifer at the party ain't the worst thing to roll through those tables."

I laughed. "Probably not."

I hopped down, rounding Titan to help Travis bring the calf down. This part of the job was easy. The momma followed right in after her calf, checking to make sure we hadn't hurt it on the ride back.

"You gonna stick around?" Travis asked, leaning against the gate.

It was on the tip of my tongue to say no when I heard a voice that stopped me dead. "Are you accusing me of cheating, Keith?"

"You've gotta be shittin' me," I muttered, grabbing Titan's reins and heading to the front of the barn. It was still lit up, with tables lined along the alley and music playing. Most of the horses had their heads outside the stalls, hoping for some drunk cowboy to take pity on them and give them treats.

And there, in the middle of it all, was Lennox sitting at a table with a stack of chips. She stared at poor Keith while his gaze flitted between the hand he'd been dealt and the pot in the middle. Callie sat at her feet, munching on a big old bone. There was no telling where she found it. The pair of them had gathered a crowd. Most of the hands watched curiously, likely wondering what the boss's daughter was doing out here with them.

I had the same goddamn question.

Callie lifted her head when she saw me, quietly humming with excitement, but her owner didn't even move as I led Titan inside. "Nice of you to finally join the party, Bish."

We stopped right behind her. I leaned down, placing one hand on the back of her chair and the other on the table. "What do you think you're doing?"

Lennox smirked. "Well, we're supposed to be playing poker, but Keith's been staring at his hand for the last five minutes, so now I'm just waiting."

Keith shook his head and took a sip of beer. "She's won the past four hands."

"I can see that," I muttered, looking toward her pile of chips. "I meant, what're you doing *here*, Lennox?"

She rolled her eyes. "As opposed to twiddling my thumbs in the house? No thanks. I'm having more fun here."

I didn't give a shit that she was here. All I cared about was getting home, showering, and losing myself in Lennox before tomorrow.

"It's late," I said.

"For you, maybe," she quipped back. "I know you need your sleep, Grandpa."

The boys hooted and hollered as I straightened up. When she finally looked up, her blue eyes were teeming with mischief. While she couldn't possibly take credit for forcing a heifer into labor, I couldn't help but wonder if this wasn't her plan all along. She'd already mentioned getting together with the boys, and now she was at their next tournament.

She knew I needed a push.

God-fucking-dammit.

"You gonna pull up a chair, B?" Keith asked before throwing his hand down. "Because I fuckin' fold."

Three sevens, the king of spades, and the five of hearts made a solid three of a kind.

Lennox clicked her tongue before reaching for her cards and turning them over. "Oh Keith... If you'd just stuck to your guns a little bit longer."

Two aces, the queen of hearts, the three of diamonds, and the five of clubs.

Keith groaned and hung his head as one of the other hands clapped him on the shoulder. "Don't feel bad. You're not the only one she's pulled a fast one on tonight."

My girl placed her hand over her chest. "Little ole me? I would never."

"Yeah, right," I snorted, leading Titan away from the crowd. "Y'all have fun." Before I did anything else, I needed to take care of him, and he'd earned his fair share of extra treats tonight.

"You scared, Bish?" Lennox called out, halting me. "I get it. You're afraid to lose—"

"I have things to do. Animals to take care of." I narrowed my eyes, which only seemed to excite her. Nothing scared the woman. I was sure the prospect of punishment overrode her hesitation to push my buttons.

If it was anyone else, I would've said no. If it was anyone else, I would've told them to fuck off. But it wasn't anyone else. It was Lennox, and I seemed incapable of telling her no.

Keith grabbed Titan's reins from my hands as if on cue and nodded to the bathroom behind me. "I'll take care of him if you wanna clean up and grab a beer. You deserve it after the day you've had."

"What I deserve is a hot meal and a shower," I mumbled, pinching the bridge of my nose. "You just want me to stay and get my ass kicked."

Keith shrugged. "Eh, it might make me feel better, but there's only one way to find out."

There was no way I was getting out of this shit now. All I had to do was ride it out. I dropped my head. Lennox was fucking in for it when we were finally alone.

"Deal me in," I sighed, letting Keith take Titan. "But throw in some extra treats for him."

lennox

. . .

WAS it a bit reckless to push Bishop and force him to socialize? Maybe. Was I going to pay for it later tonight? Without a doubt. Would I regret it?

Absolutely the fuck not.

If there was one thing I knew about the grumpy asshole walking my way, it was that he never backed down from a challenge. In fact, he was worse than I was. I was competitive, sure, but Bishop *hated* to lose. I didn't know what drove him to try and top everyone around him, but I liked it.

For a half-cooked plan, everything was working out in my favor. When I ambled up to the barn this evening, I'd been a woman on a mission. My man had gone missing, and I was determined to find him. Bishop hadn't texted me since this afternoon, and it was just a quick one-liner to let me know he was headed in. That'd been hours earlier.

I'd been around cowboys long enough to know that shit happened, and sometimes they got hung up. It was just a way of life. I didn't know how often Dad was late for dinner because he'd gotten to the barn and saw something that needed fixing before he called it a day.

But as the sun began to dip and the air cooled, I started to get a little antsy. Not even Callie's soft, sweet nudges could calm me down. I know she meant well, but all I could think of was the famous TV moment when Little Timmy fell into the well, and Lassie went to get help.

Just because someone was tough as nails didn't mean they couldn't get hurt on the job. I'd seen it plenty of times before. Most accidents could've been avoided by keeping a clear head, but some things were out of our control.

By the time I reached the barn, I'd come up with a million different horrible situations about what was keeping him out. They ranged from Bishop getting trampled by an angry stampede to him stumbling on an undiscovered, highly poisonous snake and being bitten. Each scenario grew wilder the longer he was gone.

It wasn't until I'd found Keith at the barn that I calmed down. I tried to sound annoyed when I asked where the grumpy bastard was, but I thought Keith saw right through me. He just laughed and told me Bishop was stuck with a calving mother and new hire in the pasture, which was much better than the shit going on in my head.

I was on my way back to the big house when Keith asked me if I wanted to stay. Knowing it would get under Bishop's skin, I said yes. He'd have to come here first anyway because of Titan, so I might as well have a little fun while I waited around for him.

Truth be told, I didn't know shit about Texas Hold'em. Dad played from time to time, so I knew a royal flush beat everything else. Did I know what it was, though? Nope. Sure didn't. The only thing I had working for me was the fact that most of the men on this ranch were too damn polite to call me on my bluff. I didn't ask why, nor did I care.

If their southern charm was why it happened, who was I to tell them they'd been duped?

Callie stayed by my side, thoroughly enjoying herself. I swore she was in doggy heaven. All the guys doted on her. I didn't even want to think about how many treats she conned them into. If Bishop wanted to point fingers at someone, he could point them at her.

After a few hours and a couple of beers, I'd nearly gone up against everyone. There was no real structure here, and some played me twice just for the hell of it. I was pretty sure they thought I'd been blessed with some kind of beginner's luck, which was totally right.

Dad had tried to teach me the ins and outs of poker multiple times, but I lost interest too fast to retain anything. Now that I realized how much fun it could be, I kicked myself for not taking him up on it sooner. I could've been out here swindling cowboys and paying off rodeo fees without so much as a blink of an eye.

But with Bishop here, everything seemed to change. The air was thicker, the pressure was higher, and my bravado was slipping. Pesky butterflies flitted in my stomach as he walked out of his office in a fresh t-shirt.

Why I waited so long to act on the feelings between us was a mystery to me, especially when he looked at me with that cocky expression of his. Yes, he could be an ass, but that was something I'd grown to appreciate. It made those rare moments of vulnerability much sweeter. Maybe that was a dealbreaker to some, but it kind of sealed it for me.

My gaze dropped, slowly scanning down the length of his body. I didn't care who saw it. Whether we wanted to admit it or not, the sexual tension between us had been there for years. It wasn't anything our crew hadn't seen before.

"Is that your wallet, or are you just happy to see me?" I asked, focusing on the bulge at the front of his pants.

If he cared, he didn't show it. "Don't have my wallet, but I am happy to see you."

"Why's that?"

Bishop reached forward, his corded forearm flexing as he gripped the foldable metal chair and pulled it back. My mouth had gone dry before his ass hit the seat. As if he knew it, the bastard smirked, letting one arm rest on the table and the other on his thick thigh.

"Because I'm gonna enjoy the hell out of knocking you down a peg." He leaned forward slightly, keeping his voice low over the hum of conversation around us. "You know, if you wanted to play cards, we could've played strip poker at home."

Oh, I was so fucked.

On the outside, I was trying to seem cool, calm, and collected, but inside, I was screaming. Our game would be nothing like the others because, unlike the others, my cowboy knew me better than anyone else. He was too observant, too careful. He'd likely spent way too much time studying me for any sign of weakness during our years of bickering.

If that was all it was, I might've even stood a chance, but he knew me in other ways now, too. Ways he could, and likely would, exploit to see me squirm.

I cleared my throat. "Well, I know it's past your bedtime, so we can make this quick—"

"Oh no," he said slowly. My gaze dropped to where he drew lazy circles around the lip of his beer bottle. "You've talked too much shit for me to let you off easy."

"Is that right?" I lifted a brow in challenge. "I haven't lost yet."

"I guess it's an honor to be your first." His lips curled slightly, but not enough for anyone to catch on to the possible innuendo. "Because you will lose, killer."

Something about the nickname rolling off his tongue drove me crazy. My thighs clenched together on instinct, which didn't bode well for me, seeing as we hadn't even begun yet. "You sure are cocky for a man who didn't even wanna play ten minutes ago."

"Call me inspired. Maybe I wanna be the one to put you in your place since you've been swindling my boys here." He nodded to the stacked deck between us. "Winner deals out."

I crossed my arms. "I'm not any good at shuffling."

He lifted his shoulder. "Don't care. You're playing with me now and as the reigning champ... I insist."

I reached forward, grabbing the deck with more force than was necessary. "Fine, but I don't want to hear you complain if I do a shitty job."

"I won't hold it against you. Maybe it'll work in my favor."

"Or it'll make me look like an idiot..." I muttered under my breath.

"What was that?" he asked, leaning forward.

I flipped him off because I wanted to, and it seemed like something the old Lennox, the woman who didn't know how good Bishop's hand felt on her body, would do. Cutting the stack in two, I let the cards sift through my hands. It was awkward, and I fumbled on more than one occasion. After five attempts, I was finally satisfied.

"What're we playing for?" I asked, tapping the deck against the table. "You already said you don't have your wallet, so money's out."

Bishop scrunched his nose and shook his head. "Naw, I don't need to steal your money, killer."

"What do you need then? A La-Z-Boy recliner and all fourteen seasons of *Dallas* on DVD?"

There was a quiet "damn" drawn out by one of the guys before the silence broke with hushed laughter. Others hid their smiles behind their drinks. Bishop didn't say anything, which might have been more concerning than anything else.

I was almost starting to regret my decision to smart off.

Almost.

"Nope, don't need that either," he chuckled, sipping his beer. Condensation dripped down the glass. I watched a single droplet travel down his tan hand, wishing like hell we weren't in a room full of people who had no idea we were fucking behind closed doors so I could lick it off. "What about you? What're you betting?"

"I have money to burn." I gestured toward my winnings for the night. There was about five hundred dollars there. I'd already decided that any money I won tonight would go into something for the crew. I didn't need it, and I'd kind of crashed their guys' night, so I wanted to make sure it got back to them somehow.

Bishop hummed before pulling out a twenty from his pocket and throwing it down. "We'll start there, then."

"I thought you said you didn't have money."

"I said I didn't have my wallet. There's a difference."

"Twenty bucks isn't gonna get you far, especially since this is only the buy-in." I tossed an identical bill down beside his. "What're you gonna do when you can't add to the pot?"

"Just deal the fucking hand, killer. Let me worry about what I'm gonna do," he drawled, setting down his beer with a little more force than usual.

I'm sure the crew thought he was mad—and he might've been to some degree. After all, he was fighting a losing battle when it came to my smart mouth and his inability to do anything about it.

The room was silent except for the occasional hoof stomp or tail swish. As cards were dealt, I could feel everyone's eyes dart between Bishop and me. I watched enough games tonight to know the general order of things. Two cards face-down for the pair of us and five community cards in the middle.

Carefully, I peeled back the corner to see what I had. Two aces off the bat, which had to be good, right? Weren't they supposed to be the highest cards or something? Glancing up, I noticed Bishop smirk as he checked his. He studied the first three cards and turned over cards in the middle—a three, seven, and a jack of spades.

"What's your call?" he asked.

I had no idea what I was doing, but I said, "I'll raise," and tossed another twenty in.

"Doubling the pot, huh?"

"You could always fold," I said, smiling sweetly. I couldn't lose to him. If I did, I'd never live it down. I hoped I could get by faking it until I made it because that's what I'd done most of my life when I got into a tough spot.

"Naw. I have a few bucks left. I'll match."

I reached for the fourth card and turned it over. The queen of hearts. He was staring at the cards like they'd personally offended him, which maybe they had. Or maybe, just maybe, this was his attempt to throw me.

When his eyes lifted to meet my own, he gestured toward my money pile. "What's it gonna be this time, high roller?"

"Same as before," I said, tossing my hair over my shoulder. "I'm not scared."

"You should be," he said. "You're welcome to fold anytime."

I narrowed my eyes. "You wish."

Bishop chuckled as he reached for the last unturned card. A two of fucking diamonds. He tapped his fingers along the table, blowing out a breath in a slow, steady exhale.

"Last chance," he said, rubbing the back of his neck. "I'll even let you go without saying shit about your hold'em skills."

God, he was infuriating. I pointed in his direction, wagging my finger. "This isn't going to work, you know? I'm not going to suddenly decide to listen to you only for you to be bluffing."

"If you think I'm bluffing, then call it."

That was the problem. I wasn't one hundred percent sure. I'd rather go down swinging than roll over like a dog with a bone. As it was, Callie seemed to have already wandered over to Bishop's side. She lay down at his feet, her tongue lolling out the side.

"Let's just fucking do it." I flipped the cards over, ever aware of our audience drawing closer. They stared at both hands, and Bishop grinned so wide I thought he was going to combust. He clicked his tongue. "Ooh, one pair. Guess that beginner's luck might be wearing off."

"What do you have then?" I snapped, leaning over. He was holding a four and a queen of spades.

"A flush. Same house, see?" He reached for the pot, plucking the cash and setting it aside. "Well, this was fun—"

"Again," I said, picking up the cards and setting them in front of him. "Winner deals, right?" He nodded. "Good. So, deal."

Bishop picked up the cards and began shuffling. It came as no surprise that he was good at it. After all, I knew how talented those fingers were. No one had ever made me come like he had.

We played the next three games hard and fast, not stopping for pleasantries or small talk. So far, Bishop and I were tied at two wins a piece. Our last hand would be the tiebreaker—a winner-takes-all kind of bet.

I chewed on my cheek, watching Bishop deal out one final time. If I'd lost to anyone else, I wouldn't have cared. Losing to him after all the shit I'd talked was out of the question.

"Alright, last one," he grumbled, raking his hand through his hair. "And then everyone goes the fuck home and gets some rest. I don't wanna see a single yawn tomorrow."

He was met with a chorus of "Yes, Boss" as they settled in to watch our final showdown. Sitting between us was a five of clubs, a four and five of diamonds, and a nine and Jack of hearts.

Nerves fluttered as I peeked at my hand, letting my bravado slip just a hair. Bishop, on the other hand, looked like a kid in a goddamn candy store. He was waiting for me to place my bet. I mean, I didn't care about losing the pot. But I wanted to antagonize him a bit longer by making him wait.

"Come on, Lennox. The cards aren't gonna change just because you're staring at them. Make a bet so we can get this over with," he snapped, patience fraying.

"I don't see what's wrong with taking my time. Heard some guys like that?" Bishop's cheeks flamed beneath his beard, but the cowboy-sized shadows hanging over us hid them well. "I guess I'm all in?" I pushed the rest of my winnings in the middle, watching Bishop's eyes flash with something that looked a hell of a lot like unease.

"Want to show me what you've got there, killer?"

"Not particularly," I said dryly. "But let's get this over with."

I flipped my hand, holding my breath as Bishop's eyes darted from my cards to the two he had. "Holy shit," Keith laughed, slapping Bishop on the shoulder. "She fucking won."

"What?" I asked, looking down at the cards I'd dropped on the table. "I did?"

"It's the luck of the draw," Bishop muttered, tossing his own. "Doesn't mean anything."

I pouted, trying like hell to keep the excitement out of my voice. "Aw, Bishop. Are you upset the cards didn't favor you this time?"

If Bishop had rolled his eyes any harder, I swore they would've popped out of his head. He stood, downing his beer before tossing it in the trash. "Time to wrap it up, boys."

They started gathering their things and cleaning up as if waiting for his orders. I moved to fold up the table, but Bishop stopped me. He bent down, leaning into my ear, and whispered, "Not you. Let's go, killer."

"I—I should help clean up," I stammered. "I mean, I helped make the mess after all."

He shook his head. "Oh, no, you don't. You may have started this war, but I'm gonna fucking finish it. Outside. Now."

"Jeez, okay!" I said as he poked my side. "I'll see you tomorrow, boys!"

There was a chorus of goodbyes as we walked outside. "Pack up and get outta here," Bishop called over his shoulder. He ushered me around the barn and toward the woodshed. "Remember what I said about tomorrow. Y'all did this to yourselves, staying up so late when we've got shit to do in the morning."

"Are you always this much of a killjoy?" My giggle turned into a yelp as he lifted me up and pushed me against the small building, concealing me from prying eyes. His mouth found mine in the darkness, swallowing my moans as I ground down on the bulge in his jeans.

"I've been wanting to punish that fucking mouth all night," he said breathlessly, pulling away only to trail kisses down my neck. "Christ, you drive me nuts."

"Maybe you should shut me up then," I challenged, panting as hard as he was. There wasn't a single thing he did that didn't absolutely consume me. I was always searching for some reason to get his hands on me somehow.

"You'd like it too much," he bit out. "You don't deserve a fucking reward right now. Not after I sat through an hour and a half of the world's most grueling poker tournament with a hard dick in front of a bunch of employees."

I tried not to laugh, but I couldn't stop myself. The sound bubbled over my lips and into the world before I knew what happened. "Oh, you think that's funny, huh?"

I shrugged or tried to. Bishop slid his hands up my side, lifting my wrists until they were above my head. "What if I did?"

He hummed, low and soft in my ear. "Then I'd have to add it to your list of offenses. At this rate, I don't know if you'll ever come again."

"Wait, what?" I said, trying to break his hold, but it was too strong.

"Bad girls don't get fucking rewards. And you, killer, have been a pain in my ass all night, taunting me with that bratty mouth."

"Uh, coming is a right, not a reward. If you don't, I'll do it myself," I huffed.

"I don't give a shit if you slide a finger into that pretty pussy, sweetheart. Wanna know why?"

"I'm dying to know." I rolled my hips, loving the way his body stiffened against mine.

Bishop leaned in, pressing a kiss to my jaw. "Because you'll be wishing it was me—that I was the one strumming your clit and making you come so hard you saw fucking stars. How long do you think you could go without begging me to fuck you?"

Suddenly, Bishop stepped back, and I was falling. He steadied me, the stupid prick. I wish he'd let me fall. Maybe it would knock me out of whatever haze he had me in. "This is cruel and unusual punishment, you asshole," I said, pulling out of his hold.

He tipped his head back and laughed. God, I loved when he did that. It wasn't often, but when it happened? It almost made me forget why I was mad at him in the first place.

"You know I'd give you whatever you want," he said, taking my hand and intertwining our fingers. I stared down at the contact, fighting the urge to pull him back into the darkness. "All you have to do is ask."

"Ha ha, nice try."

Bishop tugged me out of the woodshed and toward his cabin. We took the long way, strolling beneath the moonlight like two lovers without a care in the world. He tucked me into his side the moment I shivered. Sometimes, he'd press a kiss to the top of my head while I talked. I was burning up with all the physical contact. My body was a goddamn live wire, and it was only a matter of time before I burst into flames.

By the time we stumbled into his bedroom, the word "please" had left my lips, and we were tangled between his sheets.

bishop

. . .

THE NEXT TWO weeks were pure bliss.

Since she stormed in like a goddamn hurricane, Lennox had spent nearly every night sleeping in my bed. On the rare occasion she couldn't, we were typically up too late on the phone—which gave her far too much ammunition to tease me about my age.

"Why won't you FaceTime?" she'd asked me one night. I just shrugged and told her I didn't know how or what the difference was. It wasn't like I was missing out on anything, and the thought of us just staring at one another seemed strange.

At least, that was what I thought until Lennox called me the next day while I was eating lunch, and I'd opened the screen to her spreading her legs and playing with her pussy on my fucking desk. It'd taken me all of twenty minutes to ride back to the barn as fast as I could to sit down for dessert.

Lennox and I had fallen into this weird sense of domesticity, and it actually felt *nice*. All my life, I'd been quick to shut that shit down before it had a chance to grow into anything, but now I felt like a goddamn teenager again, smiling and laughing and feeling like I was walking on air. I really needed to turn it down because I was starting to get weird looks when someone asked a question, and I responded without barking orders or scowling in their direction.

Neither of us had mentioned our relationship to her family because we were trying to sort it out first. Was this just a fling? It sure as hell wasn't for me. I honestly didn't think it was for Lennox either. Her concern lay in my penchant for shutting down and walking away, while mine was undeniably selfish.

If the worst-case scenario happened, if Doug fired me and kicked me off his land, where the hell would I go? I didn't know anything outside of this life. And again, if that happened, would Lennox and I survive it? Or would the emotional wound left behind fester and ruin the last good thing I'd have?

We promised to give ourselves one month of whatever this was, and then we would decide. While I wanted nothing more than to climb up to the highest point on Black Springs and tell the world that Lennox Hayes was mine, I was also pathetically terrified of stepping outside this little paradise we were living in.

Even now, as we lay in the middle of a field staring up at the sky, I worried about the noise from the outside world. Lennox had her whole life ahead of her. I'd listened to her talk about getting back out on the circuit and winning titles she'd always dreamed of, seen the animated joy in her face when she spoke. If we decided to give this a go, it meant we'd be apart more than we'd be together, and I wasn't too sure I liked that.

I knew what happened in the rodeo circuit. I had plenty of experience with ranch hands telling stories about it around the campfire. The partying, the sex, the loneliness. It could get wild as hell. While I trusted her explicitly, I didn't trust all the fuck-boys who'd take any chance they could to shoot their shot while I was stuck here running the ranch. They'd whisper pretty words in her ear, telling her how she could do better.

I just hoped she never realized it herself.

"Have you ever traveled outside the country?" she asked, reaching for the bag of grapes between us. She threw one in the air, catching it in her mouth with a juicy pop.

It was a Friday afternoon, and we'd both snuck away under the pretense of scouting the trail for any cows that had strayed from the herd during our round-up. Instead of heading back, Lennox had packed a little picnic basket for us to enjoy. We'd laid out under the sun for a good hour now, chatting about everything and nothing.

The sun was slowly going down, and we would have to get back soon for family dinner, but I wasn't ready yet.

I shook my head, laughing. "Sweetheart, the only times I've even been out of the state were because your dad needed help while doing the traveling clinics."

"I think I want to go to Europe one day. There's so much history there, you know? I loved learning about it in school. And it's crazy to think that some buildings have been around since the medieval ages."

"I didn't pay much attention in history class," I admitted. "Didn't pay much attention to most of my classes, honestly."

She rolled onto her side, propping her head on her hand. "Really?"

I nodded. "I focused more on working after school, trying to help care for my mom and save up a little for me."

"What were you saving for?" she asked, running her fingers along my arm.

Something I'd learned over the past two weeks was how physical Lennox was. It wasn't always a sexual thing, although we spent a lot of our free time tangled in the sheets. But it didn't matter what we were doing; she always had to touch me somehow.

I was surprised at how much I loved it.

"A truck. We only had one vehicle, and my mom worked out of town. If I wanted to go somewhere, I had to find a ride or walk. Mostly, it was the latter. I didn't like anyone knowing where I lived."

"Why?"

I hesitated for a beat, old insecurities rearing their ugly heads like they did when I was a kid. Lennox knew the kind of life I came from and how it made this place look like one of the fancy European castles she was talking about. "Oak Point Trailer Park," I said, focusing on the clouds above. "We lived on the back lot, kinda hidden behind the trees. I tried to take care of it the best I could, but it was a lot for a scrawny teenager that didn't know his ass from his elbow. And Mom, well, she didn't do much when she was home. She just kinda sat in the recliner and smoked her cowboy killers while watching reruns of some old soap opera."

I reached for the pack I often stuffed in my pocket without thinking about it. I didn't smoke, not anymore, but I kept them out of habit. Maybe as a reminder of my old life and what it could've been like if my mom hadn't kicked me out. It was something I thought about a lot, and honestly, it made me a little sick to my stomach.

"Where is she now?" Lennox asked softly, stealing the breath from my lungs.

"I don't know," I answered honestly.

She hummed. "When's the last time you saw her?"

I'd never spoken about my mom to anyone other than Doug, which only happened once. But if I had any chance of making this work, of maybe understanding why I was the way I was a little bit better, I had to share that part of me. "About twenty years ago."

Her hand stilled on my arm, but she didn't take it away or recoil at my touch, so I took it as a good start. "I know that probably seems crazy to you, seeing how close you are with your family, but not everyone has that. I sure as hell didn't. My childhood wasn't filled with happy, loving memories but the stinging knowledge of being a disappointment," I said, blowing out a breath and sitting up. I leaned forward, resting my elbow on my knee and playing with a broken blade of grass.

"I think it was about one year after coming to work on the ranch. Your dad brought me to the feed store to pick up a delivery. We stopped at a diner before heading back and were halfway through our meal when a woman walked by, reeking of cigarettes and cheap perfume. I recognized her by the scent. Had given it to her as a present for Christmas one year." I shook my head, forcing my voice to remain steady. "I'd heard her talking about it on the phone one day after school. How she thought it smelled fancy and that maybe if she wore it, people would think she had money. So, I emptied my savings and bought it for her. She was so mad. Told me I was a wasteful little shit for spending our money on this when we had debt collectors breathing down our backs."

Lennox's nails dug into my arm, but I didn't look at her. I couldn't. Not without losing everything I'd held in for so long. Because her heart would break for what was left of mine, and I couldn't let that happen. That was something I realized she and I had in common.

She put on this front for the world, making those who knew her on a superficial level believe she was this reckless, wild child, but that couldn't be farther from the truth. I was beginning to realize that Lennox loved fiercely, far more than anyone else I knew. There wasn't anything she wouldn't do for those in her inner circle.

I cleared my throat, pushing forward. "She was at the bar, chatting with the cook behind the counter. Things hadn't changed that much. There were stains on her baggy clothes, holes in the fabric from years of wear and tear. The T-shirt was another gift I'd given her years before. Her hair had more grey than I remembered. It was pulled out of her face, and I could see black smudges under her eyes.

"When she dug into the pocket of her jeans, pulled out a handful of loose change, and began counting it out on the table, I felt so goddamn sick. I couldn't see much, but I knew she barely had enough for a cup of coffee, let alone a full meal. She was so much skinnier than she was before I left. I felt guilty, you know, for not checking in sooner. Here I was, never having to worry about where my next meal would come from or if the electricity would cut off in the middle of the night because I hadn't paid a bill."

I couldn't stop the tears from coming, lining my eyes and burning as I tried to will them away. "She'd kicked me out, and I hadn't tried fighting back. And I never thought to check in after I got settled here. She told me she didn't want me, that I was a burden, a disappointment. That I'd ruined her life. I figured maybe having one less mouth to feed or worry about would make it better, but I think I damned her instead."

I wiped my nose. "I don't know how long I watched her, but my food had gone cold when the check arrived. I didn't have the appetite to finish it anyway, which only made me feel worse after seeing how she'd struggled. When our waitress came over to take our ticket, Doug pulled a fifty-dollar bill from his wallet and told her to make sure the woman at the bar left here with a full belly."

This time, I couldn't stop myself. I looked over, noticing that Lennox's eyes were just as red-rimmed as I was sure mine felt. There were tear tracks down her cheeks, and I hated myself for putting them there.

"When we got in the truck, I lost it. I cried the entire way home. Or so I thought. Instead of pulling to the barn like I thought, he kept driving until we pulled up here." I gestured to the open pasture. Most of the ranch was flat land with a few trees here and there, but this was one of the few natural ponds left on the property. A small creek flowed into it, keeping the water from going stagnant.

"I really thought he was going to fire me. I thought he'd tell me I wasn't the man he hoped I'd be and send me packing, but he didn't do any of that. Instead, he hopped out, lowered the tailgate, and sat on the bench. He patted the space next to me, and we spent the next hour talking about what I wanted in life."

Lennox chewed on the inside of her cheek. "What'd you want?"

I took her hand, bringing it to my lips for a chaste kiss. "I wanted the things I never had. Stability. Comfort. Peace of mind..." I trailed off, meeting her eyes because she needed to understand this next part. "Love. And god willing, a family to call my own."

She gave me a watery smile. "You deserve all of that. You deserve more, and—"

A shrill ring sounded through the otherwise quiet and peaceful spot, jerking us out of whatever faraway trance we'd been lost to. I looked down, noticing Doug's name flash across my screen. Lennox's brows furrowed as I lifted my phone to my ear.

"This is Bishop," I said, shifting my weight.

"Where the hell are ya, son?"

"Sir?" I asked, looking at my watch. It was only half past five. Dinner wasn't until seven.

"Well, I went looking for ya in the barn, but Titan is gone. I was gonna ask you to help me with dinner. Ruby wants steak, and it'd be cruel to make a man who can't eat one make them by himself," he said. It sounded like he was still annoyed about the strict diet restrictions the doctor had him on.

"Oh. Well, that makes sense. I'm out in the side field checking for stragglers, but I was getting ready to head in. I can be there in about thirty minutes."

I wasn't sure what he was doing, but I could hear Ruby yelling at him for something in the background. "You sure you can't do twenty? These women are driving me crazy. It's all 'Doug, don't do this,' and 'Dad, you can't do that.'"

Lennox covered her mouth as I laughed. "Where's Lincoln? Can't he save you?"

Doug let out a long exhale. "I'd very much like to keep my thoughts away from what he's doing right now if it's all the same to you."

That sent Lennox rolling. She kicked her feet in the air, trying and failing to keep quiet. Lincoln had just gotten back from a clinic, which meant he and Josie were probably locked away in their little cabin right now, fucking like bunnies. "Uh, yeah. Got it. I'll go as fast as Titan'll let me."

"Fine," he muttered. "I'll try to hold on a little longer then."

When the line went dead, I looked over at Lennox whose face was beet red from laughing so hard. "Duty calls," I said, pushing to my feet and holding out my hand for her to take. The moment she was standing on two feet, I pulled her into me for a deep, long kiss. "Thank you for listening." I bent down and pressed my forehead to hers. "It means a lot."

Her hand came up, swiping beneath my eyes. "I'll always be here to listen to you."

I wasn't sure how long always would last, but for right now, it was pretty damn perfect.

lennox

. . .

"BOUT DAMN TIME," Dad grumbled as the back door opened. "Was beginning to think you'd never surface for air."

All eyes turned to my sister and her boyfriend standing in the shade. Josie's cheeks flamed bright pink as Lincoln wrapped his arm around her middle. "Sorry. Lincoln had to… unpack."

Dad snorted, leaning against the cedar pillar near the grill. "That what the kids are calling it these days?" He shook his head. "Back in my day, we just called it knockin' boots."

"God, Dad. Please stop," she said, turning to bury her face in Lincoln's chest. He wasn't fazed in the slightest. If anything, he looked proud.

"I'm just saying!" Dad said, raising his hands. "I don't like hearing it any more than you do, but if you're grown enough to do it, then you're grown enough to call it like it is."

He walked over, pulling Josie from Lincoln's arms and kissing her forehead like he hadn't seen her earlier. Then he and Lincoln shared the typical dude embrace, which wasn't quite a hug or a handshake. Bishop followed, doing the same thing. "How was your trip? Tell me all about it!"

Callie lay at my feet, snoozing away while I watched Bishop

from my seat on the patio, bringing a cold beer to my lips. He looked so happy here with everyone, laughing and joking while tending the grill. Every now and then, my dad would clap his shoulder, and I swore I saw him stand a little taller.

I'd known a little bit about Bishop's history from overhearing Mom and Dad talk from time to time, but I'd never known just how tough he'd had it. I couldn't stop thinking about his childhood while we packed up the picnic and rode back to the barn. He was right. It'd been a hard truth for me to listen to when my parents were truly special.

Growing up, they had a very open-door policy. We could come to them about anything bothering us, and they always agreed to help us sort it out. I'd never had to think about what the alternative looked like because it never applied to me. How privileged I was to never worry about money or hear sharp words wielded like weapons by the people who raised me.

Bishop deserved so much more than the hand he'd been dealt, but I wondered if somewhere along the way he'd gotten too mixed up in it to appreciate what he might draw next.

When he talked about wanting a family earlier, a place to call his own, I wanted to shake him and tell him to look around. I mean, he'd attended every Friday night dinner since I could remember. Dad wouldn't have invited him if he wasn't family. There wasn't a person on this ranch who didn't care for and respect him.

And I was no exception.

As if he could feel my stare, he looked up and winked before continuing his conversation. It was quick. So quick that I might've missed it if I hadn't been paying attention, but I think I always had been.

Whenever Bishop walked into a room, I gravitated toward him, keenly aware of his every move. If he glanced my way in a crowd, I felt his gaze like static skittering along my skin. It was something I'd shrugged off as an annoyance. Of course, I knew where the most aggravating person I'd ever met was.

But it was more.

It'd always been more.

Josie and Cleo plopped beside me, talking about the branding. It was always a big weekend around here. All hands would be on deck to move through the calves as quickly as possible. Last I checked, we had about 175 to push through, which was more than we'd seen in previous seasons.

"Any of your old boyfriends coming to help?" Josie asked, kicking me under the table.

"What?" I asked, focusing back on their conversation. My gaze drifted over her shoulder to where Bishop was standing. If he'd heard anything, he didn't show it.

Josie rolled her eyes. "I asked if any of your old boyfriends are coming tomorrow? You know… To help out?"

"Uh, I don't know," I answered honestly. "Haven't talked to anyone, so I guess we'll see."

Usually, I wouldn't think twice about who would be out here, but I'd already seen how possessive Bishop could get. Honestly? It was a turn-on. Did it make me a bad person if the thought made my panties wet?

Cleo leaned back in her chair and sighed. "At least we'll be eating good tonight, because tomorrow will be hell. I always hated branding days. Tensions are high, and there's always a lot of yelling."

"Yeah, but most of that came from Dad, and he's sidelined this year," I said.

She raised her brows. "And you think that'll stop him from yelling?"

"Fair point," I chuckled. "I think it's going to kill him to just watch. I'm sure Lincoln and Bishop will get a talking to on Monday about how they could've made things run smoother."

"I love Dad, but I really hope the boys surprise the hell out of him," Josie said, dropping her chin on her palm. "Lincoln always gets crabby when he thinks Dad's mad at him."

"Bishop, too," I added, taking a sip. When I set the beer down, both my sisters were staring at me like I'd lost my mind. "What? Is there something on my face?" I turned in my chair, looking around. "Oh god, please tell me there isn't a spider."

Josie and Cleo glanced at one another before my eldest sister spoke up. "No, it's just that—"

"Did the two of you finally bang?" Josie finished, whisper-shouting as she leaned on the table. Bishop choked on his beer, turning just in time to spew it out on the grass and not the steaks.

"Well, I'll take that as a yes," Cleo mumbled under her breath.

"OH MY G—"

"Cleo, gag her!"

She slapped a hand over Josie's mouth, who at least had the decency to look sorry. "Are you dick drunk or something?" I asked. Normally, I was the one they had to worry about for volume control. "Did you suddenly forget how the fuck to keep quiet?"

Over her shoulder, I saw Lincoln pat the center of Bishop's back. "I'm good, man," he said, wiping the spilled beer off on his pants. "Just went down the wrong pipe or something."

"I'm sorry. Was I supposed to not be excited that one of you had finally made a move?" she asked.

"Finally? What do you mean finally?"

Cleo threw her hands up. "Come on, Lennox. Don't act like you haven't been panting after him since you were a teenager. I distinctly remember you doodling *Mrs. Lennox Bryant* in your diary for at least a year."

"And don't get us started on the sexual tension between you two. It's nearly suffocating," Josie said, putting her hands around her throat as though she couldn't breathe.

Oh, I was going to kill her. Actually, I was going to kill them both. From that moment on, I was a single child.

Especially as Bishop's shoulders shook with restrained laughter.

"I hate you both," I hissed between my teeth.

Josie waved me off. "No, you don't."

I crossed my arms over my chest. "I beg to differ."

"Dinner's ready!" Dad called, mercifully changing the subject and giving me a chance to escape this new-found hell.

"Don't think we're done talking about this!" Josie called over her shoulder as I grabbed the trash they had left behind.

"Yes, we are!" I shouted back. We were so done, and I had no problem pulling the barn sex card on her if I needed to get out of it. At least when Bishop and I were in my loft, we were alone.

Except for poor Callie.

I'd have to buy her all the chew toys and treats she wanted to make up for what she'd seen.

I looked up, breath catching, as I saw Bishop staring at me through the window. His eyes were soft, the edges around them slightly crinkled. Something about the sight made all my frustrations fade away.

The word *mine* echoed in my head with each steady beat of my heart. For the first time, it didn't scare me. It didn't make me want to run for the hills and never look back. If anything, I wanted to shout it from the rooftops for everyone to hear. I wanted to claim him, to give him the comfort he was desperately searching for.

I just hoped he felt the same because I wasn't sure how to return to a world where I didn't love Bishop Bryant.

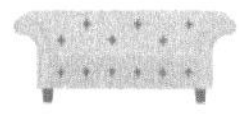

"EVERYTHING READY FOR TOMORROW?" Dad asked, scratching his goatee as he settled into his favorite armchair. Bishop and Lincoln sat on the couch beside him, beers in hand and bellies full. There was some old western show playing in the background that no one was paying attention to. I was pretty sure Dad could recite every word anyway, so it didn't matter much.

Mom peeked her head around the corner, narrowing her eyes. "How long have you been waiting to ask that question?"

"Probably since the last time he asked it when they were cooking the steaks," I chimed in before Dad could open his mouth. I came around with my arms full of empty plates, narrowly missing his playful swat.

"Smartass," he muttered.

I paused, turning around and giving him a wink. "You always told me it was better to be a smartass than a dumbass."

His laughter followed me into the kitchen, and I swore I heard him chuckle, "That's my girl."

Mom, Josie, and Cleo washed and dried the dishes as I finished putting away our leftovers. As much as I loved eating as a family, this was my favorite part. Sometimes we worked side-by-side in companionable silence, listening to Dad's antics in the next room, while others we blasted music and danced around the kitchen island drinking margaritas.

Tonight was a quiet night, which I was thankful for. This weekend would be exhausting, but I loved that Dad made a big deal out of these big events because they weren't for the faint of heart.

Brandings took a lot out of a crew. There were a lot of moving parts, and making sure the herds didn't get too anxious being cooped up. Mama cows didn't like to be separated from their babies, and sometimes that could cause trouble. We'd seen one knock down our makeshift pens like it was nothing before. On average, it was a minimum of a ten-hour day, but there'd been plenty of times we could go up to twelve, depending on the number of calves we had to go through or if there'd been any mishaps throughout the day. Dad never liked to rush things just for the sake of getting them done.

We switched from using a hot iron to freeze branding about five years ago, which meant it took a bit longer than before. There was a bit of a learning curve, but it was worth it in the long run to ensure we didn't unnecessarily harm our animals.

As we finished, Mom wiped her hands on the towel over her shoulder. "Let's go see what those boys are up to," she said.

"I'm going out to the garage to grab a drink. Y'all want anything?" I asked, backing out of the kitchen. I'd only taken a few steps when I slammed into a rigid body. A sharp exhale followed as rough hands landed on my arms and squeezed lightly.

I turned, seeing Bishop staring down at me with an amused smirk. "I've heard that walking forward can help eliminate the whole running into someone thing."

"You were clearly walking forward, yet you still ran into me, so I would say there's some fault in that argument." Stepping out of his touch felt wrong, especially when it'd been all I thought about over dinner.

Bishop was an expert at teasing me. More than once tonight, I found myself holding my breath as he squeezed past me in the kitchen. At first, I thought it was a complete accident, but then he'd kick up the corner of his lips in that same stupid little smile that had me wishing he was looking up at me from between my legs.

But we were still figuring things out, and until he'd given me the green light, I had to act like I hated him because that was what we were supposed to do. That's what everyone expected from us.

So, I crossed my arms and popped my hip out. "Are you

going to move, or are you just going to stand there with your thumb up your ass?"

There was a wicked spark in his eye, one that told me I was going to be in a lot of trouble when he got ahold of me next, but I loved bratting him. That would never change.

Especially now that I knew what punishments lay in store for me when we were alone.

Bishop widened his stance. "You gonna make me move, or are you all talk?"

I heard a giggle behind me and turned to find Mom and my sisters staring at us. The moment my gaze locked with Josie, she smacked the counter. "Yeah, are you still going to get those beers?" she asked, subtly nudging Cleo next to her.

"Oh yeah, I want one!"

I nearly died inside when my mom giggled and said, "Yes, me too! You might need someone to help you out. Bishop, be a dear, won't you?"

Bishop sighed, exaggerated and long like it was some great inconvenience. When I turned around, I expected to find a scowl, but he was smiling. It was softer than before, a little subdued, but the emotion in his eyes gave him away. Like this not so subtle nudge from the women behind me soothed a worry I hadn't known about.

He dipped his chin. "Yeah, sure. Come on, killer. Just don't murder me when I turn around." He turned and called out to Lincoln and my dad. "Y'all want a beer or anything from the garage?"

"Hell yes I do!" Dad called, rubbing his hands together. "Make it a double. I got two hands for a reason."

"You'll get water, and you'll like it," Mom said, coming around with her hands on her hips.

He huffed, looking down at the bright red water bottle Mom had gotten him. The doctor had said he needed to up his water intake, but Dad claimed it was hard since he didn't have anything to carry around with him. "Then I guess I don't need anything," he grumbled.

Lincoln looked down at his beer. "Yeah, I'll take two. By the time you guys are done, this'll be empty anyway," he said, chuckling.

"Done with what?" Dad asked, brows furrowing.

Josie's soon-to-be-dead boyfriend burrowed into his seat, smiling like a devil. "Sorry! Did I say when they were done? I meant when they're back."

My whole family was dead to me at this point. Their only saving grace was that Dad seemed to accept Lincoln's bullshit answer and run with it. Bishop put his hand on my back, giving me a little shove to keep up our pretense. The moment I cleared Dad's view, I turned and flipped Lincoln off. He gave me a little salute before turning back to the TV.

Bishop kept his hand on my back until the door to the garage was closed. All the air was knocked from my lungs as he pushed me up against the wall and pressed his mouth to mine. One hand slid around my hip, and the other landed at my throat, squeezing lightly as he took what he wanted.

I couldn't breathe, everything about his kiss and his touch consumed me until I felt dizzy. As he pulled away, we were both breathing heavily—our need for one another all consuming.

"You're such a fucking brat, killer. You love using that smart mouth to rile me up, don't you?"

I nodded, biting my lip and staring up at him innocently. "Yes, daddy," I breathed, pushing against his hold to try and kiss him again. He held me back, forcing me to stay put.

"I should turn your ass fucking red for what you said in there, but I don't have time for that," he said through gritted teeth.

I wanted him to make time for it. I wanted him to lose control just a little bit because his touch was the only thing that could take care of the ache between my legs. I wiggled in his hold as he kissed me again, picking me up and pinning me back against the wall.

Shamelessly, I rolled my hips, grinding myself against his thickening cock. My toes curled as he groaned, the sound rumbling impossibly low and sending little shocks to my core. But I didn't care, not as he met my movements with desperate ones of his own.

Bishop rested his forehead against mine, his forest green gaze heated as we moved together. "That feel good?"

I nodded, whimpering as his next thrust rubbed against my clit. "Yes, daddy, please…" God, I was so close. It wouldn't take anything at all to—

Suddenly, my stomach lurched as Bishop loosened his grip and set me on shaky feet. He backed away, leaning against my mom's car. I could see the outline of his cock straining against his zipper. "What the fuck?"

"What?" he asked, cocking his head to the side. "Oh, you didn't think I was going to let you come, did you?"

"Obviously! I was so close," I pouted.

Bishop stepped forward. Slowly. Calculating. Like a predator approaching his prey. His faint cologne filled the space, making me a little weak in my knees. "You should know by now," he said, leaning forward and whispering in my ear. "Bad girls don't get to come, and you, killer, have been a very bad girl."

And then he walked over to the fridge, adjusting his dick before he grabbed seven beers out of the refrigerator.

"Are you freaking kidding me, Bishop Bryant?"

He handed me three beers. "Not at all, killer. But we had better join the family before you throw a real tantrum and I have to spank you in front of them."

"You wouldn't dare," I said, keeping my voice low.

Bishop paused, grabbing my hand. His brows furrowed, expression growing serious. "I think you'll find that there isn't much I wouldn't do when it comes to you. I'm in the palm of your hand, sweetheart," he said, pressing a kiss to the center. "Don't crush me."

"I think you've got that backward, baby," I whispered, pausing only long enough for him to hear the words. "I'm the one who is waiting on pins and needles for you to decide if you're all in or not."

I heard his footsteps fall into step with mine as I entered the living room. The girls were still in the kitchen, gossiping in hushed tones around the kitchen island. I'd just handed them their drinks when I heard Lincoln say, "What? You're done already?"

I slid up next to my sister, handing her a beer. "I don't know who I'm going to kill first," I whispered. "You or your boyfriend."

She waved me off, pushing the drink my way. I looked down in question. "I thought you wanted one?"

Josie shook her head. "I was just giving you a few minutes of alone time," she said, dropping her voice. "You're welcome, sis."

"Is this payback for pushing you about Lincoln once upon a time?" I asked.

There was something different about her tonight, something I couldn't quite place. She'd been moping around the ranch since Lincoln had been gone, but now that he was back, there was a lightness that hadn't been there earlier.

I couldn't stay mad at her if I tried.

Josie raised her hands. "All I'm saying is that if you and Cleo hadn't, my life wouldn't be nearly as amazing as it is now. So, maybe one day you'll be thanking me for the beer."

bishop

· · ·

I LOOKED over the lip of my coffee mug, smiling as Lennox stepped out of my shitty little box shower. Beads of water dripped down her body as she hastily grabbed the towel I'd left out for her and ran it over her skin. My gold necklace glinted in the shitty lighting, and I watched as she ghosted her fingertips across the chain. She'd been obsessed with the thing, always eyeing it and me when I had it on. If it made her that happy, I'd give it to her. Looked better on her than me anyway.

She'd spent the night tangled in my sheets and my arms, and now she was in my space getting ready for the day. Neither one of us had grabbed much sleep, instead falling into our new normal routine of lazy fucking and long talks. The lack of rest was starting to catch up with me, but that's why I had coffee. I could sleep when I was dead; I wanted to spend every waking moment with her.

Lennox hummed as she wiped away the condensation on my mirror, running her fingers along the underside of her eyes. "I think you're trying to kill me," she called.

"Is that right?" I asked.

"Mmhm." Lennox stepped away from the sink and leaned in

the bathroom doorway. "Look at these dark circles under my eyes. There's no amount of concealer to cover this up."

I narrowed my eyes. "I can't tell from here. You better move closer."

Her bare feet padded against the hardwood floor, a smile slowly spreading across her lips. "Eyesight not what it used to be? Should we get you some glasses?"

I patted my thigh, and that was the only invite she needed. Lennox crawled into my lap, resting her head on my shoulder as I wrapped my arms around her. "I already have some."

"What?" she asked, looking around. "How come I've never seen them?"

I shrugged. "I don't wear them much. They get in the way at work."

"Why don't you use contacts then?"

"Never much liked the idea of putting something in my eye," I admitted. "It kinda freaks me out."

She pulled back, scrunching her face. "You're a cowboy."

I waited for her to elaborate, but she didn't. "And?"

"So you can stick your hand up a cow's vagina to check their cervix while they're calving, but you can't put a contact in your own eye?"

"Yeah, it's my job, and can save lives. What's a contact gonna do? My eyesight isn't that bad. I just need the glasses when I'm reading."

I realized my mistake too late. Way too goddamn late if Lennox's bright eyes were any indication.

"Wait, wait, wait... Did you say read?" she asked, laughing. "What? Do you have a secret smut addiction or something?"

I shifted in my seat. "No, I read reports and shit."

"And shit," she deadpanned.

"Yeah. What's wrong with that?"

Lennox stared at me for a minute before hopping to her feet

and shuffling toward my nightstand. "What're you doing?" I asked, trying to keep my voice even.

"Condoms, lube, batteries," she murmured, rifling through my stuff. "But no glasses." She shut the drawer, turning and looking around. Her eyes settled on my dresser, and I knew she'd figured it out.

We both moved at the same time. For a man of my size, I should've made it there first, but Lennox was surprisingly fast. Her fingers curled around the knob and pulled the top drawer open.

At first glance, it looked like your average underwear and sock drawer. I hoped it was enough to keep her away, but I knew better. She began rifling around, messing up any semblance of order I had. My stomach dropped when she let out a triumphant little shriek, holding up a little black glasses case.

"Okay, so we have the glasses," she said, lifting the corner of her lips. She sat them on top of the dresser and went in for more.

"What more are you looking to find?" I asked, shifting on my feet. "You found my glasses already."

"Nuh-uh," Lennox said, shaking her head. "There's no way that's all—aha!"

And then she pulled out the small e-reader, smiling as she held it between us. "You don't know how to FaceTime, but you have one of *these*?" She pressed the button, swiping up to go to my library. I closed my eyes as she began scrolling through the titles, praying to any higher power out there to swallow me up so I could die in peace.

"Holy shit, you're a secret smut slut!"

I peeked through one of my eyes, watching Lennox light up as she scrolled through my limited library before I snagged it from her hand. "Alright, that's enough of that."

"Hey! Give that back!" she said, jumping for it, but I held it above her head. There was no way for her to reach it. "That's not fair."

"Fair?" I asked, looking pointedly at the drawer that was currently disheveled. "You literally just rifled through my shit for something that you didn't even know was there until five minutes ago."

Lennox tightened her towel grip and tried jumping to reach the e-reader. All it'd done was draw my eyes to the tops of her breasts, and we really didn't have time for me to get distracted like that. "Okay, but how am I supposed to just let this go? Bishop, baby, you have porn hidden away in your underwear drawer," she said, cupping my face and giving me a chaste kiss through her giggles. "I mean, that's so cliche."

"Cliché, huh?" I said, tossing the e-reader on the dresser and grabbing Lennox around her waist. She yelled as we both fell on the bed. I captured her hands in my own, pinning them above her head, while the other slowly moved her towel out of the way. "Sweetheart, it's not cliché if I'm learning from it."

She raised her brows, lips parting in an O shape. "Really?" I nodded, dragging my fingers slowly over each of her taut nipples. "Maybe you should show me what you've learned."

"We don't have time," I said, dipping my head and inhaling deeply. She'd used my body wash this morning. The fact she smelled like me awoke some deep instinct, I felt like a damn wild animal.

Moving to the edge of the bed, I got down on my knees and pulled her body closer. Nothing had changed. We didn't have time, but I didn't care. I may have acted like I was in charge around her, but it couldn't have been further from the truth.

I may not have known much, but I knew one thing.

Lennox Hayes was mine, and I wanted to make sure she stayed that way.

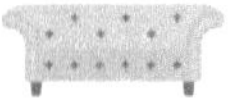

"HOLD HER STEADY," I called, pressing the copper brand against the calf's left hip. I gently rotated the brand, rolling it in small circles to keep it in contact with the skin.

"Yeah, that's a good girl," I said, patting her neck. I put the brand back in the cooler with the brand mixture, letting it cool down for the next go. "Tag her and switch!"

This was the first branding we had since Lincoln had joined. We both manned a line to try and get through as many as we could today. Our goal was to run through a hundred, but it always took us a minute to get back in the swing. Other ranch hands worked on tagging the calves with a number and marking them as complete, or shearing the hair where the brand would go.

With a single nod, Lennox pulled the lever and released the calf from the chute. We had workers ready to usher it into the arena with the others we'd gotten done. There was only one left in our line until we were calling it for lunch. Cleo and Ruby were by Cook's wagon, laying everything out to move the workers through as quickly as possible.

I lifted my hat, wiping away the sweat beading along my hairline. It may have been nearly December, but it was one of the hottest days in weeks. It was barely one in the afternoon and damn near eighty-five degrees.

Lennox swung her braid over her shoulder, removing her hat to fan herself. "You sure know how to pick the best days to do this shit," she muttered.

"I don't control the weather, killer," I shot back, closing the gates as the last cow ran through. "This was all supposed to be done by now."

"Alright, let's just get this one done so I can eat," she said, jerking her chin toward the wide-eyed animal staring at us. "Someone forced me to skip breakfast this morning."

"That's such a shame," I said with a wink. I grabbed the spray bottle filled with alcohol and doused the cut area thoroughly. "My meal was fucking delicious."

She threw her head back in laughter. "God, you're shameless."

I turned to grab the iron, lining it up in the sheared square, pressing it to the skin, and repeating the same process I'd been doing all morning. It was all muscle memory at this point. "Only for you."

Lennox looked over, narrowing her eyes slightly. "Who are you, and what have you done with Bishop Bryant?"

"Dunno," I said, ducking my head so I didn't have to look at her. "Heard he went and fell in love."

I was silent under the weight of her gaze as I focused on rolling the iron. At forty-seven seconds, I pulled it off and stuck it with the rest. Lennox didn't need any direction as she noted the tag number before releasing the animal with the rest.

The work kept me busy, kept my mind occupied so I wasn't agonizing over the words to say, but now we were breaking for lunch, and I couldn't hide anymore. Lennox still hadn't said anything, though. Not even as we fell into step with one another on the way to grab food.

God, I was so stupid. I didn't know why I said it. What if she wasn't ready? I had no idea how to tell a woman I loved her. I had no previous experience to draw on.

All I knew was that I loved her and didn't want to go another day without her knowing. I'd wasted too much time already with my back-and-forth bullshit. At least I'd laid myself on the line, now it was her turn to decide what she wanted.

I let her go in front of me to grab food. Even if she didn't feel the same, I was still a gentleman. She grabbed things here and there but didn't fill her plate as much as I expected her to.

When we reached the end of the line, I opened my mouth to ask her to sit with me, but she bounced off toward her sisters before I could.

Lincoln clapped me on the shoulder. "Come on, boss man. You're coming with me."

It went against every urge screaming at me to follow Lennox, but I fought it, letting Lincoln steer me toward one of the few empty tables left. Neither of us spoke at first, content to listen to the surrounding chatter.

From where we sat, I could just make out Lennox talking to Josie. She pushed her food around on her plate, sighing as she finally pushed it away. My own meal turned to ash on my tongue, and I did the same.

"Trouble in paradise?" Lincoln asked, shoveling a spoonful of beans into his mouth.

"Stay out of it," I muttered.

"I guess you still don't wanna talk about it," he laughed. "I'd always wondered what happened that night, but true to my word... I kept my mouth shut and never asked."

I remembered it well. It was the morning after Lennox had stormed out. Lincoln was walking up to the house for breakfast and saw the showdown on my lawn in real-time. I'd told him I hadn't wanted to talk about it, and he hadn't brought it up until today.

"Not even to your better half?" I asked, glancing back toward Lennox and Josie. Lennox wrapped her food up, setting it down on Keith's truck before they headed into the barn.

He shook his head. "Naw. If Lennox wanted Josie to know, that's on her to tell her. I don't get involved in anything happening between the sisters."

"That's the first smart thing I've ever heard come outta your mouth."

"Aw, I knew you liked me," he said, butting into my shoulder with his own. "My point is... Same offer stands as before. If you need to talk about anything, or *anyone*, I'm here."

I chewed on the inside of my cheek, letting his offer hang between us. This was strange for me. Sure, I might've had friends over the course of my life, but none that I wanted to sit and talk about this shit with.

But I wanted to make this work with Lennox, which meant I should probably open up a little bit. He'd done the same to me. After all... If everything worked out between us, Lincoln and I would be like family, right?

"I dunno what the fuck I'm doing with her," I whispered. "I feel so out of my depth. It's not even funny. She says jump, and I say how high. I don't know how to stop feeling this way, but I also don't want to stop? I'm in over my head! I'm—oh god, I can't even say it."

"What's wrong?" Lincoln asked, a hint of worry in his tone. "You're what?"

I sat my hand down on the table, scrubbing my face with my hands until the skin felt raw. "I'm just like you! I'm a lovesick fool that she's got wrapped around that dainty, infuriating finger of hers, and I don't know what to do with that. I'm terrified of fucking everything up with her, and—are you seriously laughing right now?"

Lincoln was beet red from trying to hold in his laughter, but the shake in his shoulders told me he was losing the battle. "I'm sorry," he said, waving me off. "Oh man, this is great."

"It is not!" I said, lowering my voice the moment I realized how loud I was being. "I'm so fucking gone for her."

He wiped beneath his eyes. "Have you told her?"

I looked down at my hands. "I may have said something before lunch?"

"Just now?" he asked, brows furrowing.

"Maybe."

"You just dropped the L bomb and ran?"

I blew out a breath. "This was a terrible idea. I don't know why I thought talking about it would help."

"No, stop. Sit your grumpy ass down, grandpa, and let's talk about your feelings," he said, pushing me back into my seat.

"I'm only four years older than you."

"Yeah, but most of the time, you act like a sixty-year-old who yells at kids to get off his lawn, so it fits," Lincoln said, shrugging. "Listen, I can't tell you anything you don't already know, but I can say you aren't fucking anything up. Relationships are hard. Putting yourself out there is hard. Giving someone that kind of control when you're used to holding the reins is fucking hard. But goddamn, is it worth it."

"Of course, you're gonna say that. Everything worked out for you."

"And who said things weren't gonna work out for you? I may not have known everyone as long, but Bishop... You've gotta be the dumbest son-of-a-bitch I've ever met if you don't think that woman is head over heels in love with you. There are literal hearts in her eyes when she glances your way."

"What? No. I mean, I know she cares, but—"

"Has she done anything that'd suggest otherwise?" he asked, cutting me off.

I closed my eyes, feeling every bit as stupid as Lincoln claimed I was being. I thought back, wondering if I'd missed any red flags, but came up empty-handed. Lennox always followed my lead. She may have pushed my buttons and smarted off, but if I said to pump the brakes, she did a hard stop.

"I'm gonna take your silence as confirmation that you're just being a dumbass," Lincoln said, finishing off the last of his lunch.

"Fuck off. I didn't expect you to make sense," I grumbled.

"It has nothing to do with making sense and everything to do with opening your eyes." Lincoln adjusted his chair so that he was facing my direction. "Listen, I don't know much about your history other than what you told me on my first day here. I get that opening up and trusting others isn't easy, but if you want to have a good life, then you're gonna have to. Look at Josie and me... Neither one of us had a reason to trust the other. After a year, I showed up out of the blue, and she was with someone else. Tell me, what would you have done if you'd been in my boots?"

"Well, I wouldn't have waited a goddamn year like an idiot."

He waved me off. "Yeah, Yeah. I'm stupid. I've had this fight with Josie a thousand times, but unlike the others, I'm not gonna get make-up sex after you and I are done talkin'. Just answer the question."

What would I have done? For starters, I probably wouldn't have even been in the position. I wouldn't have fallen in love after a five-night stand, and I damn sure wouldn't have pined after that person for a year after no contact and showed up randomly to get them back. Every decision I made was cautious. Careful. There was nothing I wanted to risk this life for.

Until now.

Until *her*.

Until I'd done something reckless, entirely out of character, and selfish.

Kissing Lennox Hayes for the first time had been life-altering. It made me want things I'd only dreamed about. It'd given me hope for a future—a better one where I could move away from my past and do something for myself.

My whole life has been spent taking care of others. I worked myself to the bone, earning enough to cover the bills my mom couldn't—the ones my father should've been there to take care of. I never participated in any sports or activities, barely passing high school enough to graduate.

Even after she kicked me out, I immediately jumped in head first here at the ranch. I was grateful for the work. It gave me a purpose—a way to move past the shitty hand I'd been dealt and make something of myself.

But over the years, I grew jaded and reclusive. I'd become so laser-focused on being important to the people around me that I'd forgotten any dreams of my own. Maybe that's why I'd given Lennox so much grief over the years.

I'd never felt dislike or even distrust toward her.

No, I *envied* her.

She was the opposite of me in so many ways and the embodiment of everything I wanted to be. I'd never met anyone with a wilder spirit or a harder worker. Her stubborn streak rivaled my own, but it was never out of selfishness. At the end of the day, she knew how good she had it, even if it took her a minute to realize it sometimes.

She knew what she wanted. If she didn't, then she faked it until she made it. I could do that, worry less about others' thoughts and take what *I* wanted.

And what I want is her.

There was no denying it. I wanted her snark, her bite, her unimaginable wit. I wanted to work beside her, to cheer her on, and vice versa. I wanted a relationship like Doug and Ruby, one filled with love and laughter and enough memories to last us a lifetime.

Goddammit, I wanted it all. And there wasn't anything stopping me from having it except for me.

I was my own worst enemy.

"Ah," Lincoln said, dragging my attention back to him. "There it is."

"There what is?" I asked.

"You found your answer," he said, pushing to his feet. He jerked his chin toward the barn and grabbed our plates, tossing them into the trash. "Go get your girl, Bishop."

"We've got the branding. I can't just take off."

He rolled his eyes. "Yeah, dumbass. You'll have to come

back, but we have," he looked down at his phone, "about twenty minutes before break ends. I think that's enough time to tell the girl you love her, eh?"

I stood, tucking the chair away. "It didn't go so well the first time."

Lincoln held up his hands in surrender. "Listen, if you don't wanna do this now, I'll trade lines so you can both get some space, but I think you both need to squash this shit before it gets outta hand." He began walking away but paused. "I waited a year before I got the nerve to seek Josie out, and it was almost too late. That's my advice. Take it or leave it."

bishop

. . .

I **WAS** out of breath by the time I reached the barn. Not because it was a far jog but because it felt like I was on the verge of a panic attack.

I'd never had one before, but that's what it felt like. My heart felt like it was going to beat out of my chest, and my palms were dripping with sweat. I wiped them on my jeans as I slowed my gait, looking up to see Josie and Lennox headed down from the loft. The lighting was dim, but I swore the girls had tears in their eyes. They both stopped at the bottom of the staircase when they saw me.

"Hey, Bishop," Josie said, sniffling. She gave me a small smile. "Sorry, we lost track of time. We'll be right there."

"No," I said quickly. "I mean, I just wanted to talk to Lennox if that was okay."

"Sure. Of course. I'll see you out there." Josie squeezed her sister's hand and walked away, leaving us alone.

Lennox nodded, gaze slowly sliding my way. She leaned against the railing, the light from the large window upstairs silhouetting her body. "What's up? Is something wrong?"

"No," I said, stuffing my hands in my pockets. "I just wanted to talk to you about earlier—"

"I was waiting for this," she said with a sigh. "Look, Bishop, it's fine. I know you didn't mean it. We don't have to make a bigger deal out of this. Let's just forget it."

Forget it? What the hell was she talking about? "No. That's not what I want—"

"I really don't want to do this right now, okay? We have too much going on this weekend, and I can't handle you walking away again, so if you could wait to end things, that'd be appreciated."

"Wait... That's what you think?" I asked, rocking forward onto my toes.

Lennox wouldn't even look at me. She stared at Titan's stall with tears welling as she crossed her arms over her body. "I get you're trying to be a gentleman, but—"

Enough of that.

I surged forward, tossing her over my shoulder and storming into my office down the hall. She called my name, beating her fists against my back like she did every time, but I wasn't going to stop. Not until she fucking listened to me.

I slammed the door and flipped the lock before setting her down on my desk. The room was a mess and smelled like leather and horses, but what else was a cowboy's office supposed to smell like? I rarely used the room.

"What the hell, Bishop?" Lennox shouted. She tried to hop off, but I stepped between her thighs and trapped her.

I reached out and gripped her chin, forcing her to look at me. Her blue eyes were red-rimmed and slightly glassy. Had she been crying? Was she bitching about me to Josie? The thought alone made my chest ache. I felt like a massive dick.

"I tell you I'm in love, and you automatically think I'm breaking up with you?" I whispered harshly. "What kind of fucked up logic is that?"

"Because you didn't mean it, and that's okay. I know you're preparing to run. I can feel it. Right here," she said, slamming her hand over her chest. Her heart. "Please let me walk away with some dignity before I lose it."

"I'm not letting you walk away at all, sweetheart," I said, tightening my hold. "Not now. Not ever. You are fucking *mine*, and I'm gonna prove it."

Her lips parted, a whimper slipping through before I crushed my lips to hers. I didn't want to be soft. I wanted her to realize that I wasn't running away.

Lennox wrapped her arms around my neck, pulling me closer. Her legs parted and I settled against her center. We paused momentarily, looking at the other for a signal to stop. If that's what she wanted, I'd walk away right now.

But god, I prayed she didn't.

"I want you to listen to me when I say this, killer..." She nodded, and I continued. "I am so disgustingly in love with you that nothing could change that. You could tell me to fuck off, and I would, but nothing can change the way this stupid thing in my chest beats for you."

"What if it's just really good sex?" she asked. "I mean, we have a lot of fun, but—"

I tried not to laugh, I really did, but I couldn't help it. "Trust me, killer... it's more than just sex. It's the way you make me feel like I'm worth something. You see me in a way no one else fucking has, you know that? I'm all in."

"You're all in?" She repeated the words like she was trying them on for size.

"Mmhm," I said, nodding. I let my hands run over her thighs. "Until you tell me to go away."

Her breathing hitched as my fingers inched their way up her body. "What if that never happens? I mean, what then?"

"Then I guess we'll have to figure something out. My cabin's gonna get cramped by the time you move in all your shit, and—"

"I don't have that much!" she said, swatting my arm.

"You've got more than I do. That's for damn sure. And we'll have to make some compromises on the decorating shit, because I dunno how I feel about letting you move in an orange couch and disco balls."

Lennox stuck her bottom lip out in a pout. "What if I get on my knees and beg?"

"You know… On second thought, maybe I could use some color after all," I said, leaning in for a kiss. Lennox met me halfway, keeping her arms locked tight. Her hips tilted, seeking friction, and I groaned as I pulled away and dropped my head against hers. "We don't have time for you to be grinding that hot little pussy against me."

"Please, baby…" she whined. "We can make it quick."

"It's never quick with you," I said. "You make me crazy, and then I can't stop. I can't get enough."

She paused, looking around the room, eyes lighting up when she landed on something in the corner. I followed her line of sight, interest sparking when I realized what it was.

My rope was hanging on a hook by the door, looking mighty tempting. I turned back toward Lennox with my eyebrow raised. "That doesn't seem like it'd be quick."

"It'll keep my hands busy so I'm not distracting you…"

She had a point. And maybe it'd give me some ideas for later because I knew I wouldn't ever get the sight of her bound out of my mind once I'd seen it. "I have a better idea for today," I said, reaching forward and grabbing a ball of baling twine from the top drawer of my desk. "Give me your hands," I said, making quick work of a handcuff knot. She slipped her wrists inside, and I pulled on them. "Good?" I asked.

"Great," she breathed, testing the binding.

My fingers flew to the button of her jeans, pulling them down until she was bared to me. I wanted to savor her, to take my time, but that wasn't a luxury we had right now. "Bend over the desk, killer. And keep those hands where I can see them."

Lennox did as she was told, just like I knew she would. The sight of her ass and bound wrists made my cock fucking ache. She was better than any drug. I was going to combust if I didn't get inside her soon.

"So fucking pretty," I said, undoing my jeans and pulling my dick out. She was already dripping. "And all mine."

In one quick motion, I was inside of her, stilling only for a moment before my hips picked up the pace. We were fucking like it was our last time, even though it felt like it was our first. Maybe it was in a way. It was the first time we'd genuinely acknowledged this thing between us, admitted that it was something life-changing.

"Yours," she breathed, sliding flat on the desk. Her arms were bound in front of her, grabbing at the air, searching for purchase, and being denied by design.

Lennox's ass bounced with each thrust. There was nothing soft or gentle about what we were doing. We didn't have time for that. It wouldn't take long for someone to come looking for us, but right now, I didn't fucking care. Not when this perfect woman was all mine and writhing beneath me.

I reached around for her clit, stroking it hard and fast how I knew she liked it. "Are you gonna come on my desk like a good little slut?"

"Yes, yes, yes," she cried, squeezing her eyes shut.

"I can feel you squeezing me. Goddamn, that pussy loves my cock, doesn't she?" I gritted out, upping my speed.

The sounds coming from us were lewd. A mixture of low moans and slapping skin filled the small space, keeping the tempo until I knew we were both reaching our peak. "That's it. Come for me, sweetheart."

Lennox was squirming beneath me, begging for more. She

cried out as I applied more pressure, her cunt strangling me as she barreled toward release. "Bishop!"

Her orgasm hit me like a freight train, sending me over the edge with her. My hips stuttered, the movement faltering as we fought to catch our breath.

"Shit, sweetheart. I think you really are trying to kill me," I said, looking down at where we were still joined. When she laughed, she squeezed me tighter, and I groaned. It was too damn sensitive. "Fuck," I cursed, slowly pulling out and watching my cum slip free. I reached down, gathering it on my fingers before slowly pushing it back where it belonged.

"You know I'm going to go to the bathroom to clean up, right?" she asked, holding her hands out for me to remove the rope.

I undid it quickly, rubbing her wrists to make sure her circulation wasn't cut off. I hadn't drawn the rope tight on purpose, but that didn't mean it couldn't have gotten twisted at some point.

"If it was up to me, I'd make you leave it there all day, making a mess in your panties until I was the one who cleaned it away tonight."

Lennox righted her clothes and combed through the strands of her hair framing her face. "As hot as that sounds," she began, pushing to her toes to give me a chaste kiss, "that's a surefire way to end up with UTI. I'll be quick, okay?"

"Whatever you say." I swatted her ass on the way out, loving the way her cheeks flushed as she ducked into the bathroom between the offices.

I cleaned up while I waited, picking up the papers that'd been strewn across the floor during our frenzied fucking. It was an organized chaos, and there wasn't much of a method to my madness.

When Lennox stepped out, she motioned toward the door.

"All yours. I'm gonna head back, though, so it's not too obvious what we've been doing."

I grabbed her bicep before she could go, pulling her in for a kiss. "That's fine right now, but I'm done hiding, sweetheart. You deserve a loud love. Besides," I said, leaning down with a smirk. "It's getting too damn hard to keep my hands off you."

She smacked my chest and laughed. "Behave. You'll get your hands on me tonight."

I watched her leave the barn, focused on the sassy swing of her hips and the bounce in her step. It was like a night and day difference from the girl who'd walked into this barn with a heavy weight on her shoulders.

Once she was out of sight, I stepped into the bathroom and washed my hands. I already couldn't wait to get this day over with. It was going to be hard not walking around with a hard-on when all I could think about was how good her body would look bound by my rope and the sounds she'd make when I'd take my time drawing out every ounce of pleasure.

I grabbed a paper towel to dry my hands and tossed it into the can at my feet, but it bounced off the edge. As I bent down to throw it away, I noticed something sticking out of the trash. I knew what it was. I wasn't stupid. And yet, I still couldn't stop myself from reaching forward, grabbing the end, and pulling it free.

My heart dropped as I stared at the two pink lines on the window.

Pregnant.

I thought back to each time Lennox and I had sex. We'd never used protection. She had an IUD, so I assumed we were protected, but what the fuck did I know? A quick Google search told me they were more than ninety-nine percent effective. That seemed great at first, but what about the less than one percent?

Was I going to be a father?

Lennox couldn't have taken it just now. There was no way. She'd been too quick. So, when did she have the time? Unless...

She'd been crying when you walked in, you idiot. Probably because she was stuck with you and thought you didn't want anything to do with her anymore.

Surely, I'd put her worries to rest. Kid or not, I was all in with Lennox. There wasn't a single thing that could tear us apart. If she was pregnant, I'd be the best damn dad any kid had ever seen.

Even though my childhood had been shit, Lennox's was not. I'd learned a lot from Doug over the years about what it was to be a man, a friend, and a partner, but I had a feeling that learning to be a father was going to be the most gratifying lesson he'd teach me.

I stared down at the test in my hands before stuffing it in my pocket. I didn't want to throw it out. People kept them for announcements and shit, right? I vaguely remembered watching a movie one time where they did. Lennox could take another one if she wanted to, but I liked the idea of using this one, especially if it was the one she used to find out.

There were so many things racing through my mind that I barely heard Lincoln shouting my name. "Bishop! Are you taking a shit in there? Let's go, man!"

"I'm coming, I'm coming!" I called back, finding him waiting by the sliding doors.

"Everything good?" he asked, falling into step beside me as I stormed past him. "Lennox sure looked like she was in good spirits when she re-joined the group."

I gave him a smile. "Yeah, I think everything's gonna be great."

And for the first time in my life, I felt like it was true. I was well on the way to making all my dreams come true, but first, there was something I needed to do.

lennox

. . .

I STARED at Bishop from across the campfire. He was tapping his fingers rapidly against the beer bottle in his hand, staring off into the distance like it held all the answers to life's greatest mysteries. Callie lay at his feet instead of mine—the little traitor. Why did all my animals betray me for him?

It'd been nearly a week since the branding, and he was acting strange. At first, I thought it was all the love talk, that it really had bothered him more than he'd let on, but that theory promptly crashed and burned. The man constantly told me he loved me. He reminded me of a toddler who'd just learned a new word and couldn't stop saying it. It was cute. Adorable, even. It still didn't explain the weird behavior.

When we were at work, he constantly hovered around me. If I tried to lift anything heavy, he swooped in and did it for me. When we rode horses, he kept his pace slow and steady instead of the races we were used to having. It didn't matter how many times I tried to taunt him into it. He wouldn't budge.

It was the same when we were alone.

He started cooking dinner nearly every night, which was

great. I didn't know he was such a good cook, but every single meal was incredibly healthy. They were filled with lean meats, protein, and vegetables. It was great, but honestly, I didn't think I'd ever seen Bishop willingly eat a vegetable besides family dinners. Even then, it was mainly a potato and the occasional broccoli floret.

I mean, he had the nerve to side-eye me when I brought a bottle of wine with me a few nights ago and asked if I should be drinking that. My only response was to pour a glass and keep eye contact as I took a sip.

It didn't matter how many times I'd asked him what was wrong or told him he was being weird, he wouldn't say a damn word. Not even as he and Lincoln had headed into town this morning on what the latter described as, and I quote, a "secret mission."

"Still pouting about your grumpy cowboy over there?" Josie asked, stepping in front of me to block my view.

"Maybe. Though, you make a better door than a window," I grumbled.

"Thought so," she said, kicking my boot. "Scoot over."

I opened my arm, letting my sister slide beneath the blanket wrapped around my shoulders. Dad decided to do family dinner differently tonight by building a bonfire and roasting hotdogs over the open flame. We'd found these chicken sausages that were approved by his doctor, so he didn't have to feel too left out. But it was chilly this evening, and we were all bundled up tight and huddled around the fire.

"Is he still being weird?" she asked, burrowing into my side.

"Yup," I said. "And he won't tell me why. It's like saying that we love one another changed everything. Now he's eating chicken and salad instead of steak and potatoes. It's freaking weird. And that's the first beer he's had all week!"

"Do you think it's the age thing? Maybe he's trying to make sure he can keep up with you."

I turned toward her, rolling my eyes as she fought to keep a straight face. She'd been teasing me about our age gap every chance she got. Usually, I wouldn't even mind the ribbing, but with him acting so weird, it wasn't very appreciative.

"Alright, I kid!" she said, elbowing me in the ribs.

I wrapped my portion of the blanket tighter around me. "Well, I don't find it funny."

"Yes, you do. Maybe not right now, but you'll laugh at my puns again once all this blows over."

"What if it doesn't blow over, though? What if something got into his head, and he's changed his mind? He seemed so eager to tell our big secret. Even made sure I knew he didn't want to hide anymore, but now he's back to being weird about it. The other day, I asked him when he wanted to do it, and he just mumbled something about him not being ready and then went back to looking at his phone."

"Alright... That's concerning."

"Thank you!" I said a little too loud. Bishop's head jerked my way, eyes blazing a trail over my skin like he was trying to see if I was okay. I focused my attention on him, silently begging him to come over and sit with me, but he didn't move. "See what I'm talking about? What's the point of even being in a relationship if we're not going to act like it?"

Josie pursed her lips. "Bishop isn't used to this, though, Len. He's not the flashy, in-your-face kind of guy."

"That doesn't give him any right not to tell me what's happening."

"Touché," she said in total surrender. "But if you'll let me play devil's advocate for a second—"

"You always do," I muttered.

Josie didn't miss a beat. "I've been in his shoes before. He probably thinks whatever he's doing is best for you guys. I'm sure he doesn't mean anything by it."

"How are we supposed to work if Bishop won't talk to me?"

She nudged my shoulder. "You do what you do best. You be your infuriatingly pushy self. Sometimes, it has its perks."

"I don't want to scare him off. If I push him too hard, he'll walk away."

"He won't," she said quickly. "If he was going to, he would've already done it. You might not see it, but that man has been pining over you for years."

I scoffed, watching Callie nudge Bishop's boot with her nose. "He has not. It's a new thing for him."

"Please tell me you don't actually believe that." Josie laughed, patting my hand when she saw my quivering lip. "Oh, babe. No, no, no. Don't cry. Don't do that to me right now."

God, I felt so emotional. I wasn't much of a crier, but I couldn't help myself. For the first time in my life, I had felt secure in the love of another and dared to dream of my future. It felt like it was all slipping from my fingers, and I couldn't do anything to stop it.

Josie opened her mouth to say something, but Bishop's voice cut her off. "Can I have everyone's attention?" Everyone turned his way as he stood. He sat his bottle down, wiping his palms on his jeans.

"What is he doing?" Josie asked, shifting on the stone bench.

"I have no clue," I said, wiping beneath my eyes.

"What is it, son?" Dad asked, tucking Mom to his side.

Bishop sucked in a breath, letting his gaze drift across our family until it landed on me. He was walking my way before I could ask him what was wrong.

"What're you doing?" I whispered as he stood in front of me. My eyes darted toward my parents, who looked extremely confused as they watched us. Meanwhile, both my sisters were wide-eyed with glee. I could practically feel Josie vibrating beside me. Even Lincoln had tears of joy in his eyes.

And then he dropped to one knee.

The *fucking knee.*

The one that promised a lot more than we had ever talked about, especially considering we hadn't even told my parents about our brand-new relationship.

"Bishop," I said, sucking in a breath. "What're you doing?"

He reached out for my hand, taking it in his. "I don't really know," he confessed, letting his thumb trace over my knuckles. "Honestly, Lennox, I've been trying to figure out the best way to do this. I want to tell everyone what you mean to me and hopefully what I mean to you."

"Lennox?" Dad asked, brows furrowed. "What's going on?"

"I know I'm an idiot. I've dragged my feet when telling you and everyone here tonight how much you mean to me, but I don't wanna wait anymore, sweetheart. Not with our family growing and—"

"Oh, shit," Josie said, closing her eyes.

"Bishop…" I said, squeezing his hand.

"No, I don't want to hide this anymore, Lennox. Not with everything we'll have coming up. I know I've been acting weird this week, but I've just been trying to show you I can handle whatever news you throw at me. I'm all in."

Dad stepped up, hands on his hips, staring down at us. "Alright, will someone tell us what the fuck is going on here? I'm old. My hearing ain't what it used to be, so from where I was standing… It looked like you were proposing." He laughed, and my eyes slid closed.

I was going to die.

Bishop looked up. "I am, sir. I know it's gonna come as a shock, but I love your daughter very much—"

"That's fucking obvious, son," Dad scoffed. "I'm deaf, not blind."

"I want to marry your daughter, sir," he said. There wasn't a hint of doubt in his tone. If this wasn't so wild, then it might've been romantic.

Dad scratched his head, gaze flicking between Bishop and

me. "A heads up would've been nice. I didn't know y'all were dating..."

"We're starting a family and—"

"*Josie*..." I whispered.

"You're pregnant?!" my mom screeched, throwing her arms around my shoulders. "Oh, Lennox!"

Josie pushed to her feet, throwing our blanket to the ground before yelling, "It's me! I'm the one who's pregnant, not Lennox."

The noise stopped as everyone grew silent. They all stared at Josie, who'd gone as white as a ghost. But my gaze went to Lincoln, who stumbled forward, eyes softening as he said, "You're pregnant?"

She nodded, a single tear falling down her cheek. "About six weeks. I have a doctor's appointment next week to make sure."

He surged forward, gathering her in his arms. "Darlin'..." he whispered, peppering her with kisses. "Why didn't you tell me?"

"I just found out last week. Lennox was feeling some type of way about her situationship—"

"Situationship?" Bishop asked. "What is that?"

"Undefined friends with benefits," Lincoln offered.

Josie blew out a breath. "Anyway, she shared her secret, so I shared mine. We were together when I took the test." She looked up at Lincoln. "I wanted to tell you, but I was going to wait until I'd had a blood test to confirm it, so I didn't get your hopes up."

"Oh, Josie..." Our mom stepped forward, wrapping her in a hug next. "Oh, I'm so happy for you."

As our family took turns prying Josie from Lincoln's grip, Bishop stared at me, open-mouthed and still on one knee. "Wait, so you're not...?"

"No, you idiot," I said, leaning forward to kiss him. "If you'd just talked to me—"

"I wanted to surprise you," he mumbled, pushing to his feet. "I wanted to show you I was serious about us, about a future."

"Baby... I don't need all this to know," I said, following suit and wrapping my arms around his waist. "I just need us to talk to one another."

"That I can do," he mumbled against my hair.

I grinned at him mischievously. "You sure? You seemed pretty prepared."

"I was rising to the occasion! But that's a big occasion." He swiped at his forehead. "Phew!"

"What? You don't want to marry me now?" I asked, pulling back to stare at him.

Bishop winced. "No, no! I do!"

"I'm just messing with you," I said, laughing. "I love you, but it's way too soon for that. We can start by moving in together. Orange couch and all."

He placed his finger beneath my chin and tilted it up. "I do want to marry you, though."

I leaned in for a kiss, enjoying the tenderness of his lips moving against mine. "I think I'd like that very much."

"Yeah?" he asked, green eyes sparking.

"Mmhm."

"Hate to break up this moment," Dad said, stepping closer. He observed Bishop and me. "But I think you and I need to talk, son. Especially if you're gonna ask to marry my daughter without so much as a warning. I have a weak heart, ya know."

Bishop smiled, dipping his chin. "Yes, sir. I think that's warranted."

"I'm gonna be a father!" Lincoln whooped, throwing one hand in the air as he kept the other on Josie's back. We all laughed as he pressed a sloppy kiss to my sister's temple. "Bishop! Did you bring the present?"

All eyes turned to us. I watched Bishop's cheeks turn the deepest shade of red as he walked over to his chair by the fire and picked up a small yellow bag with a ribbon. He held it out to Josie. "Here you go. I, uh, think this is yours."

"What is it?" I asked, trying to peek.

Josie's brows furrowed as she reached into the bag, pulling out a small wooden box. "Is this my pregnancy test?"

I turned toward Bishop. "*That's* how you found out? You dug that out of the trash?"

He rubbed the back of his neck. "I thought it was yours and wanted to make something for us to remember…" He cleared his throat. "Lincoln helped."

Be still my heart. What a freaking man.

"Oh Bishop…" Josie said, lip trembling as she ran her fingers over the simple oak box. "This is perfect."

"Let me see," I said, stepping out of Bishop's arms toward my sister. She handed it over, and the thoughtfulness of the project stole my breath. The casing was simple. The oak border was plain but beautiful. Inside was a different matter entirely.

Bishop had chosen a beautiful rustic red fabric as the background. The pregnancy test was laid diagonally across the space, still showing faint, positive lines. It wouldn't stay that way forever, but it didn't matter. At the top, Baby Hayes was spelled out in loopy cursive with twine, ending in a lasso at the end of the last letter. And there was a small, yellow frame for the first sonogram picture.

He'd thought of everything.

"Thank god you dug through the trash, huh?" Lincoln joked.

"I didn't dig through the trash," Bishop mumbled. "It was sticking out."

"And then you picked it up."

"Because I thought it was Lennox's!"

I laid my hand on my chest. "I love that you kept something you thought I peed on in your pocket. That's so romantic, baby."

Josie gagged. "Okay. This," she said, pointing between Bishop and me, "is weird."

"Well, you better get used to it," Bishop said. His eyes found mine, the skin surrounding them crinkling along the edges. I'd come to love those wrinkles. They only came out when he smiled, and those moments were rare. "Cause I have no intention of stopping."

epilogue

. . .

Bishop

"COME ON, come on! Move your asses," Cleo muttered as the people in front of us finally stepped out of our way.

"Slow down. We don't need you making headlines for pushing people outta the way," I said, shaking my head as she took the stadium stairs two at a time. She was rushing back to our seats as the music kicked up and the announcer began calling out the lineup for the evening.

"And last, but certainly not least, is Lennox Hayes on Strider! This duo is currently sitting at that hallowed first place spot, which isn't much of a surprise to anyone familiar with them. They traveled all the way from Ashwood, Texas to be here tonight."

"I'd expect nothing less from Doug Hayes' daughter. He was a force to be reckoned with, and Lennox is stepping into his shoes with ease," the other announcer commented.

I smiled as the crowd went wild for my girl, screaming until I barely heard anything over the thunderous applause. My ears were ringing by the time it died down, but my heart had never been happier.

I'd been to a lot of rodeos over the course of my life, but

none that quite matched this one. The Calgary Stampede was in a league of its own. I understood why the ten-day event was as celebrated as it was. People from all over the world came to see the best of the best battle it out on the rodeo grounds, and Lennox was one of them.

After the holidays were over, Lennox and I had spent a lot of time talking about our future and what it would look like. Nothing had changed with my job. The ranch was still in a transition period and needed me more than ever. With Doug finally embracing retirement, Lincoln and I were still figuring out how the ranch would be run.

He'd been cramming his schedule full of clinics and events across the country so that he could take time off once Josie had the baby. It didn't leave a lot of time to help me run the day-to-day operations at the ranch. We'd built a good crew who could take care of most of their shit on their own, but I'd been the one struggling to keep up.

Letting go of the reins, even a little bit, was still something I was struggling with, but it was getting easier with time. Lennox and Lincoln were the only two people I felt comfortable enough with to ask for help. Even then, it was normally on a small scale, but they were both patient with me.

Doug and I had talked about it, too. Though he still gave me a hard time about it, he'd told me he understood how difficult it could be to lean on others. It was something that had taken him a long time, too, but he'd realized that nothing in this life could run smoothly with a single person running the show. Doesn't matter how big or small the task was. Life was easier, better in every way, when you had someone to lean on.

I suspected his lessons were about much more than running the ranch, but he didn't push it and neither did I.

Honestly, if it hadn't been for Lennox, I wasn't sure I could've done everything I needed to. She was always the first to jump in and sort out any issues that came up if I was out at a cattle auction or in the middle of a pasture with a herd and no cell reception. We talked over a lot of decisions for the ranch as a team, even though we always ran them by Doug and Ruby afterward.

The pride that filled their eyes when listening to their daughter sparked more joy than I could've ever imagined. Not that they would ever admit this out loud, but I suspected they were worried about their youngest daughter and what role she would settle into at the ranch. Lennox had her barrel racing, and while she loved what she did and had ambitious goals to meet within the confines of the sport, I had a feeling it wasn't what she wanted to do forever.

She'd taken on a lot of responsibilities over the past seven months. Josie had spent the first trimester of her pregnancy hunched over the toilet, so Lennox had stepped up alongside Ruby to take care of the office work. There'd been a bit of a learning curve, which meant Lennox often held her tongue while Josie criticized her attempt at file organization through the thin bathroom door, but they both made it through somehow.

In addition, Cleo had come to Lennox about starting up a kid's camp over the summer. She said parents at school had asked if she knew of any in the area that involved horse riding and fundamentals, because they were having difficulty finding any. Lennox loved the idea, and the two of them had spent all their free time coming up with a presentation for Doug and Ruby to give the greenlight.

But all of that left little time for Lennox's plans to return to barrel racing. The Women's Professional Rodeo Association started calling in January, asking her if she was returning to the circuit. She'd given them some bullshit answer about being undecided, which would've been fine if her shoulders hadn't slumped forward every time she hung up the phone.

When I tried talking to her about it, she used the ranch as an excuse as to why she couldn't go back. Josie and Ruby needed her in the office. I needed her on the back of a horse. Doug needed her to occasionally drive him to doctor's appointments. Cleo needed help with the camp. The list she came up with never ended. The girl had an excuse for everything, but I saw right through her.

Lennox had a myriad of championships and trophies under her belt, but she'd talked about winning one more before hanging up her rodeo hat, and I'd been determined to make sure she had the chance to do it.

Was going to Doug and telling on her a low blow? Maybe, but it worked.

He'd been red as a tomato when telling Lennox to put herself first, and how much he hated that she'd even considered walking away before doing everything she wanted to do. "Rodeo's a fast sport, bug," he'd told her. "Gotta grab the bull by the horns while you still can."

The next time the WPRA called, Lennox told them she'd see them at the Calgary qualifier in Salina, and then she won the damn thing. I hated that I couldn't be there to cheer her on, but I didn't doubt her abilities for a moment. She had what it took to compete with the best of the best and now she was proving it.

There was no way I was going to miss the Calgary Stampede, though. Not when I knew what it had meant to her. It was the first time asking for help had been easy. Doug and Lincoln both cleared their schedules to make sure they could cover for us while we were out.

When Lennox told me she wanted to travel, I was worried I'd hold her back. The life of a rancher didn't leave a lot of time for lavish European vacations, and she'd sounded so damn happy when she talked about it. I'd barely been out of state, let alone the country, but Calgary seemed like a good place to start.

"Oh my god. Summers here are so much better than Texas,"

Cleo said, happily sipping a beer by my side. She tipped her head up toward the sun, basking in the spring-like weather.

"I'm glad you're enjoying yourself, but can you put the phone in the holder already? You're making me nauseous with all your shaking," Josie asked, her shaky voice coming through the earbud I was sharing with Cleo.

"Oops, sorry," Cleo said. She sat her phone in the small tripod we'd brought along so that her family could watch from home. Thank fuck for technology.

Since she was on summer break, Cleo was the only one who'd been able to tag along. Doug wasn't cleared for a thirty-hour car ride to Canada and Josie's due date fell right in the middle of the trip. Ruby and Lincoln stayed behind to take care of everyone while we were gone.

"There she is!" Cleo exclaimed, pointing toward the alley between the chutes.

Lennox's black hat was pulled down, so I couldn't make out her face but the hot pink long sleeve she was wearing stood out against the darkness. Strider pranced at the starting line, champing at the damn bit for his rider to let him run.

She ran her hand over his neck in three slow strokes, ending the last on a final pat. Her chin lifted just a fraction, but her eyes seemed set on the targets in front of her. I loved seeing that side of her. The laser sharp focus. The sheer determination.

For so long I'd made the mistake of thinking she was just a good time girl, the kind that didn't take much seriously and laughed their way through life without so much as a care in the world, but I was so fucking wrong. Shame was my best friend whenever I remembered the way I'd dismissed her, but I was dead set on making it up to her.

Even if it took the rest of my life.

The moment Lennox gave him the greenlight, Strider took off at a run, veering toward the left at a staggering speed. She guided the Quarter Horse with expert precision, keeping herself low in the saddle. He hugged the first barrel without so much as a bump and took off for the second. Clouds of dust kicked up behind his thundering hooves with each long stride, and at one point I'd lost sight of them completely.

"Come on, killer. Come on!" I yelled as they cleared the second. I glanced at the clock. Their time was neck-and-neck with the last racer who crossed at 14.237. Whoever had the fastest time would take it all, and I wanted that for her. I wanted her to feel fulfilled. To not wonder what she could've done when she'd had the chance.

As they rounded the third barrel, Lennox urged Strider into a dead run for home. I couldn't breathe, couldn't think, as I watched them fly. Even the crowd seemed to hold their collective breaths as the pair crossed the line.

14.224 flashed across the screen and the entire stadium went wild.

Cleo jumped up and down, grabbing the phone from its stand. "Did y'all see that?" she screamed. "She won! She won! She fucking won!"

I could barely make out the sound of Doug's tearful chuckle over the line as Cleo and I celebrated. "That's our girl."

"We'll call you when we're down there, Daddy!" Cleo said quickly. She didn't even wait for a reply as she grabbed our things. Beer sloshed over the rim of her cup and onto my boot. Normally, I would've cared but today I didn't. Not when I was so goddamned happy.

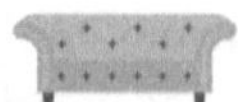

"THERE SHE IS!" Cleo sang as we clocked Lennox across the back lot.

Lennox was standing near Strider at her table, talking to two men in cowboy hats. One was around Lennox's age and the other was older. I'd wager a father and son. Each of them smiled down at her like she was a million fucking bucks. Not that I blamed them, because to me she was, but I'd be a damn liar if I said my hackles weren't raised just a smidge.

Now that Lennox was mine, I didn't get as jealous as I used to. There was no point in it. She was my girl, and she'd be coming on my fingers, my tongue, and my cock later tonight. There wasn't a motherfucker here that could change that.

Cleo yelled her sister's name, and Lennox turned over her shoulder. Our eyes locked and her lips curled into the biggest smile. The sight sent my heart into overdrive, and I let adrenaline take over. I picked up my pace, jogging behind Cleo as she bounded toward her sister.

"We'd love if you considered joining our pro team," one of them said, giving a tentative nod at our approach. "I know we talked about it before your hiatus, but—"

Lennox, as cool as ever, gave them her megawatt smile. "I appreciate the offer, but I'm taking on responsibilities around the ranch, what with my dad's retirement and all. This was the last thing on my rodeo bucket list to cross off before I hang up my hat."

The younger one frowned. "You're not seriously talking about throwing away this kinda money, are you?"

The older of the two patted the other on his shoulder. "Pay no mind to my son," he said, giving a soft chuckle. "He don't quite understand the allure of ranch life like some people. It's all flashy lights and pretty smiles for him."

The son mumbled something under his breath, but Lennox paid no mind. "If you'd told me two years ago I'd be walking away, I'd probably have told you the same thing."

"Who's taking over at Black Springs now? I heard Doug has some new buck on the training, but I've done business with your dad on the cattle side of things for longer than I care to admit."

I stepped to her side, placing my hand on the small of her back as I kissed her temple. "That's actually why I'm stepping away. My fiancé and I will be taking over," she said, tucking a piece of hair behind her ear. The diamond engagement ring on her left hand sparkled beneath the Canadian sun, and I tried my best not to puff my chest in pride.

I may have jumped the gun with my first proposal, but I made up for it later after she'd won the qualifier at Salina. We weren't rushing the wedding, but the ring had been burning a hole in my pocket since the day I bought it. I didn't want to wait another day to make her mine, to show her I was all in.

The old man smiled. "Well, in that case, I look forward to working with you in some capacity." He reached out, offering his hand to both of us. "It was a pleasure meetin' you both."

The moment they were gone, Cleo wrapped her arms around Lennox's waist and gave her a squeeze. "There's our star! You freaking did it!"

"Oh my god, I know!" Lennox squealed. "I'm not gonna lie, I didn't think I'd make it there for a second. This old guy," she said, throwing her thumb over toward Strider, "was a little slow around that first barrel."

The horse let out a deep sigh like he was calling her out for her choice of words.

"Don't listen to her," Cleo said, looking over her sister's shoulder. "You did great, boy." She pulled her phone out of her pocket. "Dad and Josie have been blowing up my phone. I told them we'd call when we got down here but they're being impatient. One sec."

As Cleo stepped to the side to call home, I sidled closer to Lennox. She slid her arms around my neck, pulling me in for a hug. I couldn't help but tear up a bit. "You fucking did it, killer," I whispered. "I'm so goddamn proud of you."

She pulled back, eyes softening as she took in the state of

me. "Are those tears for me, baby?" she asked, wiping away a stray tear.

"Nope," I said, shaking my head, but I wasn't fooling anyone. "Must've gotten some dust in my eye."

Lennox smiled, keeping one arm around my neck as the other plucked the hat off her head. She sat it on mine before closing the distance and kissing me deeply. It was too small, but neither of us cared. It was the implication that mattered. "I can see through the dust, cowboy. You're not fooling me."

"Is that right?" I asked.

"Mmhm."

"What do you see then?"

She was quiet for a moment, contemplating her answer before she gave it. "You. I always see you. Your love for the ranch, for our family, for me. How you're the first one at the barn in the morning and the last one to leave at night. The way you put everyone and everything before yourself."

Goddammit, now she was really gonna make me cry. "You see all that, huh?"

Lennox nodded. "I see more than you know."

I grabbed her left hand and brought her ring to my lips, kissing the shimmering gem. It was beautiful. A large marquise cut diamond time atop a golden band. I didn't know shit about rings, but Josie and Lincoln had both helped pick it out.

I wasn't quite sure where this life would take me, but there was one thing I knew for certain.

"All I see is you, sweetheart."

want more?

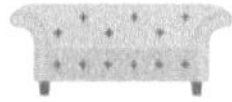

Want to find out how Bishop finally popped the question? 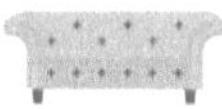 Head over to my website to receive the bonus scene!

Eager to find out what happens when the eldest Hayes sister meets up with the first man to break her heart? Keep reading for a sneak peek!

cleo

. . .

After the Rain Sneak Peek

"JUST BREATHE, Cleo. You're safe here." I closed my eyes, unable to stare at the tiny video screen on my computer anymore. My hand wrapped desperately around the stress ball my therapist sent me years ago after our first session. Once upon a time, it'd been a pristine white and yellow daisy—one of my favorite flowers. Now, it was split and faded after easing me through yet another therapy session.

"We're getting a divorce. Thomas is staying in Montana with his brother, or at least that's what he told me. I don't know, and I don't care. He can rot in hell."

Memories of last night hadn't stopped haunting me since I retreated to my childhood bedroom in the early hours of the morning and cried. Announcing my divorce at the dinner table might have seemed out of left field to my entire family, but it'd been a long time coming.

I wanted to say it lifted a weight off my shoulders, but that wasn't true. If anything, I felt heavier—like the truth only added to the burden of shame I constantly carried around. It was one more thing I'd failed at. One more thing for people to pity me for when they passed me on the street.

Ashwood, Texas was your quintessential small town—complete with a picturesque town square filled with local businesses, two barely passable dive bars, and a population of busybody gossips who made it their mission to stick their nose in everyone's personal lives.

I'd been back in town for six months, and I was still pelted with questions in the produce aisle. The interrogators fell into one of two categories—catty mean girls I went to high school with or little old ladies who'd known me since I was born. It was why I never went shopping alone anymore if I could help it. Getting asked why I moved home or when my soon-to-be ex husband would be joining me wasn't my favorite topic of conversation. I thought if I kept my answers simple, people would ignore me and move on, but it only added to the intrigue.

It was why, after months of near silence about my unexpected return, I decided to blurt it out at the dinner table. I think on some level, my sisters, Josie and Lennox, already knew something had happened between Thomas and me. Other than a random question here or there, they knew I was a private person and respected that. Even my dad had bitten his tongue when it came to the whole surprise return thing.

My mom, bless her, was the opposite. The moment she smelled something sour, she was determined to find the source. I had a bit of a reprieve at the beginning of summer when she'd gone out of town for a month. Ever since she'd been back, she'd subjected me to an inquisition nearly every week.

"How long are you staying?"

"When is Thomas joining you?"

"Why hasn't he called or come to visit?"

I don't know, Mom. Maybe because he is an abusive piece of shit who gambled away his inheritance and drained our savings before taking out his frustrations on me?

"This isn't working," I said through gritted teeth. "It feels like I can't squeeze hard enough to take the edge off."

I could hear Rachel, my saint of a therapist and best friend, rustling papers on her desk. "Then throw it at something."

"What?" I stopped mid-squeeze, cracking open an eye. "Throw it at something?"

She shrugged. "Why not?"

"What if I break something?"

I looked around my room at my parents' house. It hadn't changed much over the past eighteen years, but it never really had to. Other than the cheesy boy band posters that'd been promptly removed the first summer after college, my style hadn't evolved much. The walls had always been a pale shade of powder blue—still one of my favorite colors—and I'd bought a white linen comforter set when I'd moved back in. There were two bookcases on the wall opposite my bed, filled to the brim with shelf trophies of my favorite books.

"What if you do?" Rachel asked, bringing my focus back to the computer. "What would happen?"

"You know, sometimes I feel like you don't know me at all," I said, dropping the stress ball onto the table with a sigh.

Her laugh was soft, like tinkling bells. "You and I both know that isn't true. Perhaps it upsets you that I know you better than most."

Rachel and I had known each other since college. Our dorm rooms were right across from one another, and we'd often found ourselves locked out on the weekends when our roommates brought "friends" over to spend the night. After the first few weeks of camping in the hallway, we decided to form a two-person study group in the common area instead, and the rest was history.

After we graduated, we went our separate ways like most do. We'd checked in on one another through social media from time to time, but never stayed in touch past that. It wasn't until I saw she'd opened her own practice that I decided to reach out.

Making that first call had been one of the most difficult things I'd ever done. I wasn't used to asking for help of any kind. In fact, it was the first time I'd done something just for me in years. The thought of adding my issues to someone else's plate nearly broke me out in hives, but I did it anyway.

It turned out to be the best thing I'd ever done. There were a lot of things I needed to work through, but my progress had been great. Looking back, I knew I wasn't the same person I was when I started. But just because I could admit the therapy was working didn't mean I always liked it. In fact, sometimes I ended the session hating Rachel just a little and wished I'd never reached out.

It was almost comical how processing trauma in a healthy way could be more painful than locking up the vault of memories and throwing away the key.

Almost.

"What're you scared of, Cleo?" she asked, gently prodding me. "Talk to me. That's the point of these sessions."

I rubbed my temple. "I don't want to break something."

Rachel nodded, urging me to get to the point. "And why is that?"

I grabbed the daisy, staring at it in the palm of my hand. There'd be no fixing it. No amount of cleaning could undo the damage I'd done to it. It'd be easier to get a new one. Maybe I should. Maybe it didn't work anymore because it was broken and—

"Cleo."

I forced myself to meet Rachel's gaze. "Sometimes broken things can't be fixed," I admitted quietly, looking back down at the stress ball. "Sometimes they stay broken."

That was how I'd felt lately.

Broken.

I loved being home, but sometimes it brought out a side of me I didn't care for. The moment I crossed the property line of Black Springs Ranch, my dad's pride and joy, I reverted to my role as the eldest daughter just as I'd always done.

It scared me how easily I fell into the swing of things again. Even though I'd been gone for years, it was almost like I'd never left. I loved spending time with my family, especially my sisters. There'd been too much of an age gap between us to bond when we were growing up, but it'd been different as adults.

Watching Josie and Lennox grow into themselves was strangely rewarding. I wasn't their parent, but the seven and nine-year age gap between us meant that I sometimes struggled to balance the relationship between sister and caregiver. We'd fought about it so many times. It was always the same. I tried, in my own way, to make them understand things about life I wished I'd known when I was their age, but it always turned into someone screaming at me that I wasn't their mother and couldn't tell them what to do.

I'd be a liar if I said I didn't feel a little pride at the strong young women they turned into, even if it meant I wasn't as close as they were.

Knowing we were going to be together again as adults had been a bright spot in my otherwise gloomy life, but the one thing I wasn't prepared for was the reality that their lives were more on track than my own right now.

Josie had recently fallen back in step with her five-night summer fling from last year. They were inseparable. Where one went, the other followed. Before they'd got together a few months ago, Josie had been dating the king of the douchebags. No one liked Ellis, and for good reasons, but Lincoln Carter was different.

Even though it hadn't been long, anyone with eyes could tell the man was helplessly in love with her. It bordered on obsessive, but Josie had deserved someone who would put her first every single time.

And Lennox? Oh, my baby sister hadn't so much as uttered a word about her love life, but I had a sneaking suspicion that she and our ranch foreman weren't too far behind. Lennox and Bishop were always fighting and bickering, but there was this electrifying tension, too. They were probably the only two people who didn't clock it, choosing instead to live in oblivion.

And then there was me. Going through a messy divorce at thirty-five and living in my childhood bedroom. Clearly, I was thriving.

No matter where I looked, I was surrounded by people maddeningly in love, chasing the rush of euphoria they seemed to be consumed by. When it was only my mom and dad's over-the-top public displays of affection, it was easy to shrug off. They were my parents; in a perfect world, that was how it was supposed to be, wasn't it?

They were the best role models I could've asked for. Kind, patient, and loving. More importantly, though, they showed us what a healthy relationship looked like. And not just the good parts, either.

As we grew up, they made sure we knew life and love wasn't all sunshine and rainbows. Sometimes, it was going to be hard to put one foot in front of the other. Relationships of any kind were hard without proper nurturing, but it didn't matter because at the end of the day, the thought of living without your person was too much to bear.

Seeing my parents' devotion to one another filled me with the hope that maybe I could have that one day, too, but it wasn't their fault that I let myself be duped by love.

I wanted to be blind with passion. I wanted to feel free, to soar high in the sky like a bluebird spreading its wings. I wanted to know that if I fell, someone would be there to help me back up again.

Honestly, I wanted a lot of things I knew weren't in the cards for me anymore.

I'd been close to having it all. Twice, actually—though I never spoke about it. Thomas and I met my senior year of college. After four years of keeping my nose in textbooks instead of putting myself out there, I let Rachel convince me to go on a blind date. We were both seniors at the University of Texas and would graduate soon. I almost stood him up, but my curiosity had won out. After all, maybe she was right. I needed to do something that was just for me.

He'd been cute. Stupidly, so. I was charmed by his boyish good looks and green eyes that promised mischief.

The rest of our story? Well, it was much more complicated than I ever let anyone know.

When things were good between us, they were *good*. Great, even. The first six years were some of the happiest of my life. When things started going south, I told myself it was just a part of life we needed to get through. A storm to weather. I was more than willing to step up and be whoever he needed me to be if it took some of his stress away.

But Thomas saw that as my being a doormat. It didn't take him long to wipe his dirty boots against my dignity, to dig in his heels and tear me apart at the seams so that he was free of whatever debris he had clinging to him.

It would've been easy to blame my parents for why I stayed in my marriage for so long. Or I could've looked at the men who continued to haunt me, laying the blame at their feet instead of my own. After all, I'd been whole once upon a time before they came into my life like wrecking balls, caused havoc, and left me standing in the wake of their destruction. But pointing fingers at others never did any good. Especially considering I was the common denominator tying everyone together.

There were parts of me missing. Parts I still didn't know how to get back, even after intensive and continual therapy. Some mornings, I didn't recognize who I was. It was like I was staring at the empty shell of someone I once knew.

I normally kept that to myself. The only person I'd ever admitted it to was Rachel, but that'd been after many tears and just as many vodka tonics. To this day, she was the only person who knew every part of my story, even those secrets I'd kept close to my chest.

My therapist needed to know those things, right?

It turned out complete honesty can backfire, though. Rachel had been hooked on that one single thought for months now. No matter how hard I tried, I couldn't shake her off it. Thankfully, she didn't bring it up every session. She had me figured out pretty well, knowing when to ask, and when to leave it be, but it was still her job to help me process whatever the hell was going on in my twisted brain.

There were days I dreaded my sessions. I swore I had a sixth sense when it came to this stuff. It was like my body was preparing for the inevitable crash that came after the screen went dark. The train of thought cast a dark cloud over my mood and no matter what, I couldn't shake it.

I knew today was going to be a heavy appointment. Rachel had been begging me to tell my family about the divorce since I'd got home, but I kept pushing it off. Last night, I'd finally snapped under the weight of my parents' curious questions. Spilling the beans before my dad's birthday bash—his words, not mine—hadn't been the best move.

Earlier in the year, my dad's health had given us a major scare. Apparently, not even the world's best dad was immune to a sick heart. Seeing him in a hospital bed was an image I'd never forget. It'd been a wake-up call—one we severely needed because we had never talked about what would happen after he was gone.

When Mom had told me the news, I'd slid down the wall and cried. I hated myself for the fleeting sense of relief I felt at my dad's expense. It was the out I'd been searching for, my reason for leaving Montana and never looking back.

"Do I need to take off my therapist hat and put my friend one on instead?" Rachel asked, crossing her arms. "I can feel you shutting down."

"No, I'm good," I said, straightening my shoulders and forcing a smile. Her pursed lips told me she wasn't buying it. "I'm just thinking about all the things I need to do today. You know how it is."

"And now you're deflecting," she said, sitting back in her chair. "Look, I want to make it clear how proud of you I am. Telling your family what happened with Thomas couldn't have been easy. I know we practiced the speech together, but I want to stress the importance of this achievement."

"Thank you—"

"But by rehashing the details of your relationship, I'm worried you might be slipping back into your self-imposed guilt."

"Well, no one can make me feel worse about myself than I can," I said, trying and failing to inject a dash of darker humor into our conversation. Sometimes, it worked, and Rachel would change topics, but today was not the day.

"Cleo—"

"It's fine. I'm fine," I said, holding up my hands. Then I grabbed my ball and gave it one long squeeze. "See? Just like the doctor ordered."

"I regret giving you that fucking ball," she muttered, shaking her head.

"That's not very therapist-y of you."

"Yeah, well, our official session was over fifteen minutes ago, so now I can be a little freer with what I say," Rachel snapped back. "Cleo, I'm seriously worried about you. Are you sleeping? Like at all? The bags beneath your eyes are like dark pits of despair."

Okay, ouch.

"I'm so glad I decided to go with my best friend instead of a random stranger as my therapist. It's so much fun."

Rachel snorted. "Yeah, well, anyone else would beat around the bush, and that's not my style. I know you. Sometimes you need a little tough love. Even if it hurts."

"It's okay to keep some thoughts inside, though. Just for future reference. Yes, I'm sleeping." *No, I wasn't.* "Yes, I'm eating." *Not nearly enough.* "So, thank you for your concern. As for the 'pits of despair,' nothing seems to work. Makeup won't cover it, and I'm convinced those stupid under-eye patches you love so much don't actually do a damn thing." I said, staring at the gold remnants of the pair I'd used this morning.

She waved her hand. "That's because you don't believe in the power of self-care. Seriously, when's the last time you went to the spa or had a massage?" When I said nothing, her eyebrows shot up. "A manicure? A pedicure?"

"None of the above," I said. "You know I don't like people touching my feet, and getting my nails done while living on a ranch is useless. They always chip within a few days, so it's a waste of money.

"And the spa?"

"Never been. Unless you count the one we went to for your bachelorette party over a decade ago."

Rachel scrunched up her nose. "Oh god. Please don't remind me of that disaster. I still can't be in the vicinity of anything green apple flavored without wanting to puke."

"You were the one who thought taking shots before sitting in a sauna was a good idea," I said with a laugh. "What the bride wants, the bride gets."

I still couldn't think of that day without a stabbing pain in my chest. While I'd also been a victim of the *Smirnoff Disaster of '13*, my pain was for an entirely different reason.

"Have you seen him again?" Rachel asked, knowing exactly

where my mind was drifting to. Her voice was soft, almost a whisper. It was night and day from the tone she'd used earlier.

"Who?" My lips curled into a small smile but fell flat when I noticed her cutting glare.

"You know who."

I did, but I wasn't ready to talk about him, so I shook my head. "No. Not since the run-in at the bar four months ago. Probably for the best. I mean, he's probably on tour."

With his beautiful wife, was the thought I kept to myself. I tried not to keep track of the first boy who broke my heart, but it became increasingly difficult when he shot to the top of country music charts and became somewhat of a local idol.

Rachel drew her brows together. "No, haven't you heard?"

"Heard what?"

"Cleo!" My name came from the hallway, and the sound of a banging fist against my door sounded a moment later. "I know you're awake," Lennox sang.

"I gotta go, Rach," I said, cutting off whatever she was about to say. "Duty calls."

My friend narrowed her eyes. "I'm going to send you texts every hour. If you don't respond, then I'll call in the cavalry."

"Oh, I'm so scared," I said, placing my hand over my chest in faux shock.

"You should be."

I screamed as I heard Lennox's voice behind me. "You little shit," I said, turning around. "How'd you get in?"

"The master?" Lennox asked, holding up a small silver key in her hand. She peered over my shoulder and waved at my friend. "Hi Rachel!"

"You have a master?" I asked, trying to rein Lennox in.

She shrugged. "Yeah, I had it made years ago so I could break into Josie's room. Did you know she used to hide liquor at the back of her closet? Completely unrelated, of course." She plopped down on my bed. "Anyway, I'm the cavalry, and we both know what a pain in the ass I can be."

I turned back to my friend. "You wouldn't dare."

"Oh, I would. Every. Hour." She punctuated the last two words with a clap before pushing to her feet. "And I'm not kidding, either."

"Yes ma'am," I drawled, giving her a little salute before the screen went dark. "Whatever you say."

Lennox was quiet for a second before asking, "I already know the answer, but I feel it's my sisterly duty to ask if you want to talk about it."

Despite her loud and extroverted personality, there was no one who loved as fiercely as Lennox. She'd fight a fence post if she thought it'd wronged you somehow.

I pushed from my chair, going over and laying my hand on top of hers. I wasn't big on physical contact, but she was. "No, I'm good. Thank you, though."

She nodded. "You know I'm always here, though, right?"

"I do." It was the first genuine smile I'd given in what felt like weeks. "And you know the same goes for me, right? If there's anything, or anyone"—I nudged her leg—"that you want to talk about…"

"Nope," she said, hopping down. "Not until there's something, or someone, for *you* to talk about." She gave me a pointed look, and I raised my hands. "Alright, then. But don't think I won't call Rachel if I need to!"

"That won't be necessary," I said, pushing her toward my door and down the hall.

All I had to do was make it through a day without thinking of the first boy that broke my heart, which was easier said than done these days.

cleo

. . .

After the Rain Sneak Peek

"DAMN, IT'S HOT FOR OCTOBER," Cook said as he leaned over the massive portable BBQ pit and grabbed a foiled baked potato. "Thought the news said it wasn't supposed to be so hot?"

I laughed, putting my hands on my hips and surveying the space. Cook was right. It was hotter than hell, but that didn't seem to stop people from showing up. Today was one big celebration. Dad's party was in full swing. Cars had been pulling through the Black Springs gate all day, and they were still coming.

Red and white tents filled the pasture, giving people a place to escape the sun and grab a drink to cool off. Lennox and Lincoln's carefully curated playlist played softly over speakers placed throughout the masses. Tonight, there'd be a live band playing, though no one knew who. Dad had kept that one a secret from everyone.

Knowing him, I wouldn't have been surprised if it was some drifter with a single guitar who only played Conway Twitty covers.

My dad loved to give back to the community and had invited

damn near everyone he knew, which meant most of the Ashwood population was going to be out at the ranch. Even our employees got the day off, thereby giving the Hayes family a busy morning to try and pick up the slack.

After Lennox dragged me from my bedroom this morning, I wandered over to Cook's tent to help with the food prep. Most of it had already been taken care of—he was a bit neurotic when it came to his craft—but there was still plenty of setup to account for.

I was the only one of my siblings working today, which was fine. I didn't mind. It gave me something to do instead of crashing out while watching cowboys wrestle steers. It wasn't like they were in short supply, and I'd seen enough of them to last a lifetime.

I looked toward the table where my family sat. Mom and Dad had been by multiple times, trying to get me to hang up my apron and join them. I made up some excuse, telling them I felt bad leaving everyone else to deal with Cook's wrath. It wasn't completely a lie.

For someone who listened to nothing but Hank Williams and spent his weekend fishing, you wouldn't think he'd be such a snob, but I'd seen Cook get worked up over the order of toppings on a burger. I could still remember the time he had the audacity to criticize my great-great-grandma's banana bread recipe in front of my mom. She didn't talk to him for at least two months because he remained steadfast in his opinion.

Honestly, it was still a hot button topic. I didn't think they'd ever been the same.

"You know how Texas weather is," I said, refilling a roll of paper towels. "No one can predict what it's gonna do."

"It's days like this I wish I'd taken a job in a state that actually has seasons," Cook muttered. "This is bullshit."

I paused, turning over my shoulder to look at him. "And you've lived here how long again?"

His eyes darted to the side. "My whole life."

"That's what I thought," I laughed. "You had the chance to leave, and you didn't. Just think about all the places you could've worked if you'd followed your food loving heart."

"I couldn't give up fishing."

"You realize there are lakes and rivers in other states, right?"

Cook nodded. "Yeah, but your dad keeps y'all's stocked, so I don't have to worry about running out."

I shrugged. "I guess that's the price you pay." I picked up the case of sodas, ready to walk past him to refill one of the coolers, when my stomach let out a horribly embarrassing growl.

Before I knew it, the drinks had been plucked from my hands and there was a very large, angry man standing in front of me. "When's the last time you ate?" he asked, narrowing his gaze.

"I've been busy," I said, shrugging him off and reaching for the case once more. He raised it above his head, looking down at me with an expression that screamed trouble.

For all his strong opinions—and believe me, there were many—nothing got Cook more fired up than people going hungry. When he wasn't on duty at the ranch, he was often volunteering, donating his time and talent to those in need of some help and a good meal.

"Get the hell outta here until you've gotten some food in your belly, girl. Anthony!" he barked, looking over at one of the employees he'd taken under his wing.

The kid came running up. "Yes, sir?"

"Get Miss Hayes a plate. Load it up with everything, but make sure to put the BBQ sauce on the side," he said.

I couldn't help but smile. "You always take good care of me, Cook."

He huffed, but there was a flush on his cheeks. "I still remember you throwing knock down, drag out fits when your mom poured it all over your chicken. If I can avoid a mess, then

I'm gonna do my best. I even made the spicy sauce you love so much."

It was true. I hated most condiments, but I was pickier about BBQ sauce. Most were too sweet. After a lot of hysterical moments and refusing to eat meals, my parents finally learned what worked and what didn't.

And Cook made one hell of a sauce.

Anthony came rushing back, plate laden with food. "Here ya go, Miss Cleo," he said, dipping his head.

I thanked him, taking the plate so he could get back to work. Cook gestured toward the table. "Now, you go sit down and enjoy all your hard work."

"I'll be back," I said, pointing in his direction. "You won't get rid of me that easily."

"You should be partying it up!" he called. "Not hanging out with me."

"You're not such bad company," I replied. He just waved me off and started barking orders at everyone else.

Now that I actually had food in my hand, my stomach was going crazy. Hunger hit me like a sharp knife to the gut. I surveyed the table, clocking an extra seat beside a pissed off looking Bishop. The foreman constantly wore a scowl, but he was staring down Lincoln like he'd personally offended him.

I dropped into the empty space, groaning as the stress of the day began to show. I was running on adrenaline, denial, and an ungodly amount of coffee. "God, I'm starving," I said, immediately digging into the food before me. I groaned as the first taste of homemade mac and cheese hit my tongue. It was so good. Honestly, Cook should've been in some Michelin star restaurant rather than working on our ranch.

"Remind me never to volunteer when Cook asks for help. I don't know how anyone keeps up with him and his standards. He's nuts!" It was only half-true. He could be a bit extreme, but I kind of enjoyed his company.

Bishop chuckled beside me. "Naw, I think you'll still help. That's just who you are."

For some reason, his comment took me off guard. I'd always felt like my niceties did more harm than good—at least when it came to my own well-being. Rachel and I had joked about oldest sibling syndrome in college, but it'd planted a seed in my mind that continued to grow.

Neither Mom nor Dad were exceedingly strict parents. There were basic expectations—manners, respect, and honesty were big in our house—but they didn't ask for anything they didn't give in return. They never pushed me to do something I didn't want to or told me I needed to improve at something I loved. I think it was just a matter of loving them so much that I didn't want to disappoint them.

Rachel said I was a people-pleaser with a heightened sense of responsibility and crushing need for perfectionism, which was a fancy way of telling me I never said no and needed to learn how ASAP. In my defense, no one had taught me to be this way. It just kind of happened.

Without realizing it, the traits people had found endearing became something they expected from me. When I tried to break out of the habit, they pushed back, and guilt struck. Eventually, I found it was easier to just do what they wanted rather than live with their disappointment.

"Well, maybe I don't want to be that person anymore. Being nice doesn't get you anything," I grumbled, staring down at my plate.

I didn't know why I said it. Clearly, I was still in some kind of funk from my therapy this morning. I was too damn tired to care, though. Bishop was one of the few people I could speak to plainly.

He was a straight shooter and didn't entertain bullshit or offer comfort because it was the polite thing to do. What you saw was what you got, and there was something refreshing about that.

Not that I'd ever say that to him. I didn't think I'd survive the scowl he'd give me.

He didn't push the matter, instead turning the conversation toward complimenting my cooking skills and laughing about my mom's obsession with those stupid handheld vegetable choppers. We were still going by the time the woman in question wandered over to the table and dropped into the seat next to mine.

"What time does the band go on?" she asked, taking a sip of her wine. "I'm ready to hear some live music."

"Around seven, I think," Dad said, checking out the stage. I followed his gaze, noting two white vans peeking out from behind the structure. "I dunno. It was all a little last minute, so I think they're just making sure everything is good to go."

Josie leaned forward in her seat. "What do you mean, last minute? This thing has been planned for months."

Dad sighed. "The band I originally booked canceled a few days ago. Said they'd broken up. Guess our little shindig had gotten missed when they made their cancellations."

"That sucks. You seemed excited about them."

"Who'd you get instead?" Lennox asked.

I knew my family was excited, but I really couldn't care less about music, especially the live kind. On the off chance I let one of them drag me to a concert, I usually sat at the back with some kind of noise cancelling headphones. Though, my reasoning had nothing to do with the decibel level, and everything to do with the memories attached to music in general.

Dad splayed his hands on the table. "Well, I guess the kid I spoke with was the singer. He seemed pretty confused about why I was even calling at first. I explained the situation, and he said he'd refund the full amount I paid and still do the set."

Goosebumps prickled across my skin as internal warning

bells began ringing out. "That's nice of him, but how's he going to do that if the band's broken up?" I asked.

Dad shrugged. "I don't know. Guess he made some calls And they agreed to do one last show. Ain't that cool?"

Lennox's smile looked painful. I could feel her eyes scanning my face for a reaction, but I had nothing to give. I was frozen. Locked up on the spot and unable to think or breathe. "Sure is, Dad. Out of curiosity, what's the name of the band?"

No. No, it is very not cool, I wanted to scream. I couldn't, of course. Only my sisters knew a fraction of my history with a certain country music star, and it needed to stay that way.

My mind was just being a dick. It was jumping to conclusions like it always did, because there was no way in fucking hell—

But then a tall figure blocked out the sun and cast a too-familiar shadow across our table. I looked up from beneath my lashes, hoping like hell my heart would stop jumping in my chest.

"Lawson! How the hell are you?" my dad asked, rounding the table to shake my high school ex-boyfriend's hand.

Fuck. Me.

also by amber palmer

acknowledgments

To say this past year has been a wild ride is an understatement. The amount of love and support given to this little cowboy series is staggering, and I am honestly so grateful for each and every person who has helped me along this journey.

To my husband, thank you for your constant support. I don't say it enough, but I could not do this without you.

To Heather, thank you for always being in my corner, for helping me find my voice and use it, for making me a stronger writer, a stronger friend, and a stronger person. Thank you for forcing me to cry when I needed to get it all out.

To Lauren and Holly, thank you for your never-wavering support. Thank you for gassing up Bishop and Lennox, for encouraging me to follow the road these characters took me down.

To my Brittney, thank you for advocating for me when I didn't know how to advocate for myself. Thank you for believing in me and allowing me to pester you with one million questions.

To Liz and Rose, thank you for being the very first eyes on this book. For telling me it wasn't a heap of garbage when I second-guessed myself, and always hyping me up.

And last, but certainly not least, thank you to every single person who picked up this book. It has been a wild ride in the best way possible. I hope you loved Lennox and Bishop like I do.

meet amber

Amber Palmer is an American fantasy romance author. She was born in Arizona, but raised in Texas. She is the proud parent of three (evil) cats and one puppy dog, and when she isn't nose deep in a spicy fantasy novel, she's listening to her bookish Spotify playlists and making notes for her next project! A passionate advocate for mental health, Amber features characters processing various traumas in her work. She is an unapologetic lover of anything spicy, while also making time to game with her husband.

www.ingramcontent.com/pod-product-compliance
Lightning Source LLC
Chambersburg PA
CBHW030754310726
48969CB00005B/1400